THE DEATH OF ANTAGONIS

When Volos heard the order, he didn't feel surprise. Instead, he felt that he was being told something he had already known at a subconscious level. He turned from the dead to bring his flamer to bear on Robbes. He saw a woman fighting heroically for her life and those of her friends. His finger hesitated on the trigger. His peripheral vision caught the rest of the squad re-orienting their weapons, also on the horns of that terrible moment when orders seemed wrong.

Robbes turned her head to look at him. Volos pulled the trigger.

But he was too late. Everything was too late. The plague reached maturity, and the change began.

In the same series

RYNN'S WORLD
Steve Parker

HELSREACH
Aaron Dembski-Bowden

HUNT FOR VOLDORIUS
Andy Hoare

THE PURGING OF KADILLUS
Gav Thorpe

FALL OF DAMNOS
Nick Kyme

BATTLE OF THE FANG
Chris Wraight

THE GILDAR RIFT
Sarah Cawkwell

LEGION OF THE DAMNED
Rob Sanders

ARCHITECT OF FATE
Edited by Christian Dunn

WRATH OF IRON
Chris Wraight

THE SIEGE OF CASTELLAX
C L Werner

THE DEATH OF ANTAGONIS
David Annandale

Audio Dramas

Download the MP3s exclusively from blacklibrary.com

BLOODSPIRE/DEATHWOLF
C Z Dunn & Andy Smillie

THE STROMARK MASSACRE
C Z Dunn & Andy Smillie

THE ASCENSION OF BALTHASAR
C Z Dunn

A WARHAMMER 40,000 NOVEL

THE DEATH OF ANTAGONIS

DAVID ANNANDALE

BLACK LIBRARY

For Margaux, who believes.

A Black Library Publication

First published in Great Britain in 2013 by
Black Library,
Games Workshop Ltd.,
Willow Road,
Nottingham, NG7 2WS, UK.

10 9 8 7 6 5 4 3 2 1

Cover illustration by Slawomir Maniak
Maps by David Annandale and Adrian Wood.
Colour illustrations by Rhys Pugh.

© Games Workshop Limited 2013. All rights reserved.

Black Library, the Black Library logo, The Horus Heresy, The Horus Heresy logo, The Horus Heresy eye device, Space Marine Battles, the Space Marine Battles logo, Warhammer 40,000, the Warhammer 40,000 logo, Games Workshop, the Games Workshop logo and all associated brands, names, characters, illustrations and images from the Warhammer 40,000 universe are either ®, TM and/or © Games Workshop Ltd 2000-2013, variably registered in the UK and other countries around the world.
All rights reserved.

A CIP record for this book is available from the British Library.

UK ISBN 13: 978 1 84970 318 5
US ISBN 13: 978 1 84970 319 2

No part of this publication may be reproduced, stored in a retrieval system, or transmitted in any form or by any means, electronic, mechanical, photocopying, recording or otherwise, without the prior permission of the publishers.

This is a work of fiction. All the characters and events portrayed in this book are fictional, and any resemblance to real people or incidents is purely coincidental.

See Black Library on the internet at
www.blacklibrary.com

Find out more about Games Workshop and the world of Warhammer 40,000 at
www.games-workshop.com

Printed and bound by CPI Group (UK) Ltd, Croydon, CR0 4YY

It is the 41st millennium. For more than a hundred centuries the Emperor has sat immobile on the Golden Throne of Earth. He is the master of mankind by the will of the gods, and master of a million worlds by the might of his inexhaustible armies. He is a rotting carcass writhing invisibly with power from the Dark Age of Technology. He is the Carrion Lord of the Imperium for whom a thousand souls are sacrificed every day, so that he may never truly die.

Yet even in his deathless state, the Emperor continues his eternal vigilance. Mighty battlefleets cross the daemon-infested miasma of the warp, the only route between distant stars, their way lit by the Astronomican, the psychic manifestation of the Emperor's will. Vast armies give battle in His name on uncounted worlds. Greatest amongst his soldiers are the Adeptus Astartes, the Space Marines, bio-engineered super-warriors. Their comrades in arms are legion: the Imperial Guard and countless planetary defence forces, the ever-vigilant Inquisition and the tech-priests of the Adeptus Mechanicus to name only a few. But for all their multitudes, they are barely enough to hold off the ever-present threat from aliens, heretics, mutants - and worse.

To be a man in such times is to be one amongst untold billions. It is to live in the cruellest and most bloody regime imaginable. These are the tales of those times. Forget the power of technology and science, for so much has been forgotten, never to be re-learned. Forget the promise of progress and understanding, for in the grim dark future there is only war. There is no peace amongst the stars, only an eternity of carnage and slaughter, and the laughter of thirsting gods.

CHAPTER 1
THE DUTY TO PROTECT

THE WARS OF Lamentation did not come to Elias Tennesyn in the person of the Dragon or the Gorgon. Those figures would come later. Visited upon him by the Wars, they would, for his sins, drag him through the hellscape of what had once been his life's work. But if they were the avatars of war, they were not its herald. That role (and oh, by the Throne, had Tennesyn only known it) fell to a man whose smile told a tale of a soul eternally surprised by joy.

The herald was called Cardinal Rodrigo Nessun. Though he wore a gold medallion in the shape of a wide, almost circular eye suspended over the hilt of a sword, his robes had none of the adornment Tennesyn would have expected of a senior ecclesiarch. Instead, they were a blinding, quasar white, and their every fold winked, their every billow laughed. The movements of the clothing were the reflections of the man's pale blue eyes, eyes whose sparkle was a flourish of delight in the universe. His hair was as white as his robes. There were moments when Tennesyn couldn't distinguish one from the other, as if the hair that fell in a thick cascade down Nessun's back spread and shaped itself into vestments. The cardinal's skin was white, too, a beyond-albino chalk. He could have been a ghost, and he did, it was true, seem to walk a few centimetres off the ground. He could have been a ghost, but he was much too happy.

And on the day the Wars of Lamentation began in the Phlagia system, on the planet Antagonis, Nessun wasn't just floating. He was *dancing*. Tennesyn's mood was darker. The xeno-archaeologist was happy that his sponsor was pleased. But now, on the very day that the dig site seemed bound to validate his theories, Tennesyn was having to rush off back to Aighe Mortis in the neighbouring Camargus system. Another of his best researchers was being conscripted into the Imperial Guard. It was the third time in a week. Tennesyn had no quarrel with duty to the Emperor, but there were different ways to serve, and how was he supposed to do any work of real value if his staff kept being poached by the Departmento Munitorum? If Tennesyn wanted to reach Aighe Mortis before his protégé was bundled off-world, no doubt to die fighting over a rise of rock that no one could possibly be interested in were it not for the other people who couldn't possibly be interested in it, then he had to leave, and right away.

At this point, Tennesyn thought he knew the impact war would have on his life: problems with excessive staff turnover.

He had no idea how deep his naïveté ran.

So on the day the Wars came to Antagonis (but not to Tennesyn yet, not just yet), Nessun asked, 'The site is completely revealed, now?'

'It is.'

'And the alignment is…?'

'Tonight.'

The herald of war clapped his hands in excitement. Not at all seeing what waited in the wings, Tennesyn took his leave, and started down the road where the Dragon and the Gorgon waited.

IN A WEEK, a world can fall.

VOLOS JOLTED AWAKE. He sat up. His feet sought the reassuring reality of the *Immolation Maw*'s deck. His hands squeezed the iron frame of the cot as he fought to steady the vertigo of his spirit. Volos did not dream, nor had he now. No images engaged in a fading dance through his mind. Yet his heart was sick with the perfect, absolute, unalterable knowledge that his hands would soon carry stains from an ocean of innocent blood.

MELUS WHISTLED, HIS helmet speaker distorting the sound into a high-pitched whine.

'If you don't mind, brother,' Toharan said.

'Apologies, brother-sergeant. I was just thinking…'

'The same thing I am,' Toharan finished.

They were standing in the doorway to the huge, shallow bowl of the refuge. The space was spare and unadorned, a coldly functional, open-plan bunker.

There were at least a thousand people staring back at them with a mixture of fear and hope.

The orders had been to sweep the capital city for survivors. More specifically: hit the palace of Benedict Danton, high lord of Antagonis, and rescue what portion of the planet's government might yet draw breath. If there were any encounters of opportunity along the way, lend help and gather civilians where possible, but get Lord Danton and his family out of there. Squad Pythios of the Black Dragons Second Company had gone in, working with the Fourth and 25th Companies of the Imperial Guard's Mortisian Regiment. And here, in the sealed basement of the palace, hiding from the walking corpses that, as far as Toharan could tell, comprised the rest of the city of Lecorb's population of twelve million, was everyone they could reasonably expect to find. And more. Toharan ran his eyes again over the huddled figures. His first estimate had been correct: a good thousand souls.

'Too many for an airlift,' Melus said.

'Yes,' Toharan agreed. 'We're walking out of here.' He wasn't worried. Between his squad and the thirty thousand Mortisians, there was more than enough force on hand to act as escort, especially given how non-aggressive the dead were. They had completely ignored the Dragons and the Guard on the way in, even though their behaviour was otherwise more frenzied than Toharan had seen before. The corpses ran, howled, tore at themselves and each other, clawed at walls, and beat their own heads to pulp. But they did not attack.

A man stepped forward from the crowd and approached

the two Space Marines. Toharan pegged him as being in his early sixties, standard. His lined, patrician face showed no signs of augmetic or juvenat treatment, which was unusual. His suit was elegantly austere, a simple black adorned by the vermilion sash of his office. There was a child, a girl of about ten, peering out from behind his legs. He had a protective hand on her plaited hair. 'I am Lord Danton,' the man said. 'And this is Bethshea. I've been trying to tell her that you have come to help us.'

Toharan turned his gaze to the girl. 'That's right. We have.'

Bethshea did not look reassured. She shrank further behind Danton.

'She thinks you're monsters,' Danton explained.

Really? Toharan thought. *The Black Dragons? Monsters?* Towering head and shoulders over every human in the room, clad in black power armour emblazoned with a silver dragon, armour whose snarling helmet grilles were designed to strike fear into the enemy – why in Terra's name would they seem like monsters to a little girl?

'Don't be afraid, child,' Melus said, and started to unclasp his helmet.

Toharan raised a hand to stop him. 'Allow me, brother.' No point traumatising the child any further. He removed his own helmet and let Bethshea see his very human, if outsized, face. She appeared to relax. Slightly.

'Well done,' Melus said over the vox-link when Toharan had replaced his helmet. 'My face would not have helped.'

'That was my thought.'

'Could be worse. I could be Volos.'

Toharan chuckled, then switched to his speaker. 'People of Lecorb,' he announced, 'we have come to lead you to safety.'

SQUAD PYTHIOS BROUGHT the survivors out of the bunker. They mustered in the square of the palace compound, then joined the waiting ranks of the Mortisians. The convoy moved out from the palace walls, out onto Admiral Kiershing Square, with the Space Marines taking point.

And the dead attacked.

The change was instantaneous. The random wandering, despairing moans and acts of self-destruction turned into a furious charge. Five great avenues fed into the square, and from all of them came a storm surge of bodies. The dead ignored the Space Marines and slammed into the Guard. The Mortisians were fast. A wall of stubber and las-fire met the onrushing dead, but the momentum of tens of thousands of bodies wasn't going to be halted. Five collective battering rams struck, and the Imperial lines buckled. Toharan turned, and saw the impossible. Already, within the first second of the battle, as the Mortisians found themselves in full melee, men were changing, their eyes blanking into mindless hunger and rage as they fell on their comrades.

'Diamond,' Toharan voxed. 'Out then in.' Squad Pythios plunged into the fight. They scythed through the dead with chainblade and fist, decapitating and crushing. It was like wading through molasses. The dead were so focussed on clawing past the Mortisians to the civilians that they barely reacted to the Dragons advance.

Toharan forced a reaction. He and his brothers became the moving rocks against which the death tide broke. They split into two groups and worked their way around the defensive island of the Guard. They slashed across the flow of the dead, hundreds falling before them like threshed wheat. Halfway around the Mortisians' perimeter, the Dragons split again, with one half of the squad moving to the rear lines, and the other heading to the front, tearing apart another rank of the enemy. The momentum of the dead stalled. There was a pause while the flood of reinforcements continued to pour in from the avenues, and the charge built up its strength again.

The Mortisians had the measure of their opponents now, though Toharan already had his doubts about what difference that would make in the long run. The reality of twelve million damned souls was sinking in. But for now, the massed power of the Imperial Guard unleashed a horizontal rain of projectile and las-fire. The barrage was continuous, and it pushed back the army of the dead before it could surge again.

Breathing space. Time to move.

'Go!' Toharan shouted over vox-link and speaker, and the caravan took its first, lurching steps. The Dragons moved to the interior perimeter. Toharan disliked not being on the front lines, but he had his orders, and the mission dictated strategy. It was not the Dragons remit to take on an entire city. Their battle, in this moment, was to save as many civilians as possible. The people would be needed after the next stage of the war, after the Black Dragons and the other vectors of Imperial might had purged Antagonis of its taint. There had to be a population to reclaim the planet, to celebrate the victory and prove that it was not pyrrhic. So Squad Pythios moved to protect the unarmed. As big as the area was that the thousand civilians took up, it was one whose bounds the Dragons could keep patrolled. The refugees marched, and the Space Marines circled them at a constant run, bringing bolter and chainblade to bear wherever the Mortisian defences needed shoring up.

Toharan paused in his run to jump up on the lead vehicle, a Hellhound. Colonel Burston Kervold, heading the joint command of the Fourth and 25th companies, rode standing in the roof hatch, magnoculars around his neck. His chin was a steel prosthetic. It was scratched and pitted as if he really did lead with it. Kervold's cap perched on a head that was a phrenological map of his tours of duty. His eyes were narrowed flints, staring at the dead with a contempt so strong it should have blasted a path clear to the outskirts of the city. But when Kervold turned his head to face Toharan, the Space Marine thought he saw the tightness of fatalism in the officer's gaze. Kervold had seen and noted the same things, then. The behaviour of the dead was unusual, unlike any plague of undeath Toharan had fought before. Even more than the speed of the dead, it was their focus that was alarming. There wasn't just hunger in their frenzy. There was anger. There was passion. And then there was the rapidity of the contagion.

The elements were all wrong. Vital information was missing. The mission had the earmarks of a disaster.

'If we stop,' Kervold yelled over the roar of the inferno

cannon's spray of ignited promethium, 'we'll be finished.' Ahead of them, the dead looked like a solid mass.

'Then we don't stop,' Toharan replied. 'Not for any reason. How is our route?'

'We'll stick to the big avenues for as long as we can. But once we're into the hab zones...' Kervold's shrug was humorous in its understatement of despair.

Toharan nodded. 'Then we fight harder. And we still don't stop.' He dropped back to the ground and resumed destroying. Already the defences were being strained again. Already Guard lines were thinning.

Kervold was right. The hab zones were worse.

As long as the caravan was in the administrative centre of Lecorb, on streets five hundred metres wide, the defenders held their own. Flame, faith and will kept them moving forward. Wheels, treads and boots crunched over the flattened and burned bodies of the twice-killed. Though the dead massed in the tens of thousands in the open spaces, there were only so many that could attack at once.

The hab zones were another story. The streets were narrow and none carried on straight for more than a few blocks. Lecorb's history was preserved in its patchwork layout. Fragments of districts layered each other, the new never completely replacing the old, as if pieces from a random collection of jigsaw puzzles had been forced together, whether they fit or not. It was impossible to see what was coming. Each sharp corner slowed the caravan down, giving the dead, now a wall of meat in the confined corridors, longer and longer to press their attacks.

Bad as the streets were, the real nightmare was the architecture. Lecorb's growth had been haphazard, its one burst of urban planning happening in M38, when Lord Hosman had ordered the centre of the city razed to make way for the new administrative complexes. Its style of construction, however, had remained unchanged since the Great Crusade. At some point, the tradition of using pilotis and open façades had become linked, in the cultural imagination, with the act of obeisance to the Emperor. Load-bearing walls had become heretical. But the preservation of any particular structure was unimportant. As a result, apartment had been built atop apartment, new growths of pillars sprouting out of decaying roof gardens to support a new building, whose roof would in turn birth another.

Some buildings overlapped the roofs of several smaller ones, and the façades, freed of the need to do something as mundane as hold the structures upright, had turned into a crazy quilt of murals, stained glass windows, or sullen, stained rockcrete. The zone was a lunatic collection of boxes on stilts that looked, at first glance, like a forest of spindle-legged Titans and Dreadnoughts in collision. Time, smog and decay had rotted the faces of the buildings, and what might once have looked festive, with strident colour offset by the sober grey of unadorned walls, was now a study in dour mud.

And from every one of the myriad openings came the dead. They were like insects streaming from the opened pores of a stricken giant. From all sides, from all floors, from directly above, they fell upon the caravan. Over the neural link, Toharan's helmet transmitted threat detection so universal that he tuned it out. He simply struck at whatever was nearest, and he shattered bodies with every movement.

As the caravan dragged itself forward, the Dragons gave up their rotating patrol and each took ownership of a sector inside the Guard lines. The dead were a terrible hail coming down on top of the refugees, and the Space Marines had to move from the perimeter to the centre of the huddled survivors and back out again within seconds. It was like swatting individual insects in a swarm. They smashed many.

They didn't smash nearly enough.

Two Chimeras ran into a stream of dead who threw themselves under the APCs' treads. The corpses piled higher, more and more sucked in beneath the vehicles, blood and bone-shrapnel spraying. Within seconds, the Chimeras had sunk into a quagmire of gore metres deep. Their crews piled out and were dragged down into the muck.

The casualties mounted. The dead pressed harder. The streets narrowed and the buildings crowded in. Mortisians transformed into howling creatures and clawed at their neighbours, spreading the contagion. But the civilians didn't turn. The dead simply ripped them to pieces. This wasn't battle, Toharan thought as he tore the head off a man whose idiot face was covered in the foam of his rage. This wasn't even a retreat. This was a race against Chaos itself. There was honour in the effort, but his mind was troubled by the hard, insistent possibility of failure and futility.

Snarling, a man threw himself out of the third floor

window just ahead and on Toharan's left. The creature's hands were hooked into talons of hate and hunger, his eyes locked on a sobbing Bethshea. Toharan snapped out a ceramite-clad fist and smashed the corpse aside, caving in the head. Another one down. Another drop in a limitless ocean. But a glance at Bethshea renewed the calm of perfect duty. Since Toharan had shown her that he was a giant, not a monster, she had cleaved close to his legs. She had to run to keep pace with his every stride, but she managed, a tiny remora to his black, remorseless shark. Toharan roared his encouragement to his brothers and the Guard.

They passed a side street. It was empty when Toharan looked down it. But as the rear elements of the caravan went by, they were hit by a sudden, shrieking, frenzied mob of the dead. A torpedo of damnation, uncountable thousands strong, shattered the lines. Toharan looked back to see Brother Xorion caught. The dead ploughed into and onto him in an unending tide. Only Brother Guerign was close enough to help. He waded in and, standing back to back, the two Black Dragons felled hundreds. Toharan and the rest of the squad supported them with a stream of bolter fire, but no amount of firepower was enough against the rushing, frothing wave of corpses. Xorion and Guerign died. Even ceramite could be crushed by the sheer weight of dead flesh.

As Toharan watched, helpless, his soul sickening, what made the scene even more horrific was the single-minded focus of the dead. Even now, the Space Marines weren't actual targets. The dead hadn't attacked Xorion and Guerign – they had run them down. The corpse faces, mindless slackness mixed with idiot hunger, all faced in a single direction. Their blank yet raging eyes were fixed on the herded survivors. They didn't care about the Dragons. Toharan's brothers had simply been in the way.

Had the enemy been sentient, there could have been no greater insult.

Toharan turned from the disaster. A quarter of the civilians gone. The Mortisians weakened by at least that much. An awful reality, but it changed nothing. The orders still stood. The mission was not done until there was victory. 'Forward!' he cried. To the refugees who stood still, mesmerised by unholy loss, he said, 'Honour your dead and honour your planet. Survive and reclaim! Go!' They did, one foot in front of the other, and, to their very great credit, without panicking.

They honoured their protector, too.

HARRIED AND CRUSHED, diminished and scarred, the caravan emerged from the hab zones and gradually left the city behind. The apartment warrens, now hives of the dead, gave way first to the manufactoria, and then to still-unspoiled forest. The survivors and their guardians picked up speed, and for a little while put some distance between themselves and the greater part of the city's undead millions.

Ahead, the landscape rose in gentle foothills until it reached the jarring interruption of the Temple Mountains. The chain thrust from the earth like sudden, granite judgement, its faces vertical, towering, defiant. From there, the sanctuary of Lexica Keep was less than a day's forced march away. The keep would be blessedly inaccessible to the dead horde on its cliff side, and the route to it wound through a long, narrow pass several kilometres long. If they could reach the pass, Toharan was confident he could see his charges to safety. The mountain walls of the defile were so close together that the dead would be streamed into a line that could be held off by even a modest contingent of Guard. Arrival at the pass would be a guarantee of victory.

Or of what little victory that could be claimed. By now, half the civilians were dead. The Mortisians had been decimated, reduced to barely a third of their original strength.

The tyranny of numbers caught up to them as they reached the foot of the mountains. The city had emptied, and when its masses arrived, the open spaces no longer worked in the caravan's favour. The dead formed a single, coherent mass millions strong. A tsunami of rage slammed into the Imperial forces and pushed them up against the unforgiving granite of the Temples. The caravan couldn't advance. The dead were a sea of bone and muscle, the blasted twelve million of Lecorb constricting the little flame of life until they could smother it.

On the line fighting to hold back the tide, a conscript flipped backwards and hit the ground hard and dead. His forehead was a scorched crater. He'd been hit with a las-round.

'Brother-sergeant, did you see that?' Melus asked over the vox-link.

Toharan had. He thought he'd seen the same thing

happen a few times in Lecorb, but he couldn't be sure in the confusion of confined spaces and the rainfall of dead. But now there was no doubt. The Guardsman hadn't been killed by friendly fire. The shot had come from one of the dead, who shouldn't even know what a rifle was, much less how to operate one.

Anger. Speed. And now weapons fire. All of it wrong, and Toharan seethed with frustration at the stalled advance. The entrance to the pass was barely a kilometre to the north. He could see it, a jagged shadow in the mountain wall, its contours outlined in the red glow of the setting sun. Squad Pythios could punch through the corpse legions easily on its own. The problem was doing so with even a handful of survivors. And the problem was looking increasingly academic as the siege wore on.

The Guardsmen were collapsing. Their lines were thinning, pulling back, and then disintegrating. Squad Pythios did what it could to shore them up. Toharan and his brothers ran the interior perimeter once more, dividing the circle into eight between themselves. They were not a patrol: they were a revolving scythe, a perpetual charge, blasting clusters of dead with bolter fire, pushing into the thick of the attackers with chainsword and fist, leaving barriers of inert flesh in their wake. They were relentless. They slowed the hordes down.

They couldn't stop them.

They might have, if the Mortisians were able to hold position with just a bit more characteristic resolve. These men were veterans, blooded and war-tempered by a hundred battles, but they were going down like the rawest trainees. Toharan was baffled yet again by what he was seeing. How could the infection spread so quickly? The change from loyal Guardsman to savage corpse took seconds. There was barely time for a man to die before he turned on his comrades. The virulence of the contagion was beyond unholy. And still, not one of the civilians had succumbed. They were shredded into strips of meat when they were caught, but they never changed.

The refugees howled their terror and despair. For a moment, Toharan's frustration veered into contempt. The terrible losses of this pointless mission had been for the sake of these bleating sheep? Where was the sense in that? Then his eyes landed on Bethshea, always running to be near him, looking up at him now not as a monster, not as a giant, but as a god come to keep her safe, and *there* was his answer. *There* was the sense of the mission.

His vox-link came to life. 'Pythios, this is Ormarr.'

'Volos,' Toharan said. Even through the distorting static of the transmission, the rumbling rasp of Squad Ormarr's sergeant was unmistakable. 'Tell me you have good news, brother-sergeant.'

'Would our imminent arrival qualify?'

'It would.'

'What do you need?'

'A way through to the pass so we can move the civilians.'

'You'll have it,' Volos promised. 'Fire and bone.'

'Fire and bone,' Toharan responded, returning the Dragons battle-cry, and swallowing, as he always did, the twinge of regret that the words would never hold the full meaning for him that they did for Volos. He mag-locked his bolter to his thigh, conserving rounds, and tore into grasping, surging dead with renewed purpose. The warp take the Mortisians if they weren't up to the task. The Dragons would complete the mission themselves. His sword lopped off limbs and heads. The ground beneath his boots had become a mire of blood, and some of the defending Guardsmen were losing their footing in the slickness, but he didn't lose a beat. He was an engine of precise destruction, and mowed the dead down, slicing and trampling them to their second, final end.

But still they didn't attack him. Still, with hands and teeth, they lunged only for the unaugmented humans. And as the Guard succumbed, there were more and more corpses with weapons. Many simply used the rifles as clubs. But even though there was only a tiny percentage that actually fired the guns, and there was no accuracy worthy of the name, the numbers were enough, and they were growing. The air was filling with the lethal web of hostile las-fire.

The music of the war was an atonal cacophony of howling corpse, shrieking survivor, and crying wounded, the high timbre modulated only by the *chud-chud-chud* of bolter fire, growl of chainsword and punctuating crack of bone. The steady, rotating, murderous sweep of Squad Pythios carried what rhythm there was. But now came the glorious bass: the huge, deep-throated, vengeful roar of the Thunderhawk gunship *Battle Pyre*. Flying low, it emerged from the pass, a stub-winged fist of black armour that reflected crimson sunset as the ship turned and began its strafing run. Hellstrike missiles flashed from their pods. They slammed into the undead army with a blast of purifying fire. Tiny suns rose between Toharan and the pass, and the sky rained fragmented body parts. The sponson cannons opened fire, and the ground erupted with geysers of dirt and corpses. For a moment, the pressure from the north ebbed. The Guard pushed hard, and there was movement. The refugees, their cries turning to whimpers of hope, inched towards the north.

Figures in jump packs detached themselves from the *Battle Pyre*.

Bethshea pointed up. 'Look!' she squealed. 'More giants!'

'Yes,' Toharan said. But as he watched the Dragon Claws arrive, what he thought, despite himself, and to his burning shame, was, *No, not giants. The monsters have come.*

CHAPTER 2
FIRE AND BONE

From above, the dead were an undulating carpet covering the landscape. Volos saw eddies and currents in their movement, the formal thrust of the attack giving way in isolated pockets to the purely random. But there was no lack of focus in the forces surrounding Squad Pythios and the tattered remains of the Mortisian Guard. During the seconds of his flight, Volos eyed the distance between the caravan and the pass, saw what was needed if the refugees were going to have even a fighting chance of surviving the next hour. Brother Keryon had given the Claws a good start, ploughing a purging furrow of fire with the Thunderhawk, but the dead were flowing back quickly. Time to teach them that even a corpse could know fear.

The Dragon Claws slammed into the ground, punching craters in the enemy army. They came in at staggered distances, with Volos closest to the caravan. The goal:

blast away the dead and form a chain along which the caravan could move once more. A jump pack assault normally called for close combat weaponry, but for this deployment, Volos had ordered a maximum ammo load and flamers for all. He straightened from his landing, unshouldered the flamer and let spray in a single movement. His back to the mountainside, he played the fire out over 180 degrees, incinerating the dead and pushing their masses back.

The leading Hellhound started up. Its cannon was silent, the promethium tank long since depleted. Volos stepped forward, the flamer on full, and the dead retreated still further. The Hellhound drew level with him. Volos glanced up, saw Colonel Kervold salute his thanks. Volos gave a slight nod and returned his attention to the enemy. The Hellhound passed at his back, between Volos and the cliff wall. Toharan's voice crackled over the vox-link. 'We're advancing. Fine work.'

'So is yours.' He tried to picture the journey his fellow sergeant had made. It was song-worthy.

The Hellhound stopped. Its engine stalled out. Not letting up with the flamer, Volos turned his head. Kervold was looking down inside the vehicle, his expression a jagged mix of fury and puzzlement. He opened his mouth.

The order never came. His eyes widened. Volos saw something new wash over the colonel's face, emotions that should have been foreign to that scarred stone. The first was fear. The second was doubt, and somehow, this seemed more intense and terrible than the fear. Kervold convulsed with spine-snapping force, his body shaken by the fist that was seizing his soul. His eyes glazed as his face twisted into the shape of blank fury. He thrashed himself free of the hatch and turned with a snarl towards the refugees who were just now passing the Hellhound.

His right hand holding down the flamer's trigger, Volos pulled out his bolter with his left and shot Kervold, turning his skull into mist. As he acted, he processed what he had seen. The contagion had struck from the inside of the Hellhound, where no injury had been sustained. The implications staggered him, but they would receive his attention later. The consequences demanded a response now.

The plague spread through what remained of the Mortisians with the speed of a shock wave. The last of the Imperial forces succumbed in seconds. The disease leaped from man to man without needing injury or even contact. It was as if the fall of the colonel signalled the death of the companies' collective spirit. Commissar and trooper alike frothed and lunged for the civilians.

Volos's flamer ran dry. The enemy surged with renewed strength and reinforcements. Clawing for their prey, the dead slammed in a wave against Volos, knocking the bolter from his grasp, lifting him off the ground and throwing his weight against the Hellhound. Volos slid off the vehicle's hull. The flood tried to crush him. 'Toharan!' he voxed. 'The Guard is lost! Grab anyone and *go!*' Buffeted by the infinite enemy, he vowed to the Emperor that he would give his life in the service of any victory that might yet be claimed from this day. Then he crossed his arms against his chest and flexed his wrists, fists down.

There was a familiar moment of agony so pure it bordered on ecstasy, and his bone-blades shot out from his wrists, passing over his knuckles. They were a metre long and sheathed in adamantium. He swung his arms down and out. Limbs and heads went flying. Arterial fountains burst around him, drenching his armour, covering his visor. He ducked his head and lunged forward, a maddened bull. His helmet had a large slit near the top, and from it protruded his forehead's bony growth. He had sanded it into the shape of a crescent horn, the tips and edge as lethal as the blades that grew from his arms, and here too he had added the extra kill strength of adamantium. The dead fell before his charge. His vision narrowed as the euphoria of war descended on him. He saw nothing that wasn't the next thing he was about to butcher. His fangs extended, hungry for the mangled flesh and blood whose sight and smell had become the sum total of his world. He was the destroyer, and however numerous his foes, they were pitiable in their fragility.

A moment came when he had nothing to kill, and his mind cleared with a neuronal snap. His system quivered with the residual ecstasy, but he was already thinking tactically again. Corpses in the dozens surrounded him. The army in his vicinity had staggered, and would need a few seconds before the torrent could flow again. Volos retracted his blades, recovered his bolter and vaulted to the top of the Hellhound.

The Mortisians were all part of the dead army now. There was still occasional weapons fire, but it was all sloppy, and all aimed at the refugees. There were precious few of them left. The brothers of Squad Pythios carried a civilian on each shoulder and were moving at a good pace toward the pass. They had just reached the next of the Dragon Claws. Brother Nithigg's clearing was about to collapse as the onslaught closed in, but the dead were still seconds behind, and the Space Marines were gaining momentum. Handfuls of civilians ran in howling clusters, desperation giving their sprints a speed that was almost that of the Black Dragons jog.

Moment by moment, their numbers dwindled.

Volos joined the race. He came up behind a pair of scrambling humans, a man and a woman. They had been high administrators, to judge by their shredded finery. They held hands as they ran, as if that fragment of comfort was worth what they lost in speed. The gesture was so futile in the face of inevitable massacre, and so touchingly human. It was, Volos thought, the epitome of what he had been created to protect. A group of frenzied dead closed in on the couple. Volos swatted the enemy away, pulping the bodies. He scooped up the two humans. They screamed when they first felt his grasp. They seemed hardly more reassured when they realised what was happening. They stared at him with eyes that were near mindless with fear. But they didn't struggle.

Volos ran faster, barrelling through the dead, exploding bodies with his juggernaut run. He reached Nithigg, who grabbed two civilians and joined the race. Behind, more clusters of humans fell off the pace and were swallowed by the horde.

By the time Squads Pythios and Ormarr reached the pass, the only refugees left were the ones they carried.

They held two each, except for Toharan, who had three: there was a small child perched on his head. Thirty-seven survivors. A poor showing.

The Black Dragons pounded along the broken, twisting path of the defile. Behind them, the dead raged and followed, but lost ground. The walls of the pass closed in, barely a few metres apart at moments. They leaned in from the vertical, black stone slicked with moisture. Misting waterfalls thickened the air. The Temple chain was taking the intruders into its hard embrace, hugging them tighter and closer. Even with his enhanced vision, Volos found it difficult to see more than a few dozen metres ahead. But that was enough.

They ran for hours, outdistancing the enemy by kilometres, but not slowing even then. They still didn't slow when the pass opened out into the bottom of a vast canyon. The path turned here and snaked thousands of metres up the near canyon wall. It led, at the top, to the narrow, graceful span of the Ecclesiarch Alexis XXII bridge. From this distance below, the bridge was as insubstantial as human hair. Stretching kilometres across the canyon, it was the unique access to Lexica Keep. Its lights glowering in the night, the fortress crouched against the far cliff face like a bird of prey. From between the dark wings of its walls, it peered with cold, contemptuous majesty at the warriors and their charges.

It offered no comfort.

LEXICA KEEP WAS a Ministorum redoubt. It had, at times, reserved a portion of its east wing for schola purposes, but its primary function had been as a librarium. Its collection was as famous as it was difficult to access. It was a repository of texts from all corners of the Imperium, and from all its ages. Some of its manuscripts, Werner Lettinger knew, were pre-Imperial. Still others, he suspected darkly, were pre-human. Some of his more radical colleagues, especially among the Ordo Hereticus, would give much to examine those works. Some, he knew, had traded their souls for the opportunity. He wondered if the knowledge acquired had been worth the additional cost – their lives. Given the choice, he would have pitched the entire collection into a blazing Act of Faith long ago. He took comfort, at least, in the fact that the books were under lock and key in a fastness never to be stormed.

Captain Vritras of the Black Dragons was speaking. 'We are, of course, grateful for any aid you might be able to provide, inquisitor.'

They were in a council chamber whose door opened onto the dining hall that had become the Dragons command centre. Gas-burning torches were held by iron sconces along the curved walls. These ended in a floor-to-ceiling sheet of armourglass that looked down into the canyon. The brickwork of dark grey rockcrete was so fine that the mortar was invisible. The walls looked like a single block of stone. In the centre of the chamber was a long table carved from the enormous trunk of a berbab tree, shipped from Antagonis's southern continent. The wood appeared to absorb light rather than reflect it. In its depths, bright pinpricks shone like swallowed stars. Data-slates, maps and transmission papers covered much of its surface now, and there were scars gouged by carelessly tossed weapons. Lettinger couldn't imagine the Confessors of Lexica countenancing such disrespect, but the question was moot. The Ecclesiarchy of Antagonis had been among the first to succumb to the plague. The Dragons had purged every last one of them before making Lexica their own.

'I hope you don't mind my saying,' Vritras went on, 'that I would have thought an officer from the Ordo Sepulturum would have been sent, given the nature of Antagonis's taint.'

Lettinger smiled to show he wasn't offended. But he wondered how Vritras knew with such certainty that he *wasn't* of that ordo. 'Quite understandable, captain,' he said. 'The reason for my presence here is simple. Time is clearly of the essence, given that the situation has become this grave in, as far as we can determine, a matter of days. It would take months, at best, for a Sepulturum team to be despatched, and I, like you, was in the region.'

'Quite a lucky coincidence,' First-Sergeant Aperos of Squad Nychus remarked.

Lettinger ignored the sarcasm and kept his smile. 'It would seem that the Emperor has traced a path for us to tread together.'

'I can't help but be struck by how often the Black Dragons and the Ordo Malleus seem to wind up on similar paths,' Vritras said. 'You are always nearby to come to our assistance.'

Lettinger started. Only the Grey Knights were supposed to know that there was even such a thing as the Ordo Malleus. He tried to keep his expression neutral.

'I'm sorry, but there seems to be a misunderstand–'

'Don't insult my intelligence, inquisitor. If you think we haven't had dealings with your ordo before, then you are too naïve to be much good at your allotted task.'

It was becoming difficult for Lettinger to pretend he wasn't aware of Vritras's insolence. It was harder still to keep his own face friendly, and his eyes from narrowing, the longer he had to look at the Space Marine and his sergeant. Neither warrior's mutations were extreme by the standards of the Dragons, but there was still a bony growth on Vritras's forehead like a blunt, stubby horn, while Aperos had a ridged crest running from his crown down the back of his head. The deformations were the mark of deviant genetic practice, as far as Lettinger was concerned. *Give me the proof, captain*, he thought. *Give me the proof of what we all know your Chapter is doing, and I will have you and your unclean brothers ripped cleanly from the purity of the Imperium.* With these thoughts as his strength, he simply bowed. 'As you say, captain.'

'Someone's coming,' Colonel Dysfield said. He'd been staying out of the exchange, standing by the window with his back to the room. He commanded the 25th Mortisian Rifles, but had provisionally handed over his command to Kervold so that the Guard tasked with the rescue should have the unity of a single command.

The Space Marines and Lettinger joined him. They saw the figures racing across the Alexis bridge. There weren't many. 'Throne,' Vritras muttered.

'Incoming ship, too,' Dysfield noted.

The landing lights were on, and in the darkness, Lettinger couldn't make out what sort of craft it was. He knew who would be on it, thought. 'That would be Canoness Setheno,' he said. He enjoyed the sharp looks the Dragons and the colonel gave him.

'The Canoness Errant?' Dysfield asked stupidly, as if hoping that somehow there were two canonesses with the same name, and this wasn't the one he dreaded.

'Why is she here?' Aperos demanded.

'She was in the Maeror subsector. When I heard she was part of the tithing mission on Aighe Mortis, I contacted her and requested her aid.'

Dysfield had recovered some of his composure and was trying to withdraw into cynical apathy again, implying that Setheno's arrival couldn't possibly be any concern of his. 'It's nice how some things work out,' he deadpanned. Lettinger wasn't sure who was being mocked, so he didn't respond.

'The Canoness Errant and an inquisitor of the Ordo Malleus, both of whom just happened to be in my subsector,' Vritras growled. 'Are you sure you are here simply because of the crisis on Antagonis?'

'Proximately, yes.'

'*Proximately*? What is that supposed to mean?'

'What are your questions supposed to mean, captain?' Lettinger asked. 'Since when does the Inquisition have to justify its decisions to anyone? Do you have something you would prefer to hide from us?'

'My conscience is clean and damn you for asking.'

'Perhaps your personal conscience is. I do wonder about the collective one of your Chapter.'

'Enjoy wondering,' Vritras snapped. 'I'm going to greet the warriors who have just given much for the

Imperium.' He and Aperos strode out of the chamber, the floor vibrating from the weight of their footfalls. Dysfield followed. He gave Lettinger a look that bordered on hostile, but was also wary. He knew he should be frightened of Lettinger simply because Lettinger was Inquisition and Dysfield was not. That fear was as it should be. Lettinger approved.

He hesitated over whether to head to the courtyard or hurry to greet Setheno when she disembarked. He gambled that he had another few minutes before the canoness quit her ship. He wanted to see the Black Dragons as they returned. There were two, in particular, who interested him. There was an opportunity here, a chance to gather information that might finally bring about proper scrutiny of these Space Marines.

Lettinger hurried after Vritras and Aperos, and arrived in the keep's courtyard just as Squads Pythios and Ormarr passed through the gate. The Space Marines set the refugees down, then two of them loaded up with detonators and melta bombs and headed back to the bridge. The civilians huddled together, sobbing and shaking. Dysfield's staff officer approached them, accompanied by a medicae team, who began to herd them into the keep. Dysfield walked up to one of the Dragons and spoke quietly. Lettinger couldn't hear the conversation, but he guessed that the colonel was asking about the two companies of Mortisian infantry. The Space Marine shook his head. Dysfield looked stricken. No one else would be coming, Lettinger presumed. He thought about the loss of thirty thousand men, and his heart sank. He felt sorry for Dysfield. The man's entire command, with the exception of the contingent in Lexica, had been wiped out.

Lettinger would have liked to have spoken to the colonel. He would have liked to express his sympathy, to offer what support he could to an officer taking a staggering blow. But his own duty called. He saw Vritras and Aperos talking to the two sergeants who had just arrived. That was the opportunity he had been seeking. He moved toward them, walking softly over the cobbled surface of the courtyard, doing his best to be inconspicuous. As he drew near, the Space Marines removed their helmets, and he felt a rush of satisfaction and terror.

That there were mutations in the ranks of the Black Dragons was no secret. The Dragon Claws assault teams were composed entirely of Space Marines whose Ossmodula zygote had gone berserk. The implanted organ was responsible for the enormous size and strength of Adeptus Astartes skeletons, but in the case of the Claws, it didn't know where to stop. The bones kept developing, most visibly in the form of outgrowths on the skull and, most effectively for combat, as blades, some of them retractable, in the forearm.

As far as Lettinger and many of his Ordo Malleus colleagues were concerned, it simply wasn't possible that such a desirable mutation could be a chance development. Gene tampering was tainting the Black Dragons. Yet when the Chapter (reluctantly) submitted its tithe of genetic material, the samples were always of a purity beyond reproach. They were too good to be true, as suspicious in their own way as the bone-blades.

But the evidence was circumstantial, at best. The

Dragons were careful, and had never given the Inquisition proper cause or opportunity to put them to the question. They were also very good at keeping their distance. But now the Inquisition, in the person of Werner Lettinger, was deep in the Dragons Second Company, and the warp take him if he didn't find the means to launch a full, formal investigation against this Emperor-forsaken result of the Cursed Founding of M36.

As he took in sergeants Volos and Toharan, he felt the locks to the Dragons secrets tumbling open beneath his hands. Though he didn't have any formal proof, he could see how the gene tithe passed the examinations. Toharan showed no sign of mutation at all. Underneath a mane of blond hair, his forehead was unblemished by disfiguring crest. His skin tone was lighter than that of the other Dragons Lettinger had seen. The norm was dark, lending credence to the theory that the Dragons were debased derivations of the Salamanders. But Toharan's flesh had a glow that was almost human. All the Dragons would have to do to satisfy the tithing demands would be to send in material drawn from Toharan and others like him. He was, Lettinger realised, a very special kind of mutant: the aberrantly pure-born in a world of monsters.

And beside him stood the supreme monster. More than three metres tall, Volos loomed over every other living being in the courtyard. He was so gigantic that he wore custom-made armour and used an oversized jump pack for lift. His eyes were black, glinting pits of obsidian looking out from dark grey, leathery hide whose overlapping ridges looked disturbingly like scales. His razored horn dispensed with all pretence, as far as Lettinger was concerned, of being anything other than daemonic. When he spoke to Vritras, his fangs poked out over his lower lip.

As Lettinger watched the two Space Marines, each, for a moment, returned his stare. Toharan looked him up and down, his eyes pausing for a cold second at the inquisitorial rosette on Lettinger's breast before moving up to his face and favouring him with an expression of absolute hostility and contempt. Volos barely glanced at him, and though he showed none of Toharan's antagonism, his indifference was worse. It told Lettinger that he was beneath notice. He wasn't even an irritant, merely a detail on the landscape.

There was no trace of humanity in the creature, Lettinger thought. Volos was well down the path to becoming an actual dragon. Lettinger's puritan soul demanded that he cleanse Volos from the Emperor's sight. But his craven blood quailed before the embodied power of war. He needed reinforcement.

'Inquisitor,' a female voice said behind him.

Lettinger smiled. He turned, expecting to greet his reinforcement. Instead, his smile turned into a rictus as he stared, frozen and stone, into the face of the Gorgon.

CHAPTER 3
ILLUMINATED

THE NATURE OF his work meant Elias Tennesyn was, most of the time, spared the hive experience. He lived in the field, digging up and studying the relics of a past that receded to infinity. For the traces of xenos civilizations to be preserved on a planet, there had to be regions little touched by human development. Therefore, no hives. Antagonis was a world that suited him. Its temperate zones were broad, its two principle land masses were separated by large, life-giving oceans, and its cities, though large, were not monsters. Antagonis still boasted landscapes that were not only green, but actually wild. It had forests, veldts and tundra. Antagonis had space for antiquity and its secrets. So Tennesyn resented the occasions that took him away from the likes of Antagonis to the worlds that presented the human species in its most insect-like form. And a wasted trip, as this one to Aighe Mortis was turning out to be, was a special kind of hell.

Even the briefest, most profitable stay on this planet would have carried a whiff of brimstone. Aighe Mortis was the sole inhabited planet of the Camargus system, just as Antagonis was in Phlagia. Unlike Antagonis, Aighe Mortis was a dying star of a hive world. The civilization on this planet was like a sun going red and huge before its final collapse. It had swollen to a final, absolute extremity of population density. The growth was so unsustainable that it could only be the precursor to a terminal, lights-out plunge into the wreckage of barbarism. The shallow oceans had long ago been drained and evaporated to make way for more and more ground-swallowing, sky-shrouding manufactoria. But the memory of seas lingered in the atmosphere, turning the faecal-brown and bile-yellow air into a thick sludge that sat in the lungs like pneumonic sputum. To breathe on Aighe Mortis was to drown slowly.

The closest thing the world had known to a golden era was in the Age of Apostasy, when its mineral resources had been plenty, and there had been enough space on the surface that the population centres could still boast that they were distinct cities. But the millennia passed, the cities merged into a single disease, and the mineral seams were exhausted. Misery and deprivation were a tide that rose but never ebbed. The last of the wealthy families fled early in M41. When the mining concerns were taken over by desperate, rioting workers, off-world owners decided it was cheaper to cut their losses than face the expense and effort of reclaiming valueless property.

Something between a cooperative and a criminal

anarchy had risen on Aighe Mortis, giving just enough obeisance to Imperial administrative bodies to achieve a state of mutual tolerance. The mines had tunnelled deeper into the earth, leaving exhausted regions to be remade as sunless habs, and enough new seams were found to jolt the planet's economy into a semi-functioning state of undeath. By then, the population was such that almost all of Aighe Mortis's resources were consumed by local needs for material and energy. In the end (and Tennesyn had seen enough civilizational graveyards to know that the end couldn't be far down the road), Aighe Mortis kept itself going by exporting two things. One was small arms, churned out in cut-rate but reliable form in the uncountable billions. The other was men. Human existence here was red in tooth and claw. Vicious natural selection was encouraged by gangs that recognised a valuable resource when they saw it, and a steady stream of Guardsmen and mercenaries swarmed from the hive into the rest of the Imperium

Aighe Mortis was a world that Tennesyn didn't enjoy thinking about, never mind setting foot on. But it was also an old world. Its historical records reached back to the Heresy and beyond. Hiding in the cracks and shadows between the belching chimneys and maggot-writhing hab complexes were pockets of scholarship. There were archives here that, even in their decrepit state, would be the envy of the great universitariats, were they widely known. But on Aighe Mortis, it was for the good of their continued existence that they remain forgotten and ignored.

Tennesyn knew about them. There were some scrolls

in a private collection that he had thought might help with interpreting the find on Antagonis, and he had sent Granton Fellix here to seek them out. Fellix was a native Mortisian. It had made sense, at the time, for him to make the trip. But then had come the sudden announcement of a new and massive founding, and Fellix had been caught up in the tithe. Tennesyn had come to extricate him from that obligation, thinking his own standing as senior xeno-archaeologist at Bendridge Universitariat, the most prestigious in the Maeror subsector, might count for something.

Not for the first time, he hated himself for being so ignorant.

Tennesyn had spent the last seven days meandering through the warren of the Departmento Munitorum's Mortisian palace. Now he was waiting outside the office of Jozef Bisset. He had been down so many administrative blind alleys that he had lost all track of hierarchical positions, and had no idea what Bisset's precise title was. Tennesyn knew he was a comptroller, and that he had something to do with determining how many recruits would be press-ganged from which regions of the hive. Tennesyn knew two other things about Bisset. The first was that, over a century ago, they had been students together, and Tennesyn had helped Bisset through some exams that would have otherwise finished him off. He was hoping Bisset had a long memory. The second thing Tennesyn knew was that Bisset was his last resort. He had spent too much time on this fool's quest already. He felt sorry for Fellix, but there was no point in *both* of them being gone from the dig site.

The waiting area was like every other room in the complex. The building called itself a palace because the administrative pride of the Departmento demanded it, but it was no more palatial than Tennesyn was a death cult assassin. The walls were a dark grey, damp-stained, unadorned, pitted rockcrete. The seats were metal and dug into Tennesyn's back. The lighting was dim and as filthy as the air itself. Bisset's secretary was a dull-eyed, incompetently augmented man who must have been less than half Tennesyn's age, but looked three times older. His face was so slack and apathetic that Tennesyn had, for a brief moment, mistaken him for a servitor.

After half an hour, and without Tennesyn being able to catch any sort of communication, the secretary jabbed a thumb in the direction of doors behind his scratched and rusted metal desk. 'You can go in now,' he said, without looking up from the data-slates laid out before him.

Tennesyn stood up. 'Thank you,' he said, and walked through the doors.

On the other side, Bisset's office was more of the same as the waiting room, only smaller. The only suggestion of rank was the unblemished, dark iron of the desk, and the presence of a window. Tennesyn was surprised. Disoriented, he hadn't realised he had been this close to the exterior wall of the palace. The armourglass window was about a metre high, a tenth of that in width, and so layered with grime that it offered no view at all.

Jozef Bisset walked around his desk to shake Tennesyn's hand. He was the same age as Tennesyn, but looked both younger and more battered, thanks to his decades of active service in the Guard. He'd had more juvenat work done, and the limbs that were still his own had a suppleness of movement that Tennesyn envied. But his right arm was bionic, and Tennesyn thought he heard the subtle whine of servos in at least one leg as well. The left side of Bisset's face, above the mouth, was a bronze mask. The implanted eye tracked its ruby gaze independently of the right one. 'Elias,' Bisset said. 'It's good to see you. Do have a seat.'

The chairs were the same metal backbreakers as the ones in the waiting room, but Tennesyn sat. He gave Bisset his warmest smile and most open countenance as the man returned to sit at his desk. 'Thank you, comptroller–'

'Oh, stop it. We both know I'm Jozef to you.'

'Jozef, then.' Tennesyn said. 'I suppose you know why I'm here.'

Bisset nodded at the lone data-slate on his desk. 'I have the file. I'm sorry. I wish I could help.'

Tennesyn forced himself to go through the futile motions one more time. 'This man is a valuable member of my team, far more valuable than he would be as a single green conscript.'

'I'm sure you're right. But at just this moment, utility is completely beside the point. The tensions are bad enough that the slightest appearance of granting anyone a favour could set off more riots. Or worse.'

'Riots? What are you talking about?'

Bisset blinked at him. 'What cave have you been living in?'

'This one!' Tennesyn exploded in frustration. 'I've spent the last week shuttling from office to office, napping in waiting rooms. I don't even know what day it is!'

'We've had to double the tithe,' Bisset explained. 'And it's being resisted. But Sarcannis and Perethea are a mess, and between that and the situation on Antagonis –'

'What situation on Antagonis?' Tennesyn's voice broke with a hint of hysteria.

'Throne, man, how do you function in the real world at all?'

'I should get back there.' He rose.

'Are you mad? That planet is–'

A distant, but deep, boom cut Bisset off. The room vibrated. Dust drifted down from the ceiling. Tennesyn wondered what could shake them a thousand metres up in a building of this size. 'What was that?' he whispered.

Bisset sighed, looking very, very tired. 'That, I do believe, was a bomb.'

THE REVEALED TRUTH was a gold that did not glitter. It was a gold that stole light. The Retaliator-class cruiser was a study in dark glory, bristling with flying buttresses and spires that invited the eye to think of shining triumph, but then somehow dimmed vision, threatening blindness if stared at for too long. It was a spectacle that repelled sight. It was brazen stealth.

It was paradox.

And that made it the very dear love of Cardinal Rodrigo Nessun, because paradox was the vital truth of the warp. It was a truth that had burst upon him five millennia ago. The Ministorum had seconded him to a detachment of the Inquisition's Ordo Malleus. He had been a loyal slave of the Emperor, then, and a participant in the project that had led to the founding of the Exorcists. That Adeptus Astartes Chapter was legendary for its incorruptibility. Rumour said that each had a daemon bound within his flesh as part of their initiation, making them immune to any further possession. Nessun had no quarrel with the accuracy of the legend, but he would, if asked, add a small amendment. The immune were those who had been *successfully* initiated. There had been failures. Many, during the work leading up to the founding. So many that illumination had descended upon Nessun. The failure, he had realised, lay not with the corrupted Space Marines, but in the goal itself. Those newly born daemonic warriors were the truth of the universe. That was the first paradox. He had embraced it, and them.

He had gathered his sons to him, and baptised them the Swords of Epiphany. Then they had fled to the warp, and his true education had begun. Now he had progressed far beyond the simple paradoxes of the elastic time that had granted him a semblance of immortality, or of the fact that the further his physiological transformations took him from the human race, the better he understood his former species. These were simply the perverse truths of subjectivity, limited to his own perception. They gave surprise and joy, but they weren't enough.

He was a theologian, a Hierarch, an evangelist. He had a calling. He must make manifest the beauty of the warp's truth for all to see. He would illuminate the Imperium with a scorching light, and sometimes, *paradoxically*, it was necessary to exterminate those whom one would save.

He was standing in an observation blister on the top of the *Revealed Truth*'s command spire, listening to the writhing of colours, watching the scream of space. There was a hiss as the door slid open, and Makaiel entered. The Space Marine captain's armour was the same light-dousing gold as the ship. His helm grille was a maw of angelic fangs.

Nessun smiled his blessing. 'What news, my son?'

'Aighe Mortis is reaching critical mass, father.'

To have a being such as Makaiel address him with such reverence was a wonder that Nessun never tired of savouring. The Swords would, under other circumstances, have had a Chapter Master. But it was Nessun, the simple human (well, *formerly* so) who ruled these weaponised gods. 'And our route to Flebis?' Their destination was well to the galactic south of Aighe Mortis, halfway across the Maeror subsector, in the farther reaches of the Segmentum Tempestus.

'The warp storms are minimal. We will arrive there in plenty of time.'

Good. Destiny was unfolding before him with the beauty of a stained glass flower. He would be the bringer of light, and the destroyer of worlds.

'BEHAVE YOURSELF,' TOHARAN muttered. 'That, over there, is the purity of faith made flesh.'

Volos didn't respond, but he picked up on an odd undercurrent to his brother's remark. The cynicism sounded forced, as if Toharan were using mockery to avoid facing something serious.

'Be still, sergeant,' Vritras ordered under his breath.

'Canoness,' he said aloud and nodded.

Setheno stepped forward, past the poleaxed Lettinger. 'Captain,' she said.

Volos watched the reactions in the courtyard to her arrival. Lettinger was still rooted to the spot, and that was amusing. Lettinger wore black robes and went hooded, his face in shadow with little more visible than his convoluted electoos. His appearance was carefully designed to convey danger and authority. But his studied menace was comical beside Setheno. Beyond Lettinger, there was a ripple as the other mortals moved away from the canoness. Whether refugees or Guard, they had the same tense, shoulder-hunched look of anxious prey. They did not want to be noticed, but they couldn't tear their eyes away from the hunter. Setheno had done no more than step into the courtyard and utter two words, yet she was a presence that filled the space. Volos tried to put his finger on why that was. Certainly, by any measure other than a Space Marine one, she was physically imposing. She was one of the tallest humans Volos had ever seen. At two metres, she was the same height as Toharan. Then there was her reputation.

She had been Canoness Superior of the Order of the Piercing Thorn. Minoris though the order had been, its members had made their presence felt, melding a learning worthy of the Sisters Dialogous with a commando military philosophy. They had been a sharp blade in the flanks of the archenemy. Volos had heard many stories of the Piercing Thorn and what befell it. Some of those stories told of Setheno's leadership. It was such that she had been seen as a possible contender for the vacant seat of Abbess Sanctorum of the Convent Prioris on Terra. But then the taint had come. Exactly what its nature was, and how pervasive the corruption of the Piercing Thorn had been, Volos didn't know. The stories weren't about the taint. They were about the response to it. Whatever Setheno had uncovered, she had denounced her order to the Inquisition. She had demanded its extermination. The Orders Militant had placed themselves at her disposal, and, in numbers overwhelming, had slaughtered the Sisters of the Piercing Thorn down to the last novice. Setheno herself had executed all of her prioresses. She had burned the order's fortress-abbey to the ground, and spread salt over its shattered, blackened stones.

She had refused posting to a different order. Instead, she had become the Canoness Errant, a singular position of vaguely defined, but immense, punitive authority. Her power did not exist at the official level. It emerged from an unspoken consensus that, between her unswerving, merciless faith, and her prowess at war, she was too useful to discard and too terrifying to confront.

So yes, she had a reputation that cleared rooms of all but those who knew no fear.

Her armour was another conscious echo of the dark past. It had been blasted of identifying colour. It was now the uniform grey of ash and cathedral stone. She wore a helm, and its design, Volos suspected, had cowed greater men than Lettinger. It was a woman's face, eyes ablaze and mouth wide in a howl of horror and rage. A crimson tear in the corner of the left eye was the armour's one note of colour, an emblem of brutal grief.

When she reached the Space Marines, Setheno removed

her helm. Volos blinked in surprise. The face of ceramite and the face beneath it were the same. But the flesh showed no emotion. It had the perfection and implacable impassivity of marble. It was, Volos thought, as if the frailties and passions of humanity had been so utterly scoured from Setheno's being that it was left to her armour to show emotion. Her hair was white as death, and her eyes were a limpid, frozen gold. Volos had expected to see in them the blaze of fanaticism. Instead, he saw a clarity and a depth of knowledge that were worse. He understood how she made secular and spiritual authorities kneel before her will. He met her gaze, and felt his being become part of a perpetual flow of evaluation and judgement.

Volos knew what Lettinger thought of him, but he didn't care. Setheno was a different matter. She might constitute a legitimate threat to the Chapter. He couldn't tell if that was her intent. He glanced at Toharan, and saw the same wariness in his brother's face.

'My sergeants have been informing me that the behaviour of the walking dead is unusual,' Vritras said.

'How so?' Setheno asked.

'The attacks are more directed than they should be,' Toharan answered. 'I sense a purpose behind them.'

'What sort of purpose?' Though Setheno's low, euphonious monotone didn't change, Volos sensed a spike of interest and urgency in her question.

The thunder of heavy stubber fire cut off Toharan's response. Volos spun around. The rampart turrets had opened up. He stormed across the courtyard and took the stone steps four at a time to the top of the curtain.

The others joined him a moment later. He looked down the mountain face into the depths of the valley. 'Cease fire, you idiots,' he roared at the Mortisians manning the turrets. They were wasting ammunition, spitting into an ocean. 'Blow the bridge!' he ordered.

Melus and Nithigg set off the charges. The melta bombs at either end of the bridge turned stone molten. The elegant span parted from the mountains, and there was a moment of graceful descent, as if the bridge thought to fly; then the centuries-old masterwork disintegrated in a tumbling roar. There was no longer a road to the keep.

But the dead were pouring in from the defile, streaming across the valley floor to the base of the redoubt's mountain. Volos followed the flood of corpses back as far as he could see into the pass. The dead were a swarm that put the tyranids to shame. Volos had a vision of the continental land mass tilting, funnelling its six billion souls into this one narrow passage. The dead were an army so huge that numbers ceased to have meaning. They slammed against the mountainside. Volos watched them bunch up for a few moments before he realised what must be happening. The dead were climbing over each other, crushing each other. Building on each other. Building a mound that would grow into a hill, into a mountain of flesh. A mountain that would fill the valley.

A mountain that would topple the plague into Lexica Keep.

CHAPTER 4
GOOD INTENTIONS

'A bomb?' Tennesyn demanded as he raced to keep up with Bisset. They were pounding up an endless wrought-iron staircase, heading for the roof. They weren't the only ones. Above and below them, the faithful drones of Imperial military bureaucracy were pouring onto the stairs as the implications of what must have happened at street-level sank in. The lifts in the palace had stopped working in the wake of the explosion. The evacuees flowed in both directions, some heading to the nearer roof, others to the distant ground, where riot threatened but there was less far to fall. 'Who is setting off bombs? Why attack a Munitorum building? What's happening? Where are we going?'

'Where we're going is to get you into our shuttle and off-planet,' Bisset answered. He was taking the stairs with an effortless, mechanical rhythm. 'As to who the terrorists are, they could be anyone these days. Why? The new founding.'

There was a second, deeper, thrumming boom from below. It echoed up the stairwell like a predator's roar. The building shook. Tennesyn lost his balance and fell against the railing. Bisset caught him before he pitched over. A man one landing up wasn't as lucky. He screamed as he plunged down the stairwell, body smashing on the railings. The muffled bell toll of his fall went on for a long time. Tennesyn put his hands over his ears until it stopped. Bisset tugged at his arm to get him moving again. He noticed that the stairs were no longer perfectly level.

'What's the problem with the founding?' Tennesyn asked. He wanted his mind off towers and tilts and high places. He was giving himself a puzzle to chew on, a focus to distract himself from his fear. And here was what he knew: the founding was necessary. In the galactic north of the Maeror subsector, the neighbouring systems of Sarcannis and Perethea were in turmoil, ripped apart by the unholy combination of heretical rebellion and ork incursion. The Emperor's will would be enforced once more on the benighted; of this no one had any doubt. The greenskins' Waaagh! was a minor one, disorganised and strategically brain-dead even by their standards, while the rebellious worlds were feral and poorly armed. The only thing either enemy had in its favour was the sheer force of numbers. The tactical requirements for successful pacification were straightforward; even Tennesyn could see that. All that was needed was brute manpower. Lots of it. In the Maeror subsector, that manpower was first and foremost the Mortisian Guard, and it was being overstretched. Its forces needed replenishing. The founding was necessary. Tennesyn couldn't see how anyone could dispute that, especially anyone from Aighe Mortis itself.

'The problem,' Bisset said, 'is the drain on the local population.'

Tennesyn was so nonplussed he forgot about the slant of the stairs. He almost lost his footing. 'The *drain*? On a population of how many billions? And Guardsmen and mercenaries being this planet's big export? How does that make any sense at all?'

The wall above Bisset cracked, raining rockcrete dust. The split zigzagged past Tennesyn, working its way down the levels. On the other side of the walls, from the core of the building, came groans. Tennesyn thought of iron trees creaking in a gale.

Bisset glanced at the crack as he brushed powder from his shoulders. He climbed a bit faster. Tennesyn's lungs and legs cried out, but he kept up. Fear was his spur.

Bisset said, 'You're the expert on the big historical picture, so tell me this: how stable would you say Aighe Mortis's civilization is?'

'Not very. It's terminal.'

'So there's your answer. A little push is all it takes to upset the equilibrium, and let me tell you that balance is pretty damned delicate in this latrine. One slip and we're all in the piss. And this isn't just a tithe we're talking about. It's another full founding. The second in a year.'

'You sound like you're sympathising.'

Bisset shook his head, emphatic. 'I'm not. Bunch of forsaken primitives here, is what they are, and just lucky enough to be living in what their ancestors built. It's dog eat dog and daemons take the hindmost.' He was angry, but Tennesyn thought he detected at least a trace of understanding that went beyond the purely academic.

It was an understanding he didn't share. 'I don't see how their faith can be so weak,' he said. He didn't simply disapprove. He was confused. The Mortisian regiments were ferocious in the execution of their duty to the Emperor.

'The Guard is the end result of a shaping process,' Bisset reminded him. 'All we have to start with is rabid raw material. And–'

He was cut off by the distant but ominous *whooooom* of another blast. A shudder ran through the walls and stairs. Tennesyn's knees turned to water and he clutched at the vibrating railing. Cries of alarm swept the staircase. The vibrating didn't stop. The tilt increased. There was no mistaking it now, no chance of rationalising it away as an error of perception. Then the worst thing began. The tilt diminished. The stairs levelled. They leaned the other way. Then, gradually, horribly, back again.

The tower was swaying.

'*Run!*' Bisset roared, but no one needed to be told. The crowd stampeded up the remaining flights. Tennesyn's lungs were raw agony, his legs a leaden ache, his heart a stuttering drum. But the fear was in his entire body, and it was stronger than all of his pain, and he ran, fighting to keep his balance as rockrete became giddy and drunk.

They burst out onto the roof. The four corner landing pads each held an Aquila shuttle. The aircraft were warmed up, their pilots anxious to be off. Bisset and Tennesyn were near the front of the mob, but Bisset sprinted for the furthest lander. The shuttles only had six-passenger capacities, and the desperation in the air was going to turn the scene bloody. Tennesyn's instinct had been to head for the nearest lander, but so was everyone else's, and he saw that Bisset's strategy, taking them where the crowd was thinnest, might save their lives.

They were halfway across the roof, only a handful of people ahead of them, when there was another explosion. In the open air, it sounded much louder, much sharper, much closer, and Tennesyn had a moment to wonder why the tower didn't collapse beneath him before he realised the blast had hit another target. Bisset turned his head, and Tennesyn followed his gaze to the west.

'Throne,' Bisset cursed.

Tennesyn saw plumes of smoke rising from the base of another, higher tower half a kilometre away. The harsh roar of the explosion became a deeper, more terrible, unending thunder as the tower bowed in surrender. It disappeared with an end-of-the-world cry into a shroud of its own dust, dragging its neighbours down with it. The tangle of spires was too dense, and none would die alone. All the time, the sway of the palace grew worse. It was a slow waltz with a chorus of screams.

'This is big!' Bisset yelled as they ran. 'Not just riots! Too organised!'

They reached the Aquila. It was full, and it was starting to lift off the pad, but there was just enough authority in Bisset's uniform to make the pilot hesitate another few seconds. Bisset grabbed Tennesyn with his bionic arm and threw him into the open passenger bay. Tennesyn landed hard on metal, almost slipped out, but hands grabbed him to pull him in. He scrabbled around and was reaching out to Bisset when the waltz ended.

One more blast, big and close. The palace swayed and did not straighten. The roof tilted sharply. The screams of its refugees were drowned by the death howl of the structure itself. The lander banked away from the danger. Bisset stood still for a moment. The look he gave Tennesyn was resigned, stoic, and bitterly amused, as if he had had just about enough of this day, yet still expected to see worse ones. 'Bring back help,' he called. Then he was sprinting sideways against the tilt of the building. Tennesyn saw him make a leap of faith towards an adjacent roof, and he vanished into rising dust.

IN THE CONFUSION of the near-orbit stations, Tennesyn managed to find a merchant willing to make a run to Antagonis. He was an independent runner of small arms, a supplier to mercenaries though clearly too well-fed and lazy to have known combat himself. He hadn't heard about any trouble on Antagonis, and Tennesyn didn't enlighten him. The captain of the *Trade Sail* was eager to be out of the Camargus system, and being paid to run was even better.

Tennesyn didn't need further proof that Bisset was right, that something more serious than unrest was striking Aighe Mortis. But he received it, all the same. It came in two blows. The first arrived as the *Trade Sail* left anchor. With a peremptory electronic squeal, the message took over all vox channels. 'Citizens of Aighe

Mortis,' it announced. 'Your oppression beneath the Imperial heel is ended. Your deliverance is at hand.'

Tennesyn was looking out the rear viewport at the receding planet when he saw the second proof hit. It came in the form of two ships. One was a heavy raider, of a type Tennesyn had never seen before. The other he recognised as a modified transport, warped into a shape of clawed, grasping hunger. Both were gold, and it was a terrible gold, a gold that crawled behind his eyes to scrape and infect his soul.

But worse than the gold was the coat of arms on the hull: an eye over a sword. He had seen that sign before, swinging from a chain around the neck of a laughing cardinal. He felt the sick, wrenching certainty that he had, not long past, made an awful, devastating mistake.

'How much time remains?' Benedict Danton wanted to know. It was the morning after his rescue, and he had cleaned up well. He was pale, exhausted, perhaps a bit shrunken in his suit, but still very much the high lord.

Dysfield shrugged. 'Difficult to say. Along with the forces of Captain Vritras, we are conducting some aerial sweeps to determine how big a concentration of the dead are heading this way. We have also bombed the pass. The rockfall isn't a hermetic seal on the valley, but it is slowing the enemy down. Even so, there are so many millions close at hand. A few days? Perhaps a bit longer. We could gain some time with strategic orbital bombardments, but even then...' He trailed off.

Volos stood with Squads Pythios, Ormarr and the captain's own Nychus against the walls of the council chamber. They were not taking part in the deliberations. That was the remit of Vritras, Dysfield, Danton and Lettinger. At least officially. But Setheno was at the table too, her mere presence shoving Lettinger into the background. The sergeants, meanwhile, were here to listen, and to present a silent show of solidarity for their captain. Volos watched Danton react to Dysfield's report. The Space Marine was taking the measure of the man whose life his brothers had bought with their own.

'There has been no communication with any other population centre on this continent?' Danton asked.

'None,' Dysfield confirmed. 'Nor from anywhere else on the planet.'

The lines on Danton's face deepened. He rubbed a finger against his lips and stared at the tactical map of Antagonis spread out on the council table. 'Well,' he said. He cleared his throat, straightened and faced his audience. 'Well,' he repeated, 'as abhorrent as it may be, it is my responsibility to say what must be said: Antagonis has fallen. The war is over, and we have lost.' He turned to Vritras. 'Captain, you and your men have my most profound thanks for rescuing me and my family. I grieve for your and Colonel Dysfield's losses. This is a debt that I can never–'

'No,' Vritras said. His tone was calm, quiet, furious.

Danton blinked. 'I'm sorry. I don't understand–'

'We are the Black Dragons. We are Adeptus Astartes. We are the ultimate force of the Emperor, and we *do not* surrender. Ever. This war is not over.'

In the silence that followed, Volos mentally applauded. Danton's defeatism was as sickening as it was offensive.

Volos noted that Dysfield was keeping his opinions to himself. The colonel's mouth was a hard, narrow line, but his eyes were haggard, as if he hated what Danton was saying, but could not refute his logic.

The lord of Antagonis regrouped. 'Captain,' he said, 'I mean no disrespect either to your Chapter's courage or its prowess. But no matter how formidable you and your brother warriors are, what good will that do against *billions*? Do you have that much ammunition? Do you have that much *time*?' He spread his arms before the inevitability of humiliation. 'We have, thanks to you, already salvaged what we can. There is nothing left but to retreat to orbit, and there Inquisitor Lettinger,' he bowed to the hooded man, 'can give the order to sterilise the planet, ensuring the archenemy's victory is a pyrrhic one.'

'And so, under my watch, I must see the Emperor lose another world?' Vritras demanded.

'It is hardly a strategic–' Danton began.

Vritras cut him off again, this time with a single shake of his head. 'With every clod that is washed away, the Imperium is lessened, and we are all diminished. I will not let that happen without being certain I did everything that was possible, and more, to prevent it.'

Setheno spoke up. 'Captain Vritras is correct,' she said. 'This war is not over. We do not even know why it began. Until we do, we do not permit it to end.' Her voice was low, smooth, and Volos thought it even had a certain plainsong musicality to it. At the same time, there was a merciless absoluteness to the judgements she made, as if no other opinion were even imaginable. And he had heard more emotion coming from a

Dreadnought's vox-speakers.

Setheno turned to Vritras. 'Captain, I realise that your men have already been imposed upon, rescue missions hardly being the best use of your skills.' Her pause was tiny, but withering. Danton stiffened. 'I wonder if I might test your patience a bit further. Based on the battle reports of undead behaviour,' she tapped a data-slate and her eyes flicked a quick acknowledgement to Volos and Toharan, 'there is something deep at work here. If we are to combat it, we need to know the precise nature of our enemy. I need a specimen, and I believe that only the Adeptus Astartes are able to gather one and return intact.'

Toharan murmured to Volos, 'Did I just hear an ecclesiarch say please and thank you?'

'The universe is full of wonders,' First-Sergeant Aperos whispered.

Not least among them, Volos thought, *an Adeptus Sororitas infringing on an inquisitor's investigatory purview without so much as a peep of protest from the man*. Volos took a step forward to volunteer. Setheno nodded her thanks. 'And sergeant,' she added, 'I will need the specimen to be... well... not *alive* but...'

'Viable?' Volos offered.

'Precisely.'

LETTINGER TRIED TO keep his dismay under control as he walked the corridors. He had barely had a chance to exchange two words with the Canoness Errant, and she was showing no interest at all in the problem of the Dragons. So be it. He had more than enough power on his own to do what must be done.

He stopped before a closed door. He grasped the wrought-iron handle and gave it an experimental tug. The door wasn't locked. It was heavy, the berbab wood as dense and unyielding as the long iron hinges that stretched across its entire width, but it opened without a sound. There were no torches in the corridor ahead, but there was just enough light leaking through from the far end for the inquisitor to see where he was going. Lettinger steeled himself. He felt no pride in what he was about to do. He knew the twist in his gut for what it was: shame. But there was no choice. What he did, he did out of duty. He made the sign of the aquila, drew strength from the unalterable truth that the Emperor watched over him, and started forward. He pulled the door closed behind him and moved down the short corridor, taking his time with each step so the heels of his boots didn't sound against the flagstones.

He emerged on a small balcony that overlooked Lexica's chapel. The tall, narrow, stained glass windows, portraying scenes of judgement and justice during the Great Cull, filtered the daylight dark red and blue. The colours of blood and night washed over the assembled Black Dragons. Draped in shadows, Lettinger watched the monsters at worship.

The Space Marines alternately stood and knelt over the length of the service, but they did not sit. Chaplain Massorus stood at the altar, his crozius in hand as he led the call and response. Lettinger noted that though the crozius's head was the traditional winged skull configuration, the wings were reptilian. Knobby bone growths covered

Massorus's head like armour. There were, Lettinger knew, saurians on Cretacia with skulls like that. He shuddered.

'Emperor,' Massorus intoned, 'curse Thy servants...'

Lettinger stifled a gasp.

'...that we might feel Thy shaping hand,' the Dragons chanted back.

'Forge them fire and bone...'

'...that we shall evermore mightily defend Thee.'

'Mould them, O Emperor, our Father and Saviour of man...'

'...and for the glory of Thy Name deliver Thy enemies unto us.'

'O Emperor, hear our prayer...'

'...and let the cry of our rage come unto the heretic.'

'Bless the curse!' the Chaplain cried.

'Bless the curse!' the Dragons roared back.

'It is the mark of the Emperor's touch. By it, you will know Him. By it, you are shaped into His most perfect weapon. Deformity leads to the apotheosis of war. Can you ever forget the impurity of your body? No! Then neither can you forget the need for the purity of action. And in the agony of the emergence of bone, feel the memory of the greatest purity: the Emperor's great sacrifice. Teach that memory to the enemy on the point of your most holy of blades. Fire and bone!' Massorus raised his crozius to the sky.

'Fire and bone!' the Dragons echoed, and answered the Chaplain's gesture with blades. Most held out chainswords, but the Dragon Claws, the most cursed and blessed, lifted their arm-blades. Some were retractable and shot out. Others were permanent deformities

growing out of their forearms. Angles varied. Lethality did not. The air crackled with the mortification of flesh and the ecstasy of war.

Lettinger swallowed, throat dry, and crept back down the corridor. He eased the door open, stepped through, then shut it and leaned his back against it, waiting for his breathing and heartbeat to settle. He sorted through his impressions. He felt a mix of pity and revulsion. The Dragons devotion to the Emperor appeared genuine, but the form that it took, that revelling in deformity and mutation, was dangerous. Misguided love was one of the surest routes to heresy, and Lettinger had seen that drama enacted time and again. At the individual level, it was a tragedy. But when it involved an entire Adeptus Astartes Chapter, it was a nightmare.

Lettinger sighed, wondering if the Imperium would ever be done with the nightmares triggered by the 21st Founding. So much had gone wrong with so many Chapters that should never have been created. Rebellion, excommunication, luck that would make a daemon weep with sympathy – four millennia spent trying to undo the results brought on by the hubris of the Adeptus Mechanicus genetors who thought they could improve on the Emperor's original genetic work. It was, perhaps, a saving grace that the gene flaws made further recruitment impossible. The cursed Chapters couldn't replenish their ranks. One fallen Space Marine at a time, they were dying out.

Except the Black Dragons. Isolated from other Chapters, despised by some, their home world unknown, they were still strong. They still inducted neophytes. The thought that kept Lettinger awake at nights was the threat the Dragons could present, should they fall all the way. From what he had seen, that fall was inevitable. The only question was whether they could be dealt with in time.

No, he corrected himself. There was one other question. Because as much as that ceremony had disturbed him, he had also seen a few glimmers of hope, and by the Throne, did he want to hold them fast. There was, maybe, *maybe*, the possibility of redemption. Not for all the Dragons. Volos and his ilk were damned, corrupted beyond hope, even if they didn't know it yet. But Toharan was different, and Lettinger had seen a few others in the chapel who, like him, showed no visible mutation. Lettinger thought that Toharan's blessing of the curse had been just a bit forced, not quite soul-driven.

Lettinger strode away from the door, the path of his duty clear before him. What the Inquisition must burn, it would burn, and he would see it done. He was a Monodominant, and he knew that anything mutant must be destroyed. But if there was something to be salvaged, he would see that done, too. For the love and glory of the Emperor.

He found Toharan on the ramparts an hour later, inspecting the defences and watching the dead fill the valley and slowly rise up the mountainside. The peaks cast their afternoon shadows over the corpses, turning Antagonis's growing doom into a single, dark, writhing mass.

'Greetings, sergeant,' Lettinger began.

'Inquisitor,' Toharan answered, with the bare minimum of civility.

Lettinger wasn't put off. He hadn't expected anything

different. He still felt at a disadvantage. Toharan was small next to Volos, but he still towered over Lettinger. His essential humanity was obvious only when he was next to the creatures who had lost theirs. On his own, he was a colossus built and designed for war. Even the planes of his face looked hard enough to crack granite.

'I know you don't welcome my company,' Lettinger said, 'but it is more important than I think you realise that there be some open lines of communication between us.'

'Really.' The word wasn't a question. It was a dismissal.

Lettinger ignored it. 'Important for the Black Dragons.'

Toharan hadn't been looking at him. He did now. He said nothing, but his eyes bore an unmistakable warning.

'We both know that the relations between my ordo and your Chapter have been difficult.'

Toharan broke his silence. 'Now why would that be?' he snarled. 'Maybe because we bleed and die for the Imperium, yet the Inquisition casts aspersions on our honour? We don't ask for thanks or glory, but we could do without calumny.'

'I understand your anger. But do you, I wonder, understand *why* there is a cloud over the Dragons? The Inquisition is not capricious. It doesn't persecute for the sheer joy of it. We do have rather a lot to keep ourselves busy, you know.'

'Then make me understand.'

'Forgive my bluntness, but do you have any idea just how dangerous mutation is? How closely aligned it is with the nature of the warp? The history of your fellow founding Chapters is–'

'I'm aware of that history.'

'Then you should see why the Black Dragons provoke such anxiety. There is so much mutation in your ranks. So much potential monstrosity. Remember the Flame Falcons!' Engulfed in fire that did not consume them, they, too, had embraced their mutation without fear or repentance. The Inquisition had sent them judgement.

'That slaughter was justice, was it?'

Lettinger wondered if he'd been mistaken. Perhaps there was no hope for the Dragons after all, if even Toharan couldn't be brought to the light of reason and orthodoxy. 'It was necessary. Their mutation was a sign of daemonic corruption.'

'You don't know that.'

'I have no reason to doubt the sagacity of my superiors. And tell me, given the history you know so well, what does your Chapter think it is doing by not only welcoming, but *encouraging* mutation?'

'You have no evidence–'

'*You*, sergeant, are the evidence! Don't you see? Mutation is *not* an inevitable fact of being a Black Dragon. Rather, it is being sought. Why seek something so unnecessary, so dangerous, and so likely to bring down scrutiny and shame?'

'To be impure of body is to seek purity of action.'

'But you are not impure of body. Are your actions any less worthy?'

Toharan didn't answer.

Lettinger didn't let up. 'Doesn't that argument sound like a rationalisation?'

After another pause, Toharan sidestepped the question.

'What exactly do you want of me?'

'I would like you to ask yourself this question: is your leadership really acting in the Chapter's best interests?'

Toharan's hand shot out. The movement was whip-fast, but stopped just short of Lettinger's throat. Toharan leaned forward, his huge face filling Lettinger's vision, his eyes dark with lethal fury. 'I will not strike an inquisitor,' he said. 'This time. But if I ever again believe, or even suspect, that you have counselled treason on my part, then I shall defend the honour of my Chapter, no matter the consequences. Am I clear?'

Lettinger didn't back down. This was too important. 'Your highest duty is to the Emperor,' he said. 'Remember that.'

They locked stares, neither backing down. Then a voice in the courtyard called, 'Brother-sergeant!' and Toharan looked away.

Melus stood down below. He was grinning, and if he had noticed the tension between Space Marine and inquisitor, he gave no sign. 'We're wanted in the council chamber,' he said. 'News from the field.'

'Good?' Toharan asked.

Melus's grin grew wider. 'Hard to credit,' he said. 'But it guarantees we will fight for Antagonis.'

'Then it's good,' Toharan said, and leaped from the wall. He landed beside his battle-brother with an impact that shattered flagstones. As they strode toward the interior of the keep, he glanced back once. His face was a mask of rage, but Lettinger was sure he saw something else there, too: doubt.

CHAPTER 5
SEEDS

VOLOS LEFT LEXICA with Nithigg as backup. They used their jump packs to cross the gap where the bridge had fallen, then descended the path towards a valley floor that was not nearly as far away as it had been the previous day. Now Volos stood before the rising tide of bodies. From his vantage point, looking back across the valley toward the keep, he could see the full tableau of unwavering purpose and mindless, writhing horror. The new mountain heaved. It squirmed. It filled the air with a keening wail of desperation and rage. Avalanches of mangled corpses, some still twitching, slid down the slope, bowling over climbing figures, adding them to the chaos of snapping bone and tearing meat. Cascades of blood poured down the slope to feed the crimson river at the ever-rising base. The enormous mound settled, stabilised, crushing bodies to pulp and mortar, and then reached higher.

The dead were not just marching through the pass into the valley. They were running, throwing themselves onto the hill of flesh, and then climbing to the top with the same frantic urgency, using handholds made of arms and legs. Once they reached the peak, they scrabbled at the sheer mountainside until they were crushed by those coming up behind. Every corpse that rushed past Volos bore the same expression. It was a mix of obsessive determination and what Volos couldn't help but think of as *religious* terror. And the rushing horde ignored him. Utterly.

None of it made any sense.

His old mentor had been hanging back to provide covering fire as needed. Now Nithigg rejoined him. 'Hardly the aggressive force they were on the other side of the pass,' he said.

'Looks like I wasted your time,' Volos replied.

Nithigg shrugged. 'Which one looks good to you?'

'This one,' Volos said, and grabbed the next corpse that went by. It frothed and scrabbled against him, snapping fingernails on ceramite. It was like holding a handful of snakes. Volos tightened his grip, careful not to crush the thing. He and Nithigg turned and jogged up the path.

They made the jump back to the keep, and the corpse's struggles changed. It no longer tried to escape Volos's arms. It didn't even seem to notice him any longer. Instead, it reached for the keep, clawing at the air, howling and snapping its teeth. When he saw Setheno waiting just inside the gate, Volos muttered to the creature, 'I wouldn't be so eager to get inside.'

Setheno nodded in approval as they approached.

'Thank you, sergeant,' she said. 'Would you mind bringing it to the medicae centre? Then I believe your captain has a mission more worthy of your talents.'

'THE ADVANCE OF the dead has been slowed,' Vritras announced to his assembled squads, 'for reasons that have nothing to do with our tactics, but that we *will* fully exploit. Brother Keryon reports, and Colonel Dysfield's pilots confirm, that there are pockets of resistance within the mass of the enemy.'

'Resistance?' Volos asked. 'Human resistance?' As good as this news was, he couldn't see how it was possible.

'So it would seem,' Vritras answered. 'We are clearly not the only ones who refuse to surrender this planet to the Ruinous Powers.' He spoke with grim satisfaction, his tone that of a commander eager to take advantage of a turn in the tides of battle. But Volos thought he saw, in the slight downturn at the corners of the captain's mouth, the trace of uncertainty. So Vritras, too, could see the illogic in this development. Where had these fighters come from?

'How much resistance is there?' Toharan asked.

Vritras gestured to Keryon, who answered, 'More all the time. I saw at least twice as many instances on my return pass as on my way out.'

'What form do they take?'

'They're like bubbles,' Keryon said. 'The survivors are surrounded by the dead, but at least some of them are expanding their perimeters. They're managing to push back.'

Volos studied the topographical map that Vritras had

spread out on the table. The locations of the centres of resistance had been circled. 'This is very odd,' he said. 'Never mind where these people have been and how they come to be present all of a sudden, but look at where they *are*.' He tapped a gauntleted finger on the nearest circle, just on the other side of the pass. 'This location makes some sense,' he said. 'Mountainous terrain, plenty of cover and defensible ground. But pretty much all the other sites are in the middle of low hills or prairie. The survivors should be overwhelmed in seconds. You say some are expanding their held ground?'

Keryon nodded. 'And some of those groups are in the flatlands.'

'Where are they getting their ammunition?' Nithigg wanted to know.

'Brothers,' Vritras said, 'I understand and share your puzzlement. We will dispel these mysteries, and we will do so by destroying the enemy. Dragon Claws, you will deploy to the nearest resistance pocket, secure the area and block further access to the pass. Pythios and Nychus will insert at the mouth of the valley, fight through the pass to link up with Ormarr, and consolidate their gains. From that point, Ormarr will move to the next survivor group and reinforce them. The rest of Second Company will arrive via drop pod from the *Immolation Maw* to support other pockets. Seize, hold, and link the territories. And so we reclaim Antagonis for the Emperor, with fire and bone!'

THE VIEW FROM the *Battle Pyre* was very different from the last time Volos had flown out over the foot of the Temple chain. The land was still carpeted to the horizon by raging ghouls. But this time, the focus of their frenzy was not a disintegrating caravan. This time, the combatants he saw were holding firm. There were a few dozen of them, and they were not only keeping the dead at bay, but forcing them back. He thought about how he and his battle-brothers had been stymied in their efforts to do just that. The problem hadn't really been the dead breaking through the Space Marine lines. It had been the total collapse of the Mortisian Guard, and the plague of undeath erupting within the perimeter. There was no sign of such spontaneous contagion below. There was, it seemed, hope on this battlefield.

Volos distrusted it. But the Dragon Claws launched, and they descended in the midst of the survivors like the angels of darkest night. 'Citizens of Antagonis,' Volos bellowed, his voice amplified by his helmet grille, 'we are the Black Dragons, and we bring you salvation by fire.' After a moment of paralysis, the survivors cheered and attacked the enemy with even greater ferocity. As Volos opened up with his flamer and incinerated the front ranks of the dead, he took in exactly how the survivors were waging war. They were all armed with what he took to be scavenged weapons. He saw lasrifles and combat knives and a handful of chainswords. Only two of the rifles were being fired. The others appeared to have no ammunition. Those with bayonets were being used to slash and disembowel, and the others were wielded as clubs. The fighting was savage, as all combat was, but there was a frenzy to the way in which the humans threw themselves at the dead that struck Volos as being just a little too familiar. There were moments when he found it difficult to distinguish between the combatants, especially when some of the corpses were also armed, and there was a clash of steel.

But there were differences. The survivors fought intelligently, shifting stance and tactics according to the second-by-second flow of war. And they dodged, which the corpses never did. The dead were so consumed by their hunger to destroy the living that there was nothing in what passed for their consciousness that cared for self-preservation. As recklessly as they fought, the humans were still, Volos thought, fighting to stay alive. Even so, as he reduced another phalanx of the dead to smouldering bone and ash, he used the momentary breathing space the gap created to speak to the woman at his shoulder. 'What is your name, human?' he asked.

'Sanna Robbes, lord,' the woman answered, proving to Volos that she was sentient. She came from manufactorum labourer stock, Volos guessed. She was in late, greying middle-age and stocky, her shoulders rounded from decades bent over machines, her limbs thick with muscle like knotted wood. She smashed at the enemy with the butt end of a lasrifle. She caved in the forehead of one corpse, ducked beneath the grasp of another, brought her foe down with a sweep that shattered kneecaps, then swung the rifle over her head to finish the corpse with a crushed skull.

'You fight well.' In the corner of his eye, he saw one of the dead reach for Robbes. With his finger depressing the flamer trigger, Volos stretched out his left arm, shot out a bone-blade and impaled the thing through the head.

Robbes grunted her thanks and swung the rifle again.

'I fight how I must,' she said.

The waves of the dead broke against the levee of Space Marines and dogged humans. Volos urged the counter-attack on, and the line moved forward against the dead. By promethium and bolter shell, by las and by blow, by fire and by bone, the advance moved to the mouth of the pass and inched across it, slowly cutting off the flow of the dead towards Lexica.

'Volos,' Nithigg said over the comm-feed.

'Yes, brother.'

'Did you happen to make an exact count of the humans before we began?'

'No. Why?'

'Because I think our mission might be going *too* well.'

Without breaking the rhythm of his kills, Volos scanned the formation. Nithigg was right. None of his brothers had fallen, which wasn't surprising, but none of the humans appeared to have, either. It was hard to shake the impression that there were more survivors than at the start of the engagement.

Movement to the left caught his eye. A man was using a chainsword against the dead, but he wasn't just slashing at them. He was brandishing it, weaving the blade through the air as though it were light as a rapier. He was shaping a distinct pattern.

LETTINGER WALKED INTO the medicae centre. The door to the surgery was closed. Two of the remaining Mortisians stood guard before it. In the antechamber, Dysfield was talking with Lord Danton, who was holding his daughter's hand. Lettinger nodded vaguely at the group and approached the door. One of the guards stepped in front of him.

'I'm sorry, inquisitor,' the man said. 'Canoness Setheno is at work in there.'

'I know that. I'm here to examine the specimen.'

The guard shook his head. 'She gave explicit orders to admit no one.'

Lettinger saw red. 'Are you saying *no* to the Inquisition?' he threatened.

'I'm afraid she didn't mention any exceptions.' The guard was more frightened of Setheno than he was of Lettinger.

The inquisitor felt himself deflate. He couldn't blame the man.

The absurdity of the situation was staggering. A canoness was conducting what was, in effect, an inquisition, while the inquisitor was barred from the scene. Setheno had as little business studying the corpse as he had the absolute right and duty to do so. Yet she commanded, and all obeyed. If anyone else had been on the other side of the door, Lettinger would have ordered and witnessed her immediate execution. That even contemplating such a course of action made him break out in a cold sweat was a testament to her power. The being in that room was *will* incarnate. Though Lettinger's rational mind rose in outrage at the slight to his *real* authority, his every instinct recoiled from the mere thought of moving against Setheno's wishes.

Danton gave him a face-saving out. 'Inquisitor Lettinger,' he said, 'perhaps you can convince Colonel Dysfield that I'm right.'

'About what?' Lettinger asked, turning his back to the door and joining the trio.

'About an evacuation.'

Lettinger frowned. 'I was under the impression that the war was still ongoing.' Whatever dangers the Black Dragons represented were not the immediate threat. The Chapter was still, for the moment, following the Emperor's will. There were other elements of the Ruinous Powers at work on this planet, and Lettinger didn't plan to retreat before them any more than did Vritras.

'I'm not seeking it for myself, you understand,' Danton added hurriedly. 'I was thinking of my daughter and the other civilians.'

'Any evacuation is a retreat,' Dysfield said, 'and unacceptable.' And then he walked off, leaving Lettinger to deal with the pleading.

'I don't like it here,' Bethshea put in.

Lettinger looked down at her. 'Why do you want to run away from your home, child?' he asked.

'I...' she began, but faltered.

'Is this how you do honour to the Emperor?'

'But I'm frightened.'

'That's when doing your duty counts the most, because that's when it's hardest. Do you understand?'

Bethshea looked unhappy, but nodded.

'Your family represents the hand of the Emperor on this planet. Do you think it would look good if you ran away?'

'No.' Spoken very quietly.

Lettinger turned to her father. 'I think you should stay,' he commanded. 'Don't you?'

Danton didn't answer. He looked upwards, as if he could see the sky through the stones of the keep. Disgusted, Lettinger stalked away. He wasn't needed here. He would watch the Pythios and Nychus operations from the ramparts. He was halfway there when it struck him that Danton's eyes had been filled with a longing that didn't seem to have anything to do with fear.

SETHENO WAITED WHILE the three Mortisian Guardsmen she had selected as assistants secured the male corpse to the operating table. Its legs were spread, its arms held above its head, its ankles and wrists fastened by chains. It wailed and frothed, its eyes straining from their sockets in mad rage and terror. Setheno used a scalpel to strip away the last shreds of clothing from the body. It had taken several hours to reach even this preliminary stage of the investigation. Setheno had first had to sanctify the surgery with prayer, and then prepare a network of wards across the stone of the floor and walls, on the door, and around the table. She hoped they would be enough. She placed her helm on a bench, but she was otherwise in full armour.

At first glance, the thing was a typical victim of a variant of the zombie plague. The flesh was grey, mottled with patches of green and black. The frame was withered; chest and cheeks hollow as if the skin were being sucked into the bones. It didn't breathe, but putrid gases wafted from its mouth and nostrils all the same. Its gums had shrivelled, pulling back over teeth slicked with thickened saliva and bits of blackened flesh. The flecks of meat might have come from the bodies of others, or from the creature's own dark, ravaged lips.

The thing was a mundane abomination, but for the look in its eyes. The terror that Setheno saw there was all wrong. The walking dead known to the Imperium were too brain-dead to fear anything. And then there were the instances of weapon use the Black Dragons had reported. There was intelligence, and the agony Setheno saw in the monster's expression was something more than physical. She leaned close to its face, while her aides tensed in alarm. 'You fear for your soul, don't you?' she whispered.

The creature stopped struggling. It stared at her. And then the worst thing possible happened, the thing Setheno had dreaded: a tear formed in the corner of the thing's left eye and trickled down its cheek.

Setheno took a step back. She watched the creature's chest, waiting for the inevitable. 'What are your names?' she asked the Guardsmen.

'Canoness?' one asked.

'What are your names?' she repeated.

They told her. And while they did, she saw what she had been waiting for. The creature's chest expanded. The movement was gradual, hidden, suppressed to the point of being almost imperceptible. Almost. She saw it. So did one of the others.

'Throne of Terra, it's breathing!' the soldier said.

'Yes, he is,' Setheno said. 'He's alive. Corporal Drunet, Corporal Benyamien, Major Estain, you have the Emperor's blessing for your duty and faith, and my profound regret.' She pulled out her bolt pistol, and shot each man in the head. Only one of them had time to plead *no*.

Then she turned to the weeping thing on the table and gave it peace.

THE BLADE-WIELDING HUMAN finished his gesture, and Volos recognised it for a sigil even before a cluster of the enemy two metres wide and three deep fell as if struck by a fist. Then he saw why there seemed to be too many survivors. The stricken convulsed with dislocating force, their jaws gaping in a scream the more excruciating for being silent. Then they stood, the glow of health flooding back into their features, and began to attack their former brethren

Though he didn't stop fighting, Volos had the sensation of the battlefield freezing for a moment. Everything turned topsy-turvy, and he began to realise the depth of Antagonis's damnation.

SETHENO DONNED HER helmet and loaded a fresh clip into her pistol. She pulled out her power sword and approached the surgery door. Before she opened it, she voxed, 'Captain Vritras. There has been a development.'

THE BATTLE PYRE had bombed a clearing at the mouth of the valley. Keryon was bringing the Thunderhawk back around to drop the squads when the message came through. Toharan watched Vritras receive the news. The captain's face darkened and he punched the bulkhead. 'This operation is terminated,' Vritras announced. 'Brother Keryon,' he voxed the pilot, 'return us to base, and then retrieve Squad Ormarr. I am ordering the immediate evacuation of Antagonis. Black Dragons, link up with Canoness Setheno, and kill all humans on sight unless she says otherwise.'

'*All* humans, Captain?' Toharan asked. He was thinking of Dysfield and the remaining Mortisians. He wasn't worried about Lettinger.

'Unless she says otherwise.'

WHEN VOLOS HEARD the order, he didn't feel surprise. Instead, he felt that he was being told something he had already known at a subconscious level. He turned from the dead to bring his flamer to bear on Robbes. He saw a woman fighting heroically for her life and those of her friends. His finger hesitated on the trigger. His peripheral vision caught the rest of the squad re-orienting their weapons, also on the horns of that terrible moment when orders seemed wrong.

Robbes turned her head to look at him. Volos pulled the trigger.

But he was too late. Everything was too late. The plague reached maturity, and the change began.

CHAPTER 6
DOUBTWORM

Robbes opened her mouth wide in a snarling scream, and her head folded in on itself. The skull collapsed and flowed into her jaws. The bones in her legs turned to soup, and she dropped to the ground as Volos's jet of flaming promethium passed over her. The jaws widened, unhinging like a snake's, the teeth turning into rows of gleaming needles. The legs lengthened, thickened, coiled. The torso twisted, bones cracking and muscles flowing, transforming into an incarnation of liquid and strength, reptile and desire, teeth and chaos, and eternal change.

The metamorphosis was as complex as it was instant. The shift from human to daemon took a fraction of a second. Volos lowered his flamer to send the abomination back to the warp. A leg turned into a tentacle covered in eyes. The eyes blinked and became mouths. The mouths snapped and became eyes. The tentacle whipped out and wrapped itself around the weapon, crushing it. Volos dropped the flamer and threw himself to the side as the promethium reservoir exploded. The eye-mouths of the tentacle screamed in a dozen registers as they were coated by flaming liquid. The limb curled in on itself against the pain, but the rest of the monster attacked as if unaware that it had been injured.

The daemon's body was stretching as it twisted, becoming a ropey, blinking tube of flesh. The other leg tentacle snatched at Volos, while the neck became a python, reaching for him with its gaping jaws. He slammed the tentacle down with his chainsword, pinned it and ground it beneath a boot, then lifted the blade high with both hands. He brought it down in a savage chopping motion against the daemon's maw.

Teeth met teeth. The sword's howl was Volos's rage as it ground deeper into the neck of the abomination. Ichor and blood splashed over him. The daemon unleashed an ululation that built into a choir of rage and pain before it turned into a racking, choking gurgle. The torso slumped forward. The burned tentacle snaked along the ground, not toward Volos, but to what had been the next strong point of the circle, where Nithigg was incinerating another daemon. That creature sent braided tendrils of muscle to meet the envoy from Volos's foe. The flesh linked, fused and expanded, the wounded bodies at either end shrivelling as they poured what remained of their essence into the new, larger being.

It had a less defined shape. All trace of the human was gone now, replaced by a giant, pulsating flesh sack. And still, covering its surface, the eyes that became mouths that became eyes that became mouths, watching and hungering, hating and screaming.

Volos scanned the battlefield as he yanked his chainsword from the flopping corpse. The same pattern had played out along the entire defensive perimeter. His battle-brothers had cut down the daemons before them, but the defeated monsters were all melding with the new construct. And it was growing fast. All of the humans within the circle, dozens and dozens, had transformed. Some of the daemons melted down, flesh running like mercury and racing to the greater being. Others, still moving on things that passed for legs, leaped across the ground to throw themselves into the absorbing sac.

Only it wasn't really a sac any longer. In the seconds since it had formed, though its surface of eye-mouths were nothing but staring, gnashing change and the flesh between them bubbled and dripped, the larger whole had gathered force and shape. It was long. It was a tube.

It was a worm.

Volos grabbed one of the krak grenades from his belt dispenser. He hurled it at the worm. The grenade hit the centre of the monster and exploded in a fountain of gristle and blood. The other Dragon Claws followed his example. The worm howled with its thousand voices, and rolled into the army of beings that Volos had thought were dead.

When the transformations had begun, the attacks had ceased. Antagonis's tainted millions now were standing still and wailing. Their cry was inarticulate and mindless, but it wasn't soulless. It was the most primitive, basic hymn of abject despair and regret, a song of a mission failed and of a doom inevitable. All the energy and ferocity evaporated from the creatures. Whatever need had animated them, it had fled at the moment of the daemonic transformations.

The moment when disguises had been shed.

For all the grief and terror resounding from millions upon millions of throats and stretching beyond the horizon, the tainted did not run as the worm rolled onto them. When it did, its flesh flowed over them and dissolved them. The daemonic body devoured them, taking in their mass and their essence, and grew. It screamed as the grenades blew out deliquescent chunks of its body, but it grew far faster than it was being injured. Its growth accelerated exponentially as its bulk covered a greater and greater area, swallowing up ever more bodies. And scattered over the foothills and forest were all the other pockets of resistance. Even now, from all those bastions of false hope, other worms were approaching, growing all the while, racing to fuse with the first.

SETHENO YANKED OPEN the surgery door. She saw Danton and his daughter. They turned to her. In that first second, Danton kept his aristocratically entreating smile and Bethshea was utterly the frightened little girl. Setheno didn't hesitate. She raised her bolt pistol and fired. Danton was already changing when the mass-reactive rounds hit him, but he was still human enough to have a head and a face that disintegrated as the bolts smashed into his skull and exploded. The thing shrieked with the mouths that had sprouted on its neck and palms. It staggered, flailing madly. Arms became barbed whips that slashed across the room, but Setheno ducked under them and slid forward, emptying the clip into the daemon's torso, knocking it down. She pressed the attack, knowing that she would never get the advantage back if she lost it for the slightest moment. She straddled what was still almost a chest, and slashed twice with her power sword, severing whip arms, and then stabbing straight down. It wasn't a heart that she punctured, because hearts didn't scream, but it was still something important. In the seconds that she had gained, she reloaded the bolt pistol and looked for Bethshea.

The child thing was running away, racing down the corridor away from the surgery. Setheno cursed herself for having chosen not to shoot both daemonhosts at the same time. As she pulled the trigger, the Danton creature bucked, and a pillar of twisting muscle shot out of its chest. It slammed into her breastplate and knocked her across the room. She smashed into the far wall, cracking stonework. Even as she landed, she was firing again, her bolts blowing out more of the monster's central mass, spreading it around the room. It tried to rise, but fell, thrashing. Setheno reloaded, fired again. The movements grew weak. She brought her sword to bear again.

'You are alone here, wretch,' she said as she butchered the thing. 'You have no ally to absorb. You have no succour.'

It sprouted a mouth on its shoulder and spoke to her. 'You should be one of us.' It sounded puzzled.

'I have nothing for you to feed on,' she said, and

reduced it to dead, scattered meat.

Then she ran from the room, hunting Bethshea.

THE REFUGEES FROM Lecorb had been housed in the sleeping cells of Lexica Keep. Now they gathered together and fused. They made enough noise chanting and shrieking in ecstasy that Guardsmen came to investigate. The being took them. A worm ate at the heart of Lexica, and grew strong.

LETTINGER WATCHED THE *Battle Pyre* roar back to the keep. He frowned. All he had seen it do was engage in a brief bombardment. That wasn't the counter-attack he'd been expecting. The attack craft descended to the elevated landing pad on the east side of the central courtyard. He hurried down the rampart stairs. He was halfway across the courtyard, and the *Battle Pyre* was just settling on the pad, when the keep's main doors burst open and Setheno charged out, weapons in hand. He stopped to wait for her. She ran straight at him. The impact of her armoured form sent him sprawling, lungs flattened. She crouched over him and held her bolt pistol to his temple. He heard the racking of many chambers. He stared up into the screaming face of her helmet, and beyond her at the disembarked squads of Black Dragons, every bolter aimed his way. Perhaps his terror saved his life. Setheno hesitated. She grabbed his aquila pendant and brought it to his lips. 'Kiss it,' she ordered.

He did.

'How close have you come to any of the foe?' she asked.

'I've only seen the ones in the valley,' he gasped.

Setheno paused a few more seconds, then stood and took a step away from him. 'Get up,' she said, lowering her pistol. The Dragons followed her lead.

Lettinger got to his feet, and saw a small figure dart out of the doorway. 'Bethshea?' he asked, puzzled. When he spoke, Setheno whirled, gun out.

Then the façade of Lexica Keep exploded.

IN THE DAYS that followed, the images of those few seconds would replay themselves before Toharan's inner eye. They would remain vivid in his memory, etched in lightning, in a way that the rest of the battle would not. They would stay with him because of what they represented. They were proof of how desperately wrong he could be. They were a wound, and they were a lesson.

He saw Bethshea running from the keep. He saw Setheno turn and raise her pistol to fire at the girl. He saw Lexica give shattering birth to a monstrous worm. It was fifty metres long, wider than Toharan was tall, and writhing with eye-mouths and roiling flesh. Stonework flew across the courtyard, battering Setheno's power armour. She remained standing, and Lettinger ducked behind her, avoiding the worst of the falling wreckage. He wasn't quite fast enough and an errant gargoyle head knocked him unconscious. The rain of blows was enough to throw Setheno's aim off, and her volley of shots missed the zigzagging Bethshea.

Then came the lesson. Toharan saw Bethshea turn and run towards the worm. Her speed was superhuman, and she was at least five metres from the monster when she leaped, arms outstretched as if to embrace the thing. As she flew, she transformed, elongating and distorting into a daemon of serpentine limbs and teeth, her shape changing from one fraction of a second to the next, each form flowing into the next until she hit the worm and was absorbed into its flank. Toharan remembered looking at Bethshea during the flight from Lecorb, and seeing in the girl the reason for an otherwise senseless mission. His battle-brothers and the Guard had been sacrificed, but she had been a small portion of the Imperium and its future that had been saved, and so the sacrifices had not been in vain. And indeed, he saw now, they had not been. But the deaths had been sacrifices to a monstrous cause. All of Toharan's efforts in this war, and those of his fellow Dragons, had been worse than futile. The taken-for-granted certainties had been lies.

The lesson would fester in time. But for now, all he felt was, first, a sharp drop in the pit of his stomach, and then nothing but the killing rage. Vritras yelled, 'Fire and bone!' Toharan roared it back at him, and he lived the battle-cry as he never had before. The Black Dragons charged down from the landing pad, bolters unleashing a mass-reactive hail. The worm flinched back from the blows. Each individual round was no more than a nuisance to it, but the cumulative effect of hundreds was punishing. It reared as its flesh was blasted away, and brought more of the keep crashing into the courtyard, crushing a handful of the few remaining Mortisian Guard. The leading end of the worm shaped itself into what passed for a head. It was nothing but a gigantic maw and a single, glistening black eye two metres across. It lunged forward, knocking aside Space Marines through sheer momentum and bulk.

Toharan stood his ground until the last second, firing straight into the creature's eye. A leathery membrane flicked down, covering the orb, deflecting and absorbing his shots. One got through, though. Green fluid and flickers of black flame burst from the wound. The worm squealed and jinked to the side to avoid him. As it passed, Toharan plunged his chainsword into the monster's flank, and let the creature's own motion tear open a massive wound. The blade-teeth chewed through eyes and shrieking mouths.

Toharan snarled his satisfaction at he destroyed the embodiment of impurity. Then the worm's tail curled and struck him, biting at his armour, teeth sinking into ceramite even as the blow pinned him against one of the landing pad's support columns. The pillar cracked. The tail wrapped around Toharan and squeezed. He couldn't move his arms, couldn't strike with bolter or sword. His retinal display flashed warning runes as the pressure mounted. He saw the worm thrash as the Dragons continued to pour rounds into it, but it held its ground. It whipped and snapped. It landed a massive blow, and Toharan saw Brother Ythagor's status rune switch from green to fatal red.

The thudding rhythm of a heavy bolter began, and the worm shrieked. It released Toharan, leaving the surface of his armour pitted and scored from the bites of countless mouths and the touch of corrosive flesh. He leaped clear of the tail, reloaded his bolter and started firing again. Up on the rampart, he saw who had hurt the worm: First-Sergeant Aperos was manning a turret, the pounding fire cutting the worm to pieces. Shredded, enraged, it hurled itself at him, losing pieces of itself as it forced its way through the shredding fire. A juggernaut of corrupted flesh, it obliterated an entire section of the rampart, mangling the turret. Aperos's rune blinked amber, but he emerged from the wreckage. His right arm swung loose and limp, but he drew his chainsword with his left hand and jumped onto the worm's head. He plunged the sword deep into the flesh just above the eye. The growl of the sword competed with the shriek of the worm. It spasmed in agony and threw itself from side to side in an attempt to dislodge the Space Marine. Aperos held on, his blade staking his claim to the monster, sinking in and tearing deep just as Toharan's had done, and with every movement, the wound became greater.

The worm's shrieks echoed off the mountains. With a massive convulsion, it slammed its head into the rampart again and again, reducing Lexica's defences to ruins, ignoring all other attacks as it fought the terrible being whose fang was biting lethally into its essence. Finally, it drove itself deep into the foundations of the wall, a third of its length disappearing beneath the rubble.

It stopped moving.

Aperos's rune blinked red.

The Dragons kept up the attack, the need to ensure the worm was dead now less important than taking vengeance for a hero's fall. And the worm wasn't dead. After a few seconds, it reacted to the continuing fire and jerked free of the stonework. Its maw roared over the death of its enemy, but the ten thousand eye-mouths moaned in pain. It wavered in the air, a drunken serpent. Its movements were erratic, weak. It swung its head back and forth, seeking prey and salvation.

To the front, it encountered nothing but the Black Dragons, now in a spearhead formation. Vritras was the tip, Toharan just behind and on his left. On his right, Chaplain Massorus cursed the worm back to the warp as he fired, and the monster seemed to twitch as if in fear. However it fed, Toharan realised, it could kill but not consume the Space Marines. Then the worm swung its head left. Dysfield and Setheno had organised the remaining Mortisians into a fire team under the landing pad platform. All the lasrifles and bolter rifles but Setheno's suddenly fell silent as the worm looked at the men. It did not need to touch to feed or spread its taint. Its gaze, when met by a human, was enough. Dysfield and his troops stood still. They let their weapons drop from their hands. They began walking forward, until Setheno, with reptilian mercy, shot them all.

The worm moaned. The Dragons crucified it with bolter fire, pushing it back against the crumbled wall of the keep. They did not advance, though. They retreated instead, putting space between them and the monster, at last giving Brother Keryon, in the airborne Thunderhawk, the opportunity and the clear line of fire he needed.

The worm was consumed by the justice of Hellstrike missiles. Its shrieks reached a height of pain pure enough to cut crystal, and then they cut off, and there was only the roar of flame. The worm fell. Toharan and his brothers moved to the edge of Lexica and peered down.

Thousands of metres below, the worm had smashed itself open on the hill of bodies, its impact killing the few remaining climbers. Toharan noticed that there were no more of the tainted making their way into the valley.

IN THE COURTYARD, while Apothecary Urlock revived Lettinger, Toharan asked Setheno, 'What was that?'

'It was the terminal stage of doubtworm,' she answered, as if that explained everything. 'Captain,' she said to Vritras, 'you have a very short time, if it is not already too late, to extract your Dragon Claws. The souls who formed the worm we just fought only numbered in the dozens. There is one coming into being on the other side of the pass, and it will be composed of billions.'

Toharan was neck-and-neck with his captain as they raced for the landing *Battle Pyre*.

'BROTHER-SERGEANT,' NITHIGG said as he and Volos crouched behind a boulder, 'I'm all ears.'

'I didn't say I had an idea.'

'I know. I was just hoping to prompt some inspiration.'

All trace of the mission had vanished. The worm was easily a thousand metres long, its maw twenty metres wide. And it was growing, the limitless, defeated hordes slowly walking to destruction and absorption by the beast. Ormarr had split up into pairs, darting from cover to cover, flaming the worm first from one side, then the other, shifting its attention from one team to the next, never letting it get a proper fix on its tormentors. But they were only playing for time, and Volos knew it. Every wound they inflicted on the worm was healed a hundred times over by the infinite prey. The Dragon Claws were trying to drain the ocean with spoons. And at the rate the worm was growing, it wouldn't be long before it became impossible to evade its earth-shattering blows.

'Ormarr,' Vritras's voice came over the comm-feed. 'This is *Battle Pyre*. We are coming to extract you.'

'Negative, brother-captain,' Volos responded. 'The skies are not safe at this time.' The worm would swat the Thunderhawk like an insect.

'Then make them safe, brother-sergeant. Inquisitor Lettinger has ordered Exterminatus, and we are not leaving this planet without the Dragon Claws. Arrival in five minutes.'

Volos watched the worm pound the cliff side, bringing down an avalanche as it tried to crush Braxas and Vasuk. The monster and rocks missed. Just. But in the moment of the attack, Volos found his inspiration. 'Brother,' he grinned behind his helm, 'this would not be a fitting death. We will need to seek a better one in another battle.'

'You see how to end this one?' Nithigg asked.

Volos pointed at the worm. 'It blinked.'

'What?'

'When it slammed its head into the rock, it closed its eye.'

Nithigg caught his train of thought. 'If the eye needs protection, it is vulnerable.'

'If it has an eye, it can be blinded. And where there is an eye, there is usually a brain not far away.'

'How are we going to get at the eye?' They had come equipped with short-range, area-effect weapons. They had nothing that could reach the eye, and the flamers were just about depleted. There was still some fuel left in the jump packs, but starting from the ground was impractical.

Volos scanned the slopes behind them. About a hundred metres up and three hundred to the left, a ledge protruded like a tongue from the cliff face. *'Battle Pyre,'* he voxed, 'this is Ormarr. Hold position on your side of the pass. Will advise when we are ready.'

'Make it soon,' Vritras responded.

'Acknowledged.'

Volos showed Nithigg the ledge. 'I sense divine madness,' Nithigg said. 'I approve.'

'I would give much for a melta bomb.'

'I'm sure we all would. I do still have one krak, though.'

Volos took the grenade. 'I need its head low,' he told Nithigg. 'As soon as I'm up there, get it near my position. And do try not to let it wreck the mountain while I'm still on it.'

'You are so very particular, brother-sergeant,' Nithigg said, and moved out.

Volos communicated with the rest of the squad, then sprinted for the mountainside. He didn't use his jump pack to reach the ledge. He wanted to conserve fuel for when he really needed it, and there was plenty that could go wrong with his plan. He doubted the worm would cooperate with what he had in mind. There were enough handholds to make the climb not much worse than a steep scramble, and where there was nothing to grasp, he punched the rock face until there was. It took him less than ten minutes to reach the ledge, and the worm left him alone. Nithigg and the other Dragon Claws circled and harried it. They couldn't kill it, but they swooped and stung like wasps around a grox. Their attacks had the grace and coordination of a dance. A team would burn the worm's flank, drawing its attention, then retreat as it moved to attack, and the next team would hit just as the worm was ready to strike. They kept it off balance, and prolonged the stalemate. Even with all its eyes, the worm couldn't keep up, its movements becoming more ponderous as it grew.

But it *was* growing, all the time and always faster. The point would come, and come soon, when it wouldn't even have to target the Dragons. It would simply move, and mountains would fall.

Volos reached the ledge. 'In position,' he voxed to his squad. Then, '*Battle Pyre*, begin your approach. Remain at altitude for now. Whether we meet triumph or death, you'll know.'

Nithigg was at the foot of the cliff directly below the ledge. His flamer was done, but he had a bolt pistol as a secondary weapon and he fired with it. The rounds were barely pinpricks in the flanks of the monster now, but Volos saw those pinpricks count. Nithigg targeted the eye-mouths. High-pitched wails were drowned out by the ocean-deep roar of outrage from the maw. Braxas and Vasuk joined Nithigg, and concentrated their fire in the same spots, making the three of them a target as inviting to the worm as they were irritating. It heaved its bulk toward the mountainside and ducked its head to strike.

Volos pulled the pin from the krak grenade, counted two, and leaped, riding the flame of his jump pack. His target was the upper portion of the worm's eye. As he fell, he threw the grenade ahead of him. The worm saw him coming and its membrane snapped down over the eye. The grenade hit. The membrane was thick, tough muscle. It deflected much, and protected the eye from the pile-driving impacts of the worm's lunges. But it was still flesh, and the krak grenade was designed to pierce armour. The explosion punched through the membrane, leaving the muscle hanging in ragged flaps. Volos was right behind, fists clenched. Propelled by the jump pack, he was a missile of flesh and rage. He snapped out his bone-blades and slammed into the eye.

There was the treasured moment of agony as the blades emerged, treasured because the pain was an act of faith, and an act of pure war, his body transformed into the doom of the Emperor's enemies. And on the heels of the agony came the ferocious pleasure of the deeper agony inflicted on the foe. The blades shot with the force of adamantium pistons into the orb. Ichor spewed over Volos. It was a green the shade of rotten limbs and cancerous souls, and it moved with a will of its own. It defied gravity and ran up his arms, coating and clutching at his armour. It bubbled as if it were an acid. But it did nothing. It covered his votive parchments, and then slid off, leaving them untouched. Ebony flames licked over him, and his retinal display told him that these flames were cold as the void of space. They were impotent against him. With his left arm holding fast to the corrupted jelly, he pulled his right out and plunged the blade deeper. Then he held with the right and stabbed with the left. He began to dig himself deeper and deeper into the eye.

The worm became frenzied. Its scream was as big as the world, and it writhed, an electrocuted serpent, desperate to dislodge him. Gravitic-forces pulled at Volos from every direction as the worm twisted and smashed itself against earth and mountain, but each blow only drove him in further. He punched and slashed, gouging into a morass of tissue that now held him tight despite itself. He shoved his head forward, using his horns to tear yet more of the filth apart. And as he tunnelled into the daemon eye, it spoke to him. There was no light inside the orb, but he could see all the same as visions fell upon him and voices shouted. Everything was the same refrain: there was no God-Emperor. The message was so absurd it was almost comical. There was something almost childish about the insistence, as if a big enough tantrum could make the ridiculous true. Volos began to laugh.

Deeper, darker, the pressure building, the battering of the worm growing worse. He felt snaps, and knew they were his ribs. He didn't care. His laughter was gigantic, wide and fierce as a battlefield. His enemy was in lethal torment. He was a Black Dragon, and he was the Emperor's fire and bone.

His blades sliced into something thick and knotted. He thought of tendons and nerve clusters, and he sawed with renewed savagery. The worm's throes stiffened into a vibration that threatened to reduce his armour and skeleton to dust. The visions shrieked infantile heresy at him one more time, and dropped into silence. The movement stopped with a teeth-rattling *boom*. Volos paused, embraced by suffocating nothing, and then he twisted around and clawed his way back.

He slid out of the eye as from a corrupted womb. The worm was a prone, motionless immensity. The rest of Squad Ormarr was waiting for him. Beyond them, in a space flattened by the worm's agony, the *Battle Pyre* was coming down. 'Brother,' Nithigg said, 'when are you going to limit yourself to battling foes your own size? These one-sided affairs hardly do you honour.'

Volos laughed again despite the grinding in his ribcage. Then he saw that the worm's jaw was still working. It was snapping at nothing at all, but as he watched, he realised that the motion wasn't dying away. It was getting stronger.

'Brother-sergeant,' Braxas said.

'I see it.' He had a momentary impulse to plunge back into the monster and finish things.

'Not the jaw.' Braxas pointed.

The millions upon millions of damned souls were still moving. Their strings hadn't been cut when the worm fell. The entire circle of the horizon was in motion as the tainted population of Antagonis advanced to throw itself into the twitching monster.

'No,' Volos snarled, seeing his victory being taken away from him. His lips pulled back, and his fangs pushed out. For a moment, the world blinked out of existence, and there was nothing in the universe but his black rage. Then Nithigg had his arm, yanking him back to the here and now, and was pulling him toward the Thunderhawk. The worm's body was moving again before he reached the loading ramp, and as the planet's blasted humanity poured itself into the being, it grew so quickly it was almost touching the *Battle Pyre* as the ship took off.

Toharan clapped his shoulder as he removed his helm, and Volos nodded an absent greeting. He moved to a viewing block. The worm's expansion was obscene. It seemed to come closer as they pulled away, and it took several seconds before the *Battle Pyre*'s acceleration reached the point where the Thunderhawk flew faster than the worm grew. Moment by moment, the creature's movements became bigger and more violent, and with every sweep of its body, greater and greater numbers of walking fodder were consumed, and the growth exploded.

Volos found cold solace in one fact. There was no purpose to the thrashing. The worm wasn't searching for its tormentors. For all that its body was covered by countless thousands of eye-mouths, it was blind. He had hurt it at a level that it could not heal. But even that victory didn't matter. There was nothing to save here now, and the worm didn't need to see or even think to be the end of Antagonis. Its mere existence was now destruction itself.

By the time the *Battle Pyre* reached Lexica Keep for the last time, the worm was a convulsing, coiling monstrosity that towered over the Temple chain. It rose, and it was as big as a god. It *was* a god. The setting sun bathed it red, marking it with the blood of the world it had killed. Volos sensed, for the first time in his life, the direct touch of the sublime, and he wanted to spit its obscene taste from his mouth. Then the worm fell, and it levelled mountains.

It was visible even from orbit, and still it grew.

CHAPTER 7
PURGING

It was Lettinger who ordered the Exterminatus, but only after being commanded to do so by Setheno. He had the formal authority. She had the will and the experience. And it was the Black Dragons who carried out the order. They had the cyclonic torpedoes.

Dragons, canoness and inquisitor gathered on the command bridge of the *Immolation Maw* to watch the final curtain come down on Antagonis's tragedy. The primary occulus showed the planet at zero magnification. The worm writhed across the entire northern landmass. To Volos, even at a size that changed tectonic behaviour, the worm seemed more than ever like a disease. Perhaps it was the way it moved, the smaller tremors looking like the trembling, mindless frenzy of bacteria. The worm was a warp-tainted infection. It needed to be burned out.

The Exterminatus began with an assist from the Mortisian Dictator-class cruiser, *Archon Voltinius*. It was the least bit of justice that could be granted to the decimated companies. The bombardment began with mass drivers sent in a cluster near the worm's head. Into that grouping, the *Immolation Maw* then fired the cyclonic torpedoes.

In the past, Volos had heard human enthusiasts describe the work of the torpedoes as beautiful. Those men were idiots, he had always thought, mighty war boosters who had managed to avoid combat and its inconveniences themselves. But now, he could see a kind of beauty in the work of the torpedoes. It was the beauty of inexorable, unforgiving judgement, and of absolute power. These bombs killed by reshaping worlds.

The artistry of annihilation began with a magnesium-white flare at the site of the strike. The burst was a sudden blossom, a flower from the heart of a sun. The torpedoes blasted through the planetary crust weakened by the *Voltinius*'s bombs, and drove the mantle into the fury of the storm. Its kinetic energy turned supernova-worthy, the mantle discovered a heat beyond molten, beyond incandescence. Rock became gas. The surface of the planet twisted and flowed like clouds. Mountain ranges new and old became the arms of a hurricane. Antagonis was new again, returned to its infancy. Volos saw the worm consumed by a crust that veered wildly between solid and liquid, mountain and valley. When the terrible dance of the continental plates ended, so had everything else on Antagonis. There was no life. There was no hope. There was no point.

Volos turned from the occulus to stare at a hololith of the planet projected above the strategium table. He asked Setheno, 'Canoness, what were we fighting down there?'

'An outbreak of doubtworm,' she said. 'Such events are rare, but when they occur, the result is preordained.'

'And doubtworm is...?'

'A parasitical form of daemonic possession.'

'So the walking dead...' Toharan began.

'...were not dead,' Setheno confirmed. 'They were suffering the early onset of possession. The larval stage of the worm. Did you notice, sergeant, when you first arrived in Lecorb, any signs of distress or self-inflicted injury on the part of the infected?'

Toharan nodded. 'They didn't seem interested in us at all until we were in the company of Lord Danton and the others.'

'In the larval stage, the victims' higher thought processes are dulled, but they are aware of what is happening to them. They sense their damnation, and are focussed on it, not on those as yet untouched by the plague. But the people you rescued were fully possessed, and the others attacked them in a final, desperate act of faith before they succumbed.'

'An entire planet possessed in a week?' Volos said. 'How is that possible?'

'It is possible because of human weakness. The parasite both feeds on doubt and spreads it. It is during the larval stage that it is most contagious, as that is when its effects are visible. Remember, this is no airborne virus. It is a thing of the warp, and leaps from mind to mind. For almost any human, to see a fellow fall prey to the worm is to feel vulnerable, and thus to be vulnerable. Then, during the pupal stage, the mind of the victim is active again, but only as the puppet to the daemon. During this phase, the worm will work to arrange its propagation to other worlds.'

'Which is why Danton was so insistent on an evacuation,' Lettinger put in.

'Quite. The pupal period lasts until the disguise is either no longer needed or is discovered. The final stage,' Setheno gestured at the hololith display of the shattered planet, 'is final.'

'Just so we can all follow,' Lettinger said. 'Those who appeared to have been untouched by the infection were in fact the most fully corrupted.'

'I think I was clear the first time.'

Volos didn't believe for a moment that Lettinger hadn't understood. He was making a point. There was satisfaction and triumph in his tone, and underneath, a current of grim duty. Volos thought he was pathetic.

Lettinger didn't respond to Setheno. He turned to Vritras instead. 'Captain, I thank you for your rescue and your hospitality, but I will ask now for a transport back to my ship.' When Vritras nodded, Lettinger added, 'I'm sure I will be back again soon.' Vritras stiffened in the command throne. Lettinger swept out of the strategium.

'He will return with a writ from the Ordo Malleus,' Setheno said.

'And this pleases you?' Vritras snapped.

'Merely an observation.'

'To the warp with him, then,' Toharan said. 'He does not board this ship again.'

'You would deny access to the Ordo Malleus?' Setheno

asked, her eyes of gold and ice on Toharan. The flatness of her tone made it hard to tell if the question was curiosity or a rebuke. 'You are aware of the limitless extent of its authority, are you not?'

'No branch of the Inquisition has any business here,' Massorus said. 'The faith of this company is beyond challenge.'

'I will not have him putting my Dragons to the question,' Vritras promised.

'I think you will, captain,' Setheno replied. 'And I strongly suggest you do not attempt to fight him.'

'And why, in the name of the God-Emperor, would I be so derelict in my duty to my brothers?'

'Because you will be serving the wider interests of your Chapter.'

'And how do you propose to convince me of *that*, canoness?'

'By helping you see clearly. Captain, the Black Dragons have been on a collision course with the Ordo Malleus for their entire history. This day has been inevitable, and the wonder is that it did not come long ago. Your very existence is a provocation to the Inquisition. Did you think to avoid a formal investigation forever? I do not believe you are naïve.'

'Go on,' Vritras said, his voice as quiet as it was dangerous.

'You know that I am not without influence. Inquisitor Lettinger will report on the events on Antagonis, and make the case that the Black Dragons require formal scrutiny. He will rehearse your history and present, as evidence of immediate threat, the nature of the doubtworm infestation, arguing that the fact that not a single one of you has shown any sign of succumbing to the parasite is itself near-proof of daemonic taint. Rest assured, that argument will be convincing enough, if only for political reasons, to have a formal investigation launched. I cannot prevent that, nor will I try. My influence is of a more… informal nature.'

Volos wasn't surprised to hear that. He couldn't imagine the administrative contortions that would officially grant Setheno the authority she appeared to possess. Sisters of Battle, like the Space Marines, were warriors, not rulers. But he could well imagine one hierarch after another humbled by her implacable presence.

'I am confident,' Setheno continued, 'that I can have the inquiry limited to your company and the Antagonis action. Inquisitor Lettinger is a Monodominant and he is young, and so the cooler, more senior heads in the ordo will be open to mechanisms that will keep him from going too far, too quickly. However, if you resist, then you will spread this problem to the rest of the Chapter, and the investigation will be into the deepest core of the Black Dragons. The question you will face will not be whether this company has acquired a taint, but whether the Chapter is corrupt in its essence.'

'You don't think Lettinger already believes that? You don't think he will seek to broaden the terms of his mission?'

'I'm sure he does, and I'm sure he'll try. That doesn't mean he will succeed. Particularly if my presence here adds the Ecclesiarchy's imprimatur to the proceedings.'

Vritras was silent for a few moments. 'I do find it

curious,' he finally said, 'that someone of your reputation in the Ecclesiarchy should be offering advice on how best to thwart the Inquisition.'

'Don't misunderstand me, captain. With my every breath, I do what will best serve the Emperor. There, and only there, is where my loyalty lies.'

'And I take it that you do not believe we are possessed by doubtworm.'

'I know you are not.'

Vritras raised his eyebrows. 'You know this how?'

'Because of the nature of doubtworm. However complex an organism it becomes, and however sophisticated it appears to be once it makes use of its human host, it is, at its most basic level, very simple. Its attacks are narrowly targeted, but effective. It exploits the nature of faith, and one very specific doubt. The worm's message to its victims is that the Emperor does not exist.'

Volos thought of the childish ranting he had experienced inside the worm.

'That's ridiculous,' Massorus said.

'Of course it is, but remember that to have faith in something is, by definition, to lack proof. Faith is a spiritual wager, not a certainty. To believe is to open the door for doubt. To believe is not to *know*, and the vast majority of humans, especially civilians, never have any direct knowledge of the Emperor. Thus, they can doubt. You are Adeptus Astartes, and are therefore immune to this attack.'

'You are implying that we have no faith,' Massorus said, outraged.

'Not at all. You have faith in each other, in your

captain, in the Chapter, in the all-knowing wisdom of the God-Emperor. But you do not need faith in his existence. You know he exists. Your own being is proof of his. He is not just your Emperor. He is your ultimate progenitor. Even the Traitor Legions are incapable of this doubt. They would have nothing to betray, otherwise.'

Vritras leaned forward. 'You could, of course, make this very convincing argument to the Inquisition on our behalf.'

'The name of my ship is not *Act of Charity*. It is *Act of Clarity*. I have told you what I will do.'

'You can do no more, or you refuse to try?'

'I serve the Emperor.' She picked up her helm. 'I will return to my ship for now,' she said. 'Though I have faith that we will be seeing much more of each other in the days ahead.' She turned to go.

Volos blinked. Had she just made a joke? Again, he couldn't tell. Her face and tone remained stripped of any readable emotion.

Either way, Vritras wasn't laughing. 'One question, canoness, with your permission.'

She stopped and waited.

'You, also, seem to be immune to doubtworm. How is this possible?'

'I do not suffer from illusions,' she answered, and left.

Her phrasing struck Volos as odd. There was a precision that was strategic, that said more than the surface meaning of the words. He watched the door to the strategium close behind her. *Friend or foe?* he wondered. Somehow, the former seemed the greater threat.

* * *

THE SOUNDS OF a massive body slamming against metal echoed down the corridor to Toharan as he made his way toward the training cage. His Lyman's Ear parsed the sounds, telling him that there was only one Dragon exercising, and how big that Space Marine was. The analysis was easy: Volos shadow-sparring. Good. Toharan could use some one-on-one practice, too. He needed to work off some of the tension from the Antagonis action.

Perhaps it hadn't been a defeat. Perhaps there had never been a victory to be had. But there was something bitter in his gut. He couldn't get the sight of Bethshea transforming out his head. He wasn't sure why this, of all the sights on Antagonis, bothered him the most, even more than the death of Aperos. The fact of his having been so wrong about the mission rankled, but there was no reason why he should feel particular shame.

He hadn't been the only one mistaken. Setheno herself hadn't known, even if she had suspected, until almost too late. And yet, having been wrong, having what he knew to be true become false, grated like tyranid claws on his soul. For some reason, every time he thought about that moment in the courtyard, he also thought about Werner Lettinger's obscene suggestion to him. The two scenes were locked in his mind in a poisonous symbiosis, and he didn't know why, and he wanted them out. So he picked up the pace. He would sweat them out, and, if need be, bruise them out. He could certainly count on Volos for that.

He was almost at the end of the corridor, the battle cage arena opening up before him. He could see Volos, clad in a loin cloth, working through the steps of his form.

Then a voice said, 'Are you alone, brother-sergeant?'

'I am, brother-captain,' Volos said.

Instinct brought Toharan to a halt. He stepped back, keeping to the shadows of the corridor. He waited, motionless, while Bethshea leaped and transformed again and again, and Lettinger whispered.

Vritras stepped in front of the cage. 'A moment of your time?'

'Of course.' Volos grabbed a towel as he left the cage.

'Your actions against the worm will see you in song yet,' Vritras said.

Volos shrugged. 'Not a song I would choose to hear.'

'Do you so dislike being honoured?'

'My duty is my honour.'

Vritras bowed slightly. 'Well said. In that case, I have come to ask you to take on a new duty.'

Volos stopped moving. Then he folded the towel very slowly, as if delaying something unpleasant. 'My arm is always ready to serve the Chapter,' he said, and Toharan thought he heard wariness in the sergeant's tone.

'You heard about Brother-Sergeant Aperos,' Vritras said.

Volos bowed his head. 'He has earned his rest.'

'He has indeed. But now I find myself without a first-sergeant.'

Silence. Both warriors let it stretch. Vritras's silence made his meaning clear. Volos's seemed more like evasion. A vein in Toharan's temple began to throb. Finally, Volos spoke. 'You wish me to take command of Squad Nychus?'

'I do. I want you at my side, brother-sergeant.'

Again, Volos took his time answering. Standing stock

still, a hulking dark shape with grey, reptile skin and hellish horns, he had never looked, Toharan thought, so much like a statue, so much like a gargoyle. And at the back of his mind, another word lurked: *daemon*. Toharan quashed the word before it could fully surface.

'You do me a great honour,' Volos said at length.

'And you would do me a greater one by accepting it,' Vritras answered.

'Brother-captain, I am bonded to the Dragon Claws in ways that are difficult to explain to an outsider, and forgive me for using that term. We have a shared condition.' He raised an arm and briefly extended a bone-blade. 'We are Dragon Claws because, of all the members of our Chapter, we are the most...'

'Developed?' Vritras suggested.

'Deformed, I was going to say, and I do so with a certain pride. We are the most monstrous of those who retain their sanity. That monstrosity gives us a shared purpose. We bless the curse, and our individual quests for purity of service are fused with an even greater collective one. I cannot imagine breaking that.'

'Everything you have just said is no less true of the rest of our brotherhood,' Vritras chided.

Volos hung his head. 'My apologies. I spoke with hubris and selfishness, and I spoke badly.' He hesitated. 'And now I'm going to speak badly again. There is, around the position of first-sergeant, an aura of... grooming.'

'That's true,' Vritras nodded. 'To name a Black Dragon first-sergeant is to declare him captain material.'

'And I am not that. I know my limits as a commander.

I neither seek, nor am fit, for higher leadership. Have you spoken to Toharan? He–'

'I didn't make this request lightly,' Vritras said.

'I don't refuse it lightly, if it is a request. If it is an order, then...'

Vritras shook his head. 'I won't compel you. Will you at least think it over?'

'That would be an insult to you and to the honour, when I already know what my answer would be. Thank you, brother-captain, but I cannot accept.'

'You disappoint me, brother, but I will respect your conviction.' He held out his hand.

'My sword is eternally yours to command,' Volos said, and they clasped forearms.

'And it is my privilege to do so.'

Vritras left. Volos stood alone, and shadows seemed to flow from him as he meditated. Then he climbed back into the cage.

Toharan turned and walked back down the corridor. He moved quietly. The pounding in his temple was worse. It was hard not to hit the wall with the same rhythm.

THE SHUTTLE LEFT the Viper-class scout *Dominion of Grace*. Lettinger watched through the viewport as his ship grew smaller with distance. It would be some time, he knew, before he would revisit its clean lines and sober décor. He was sending it away, to his base in the Marat system. Vritras had no right to deny him full access to the *Immolation Maw*, especially not now, but Lettinger also wanted it physically difficult for Vritras to deny him boarding rights. So he had taken the steps that would make the Dragons ship his home.

He moved to the other side of the shuttle and stared at the growing hulls of the *Immolation Maw* and the *Act of Clarity*. They rested at high anchor and in close parallel. Canoness Setheno's ship, which was also about to lose its owner, was of a manufacture that Lettinger didn't recognise. He suspected it was a Mechanicus-modified variant of the Cobra-class destroyer. Just less than a kilometre long, it was about the right size for a Cobra, but it was much sleeker. It was a grey, merciless stiletto of a craft, its profile so narrow, its colours so muted and light-absorbing, that it was hard, even this close, to see it clearly against the stars. Lettinger had no such difficulty with the *Maw*. Over four times the size of the *Clarity*, the strike cruiser was an ugly, brutal, clawed fist, its outgrowths of flying buttresses and weapon turrets a reflection of the deformed warriors who made it home. It was a ship with a very high degree of long-term self-sufficiency. It would have to be. It had no home base, and outside the zones of their frequent operations, the welcome the Dragons found was frequently frosty.

The citizens of the Imperium knew corruption when they encountered it, Lettinger thought. It was time, through his agency, that this wisdom be confirmed.

He thought about his vox conversation with Proctor Toqueville. There had been some disappointments. One was the limit to his inquiry.

'Only this company?' he had asked.

'That's correct.'

'It should be the whole Chapter.'

'Work with what you have there, inquisitor ordinary. Find the guilt in Second Company, and that thread that will take us to the taint of the rest.'

'But why begin with such a limitation?'

'Because, thanks to your diligence, the Antagonis events give us the evidence needed to investigate the Second, but only the Second.'

The rationale struck Lettinger as weak, and the limited parameters of the investigation were uncharacteristically conservative by the standards of the Ordo Malleus. He thought he could detect the stench of political manoeuvring, and his eyes turned again to the *Act of Clarity*. The Canoness Errant was not the ally he had expected. He couldn't understand why this was so. Her motivations baffled him, and he could make even less sense of her actions. He shrugged. He now had the tools he needed to purge the Adeptus Astartes of this tainted growth.

As the shuttle banked toward the talons and fangs of the *Immolation Maw*, Lettinger caught a flash of starlight off another approaching craft. It was a grubby-looking civilian freighter. He didn't know what business it had here. He couldn't imagine anything good.

CHAPTER 8
PURITY AND HONOUR

THE SURFACE OF Antagonis had been so transformed, for a moment Tennesyn thought the trader had taken him to the wrong system. But the coordinates were correct, and after staring hard and long through the armourglass of the bridge's occulus, Tennesyn could make out enough echoes of familiar land masses to know that this was indeed where he had paid to be taken.

'Are you sure this is your destination?' asked Loran Tinburne, captain of the *Trade Sail*. 'We could try again. We could leave. Now.' An immense shadow in the form of a Space Marine strike cruiser was closing on them.

Tennesyn gave him a weak smile. 'This is the place,' he said sadly. He looked at the cruiser turrets aimed their way. 'Besides, I really don't think we can leave. Do you?'

The *Trade Sail*'s vox-operator looked up. 'Message from the *Immolation Maw*,' she said. Her voice was very small. 'Heave to and prepare to be boarded.'

Tinburne took a deep, shuddering breath and nodded. He looked close to frightened tears.

Ten minutes later, there were night-clad giants on the bridge, and Tinburne was weeping while Tennesyn explained that it was he who had sought passage to Antagonis. 'I really didn't know anything this serious had happened,' he said, gesturing at the transformed planet. 'I was only just here, and–'

'When was that?' one of the Space Marines interrupted.

'A week ago.'

The silence that followed was not reassuring.

And then, while the captain and crew of the *Trade Sail* joyfully fled to anywhere that wasn't Antagonis, the giants marched Tennesyn through the corridors of the *Immolation Maw*. They passed through one gothic arch after another, down passageways lined with veined, marble-like stone. It was a deep, green-black in colour and had a texture that reminded the xeno-archaeologist of a reptile's hide.

Tennesyn wasn't a big man, and he felt like a child as he struggled to keep up with the pace of his escort. He didn't even reach the shoulders of the giants. They had barely glanced at him since taking him into custody, and he was grateful for that small mercy. Their black eyes were coldness and war, and there was precious little human in the way they evaluated him. They weren't wearing their helmets, and he wished they were. The grey skin and bone crests reminded him too much of things he had seen in fossil records. On their journey through the ship, they crossed paths with an even bigger warrior, the most saurian of them all. He was the flesh embodiment of his armour's livery. He made Tennesyn feel like a thing of twigs, so easy to snap and burn.

They took him to the strategium overlooking the bridge and left him there in the company of three figures who made Tennesyn wonder into what hell he had fallen. He faced the captain of the Space Marines, sitting on his command throne, and two humans. Tennesyn couldn't see the face of the man clearly, but the hooded robes and silver electoos marked him as Inquisition. The woman was a warrior of the Ecclesiarchy, and the chill of her expressionless face made Tennesyn long for the comparative warmth of his escort of Dragons. Of the three, Tennesyn found it easiest to keep his eyes on the inquisitor, and *there* was a sign of a day that wasn't going well. He was also aware of tension in the room that had nothing to do with him, and he resolved to keep it that way.

But then there were those last words Bisset had shouted to him: *Bring back help.* The terrors before him were that help. So after they told him who they were, which did his confidence no good at all, and they asked him who he was and what he was doing here, he spoke about Aighe Mortis. But though they listened, the detail they jumped on was the date of his departure from Antagonis.

'There was no plague when you left?' Inquisitor Lettinger asked sharply.

'Plague?' Tennesyn asked. 'No, there was nothing wrong at all.'

The trio exchanged a look.

'Incubation stage?' Vritras asked.

Setheno stepped forward and took Tennesyn's chin in

one armoured hand. She tilted his head up to face hers. He stared into golden eyes that reduced him to his itemised component parts. 'I don't think so,' Setheno said. 'His return would make no sense.' She pulled the chain around his neck, drawing out his aquila. 'Then there's this.'

'Congratulations, Scholar Tennesyn,' Vritras said, and there was a welcome shade of humour in his tone. 'You have just avoided execution.'

Setheno released him, and Tennesyn tried to swallow. He found that he couldn't. 'Will you please tell me what has happened here?' he asked. 'Everything was going so well just before I left, and the cardinal was pleased. I can't believe–'

'Cardinal?' Setheno said.

Tennesyn nodded. 'Cardinal Nessun,' he said, and the temperature in the room plunged ten degrees. 'Why?' he croaked. 'Do you know him?'

'Excommunicate Traitoris,' Lettinger hissed.

'No...'

'What were your dealings with him?' Setheno said. Her voice was quiet, but its steel almost deafened Tennesyn. 'Leave nothing out.'

'He was financing my dig,' Tennesyn began, and felt the immensity of war wrap its fist around him.

THE WORD RAN through the *Immolation Maw*. There was rebellion on Aighe Mortis. The scope and nature of the revolt was not known, nor was it clear whether the Imperial Guard would be able to suppress it. But the possibility of full-company deployment was enticing. It was the chance to cleanse the war spirit of the filth of Antagonis. Honourable retreat or pyrrhic victory, the engagement on that planet was something to recover from, and the way to recovery was through the flesh of the Emperor's foes. There was also another point of honour involving Aighe Mortis: the Black Dragons had recruited there in the past.

But the *Maw* remained in orbit over Antagonis.

Toharan found Symael of Squad Jormund in the armoury, cleaning and oiling his weapons. Symael didn't have Toharan's fair skin and blond hair, but his bald head was smooth, free of crests or horns. 'What do you hear, brother?' Toharan hailed him. He went to work on his own bolter.

'Nothing but rumour, brother-sergeant.'

'I want to ask you something. It's of a personal nature, so if I overstep my bounds, tell me so, with blows if necessary.'

Symael laughed. 'Are you going to ask if I have greenskins in my genetic ancestry?'

'I plan to, but not today.'

'Then I can't see how else you might give offence.'

'When our Chaplain commands us to bless the curse,' Toharan said slowly, 'how do you respond?'

'You aren't asking if I echo the creed at the appropriate moments, are you?'

'No.'

Symael toyed with his trigger assembly. 'Truth be told, it's sometimes hard not to feel a bit...'

'Resentful?' Toharan suggested.

Symael gave him a long, considered, guarded look. Then he nodded. The gesture was almost imperceptible.

'Excluded?' Toharan said.

The nod became emphatic. Ecstatic relief flooded Symael's face, as if he were giving in to an emotion repressed and disavowed for centuries. 'Yes, by the Throne, I damn well do. Am I any the less a Black Dragon because my bones are all inside my skin? I would kill anyone who dares aver I am.'

'Well said, brother. Well said.'

'Why do you ask?'

'Because I have been wrestling with the question of purity. It has been put to me that seeing the greatest purity in the greatest distortion is, perhaps, unsound.'

'Do you think it is?'

'I don't know,' he said, and he spoke from his soul. 'I don't know. I do know this, though: there is no such reasoning anywhere in the Codex Astartes.'

'We are hardly a Codex Chapter,' Symael pointed out.

'No, we aren't. That has certainly been beneficial, hasn't it?'

Symael didn't answer. He didn't have to. They had all experienced the suspicion of the more orthodox Chapters, suspicion that, in some cases, extended as far as a categorical refusal to fight at their side. Symael reloaded and mag-locked his bolter, then turned to go. He paused before he left. 'I think we should talk about this further, brother-sergeant,' he said.

'Yes, we should.'

'There is,' Symael said, 'another warrior who would, I think, be interested in taking part in that conversation.'

'He would be welcome.'

* * *

Nithigg was in the librarium. He had a favourite lectern. It was on the second level, facing the balcony, overlooking the marching stacks of manuscripts below. He had his nose buried in a massive folio, though he had to keep a certain distance from the tome: adamantium-tipped horns jutted from both temples and the centre of this forehead, and he had to be careful not to gouge the precious manuscript. All of Nithigg's non-combat movements had to be cautious. His blades didn't retract, and extended downward from his forearms like scimitars. Volos peered over his shoulder. 'History?' he asked, keeping his voice down.

Nithigg nodded. 'A chronicle of the Year of Ghosts.' He looked up. 'I see Epistolary Rothnove still hasn't granted my requests for tighter security at the entrance.'

'He won't. He's hoping I'll acquire some knowledge through osmosis.' An old joke. He spent almost as much time here as Nithigg.

Nithigg closed the book. 'Something?' he asked.

Volos nodded. 'Our captain asked me to be first-sergeant.'

'And you refused.'

'Yes.'

'It's hard to leave the Claws, isn't it?'

'You say that as if I will.'

'I think you might.'

Volos shook his head. 'I refused, remember?'

'So you did. The choice might not always be yours to make.'

'It has been yours.'

'Ah,' Nithigg said. 'What you really wanted to talk about.'

'Yes.' Nithigg was the unofficial, self-appointed, universally accepted historian of Second Company. He had good claim to the title, not just because of his meticulous research, but because of his age. He was the oldest Dragon Claw, and the oldest veteran in the company. He kept his exact age to himself, though Volos suspected he was at least a thousand years old. Why he had not been elevated to First Company was a mystery to Volos. The honour markings on his armour were beyond counting, as were the scars on his face. There were times when his personal memory seemed even greater, and to reach back further, than the Chapter's institutional one, and though Nithigg had frequently acted in the training and mentoring capacity of a sergeant, he had never officially been given the rank.

Nithigg reached up to place a hand on Volos's shoulder. 'Brother, I am still where I am not because I choose to be, though I do. I am here because this is where I can best serve the Emperor.'

'So am I.'

Nithigg shook his head. 'You don't know that. We don't get to decide. It takes someone who is not yourself to see your essence clearly. I stay because it has been recognised that I have no leadership skills to speak of, though I am apparently very good for morale. When the final decision about you, whatever it is, comes down from whoever has authority over your fate, please have the good grace to accept it.'

Volos sighed. 'All right.' When Nithigg clapped him on the pauldron, Volos said, 'I also wanted to talk about one of our guests.'

'That worm is an insult to—'

'Not Lettinger.'

'I see.' Nithigg lowered his voice. 'I wonder about her, too. I spoke to Epistolary Rothnove.'

'Is she a psyker?'

'He's not sure. Neither he nor the Chaplain quite knows what to make of her. They agree that she is powerful.'

'Do they think she's a threat?'

'They didn't take me that far into their confidence.'

Volos grimaced. 'So we're no further along.'

'I'll tell you what I think,' Nithigg said. 'I think she's dangerous, and so is the inquisitor.'

'You just called him a worm.'

'And we just fought one.' While Volos digested that, Nithigg added, 'I don't think they represent the same danger, though.'

'Is that all the wisdom you have to offer me, oh Ancient of Days?'

Nithigg grinned. 'All that you can take in, whelp.'

They left it there, and as Volos exited the librarium, he almost collided with Lettinger on his way in. Of course he did. The fates had so decreed.

It was the first time Volos had been brought into direct contact with the inquisitor. He looked down at the man, and though his face was shadowed, Volos could read it easily. Before him was a man determined to destroy his Chapter. Volos had expected to feel rage. Instead, he felt contempt, and something that came very close to pity. 'Your pardon, inquisitor,' Volos said, and stepped aside for him to pass.

Lettinger didn't go in right away. 'Sergeant,' he said, 'do you make much use of this resource?' His gesture took in the librarium.

'We all do.'

'And do you admit that some knowledge is inherently dangerous?'

Volos saw the trap open before him, and knew he would spring it no matter what he answered. The beauty of a certain form of Inquisition logic was that it could not fail to reach its desired conclusion. If Volos said 'yes,' then he would be confronted with some unpardonably risky sin on the part of the Dragons. If he said 'no,' he would be branded a heretic. His contempt for Lettinger ratcheted up another notch, and he spoke the truth. 'I admit that there are many instances of powerful knowledge being misused.' Lettinger would damn him for saying that, too, but he was being true to himself, and to the doctrine of the Chapter. Speech was a form of action, and should be no less pure than the most lethal blade thrust.

'That is a potentially catastrophic equivocation,' Lettinger said.

Volos shrugged. 'It's the truth.'

'Then it's a truth that could be fatal to the Black Dragons, and thus prove my point. Can't you see what your Chapter is doing to itself? Don't you see how the process that created you is corrupt?'

'It gave me the tools to do the Emperor's work. I don't see that as corrupt. And we are hardly the only Chapter to encourage mutation. Why aren't you bothering the Space Wolves?'

'You are not the only Chapter under suspicion, so do not pride yourselves on your uniqueness. But no other Chapter goes so far in encouraging mutation, and does so at such a fundamental genetic level.'

'Why are we having this conversation?' Volos said. 'Are you trying to convert me or threaten me, inquisitor?'

'Perhaps warn you. I would be sad if not a one of you sought salvation before the end.'

'I will not seek it from you,' Volos said, very quietly.

'And what will you do, when you and your Chapter are condemned?'

'What my brothers and I have always done. Fight and destroy the enemies of the Imperium. And we will not stop because of one man.'

'You would fight me? And would you fight the Ordo Malleus?'

Another trap, an even worse one. The idea of coming to blows with another Imperial brotherhood, one just as loyal to the Emperor, was horrific. Volos wouldn't grant that as a possibility. And he was tired of playing Lettinger's game. He didn't answer. He walked away.

THE SUMMONS CAME, and Toharan surprised himself by discovering that he had expected it. That made nothing better. It simply told him that he knew his own worth. He made his way from his meditation cell to the captain's quarters. He knew what was about to happen, and he tried to understand why he felt nothing but resentment.

He still had no answer when he knocked on Vritras's door and stepped inside. The captain's quarters were just as spare as those of any other Black Dragon, and were only a bit larger to make room for a table covered with maps and parchments of jottings which half-concealed three data-slates. Vritras returned his salute. The two Space Marines faced each other in full armour and under total military formality. This was no casual discussion at the training cages. Vritras's first words were just as formal. 'Brother-Sergeant Toharan, it is my privilege and honour to offer you the position of first-sergeant.'

It is my duty and my honour to accept. That was what Toharan was supposed to say. That was the protocol. Instead, he said, 'Am I the first you have spoken to?'

To his credit, Vritras didn't hesitate. He didn't even blink. 'You are not.'

'You spoke to Volos.'

'That's right.' Again, no reaction from Vritras.

Toharan said nothing. The seconds slipped by, one after another, and he didn't know why he didn't speak. Perhaps because he still hadn't found the answer to why he felt as he did.

Vritras spoke first. 'You believe you should have been my initial choice,' he said. He did not sound angry.

'I do,' Toharan said, and it was the truth, a simple one, and not spoken out of arrogance or pride. He did not resent Volos. They had a comradeship forged by decades of battle together. That was not broken easily, and he didn't believe it was broken now. He was just acknowledging truth, which was the duty of any Space Marine. He was better suited for the position. He knew that Vritras was about to ask him why, and he was asking himself the same thing, and he didn't have the answer yet, but it was coming, bearing down on him with the force of destiny.

'You can't deny that Volos acquitted himself spectacularly on Antagonis,' Vritras said.

'I don't. Nor would I ever. He has always been the most perfect of warriors, one I am proud to call my brother.'

'So why should I have come to you first?'

'Volos refused you. I will not. Therefore, Volos isn't suited to the demands that lie ahead as your first-sergeant. I am.'

'Why?'

There was the question. The answer came with a burst of insight so powerful it almost staggered Toharan. 'Because I have a vision for our Chapter. I have duties to perform that extend far beyond winning the next battle.' The truths, each more simple and pure than the last, kept thundering in on him, and his hearts expanded with hope and joy. And hunger. Everything he had been feeling, all the disturbing questions and the memories that would not leave him alone, fell into place. He understood. The pressure in his chest lifted, and he could breathe in a way that he hadn't in days.

Vritras said, 'Then I thank you for performing them as the first-sergeant of Squad Nychus, Black Dragons Second Company. Fire and bone.' He crossed both arms in front of his chest and banged armour against armour.

Toharan returned the salute. 'Fire and bone,' he repeated, and began not a duty, but a mission. A sacred one.

He would save the Black Dragons from themselves.

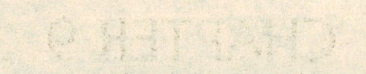

CHAPTER 9
TRACES OF EPIPHANY

THERE WERE TIMES, after battle, or during long sessions in the librarium, that Volos and Nithigg tried to untangle the web of fate that bound the Black Dragons and the Swords of Epiphany. Over the course of five millennia, they had met and clashed again and again. The black and the gold, the Emperor's night and the archenemy's light, found and tore into each other with a regularity that smacked of destiny. 'Do you realise,' Nithigg had pointed out on one occasion, 'that we know more about the Swords' history than we do of our own?' Volos had appreciated the irony, though the situation was not surprising. The early days of the Dragons were shrouded in the murk and confusion that attended anything to do with the 21st Founding. The Swords, by contrast, were evangelists. They had lessons to teach, and one of those was the story of their origins, which they spread through every system they attacked. As to why the Dragons and the Swords were doomed to wade in each other's blood, Nithigg had ideas. Both forces were the product of secretive experiments. 'We are their opposite number,' he theorised. 'We are Nemesis. We must fight until we have annihilated them down to the last memory of their existence.'

The Swords had been active on Antagonis. There was something on the planet that the traitor cardinal had desired. When the augurs revealed that Tennesyn's dig site still existed, the Dragons course became clear. A team must return to the blasted world, and pry Nessun's secret from its corpse.

And so the *Battle Pyre* touched down on the tortured surface of Antagonis. The Thunderhawk's door slid open. Tennesyn lowered himself to the ground and consulted the auspex readings. Lettinger and Setheno walked behind him, with Volos following as escort. 'This is remarkable,' Tennesyn said, his voice tinny through his rebreather. The planet's atmosphere was a toxic shadow of its former self after the fires of the torpedoes. 'The topography of the entire continent has changed, the tectonic plates have moved hundreds and hundreds of kilometres, and yet the latitude and longitude of the site haven't changed at all.' His smile was childlike in its joy in discovery. 'It's as if the planet flowed around the structure like a river around stones. Can you imagine how deep the roots of this thing must be? They must be impossible. They must be anchored in the core itself!'

Tennesyn was right, Volos thought. There was something impossible about the place. After the devastation of the cyclonic torpedoes, it shouldn't be here at all, much less be recognisable, and never mind intact. But there it was, uninterested in the changes of mere rock around it. 'What is it?' Volos asked. 'A temple?'

There was a solemnity to the structures and the spaces between them that suggested worship. Volos even experienced a touch of awe, and the sensation was novel enough that he rather enjoyed it. Set out in two concentric circles were a series of monoliths. Each was cylindrical, and tapered to a point sharp as a gladius. They all curved towards the centre. Volos pictured a clawed hand about to close.

'That's what we all guessed at first,' Tennesyn said. 'Maybe it did have some religious value to its builders, but I don't think that was all. It's too... functional.'

'An observatory?' Setheno suggested.

'Nearer the mark,' Tennesyn answered as he led the way toward the centre of the configuration of monuments. 'But what I really think is that this is a signpost. A marker.' He stepped within the circles as he spoke the last two words, and his voice dropped. When he passed into the first ring of monoliths, Volos understood why. The feeling of awe intensified. It had to do with more than size. The monoliths were big, rising thirty metres above Volos's head, but they were hardly the largest xenos artefacts he had seen. There was something else. 'How old are they?' he asked.

'We're not sure. At the very least, many millions of years. But we had a few aberrant readings that suggested they predate Antagonis itself. I dismissed those results as absurd. I'm much less certain of that now.' He gave Volos a shrewd look. 'You feel it too, don't you?'

'I do.' There was a buzzing on his skin like the writhing of a billion microscopic insects. It had started the moment he came within the grasp of the giant claws. Volos glanced at Setheno, and she nodded.

'We mustn't linger here,' the canoness said.

Tennesyn rubbed his arms. 'The effect is much stronger than before,' he said. 'And much more is exposed. Your bombardment has been very helpful after all.'

Lettinger had stopped just outside the first ring. He looked as if he had been mag-locked to the ground. 'I will not go in there,' he said. 'It is unclean.' With a visible effort, he lifted one foot, then the other, and backed away.

Volos approached the nearest monolith. He rapped his fist against it. From a distance, he had assumed they were stone, though of what sort he couldn't imagine. Tennesyn had described them as being black during the day. Now, near midnight, they were the white of bleached bone, and shone with an inner light that illuminated nothing of their surroundings. Closer up, Volos had wondered if they might be metal. They were not. Touching one revealed the density of granite. But it rang with a crystalline tone worthy of any cathedral bell. Up close, he could see that the surface was covered with a faint tracery of silver-on-white designs. They reminded him of runes, but there was something incomplete about them. 'A signpost?' he asked.

'Yes.' Tennesyn reached the centre of the rings. Volos and Setheno joined him. 'We kept experiencing a partial activation while we were excavating, enough to give a sense of what this complex was built to do. We had only just finished uncovering the top sections of all the monoliths when I left, and then...' He stopped, his eyes widening. 'Could this have caused the outbreak?'

Setheno shook her head. 'The ritual of doubtworm is very specific, and conjured by an individual, not by stones.'

'The inquisitor might disagree,' Tennesyn said, looking over at Lettinger, who had made his way back to the Thunderhawk.

'Let him,' Setheno said, and Volos wondered how two words, expressed so neutrally, could be so contemptuous. 'What happens next?'

Tennesyn checked his chronometer and looked at the sky. 'We wait just a few minutes. There is a planetary alignment currently under way in this system. All thirteen planets are in conjunction. You can imagine how rare that is. This signpost can only be read when it becomes part of the alignment. That was what Cardinal Ness–'

'He is no cardinal,' Setheno corrected.

'I'm sorry. Nessun was very excited to witness the site's full activation.'

'You're lucky you didn't share the moment with him,' Volos commented.

They waited while the stars slowly wheeled through their dance. Most of Antagonis was under a thick cloud of ash thrown up by the eruptions that had followed in the wake of the bombardment. But the air over the rings of monoliths was clear. The clouds circled around the area, but did not pass over it. Volos saw the lights of Antagonis's fellow planets move towards a point directly overhead. As they did, the buzzing on his flesh intensified. A subaural hum began, rising in power until Volos's rear teeth ached with the tension. Tennesyn was trembling, but managed to stay upright. Setheno was rigid, motionless except for a slight quiver running the length of her frame.

The monoliths flashed to life. The designs crackled, blazing with a light that Volos saw more clearly with his eyes shut. He understood now why the shapes had seemed incomplete: he had been looking at just one fragment of a massive pattern, one that ran from column to column and formed an intricate whole, one that was completed and made visible by the celestial configuration. Volos looked up. The glow of the pattern leaked into his peripheral vision, extended spider-web tendrils over the stars, and formed an image. The picture crystallised, and he realised he was looking at a pattern of stars overlaid over the real ones. The image was a map. He recognised constellations, and there was a moment of anticlimax. He wasn't looking at some unknown, unreachable sector of the universe. Given a chart, he could work out precisely where this was. At the centre of the image, one light pulsed a cold blue, and as it did, Volos became aware of a sound. It was a tuneless whistle that rose and fell with the rhythm of breathing. Inhale, and the pitch rose while the volume ebbed, exhale, and the sound gathered force with the dropping pitch. The song was a single, endless, idiot note, but behind it, Volos sensed something huge.

'How can we record this?' Tennesyn whispered, a scientist to the last.

'We won't have to,' Setheno said.

Volos looked back down. The canoness was right. The chart was emblazoned on his mind's eye. He would have no trouble reconstituting it for the *Immolation Maw*'s navigator. 'That's where they've gone,' he said. And that was where the Black Dragons would go, bringing the consequences of the death of Antagonis down on the Swords of Epiphany.

Antagonis's moon was a sprinter. It circled the planet every fourteen days. Its position was part of the alignment, Tennesyn had discovered, a small but critical element in the triggering of the monoliths, and so the Dragons had had to wait most of a sevenday after the bombardment for the moon to be right. These were lost days, Toharan thought. Second Company was in orbit over a dead planet, waiting to play with corrupt stones, doing nothing while rebellion spread and took firmer hold on Aighe Mortis. Vritras was in contact with the commanders of the Mortisian Guard regiments dispatched to quell the uprising, and the reports were troubling. But the *Immolation Maw* remained at anchor over Antagonis, waiting for Tennesyn to be able to make his observation.

The lack of action was unconscionable.

It was Symael who had suggested the meeting place. On the bottom deck of the *Immolation Maw*, in a straight line down from its chapel, was another, smaller, place of worship. It was no less sanctified, but saw much less use. It was the prison chapel. The Black Dragons did not take many prisoners. They left no wounded foe on their battlefields, only corpses. But the cells were there for those exceptional times when a target was, from a tactical point of view, worth more alive than dead, and the chapel was there for the penitent and the punished. The marble altar was stained brown from receiving centuries of justice spilled across its surface as heretics and traitors were shown the blade of mercy and truth. The aquila above it was iron-black, its edges sharp as if it would descend to scour the unworthy. The pews were rough stone. There were no viewports, and the few glow-globes gave off little more than a dim and mournful light. It was a space where faith was at its most harsh and most necessary. It was the sanctuary of brutal decision.

It was fitting.

It was fitting not just because of its severity, but because nearby was a reminder of why brutal decisions were needed. Sternward of the chapel, beyond the prison, was another set of cells. They held a special group of Black Dragons. They were the blessed, and they were the abominations. Mutated far beyond even Volos's distortions, they were monsters of spikes and horns and scales. Huge, muscled, slavering, they were trapped in a permanent predator rage, and their snarls echoed faintly down the corridors to the chapel. They were berserkers who were kept alive until they could be unleashed to find their final peace in frenzied suicide missions. Toharan had heard that the Blood Angels had a similar squad of the damned, but those warriors, however tortured their minds, were not physical grotesques. The Dragons abominations were, he believed, an unconscionable risk. Even hidden, they were a provocation to the Inquisition. They should be exterminated as soon as they developed. But they were also the logical end-point of Chaplain Massorus's theology. If one must bless the curse, then the most cursed were the most sacred. They could not be touched. Only the battlefield could end their torment and their duty.

Ridiculous. Heretical. Toharan would put an end to such perversity.

He had spoken once to Symael since their first conversation. Jemiah, a brother almost as fair as Toharan, had been part of that talk, four days ago. Now, while Volos played escort to the xeno-archaeologist, it was time for more than discussion. As Toharan stood before the altar, far more than two brothers sat in the pews. There were fourteen warriors, coming from every squad except Ormarr. Most showed little sign of Ossmodula deformation, but a few did have crests. One, Danael of Squad Neidris, had a sharp, painful-looking growth poking out just above his right eye. They all came here from different experiences, but they were united by their concern and hope. Toharan vowed he would justify the faith they had shown in meeting him here.

In his imagination, he could still here the echoes of the ceremony anointing him first-sergeant. The entire company had filled the chapel. That space was a hall of worship and honour, the blood it celebrated heroically given, not extracted from the unforgiven. There, the air had trembled with the Dragons roar of approval as he had knelt, then risen, symbolically reborn as the new right hand of the captain. The honour had been enormous, but it was also a hollow one if he didn't make use of it. The small group here was, he thought, an even greater tribute. It was a testament to the challenge and righteousness of what he was about to attempt.

'Brothers,' he said, 'I am more grateful than you can know for the confidence you are showing in me. But my gratitude will pale next to that of our Chapter once we have successfully brought it back to the embrace of the Codex. No longer will our fellow Adeptus Astartes spurn our comradeship in battle. No longer will the Inquisition cast a suspicious eye on us. No longer will our loyalty and faith be doubted. There are difficult choices ahead for us. There will be actions that we will have to take that will sever bonds of brotherhood that we have, mistakenly, valued. We will have to be strong for one another. We will need faith in what we do. And so it shall be, because not only are we Black Dragons, we are also their salvation. We are the Disciples of Purity.'

As he took part in the oaths that followed, Toharan felt no misgivings.

None at all.

CHAPTER 10
A CHOICE OF WARS

FLEBIS WAS AN orphan. It was a rocky planetoid, with an atmosphere thin as an excuse. It had no right to its own orbit around a Sol-class star, at a distance roughly equivalent to that of Mars, let alone be the only planet in the system that bore its name. Given its size, it should have been nothing more than a large moon. And once, it had been. But something had happened to its parent planet, and that world was now an asteroid belt that followed Flebis around on its orbit, keeping it in line with regular beatings. Nessun didn't know what had happened to the planet. He had his suspicions. They involved what he had brought his children to find on the moon.

Finding where the prize was hidden was easy. There was only one structure on the moon, and it was enormous. It was nestled between two mountain chains, an artificial peak higher than the natural ones on either side. Thunderhawks and drop pods streamed from the launch bays of the *Revealed Truth*, and the Swords of Epiphany gathered before the sublime. Rodrigo Nessun was the first on the ground, and he was at the forefront of the reconnaissance party that approached the vault.

Nessun wasn't touched by awe often. When he was, he was thrilled by the experience and fascinated as the emotion ran up and down the components of his being. His consciousness fluctuated between the collective mind that had taken over his body and the echo of the individual he had once been. Most of the time, there was no distinction between them, but when Nessun was in the presence of a source of wonder, the old human re-emerged, astonished into a brief existence.

There was plenty of wonder before him now. The vault's façade was smooth and raked slightly off the vertical. Apart from a seam revealing the outline of the entrance, the monument appeared to have been created using a single block of stone. It was as if a mountain had been carved into this squat shape, a mountain that did not belong here. The peaks surrounding it were sedimentary. The vault was igneous. The mountains were a light grey, covered in the dust of aeons of meteor strikes, slow erosion, and geological inertness. The vault was dark crimson. It was not made from the material of Flebis, nor from the shattered remains of its planet. Nessun tried to picture the technology required to transport a rock this huge from one system to another. He couldn't. He tried to picture the warp magic, and thought he might be a bit closer. He thought about the necessary will, and he didn't have to imagine that. He shared it.

He smiled at the scale of the vault's features. Its door frame was fifty metres high. Was that a reflection of the builders? What monsters they must have been, he thought, delighted.

Makaiel sounded less thrilled. 'How are we supposed to get in?' he asked over the comm-feed.

'Through strength, determination and power. What we seek will expect and respect no less.' Nessun used a vox he wore around his neck, but he had no helmet. He didn't need one, even in the thin atmosphere of Flebis. His chest expanded and contracted out of habit, and he enjoyed the expressiveness of sighs and laughter, but he had not had to breathe for millennia. The perpetual breeze of the moon sliced into his flesh with scalpel cold, dragging his smile wider. He strode forward, reached out and placed the palm of his hand against the seam that ran down the middle of the door. He was touching will embodied in stone. He felt a thrum in the stone, a coiled potential waiting to be unleashed.

JOZEF BISSET SAT on a level piece of rubble. He was in the shadows, away from the light of the fire and the noise of the dancing. Karl Guevion made his way over the wreckage to the comptroller with a cup of recaff. Bisset took the beverage with his left hand. His right arm was in a sling. It didn't have to be. The sling was a useful camouflage. The bionics would show through the shreds of clothing and synthetic skin that dangled from the limb. The cloth kept him covered and looking harmless. Best to keep things that way for the time being.

His leap from the collapsing Munitorum palace had

taken him to the roof of the next tower over. He had landed rolling. His momentum had brought him to his feet and he'd been up and running again. But he could not outpace ruin, and the palace had fallen against Bisset's refuge, wounding it fatally. The building had screamed and cried as he leaped down the stairs from landing to landing, but in the end the steps had disappeared beneath his feet and he had fallen, caught in an avalanche of girders and stone.

The landing had been hard, but the wreckage had tented over him as it had come down. For seven days he had squirmed through absolute darkness, several times becoming stuck, again and again narrowly avoiding being crushed as the rubble shifted. At the end of the seventh day, hands had pulled debris away and he had emerged into Aighe Mortis's brown daylight, blinking like a mole and massively dehydrated. Guevion had been in the rescue party. He had patched Bisset up and given him the sling before anyone else had come near. He was an old man, whether from years or labour, Bisset couldn't say. His hair was a lank grey, his stubble a salt-and-pepper sandpaper over a wrinkled leather hide. Bisset guessed he had some basic medicae training, and pegged him as a manufactorum patcher – one of those workers whose additional duties consisted in quickly dealing with injuries, keeping the other labourers more or less in one piece and production uninterrupted.

Guevion sat beside Bisset as the comptroller sipped his recaff. 'You're Munitorum, aren't you,' the man said. It was an observation, not a question. When Bisset didn't answer, Guevion tapped his shoulder. 'I recognise what's left of the uniform.'

'Good eye.' There wasn't much still on his frame, and what there was of it was a dust-caked mess.

'Don't worry. I'm not going to give you away.'

Bisset nodded, thankful. The crowd in the street ahead of him was chanting and dancing before the ruins of the Munitorum palace. He knew what would happen if they realised he'd been part of the bureaucracy they had just brought down. He wasn't feeling suicidal tonight. He was curious, though. 'Why did you help me?'

Guevion scratched at the bristles on his neck. 'My little shot at trying to stop things from getting worse. Figured you might be able to get our message out.'

'Which is?'

'Just leave us alone. That's all.'

Bisset shook his head. 'You can't be that stupid. This is an insurrection. You know how this is going to end.'

'Why?' Guevion pleaded. 'Why did you have to take so much from us?'

'There is no 'you' and 'us,'' Bisset told him. 'We are all subjects of the Imperium.'

Guevion carried on as if Bisset hadn't spoken. 'You already get plenty of men from us. You could just take all the ones who want to go, and everything would be fine. But no, you have to suck everything away. You take one son. I accept that. You take the other, and who's going to protect our women from the gangs? Me? And if you're putting together another regiment, then you'll be wanting all sorts of productivity up, too, and everything we make gets stripped from us. And what do we get in return?'

'The Emperor's protection.'

'From what? We need protection from you, that's what we need.'

The conversation was getting loud, even with all the shouts and whoops nearby. Bisset dropped his voice, hoping Guevion would do likewise. 'You think dropping buildings is going to help your cause?'

Guevion sighed, suddenly a very tired old man. 'Well…' he said. 'Well… I can't say that was good. No, I can't. But… Nothing else was making you listen.'

You, Bisset thought. *You, you, you*. How much of the Mortisian population, he wondered, had this mindset? It was, in its own way, an even more troubling symptom of rebellion than a dozen felled towers. Then, over the noise of the crowd, he heard the rumble of engines and clanking of treads. 'You have our attention now,' he said.

Guevion heard what was coming, too. 'Throne,' he muttered and stood up. His automatic use of the oath gave Bisset a quick pang of sympathy. He was sorry the old goat was about to die. Guevion scuttled back over the rubble, shouting. The dancing came to a ragged halt. The thunder of approaching Guard grew louder. The rebels grabbed guns and ran for defensive positions. Bisset counted about a hundred people, armed with nothing more impressive than typical Mortisian-make lasrifles. They couldn't have been the force that had destroyed the Munitorum palace. Whoever had the bigger explosives had moved on in the days since the strike. This lot was just holding a major artery checkpoint and getting drunk. They were going to be slaughtered.

Feeling more than a bit tired and old himself, Bisset

stood and worked his way deeper into the ruins, away from the street. No point getting caught in the crossfire. Might as well wait until the Guard had done its duty, and the shooting and the bleeding were over. He'd choose a calm moment to approach a Guardsman who didn't look too trigger-happy.

The thunder was now the sound of implacable law and unforgiving justice. The stubber rounds, las-fire and cannon shells slammed into the rebel positions before the Imperial Guard came into sight. People screamed. Bodies and debris fountained into the air. Pathetic return fire lanced into the darkness, and then the Emperor's hammer appeared. Tight ranks of infantry marched ahead of two rows of tanks. The vehicles were three abreast on the road, their flanks almost flush with the building façades. The rear three were Leman Russ battle tanks, and it was their high-explosive rounds that had been punching craters into the ramshackle defences. At first, Bisset thought the first-row vehicles were Hellhounds, but then he spotted the rear-mounted gas chambers. They were Bane Wolves. He scrambled back deeper into the ruins.

The Guardsmen dropped to their knees and let loose another concentrated burst of fire into the rebel lines. Bisset saw more bodies drop, but there was also a steeling of resistance, as if the inevitability of what was coming, through some perverse alchemy, transmuted despair into determination. Then the Guard moved to the side, and the Bane Wolves rolled forward. Bisset saw Guevion illuminated by the fire behind him. He was in the dead centre of the barricades. He had no chance. No one there did. There was no cover from what a Bane

Wolf fired. Bisset forced himself to watch, desperately clutching the fact that the defenders were traitors.

The chem cannons opened up, spewing a cloud of gas over the rebels. The gas was the sick green of violent plague and bad death, and its movement was a savage roiling. The screams that reached Bisset's ears were brief, but unspeakable in their agony. He saw skin liquefy, pouring off bones like candle wax. The screams had a gargling quality as blood boiled in veins and lungs. An entire swath of the street several yards deep was scoured of organic life. The purge was absolute.

The clouds dissipated. Beyond their reach, there were still a handful of rebels. They were routed. In full retreat, they were running down the road away from the Guard, disappearing into the rubble of the palace and down lanes between the buildings that still stood. Bolter and las-fire followed them, cutting more down as they fled. *Another couple of minutes*, Bisset thought, *and this will be over.*

There was a flash over his head, and a lascannon shot punched into a Bane Wolf's gas reservoir. The tank exploded, spreading its angry death for dozens of metres around it. This time, it was the men of the Mortisian Guard whose screams were awful and short, and whose skin was puddling in the road. Bisset's jaw dropped and he threw himself flat. The Leman Russ's turret rotated in his direction, and the heavy bolter sponson chugged rounds. The turret hadn't moved half its arc before a second lascannon beam blasted it from the chassis.

Armoured beings stormed past him. They were terrible, golden angels, and they fell upon the Guard with bolter and chainsword. They savaged the units that had escaped the release of the gas and tore the tanks apart. They were monsters who bore the garb of beauty. They were giants in the service of war turned into art. There were only five of them. There were a hundred times as many Guardsmen, and that was far too few. The battle was even more one-sided than the attack on the rebels had been. Within seconds, hulls had been ripped open, treads yanked from wheels and used as whips, and men scythed into shrieking meat. The Chaos Space Marines stood proudly in the carnage, gods well pleased by their allotment of blood. The surviving rebels emerged from their hiding places. They began to cheer, and the cry was taken up by more and more people pouring into the streets.

In the span of a few seconds, the insurrection on Aighe Mortis had gone, for Bisset, from tragedy to nightmare. Now he had to survive the coming minutes, long enough to tell someone off-planet what he now knew. He glanced behind him. He saw no one. He took one more look at the carnage in the street, then jumped to his feet and ran. Even as he did, he wondered what he thought he was doing. Did he want the enemy to see him? Did he think a mad dash was a smarter escape than a stealthy crawl in the shadows?

He didn't care. He just wanted space between him and the angels of terror and beauty.

He had covered about a hundred metres when they saw him. The shot came a fraction of a second before the sound of the report. The bolter slug tore a wound in the air just to his right. He started zigzagging. Rounds dug up puffs of debris near his feet. He jerked left, then left again, and this time, the round kissed his cheek. He felt the burn, heard the roar of an angry hornet. He ducked to the right and kept on going.

'You grazed him,' Raiel said to Gabrille.

'I know. Idiot feinted left twice. What kind of strategy is that? He almost ran into my shot.'

Raiel watched the man dwindling in the distance. 'Maybe give him a couple more.'

Gabrille obliged, then lowered his bolt pistol. 'That should do,' he said. 'Is there a vox for him to use?'

'They're scattered about. He'll find one. He should work for it a little bit, though.' The Sword's laughter through his helmet's grille was a handful of nails and bells. 'After all, we don't want it to look *too* easy.'

In the strategium, Toharan said, 'With respect, brother-captain, how can there be any question about where duty summons us? The Swords of Epiphany are fomenting insurrection on a planet to which some of us have genetic ties. What could be clearer? We have been made to waste time on this diversionary action here, while the primary target is falling.'

Volos understood what Toharan was saying. He felt the same urge to defend the Chapter's honour. The Black Dragons had no Chapter world. Or rather, its location and its true name were lost to them. It lived in their legends and collective hopes as Gauntlet, but whether the word stood for the planet, or the test that must be undergone to find it, was unknown. Without that centre and a stable pool for recruitment, the Dragons had been forced to become genetic opportunists, always looking for planets whose environments could produce individuals who were suitable raw material for induction into their ranks. Aighe Mortis, the hive at its most brutal, had given more than one of its sons to the transformation. The planet was not just a useful resource, therefore. The Black Dragons owed it a debt. To lose it to traitors was unthinkable.

But.

'I don't think Antagonis was a diversion,' Volos said.

Epistolary Rothnove looked up from his examination of the star charts Volos had brought to the war council. The Librarian's skin was a dark grey, and though he bore no horns, bony growths covered his head, twisting and entwining in patterns that resembled runes. His eyes were lost in shadows beneath his jutting brows. 'What was it, then?' he asked.

'What Nessun did here was designed to cause maximum destruction. He wanted us to deploy an Exterminatus bombardment. If we had cracked the planet in half, all the better. Then we would never have been able to use the xenos site, and discover his true objective.'

Vritras said, 'You contend, then, that Aighe Mortis is not that objective.'

'No. Aighe Mortis is the diversion. With the doubt-worm, Nessun was attempting to cover his tracks.' He tapped the chart. With the vision from the dig site still vivid in his mind, it had taken him less than an hour to find a match for the star patterns he had seen. 'Flebis is the target.'

'You would have us abandon Aighe Mortis?' Toharan

asked. His tone was accusatory, self-righteous.

'That would be heresy,' Massorus warned.

'I am recommending no such thing,' Volos answered. 'I am saying that I think we should proceed to Flebis first, counter Nessun there, then return and liberate Aighe Mortis.'

'We have an eyewitness report of Swords of Epiphany forces in action,' Toharan spat. 'But we should ignore that and let the insurrection grow?'

'We know of one combat squad. What I fear, brothers, is that we might let ourselves be drawn into combat on Aighe Mortis while a worse threat develops on Flebis. If we move on Aighe Mortis too soon, we could be playing into Nessun's hands, and ensuring that we *do* lose the planet.'

'Is this your opinion alone?' Toharan asked.

Volos hesitated. He could see where Toharan was going with that question, and he wondered why. He couldn't understand what had happened to his battle-brother. Toharan had been different since the endgame on Antagonis. There was a brittleness to him, a defensive inflexibility. Volos couldn't shake the impression that either something vital had been stripped away, or something just as important but toxic had risen to the surface. And now he had asked a question to which he clearly knew the answer, in order to score points in some game whose rules Volos wasn't even interested in knowing. 'No,' Volos told him, giving in to the inevitable. 'Canoness Setheno concurs.'

'Are we now turning to the Ecclesiarchy for strategic advice?' Toharan asked.

Volos refused to rise to the bait. He kept his voice calm. 'We happen to agree. That's all.'

'That isn't–' Toharan began, but Vritras cut him off.

'Thank you, brother-sergeant.' He walked around the strategium table, arms folded, eyes on the charts. 'Chaplain?' he asked without looking up.

'The taint on Aighe Mortis must be purged without delay.'

'Librarian?'

'Flebis concerns me. The circumstances are so unusual, we ignore them at our peril.'

Vritras stopped walking and thought for a few moments more. Then he moved to the command throne and faced his assembled officers. 'We make for Flebis.'

CHAPTER 11
THE PRICE OF ENTRY

'Surprise,' Vritras said, 'is the hope of fools.'

Armour-piercing rounds, grenades, melta bombs. Cannon fire. The Swords of Epiphany had not been gentle with the door of the vault. It had ignored them. It had not opened, and it had not shattered. It wasn't even scratched. Nessun ran his hand along the unmarred surface. He was impressed. He could almost enjoy the frustration, if only he weren't so aware of the relentless slipping away of time. 'This building is a sorcerer,' he said, and revelled in the further awe of that realisation. The vault was protecting itself with a shield, but not one that had any technological origin. He could feel the warp energies twisting over the stone. The Swords would have to respond with their own sorcery.

Makaiel had been away from his side, speaking to the master of the augurs. Now he returned. 'A ship has just transitioned into the system,' he said.

Nessun didn't say anything at first. He couldn't find the words. Something had happened that he considered impossible, and he was torn between excitement over the richness of that paradox and anger at the threat. In the end, he expressed his wonder and rage in one sentence. 'They've found us.'

Makaiel was less interested in the philosophical implications of the arrival. He, or the thing that inhabited him, was so boringly pragmatic. 'Father,' he said, 'you cannot remain here.'

Dull, but almost always right. Nessun grimaced in disappointment. He had so hoped to be present when the vault was opened, when its interior was revealed and the great key was found. But the Sword was correct. There was too much at stake, and he was needed elsewhere. The Flebis vault, in all its cyclopean glory, was still only one step. Nessun nodded. 'You know what to do here,' he said. 'Don't fail me.'

'The galaxy will hear our song,' Makaiel promised.

'Surprise a foe on ground that is known to him and alien to you,' Vritras said, 'and you surprise him with his victory. We do not seek surprise. We are Black Dragons. The enemy shall know of our coming and fear it. Let him prepare. Let him look to his defences. All this will grant him is more time to cower in the shadow of our looming verdict. Does he hear the thunder of our charge? Then he knows the sound of his ending. '

The Immolation Maw moved on Flebis. The long-range augurs picked up the *Revealed Truth* in geostationary orbit over the planetoid. The grand cruiser outweighed the *Maw* in size, weaponry and armour. The strike cruiser had the advantage of speed and manoeuvrability. But that wasn't the contest Vritras sought yet. He had Helmsman Maro approach Flebis with the moon between the two ships. The *Revealed Truth* didn't appear interested in an engagement either. Its engines were powering up, but it didn't move from its position, and transport craft were dropping from its bulk towards the moon.

Something small, shuttlecraft-sized, took off from Flebis to rendezvous with the Chaos ship. At the same moment, the *Immolation Maw* fired its drop pods just beyond the horizon from the *Revealed Truth*. Second Company descended in its rage.

Earth and sky: Vritras's assault would hammer the traitor in both his refuges. The attack was a closing talon. As the ground forces deployed in the low hills that marked the horizon line, the *Maw*, in the hands of Maro, accelerated, grazing Flebis's thin atmosphere as it made its predator run for the underbelly of the *Revealed Truth*. The strike cruiser whipped over the line, straightening into a climb for its prey.

A prey that was fleeing. Its engines flaring corona-bright, the corrupted monster pulled away from Flebis. The *Immolation Maw*'s turrets opened up, but the salvo was an expression of frustration rather than strategy. The *Truth*'s void shields held, and then it was picking up speed, and the choice was pursuit or support of the ground forces. The *Maw* did not abandon its own. It moved to the *Revealed Truth*'s former position. It began its scan of the battlefield. The talon closed over the Swords of Epiphany.

On the ground, the Black Dragons worked their way to the hilltops. Toharan was at Vritras's right hand. He looked over his captain's shoulder at the data-slate he was holding. Messages and picts transmitted by the *Immolation Maw* scrolled across the screen. 'The enemy betrays himself,' Vritras said. 'His ship has fled to the warp.'

MAKAIEL LOOKED UP into the Flebis night. He had received his father's farewell vox message. He saw a concentrated configuration of stars moving, and knew them as the lights of the Imperial ship. He knew that he and his passenger within were staring at their final hours in the materium. But there was work to be done first, and awe to be spread, and he knew, too, that his father did not abandon his children to be pointless sacrifices. They would not be annihilated by orbital bombardment before they could even set foot in the vault. He watched a swarm of fainter stars close in on the cluster. The *Revealed Truth* had left a gift behind. Squadrons of Doomfire bombers, escorted by Swiftdeath fighters, flashed towards the cruiser, and now it was prey.

THE HILLS OVERLOOKED a wide plain. It was perfectly flat, obviously engineered. It was a church square before the vault, a little detail wrought on a giant scale by forces that could look at planets as décor to be shaped and arranged at will. At the far end rose the vault, seeming to shoulder aside the lesser mountain peaks that flanked it. In front of the vault were the massed ranks of the Swords of Epiphany. They formed a golden wall in front of the door. Looking through magnoculars, Toharan saw that not all of the traitors were facing out. Some were doing something to the door, waving their hands and moving in harsh, jerking movements that made him think of spiders and dance. A bit forward of the vault's façade, some rudimentary trenches had been dug. They were clearly the work of a frantic few hours. So the enemy hadn't been expecting them. Good.

On the plain itself were the wretched of Chaos. Toharan's lip curled as he took in the slaves and true-believers and renegade Guardsmen. There were thousands of them, clutching rifles and spears and even clubs, and wearing crude rebreathers. Their clothes, whatever uniform or class costume they once had been, were now the expression of the Epiphany cult. Gold was everywhere, on every torn shred, and it was always a gold that was twisted, light-sucking, diseased. There was also a symbol, sewn into the clothing, inked onto flesh, carved into foreheads: a five-pointed star with rays lancing out from the corners. And in the centre, a spiral that seemed to move if Toharan trained the lenses on it for too long. He lowered the magnoculars and picked up his bolter. 'A lot of open space,' he said. 'No cover.'

'Yes,' Vritras agreed. 'They will have nowhere to hide from us.'

Toharan laughed, though he caught himself hoping that it wasn't bravado or recklessness speaking through Vritras. He banished the thought. He didn't agree with many of Vritras's decisions, but he had no cause to question the captain's tactical wisdom. Vritras had led Second Company to too many victories for that sort of doubt.

Vritras turned to Massorus. 'Brother-Chaplain, we are ready. Brother Kommodor, raise our standard.'

Kommodor did as Vritras ordered, and Massorus began to speak. 'Warriors of fire and bone!' he cried. 'See what pestilence awaits the purging flame of our wrath! March in their midst with holy violence. To the foul and the faithless, bring the Emperor's truth. To the treacherous and the corrupt, show them the only mercy they deserve. Show the finality of death without redemption. Cast them into the tomb of infinite pain. Throw them to the eternal darkness beyond the Emperor's light. For Antagonis!'

'For Antagonis!' came the shout. It was a full-throated roar, made monstrous in its volume and rage by helm speakers. It rose from Squads Pythios and Nychus, Neidris and Lanx. And then justice charged down the hill.

Four squads. Just under half of Second Company's full strength, and not one of its precious few land vehicles deployed. Vritras had held back squads on the *Immolation Maw* for possible boarding action against the *Revealed Truth*. Now forty Space Marines slammed into thousands of the warp-corrupted, about to fight their way over a kilometre of open ground toward the entrenched position of the god-warriors of Chaos. It was, Toharan thought, as he gave himself over to the fury of war, a good day.

With no home world, the Dragons had no infrastructure to produce and properly maintain vehicles. Those they had were for ultimate measures. But what did they need with vehicles when each Space Marine was a main battle tank with legs? Vritras's spearhead began its destruction of the enemy with fire from the rear. The Devastators of Squad Lanx unleashed their heavy bolters. Rounds with the destructive punch of artillery shells tore the cultists apart. A trench opened up in the enemy. The Dragons poured into it, gouging deeper into the formation. Command squad Nychus was the tip of the spear. Vritras was the sharp edge, leading his men into the sundered flesh of the foe. Toharan followed with Massorus, Rothnove, and Apothecary Urlock. Massorus's litany of salvation and destruction became more rabid with every swing of his crozius. For all its fury, language could not express the depth of his disgust with the heretics, and his religious outrage found outlet in the obliteration of the unholy. Rothnove, meanwhile, seemed calm. The Librarian was silent, but shouted all the same. His anger crackled in the bolts of warp energy that shot from his hands and incinerated the heretics.

Canoness Setheno strode beside Massorus. She was as silent as Rothnove, and if she felt, as Toharan thought she must, hatred for the enemy, it was visible only in the frozen scream of her helmet, and in the savage, spare precision with which she dispatched the cultists to hell. She fired her bolt pistol with her left hand, and in her right was her power sword. It sliced through bodies with the hiss of the sacred.

Just behind, and spread out a bit further, came the rest of Squad Nychus: five warriors in Terminator armour. They were juggernauts who crushed and pulped the foe and barely noticed that they did so. And behind them came Tactical squads Pythios and Neidris, widening the swath of destruction and beginning to train their fire on the Chaos Space Marine positions ahead.

The cultists didn't try to defend themselves. They threw themselves against the Dragons. The chattel of the Sword were joyous as they fought and died. Consumed by faith, many of them were smiling right up to the moment Toharan shot them in the face or decapitated them. The Black Dragons advance was steady and measured. The cultists were little more than a morass that had to be waded through.

They were enough. The spearhead was a concentrated, slow-moving target. The squads were halfway across the plain when the psyker attack hit. It was a steady barrage of energy blasts that were Chaos itself. They dragged claws down the veil of reality, rending its flesh, making it bleed. Colours that screamed and sounds that blinded erupted over the squads. Brother Reprobus took a direct hit to the breastplate. The Terminator staggered, but kept walking and firing. His armour cracked, the ceramite twisting itself into a spiral, but it held.

'The traitors attack with the taint of the warp!' Massorus shouted. 'Deny it and all its works! Feel the Emperor's steady hand and brush aside the shape of lies!'

They couldn't brush aside what screamed their way now. The sorcerous bolt was enormous, rolling, hungry. It devoured cultists as it came, and its howling murder of the real only grew stronger. 'Evade!' Vritras yelled and the spearhead split, its advance stopped as the Dragons threw themselves out of the way of the ball of insanity. Reprobus, slower in his armour, already wounded, took the bolt full-on. It smashed through the cracks in the ceramite and blew his breastplate wide open. He began to transform. Ripples over his body grew to a storm of flesh and bone, and his entire frame became a liquid flow of endless mutation. An arm became a claw, and then a mouth, and then a head, and then sprouting, bubbling tumours. His armour sloughed off. And through it all, as his physical identity shifted, split, multiplied and vanished, he roared, his pain and anguish transmuted into battle rage. He plunged forward a few steps, flailing. He smothered cultists with his shifting flesh until his legs vanished and he fell. For a moment, his head was visible again, eyes wide with a terrible hope as they turned to look for his brothers. Vritras answered that hope with his bolter, granting Reprobus the Emperor's Peace.

'Exterminate the sorcerers!' Massorus yelled. His shout was drowned out by a nerve-scraping shriek. It was the cry of a hawk paralysing its prey. It was the inhuman shout of Raptors. The Chaos assault unit had been held back somewhere in the mountain slopes, Toharan realised. Now, jump packs fuelling their flight, the warriors tore into the Dragons. Toharan had fought Raptors before, and was used to the mutations and body modifications that turned them into mirrors of their namesakes. The Sword Raptors were different. Though they struck with lightning claws, the gauntlet-mounted blades that were a Raptor fetish, they had not altered their feet into talons. With the oily gold of their armour and the huge arch of the jump packs, their span spread to resemble iron wings, the warriors weren't birds. They were angels who didn't know they had fallen.

One Raptor slammed into Massorus like a beatific

meteor. The two Space Marines, bright traitor and dark loyalist, rolled together. The Raptor sank his claws into Massorus's gorget. The Chaplain held on to his crozius and smashed it against the side of the Sword's skull.

Another tried to land on Toharan's shoulders. He heard the shriek, sensed the rush of the strike's wind, and sidestepped. The Raptor hit the ground in a crouch. Toharan fired his bolter at the jump pack's fuel reservoir. Multiple rounds struck in the second before the Raptor could rise. Promethium exploded, wrapping the traitor in flame. He shrieked and leaped at Toharan. The blasting fuel knocked him off-balance and he missed, his claws slashing empty air. Toharan swung his chainsword into the back of the Raptor's neck, chewing through armour and severing spinal cord.

The creature fell, but then Toharan was crouching low as heavy bolter fire scorched the air above his head. More blasts of Chaos energy rained in, and the Raptors kept slashing. Massorus had pulped his opponent's head, but another had managed to tear off the helmet of Brother Demorgon of Squad Neidris. The Raptor punched his claws into Demorgon's eyes.

The spearhead had stopped advancing. Cultists pressed in, making an offering of their bodies and holding the Dragons while the Swords of Epiphany cut at them, piece by piece.

THE CLOSING OF a dragon's talon did not mean attacks from just two sides. The grip of a dragon punctured its prey on at least three. Vritras's talon had lost one angle of attack as the *Immolation Maw* fought off bombers and fighters. The second was stymied. But there was a third. It was the stabbing thrust.

Standard Codex doctrine called for assault squads to be deployed in deep strikes at the start of an engagement to destabilise an enemy before the main attack flattened him. The simple geometry and absolute bulk of the vault, coupled with the size and strength of the defending force, blurred the line between dogma and pointless sacrifice. And the Black Dragons were not a Codex Chapter. Vritras had held back the thrust. It came now.

The Doomfires unleashed punishing payloads against the *Immolation Maw*'s void shields. The massive ship couldn't outmanoeuvre the bombers and their escorts, but the turret fire held the worst of the attacks at bay and whittled down the pack. Maro kept the strike cruiser in motion, and hit his second waypoint. He fired one more drop pod. The Dragon Claws landed in the mountains, on the opposite side of the battlefield from the rest of the squads. They raced toward the vault. Though it loomed higher than the mountains, its roof was still within jump pack reach from the top of the nearest peak. When Volos came down on the roof, the surface beneath his boots was odd. It was smooth as metal, as bedrock solid as any mountain, and yet he felt like he was walking on writhing worms. He grounded each step, careful to keep his balance.

'This is not a healthy place,' Nithigg observed.

'It will feel even worse by the time we're done with it,' Volos replied and led the way to the roof edge. The slope to the ground was near vertical and as smooth as the roof. The Dragon Claws had a complete view of the battlefield. They saw the Raptors descend on their brothers. They saw the disposition of the Swords' defensive positions. They saw the perfect angle of attack.

Vasuk's bone-blades, like Volos's, were retractable, and now he extended them, eager for flesh. 'An open invitation,' he said.

'Then we should accept.' Volos launched himself into the air.

They struck the centre of the Swords' rear line. They were fire and darkness come to crush and smother the light of false gods. As he plunged, Volos unleashed the fury of his bolter, pinning his target to the ground, blasting away chunks of armour and gouts of blood. In the last second, he mag-locked the gun to his thigh and landed with bone-blades extended. He punctured the traitor's primary heart and throat, destroying not just his life but his progenoid glands, erasing the legacy of the Sword forever.

He straightened, drawing his gun again and firing on the Sword manning the heavy bolter. The traitor grunted but stayed at his post, swinging the turret around. Volos ducked under the sweep of the barrel and rammed the Sword, horns catching the foe under the arm, cutting through the seam of the armour and slicing deep into his shoulder joint. He lifted the Sword off his feet, grabbed him and whirled him against the door of the vault. The Sword slumped, stunned, and Volos pumped mass-reactive rounds into him until he was motionless.

Something began to hum. It was a deep sound, its frequency far below what a human ear could detect, but

Volos's Lyman's ear heard it clearly. Then a huge blow knocked him sideways.

Makaiel was grappling with an Imperial, the two of them caught in an immobilising stalemate. Over the shoulder of the Black Dragon, he saw Ecanus shot to pieces against the door. He heard the hum. He also saw a change in the door. It was slight, but the seam that ran the height of the entrance was more pronounced, as if the two halves had parted less than the breadth of a hair. And so he knew what to do, now that it might be too late.

No. It wasn't too late. He lived, his vow was unfulfilled, and there was so much truth yet to propagate.

He let his knees buckle and he fell backward, dragging his opponent with him. He kicked up as they hit the ground, and knocked the Dragon over his head. Makaiel had lost his bolter during the grapple, but his pistol was still at his side. He rolled away, drew the pistol and fired. The bolts struck the Dragon in the shoulder as he rose, spinning him around and knocking him away from the vault and into the teeming plain. Cultists swarmed over him.

'Drive them back!' Makaiel yelled. 'In the name of our Father, drive them back!'

The Chaos bolts pummelled Volos. Damage runes lit up in his retinal lenses. Corrupt energy crackled and cackled over him, and the force of the hits felt as if he'd been punched by a Dreadnought. He stumbled back but kept his feet, and looked for his enemy. The sorcerer had risen from one of the rudimentary trenches the traitors had dug. He was in a direct line with the Dragon spearhead, and Volos saw the scorch marks of madness on the rock of the plain and on the avenue of bodies that ran from the sorcerer to the stalled spearhead.

Volos dropped flat and the worst of the bolts passed over his head. The sorcerer stopped his attack. Volos scrabbled forward and pushed himself up with his arms, moving to a crouch and then a leap, a burst of his jump pack turning him into a comet of hate aimed at the sorcerer. He flew at the traitor, blades out and thirsty for heretic gore. But the sorcerer had already cast another spell. He seemed to flicker in and out of being, and his movements were blurred, almost invisible with speed. It was as if Volos's leap were being dragged through a morass of time, each second stretched to an endless hour. Volos had a momentary impression of the sorcerer bringing his hands together, and then pushing his palms out, fingers splayed.

Up! Volos's intuition howled.

Another burst from the jump pack, popping him up, destroying the arc of his leap and spoiling the angle of attack. But the sorcerer clicked back into stable reality, and from his hands came a ball of nightmare, rolling over the ground to meet Volos. He flew over the inferno of change, but his blades caught the outer edge of the spell. He felt a shift, a fusing of chance and fate. Then he was on the sorcerer, and when he swung a blade, it sliced through the sorcerer's gorget like an afterthought and sent the traitor's head flying.

Volos blinked and looked and the blades protruding

from his wrists. The adamantium and the bone had run together. The blades were shaded like limestone, and veined like marble. They were something different now, and when he retracted them, he half-expected them to shoot up his arms and into his brain. The moment of agony was worse than before. Otherwise, he felt no different.

His attention returned to the battlefield. Nithigg was dispatching another sorcerer. Vasuk was down, just before a trench, but dragging himself up again. The Dragon Claws had been pushed back from the immediate area of the doorway, but the psyker attacks had ceased, and the heavy bolter was silent. The Raptors were down. The spearhead was moving again.

Volos bared his fangs behind his helmet grille. The traitor line was broken. A concentrated push now and they would crush the Swords against the wall.

The cultists were routed, too. The robed disciples were fleeing the field, running pell-mell to the vault, brushing past the Swords and heading straight to the door. The Swords must have sounded the retreat, Volos thought as he began to charge the few dozen metres back to the vault. He wondered where the heretics thought they would retreat to, and he almost felt sorry for the fools in their final seconds before being slaughtered.

Most of the Swords of Epiphany were sending a shredding hail of bolter fire at the attackers. Volos crouched low as he ran, and he took some hits, but the defence wasn't enough to stop the Dragons, only slow them a few seconds. Then he realised that the other Swords weren't even looking at him or his brothers. They were watching the cultists pile up near the door. He saw what was about to happen, and ran faster because he knew he must stop it, and knew also that he was far too late.

The clamour of bolters and grenades echoed off the face of the vault. Nessun's faithful died by the dozens. Their blood splashed up the sides of the door. The hum became a staggering blow, a seismic vibration that tried to bring Volos to his knees. Static filled the readouts on his retinal lenses. He forced himself to keep moving, though his head was filled with electric agony. The hum became a rumble that seemed to spread from inside his skull, down through his feet and into the earth itself. Then the ground really was shaking as the mammoth doors opened like twin mountains grinding apart.

The Swords of Epiphany charged over the corpses of their disciples and disappeared into the vault.

CHAPTER 12
OH, WHISTLE, AND IT WILL COME

THE BLACK DRAGONS regrouped at the entrance. The urge was to race after the traitors, guns blazing. There had been a toll of brothers' blood paid, and a debt in kind was owed. But the vault was not going to make pursuit easy.

The doorway opened onto an immense chamber, hundreds of metres high. The interior was lit by a glow that had no discernible source, as if the light simply floated inside the structure. The glow was the dark red of an infected throat. The diseased architecture also resembled a throat. The walls were slightly concave, and rose to a curved ceiling. The chamber was ribbed, and there was a smooth, curved softness to the protrusions, suggesting not the rigidity of bone but the pillowing of flesh. The floor had a single groove running down the centre, and on either side there was a low, curving rise. It was a tongue. The hall followed a gradual downhill slope for at least a kilometre, and then appeared to hit a sharp drop. There was no sign of the Swords of Epiphany. They were gone, leaving only the echoes of their march behind. The acoustics of the chamber played havoc with the echoes, bouncing the sounds around and redirecting them, amplifying and distorting them. The echoes were so loud, it was as if the traitors were present, and Volos looked over his shoulder for a moment when the thud-clang beat of boots on the stone-metal of the vault's surface appeared to come from behind. The echoes weren't dying off. They were self-perpetuating and self-generating. The sound built on itself until there were no distinguishing individual footsteps. The din became a single, space-filling tone. It seemed to Volos that it was just about to develop an actual melody when it cut out and silence returned with the blow of a fist.

'Where are they?' Toharan wondered.

'Past that drop,' Melus said.

'But how did they get there so fast?' Volos wanted to know. The Dragons had been barely thirty seconds behind the Swords. The traitors couldn't have covered the distance that stretched ahead so quickly.

Rothnove crouched and examined the floor. He reached a hand out. Energy crackled between his palm and the surface. 'There is a current,' he said.

'Of what kind?' Vritras asked.

The Librarian shook his head. 'I don't know. There is warp magic here, and it is more ancient than anything I have ever encountered. It is dangerous, but there isn't the same quality of malignity as I would expect. It is more...'

'Indifferent,' Setheno said.

Rothnove straightened. 'Exactly. We are beneath notice.'

Under his breath, Massorus began to recite the Liturgy of the Eternal Purge. It was a hymn praising the eradication of all that was not of and for the Emperor.

'If it thinks we are beneath notice, then it should learn it has erred,' Volos said. He stepped through the doorway and onto the floor. The insect writhing he had felt on the roof was much stronger, and he felt a tug towards the interior of the vault. It was as if he were setting foot into the shallows of a fast-moving river, and in another few steps he would be out of this depth. He looked back at the rest of Second Company massing at the entrance. They weren't moving. They were statues. Massorus had an arm raised in mid-gesture of anathema. As Volos watched, Massorus's fist moved a few centimetres down. Volos walked back to the entrance, and he was pressing against a force strong as a focused gale. When he crossed the threshold, Massorus brought his fist down the rest of the way.

'You have never moved that quickly, brother,' Nithigg said. 'We could barely see you.'

'There's a chronal distortion effect,' Volos said. 'Time moves much more quickly in there than out here.'

'That is warp space,' Rothnove pronounced.

Volos looked back at it. 'It seems unusually stable.'

'The words 'usual' and 'unusual' have no meaning in the warp. It is simply what it happens to be.'

'But how am I still alive? There's no Geller field present.'

'There must be some equivalent. Whatever beings constructed this vault, they had to be able to use it. This structure was not spat out from the warp spontaneously.'

'It doesn't matter how it arrived here,' Vritras said. 'Nor how it works. We have wasted enough time.' He turned to Urlock. 'How do we stand?'

'Two of the Claws dead,' the Apothecary answered. 'Four more from the spearhead.'

'Injuries.'

'None incapacitating.'

Vritras nodded, then voxed the *Maw*. 'Helmsman, status,' he said.

'All threats neutralised, captain. We sustained some damage, but all critical ship facilities are intact.'

'Good.' Vritras looked at his four squads. 'Brothers,' he announced, 'before us lies madness and death. Let it be the enemy's madness brought on by the fear we bring, and let it be his death.' He raised his chainsword high. 'Fire and bone!' he roared, and his men shouted their answer.

'Bless the curse!' Massorus called, and the prayer was repeated.

The squads reformed as they entered the vault. The echoes started up again. Vritras took the point of the spearhead once more. The Dragon Claws advanced just to the right of the main body, waiting for the orders to strike out ahead. The air seemed to thicken as they moved deeper into the chamber. Volos's helm readouts blinked on and off erratically, but if he could believe them when they were present, the temperature was rising. Second Company made good progress down the massive hall. Volos again thought of a deep river's dangerous current. The vault was too eager to welcome them inside.

'Brother-sergeant,' Vritras said over the vox, 'how much of a lead do the Traitors have?'

'Based on the time dilation I saw,' Volos answered, 'several hours.'

'Then they will have prepared for our coming.'

The Black Dragons reached the drop. The hall curved sharply for another hundred metres. Then the floor fell away while the ceiling, still high above, levelled out. At the lip, they looked out over a vast bowl, at least as big below the ground as the superstructure of the vault was above. Rising from the base of the bowl was a forest of monstrous pipes. Each was about ten metres in diameter, and their heights varied from a few hundred metres to a thousand. They appeared to be made of the same substance as the vault, the same crimson igneous rock that rang like metal. They looked twisted, as if a giant hand had turned them round and round while their stone was still molten, then yanked them to a pained vertical. They were the voices of a titanic pipe organ.

'Can you feel it?' Vritras asked.

Volos could. There was movement in the air. It was slow, and shouldn't have been detectable through power armour, but it was also strong, suggesting the motion of something vast. There were also distinct, conflicting, alternating flows. The thick breeze pushed toward the mouths of the pipes for the space of about five seconds. There was a pause, and then air would be expelled from the pipes for about the same span of time. The organ was breathing.

Linking the pipes was a network of scaffolding and catwalks that criss-crossed all the way down to the ground.

The lattice was a delicate tracery of crimson, a spider-web of stone. From this height, the thin, woven bridges didn't look strong enough to support any weight at all.

'Auspex?' Vritras asked.

'Multiple readings starting at the edge of range,' Toharan reported. 'About a third of the way down. They're using the pipes as cover.'

'Mark them,' Vritras ordered, and Toharan's auspex results flashed to the company. Volos noted the positions as they appeared in his lenses. 'There are the first ambushes,' Vritras continued. 'Neutralise them. Expand and contract the talon. Show no mercy, brothers. I expect total extermination.'

Expand the talon: spread out and encircle the enemy. Contract the talon: concentrate fire from multiple sides and regroup, obliterating the surrounded foe. The spearhead formation on this network was pointless, little more than an inviting target for a knock-out blow from the Swords.

The squads split into five-man teams as they dropped onto the bridges. They fanned out into the network. Then they began the descent. They were three levels down when the Swords began to fire.

TOHARAN USED THE pipes as cover, sprinting from one to the next with the rest of the command team. The bridges had no railings, no defensive potential at all, and they were only a couple of metres wide. To move in the open, between the pipes, was to be completely exposed. The Dragons placed their faith in speed and armour. Glancing shots smacked Toharan's ceramite, but the damage was minor and his momentum kept him running in a straight line. The assailant continued to fire, compounding his mistake. He was remaining in one place. He was giving away his position to every Dragon team, and they were all on the move, a fluid, adaptive doom descending on the traitors.

At the next pipe, a ramp led the Space Marines down another level. They were closing on the nearest Swords. Vritras pointed at the span ahead of them, and Toharan saw the opportunity. All of the squad did. Vritras didn't even have to signal his intent. His brothers had fought so many battles together, they responded to the battlefield as a single entity. Toharan exulted in the precision and art of the war machine he had joined. His elevation to Nychus was still fresh, but he found his instincts and actions meshing with the collective will of the squad as smoothly as if he had been there for a century. *How do you like your second choice, captain?* he thought as they paused, waiting for their moment.

Halfway across the bowl and one level up, a team from Squad Pythios, now led by Melus, rained bolter rounds on the Sword position. The traitors fired back. Their attention was drawn away from Nychus. The Swords had no choice, and they had no chance. They could not ignore Pythios's threat. If they did, Melus and his brothers would cut them to pieces. Instead, that honour fell to the command team. That was the perfection of the Dragon talons: lethal claws on both sides, no possible defence.

Vritras charged down the bridge, Toharan and the rest of the team at his heels. Midway across, the span passed over another directly below. They leaped. As he fell, Toharan had a split-second view straight down into the bowl. The structure of the lattice wasn't random. The intersecting lines and angles formed runes, and they stabbed at his eyes. He landed and kept moving as he blinked away the seared image.

The Swords were next to a pipe three metres from where the Dragons landed. The traitors had their backs to them. Nychus tore into them. It was ugly, brutal, satisfying. Toharan two-handed his chainsword and stabbed it down into the throat and chest of his target as the Chaos Space Marine turned around. The teeth chewed through ceramite and flesh. The sword caught, whining, on the reinforced shell of the traitor's ribcage. The Sword of Epiphany struck at Toharan, but the impact of the attack had made him drop his weapons, and his fists were uncoordinated, his wounds already disabling him. Toharan leaned on his blade, and the weapon cracked through the bone, chewing up the hearts beneath.

Toharan sensed a blur of motion at his back. He dropped with the Sword's corpse as it fell. A power whip snapped the air where his head had been with a flash of blue energy. Toharan spun, prone, pulled the bolt pistol from his side and fired up. He emptied the magazine into the traitor's face. The helmet shattered and the Sword jerked backwards. He stumbled one step too many and plummeted off the edge of the bridge. He disappeared without a sound.

Toharan stood. The ambush point had been purged. Vritras gave his men a nod and they took off again, already taking fire from another Sword position. They had their next target.

Justice, Volos thought, must taste like blood. He knew that was what it smelt like. He was covered in justice. It had jetted over his armour again and again as he and his team of five Claws massacred their way down into the depths of the bowl. This was an arena made to order for their style of war.

The Dragon Claws flew from level to level. Manoeuvring with the jump packs was tight in the cat's cradle of bridges, but they knew the force of the engines and the arc of their trajectories as they knew their own bodies, and they had flown through narrower webs than this. They waited for a group of Swords to open fire, then streaked in. They landed on top of each target like a Titan's wrecking ball. Volos sensed an unspoken contest developing to see how many traitors each Claw could smash and knock from their perches on initial contact.

He had missed his mark with the enemy he fought now. Volos's blow threw the Sword against the pipe, hard enough to jar his helmet loose. The traitor bounced back and recovered instantly, swinging his chainaxe on the return. Volos dodged, but took a ringing blow to the head from the side of the blade. He snarled and thrust with his bone-blades. The traitor impaled himself on them. The blades plunged through the armour and into his body as if they were power swords. There were implications that Volos didn't like, but he suppressed all thought of them, and redirected his worry into a killing rage. He yanked his arms wide, tearing the Sword apart.

Justice splattered him. He wiped it from his lenses. 'Next!' he yelled.

'There,' Nithigg pointed. Two levels down, toward the north side of the bowl, behind a pipe: a stream of las-fire streaking up at one of the Squad Neidris teams.

'On me,' Volos said, and jumped. He heard the other packs fire a second behind his as the team followed. They flew straight for the target pipe, whipped around it and came down on the catwalk.

There was no fire team of Swords. There was only an auto-turret. Volos kicked it over the edge and looked around. 'Where–?' he began.

The thing came down on top of him. It must have been clinging to the underside of the bridge one level up. It had once been a Sword of Epiphany. Perhaps it thought it still was. It still wore the armour, though there were huge chunks missing, as if the thing had burst through the plate. It wore no helmet, and its face was lit by the beatific smile of a being who knows a great truth and would be happy to share. Its skin was the same gold as its armour. It was huge, half again as big as Volos, and its features had been twisted by the warp into a grotesque patchwork. One eye was twice the size of the other and perched halfway up the forehead. The nose was long and tapered, like a snout. Even its arms were mismatched. The hand that held a chainaxe was normal in size, ridiculous compared to the rest of him. The other arm ended in a gigantic, chitinous claw. It was as if the creature had been holding an entire colony of daemons in its body, and now they were all bursting out, a hellish metastasis.

The monster yelled something at him. Perhaps it made

sense in the thing's language. All Volos heard was inarticulate nonsense. But he also heard the joy, and knew he had been told something the monster thought was wonderful. Then it struck. The pincer locked around Volos's head and began to squeeze. Warning runes flashed as the pressure increased. The chainaxe came down on his helm. The runes went red, then died in static. He tried to knock the creature off, but it held him fast. Its tail was wrapped around his legs. Braxas brought his boneblades, jutting forward from just below his elbow, down at the monster's head, but its reflexes were warp-honed. Its tail yanked itself from Volos's legs and whipped across Braxas's chest, knocking him off-balance. He tumbled from the catwalk.

The possessed Space Marine hit Volos again, and his helmet snapped in half. The two sections fell away, exposing his face. He spat acid into the monster's eyes. It howled and dropped its axe, clawing at its eyes. The grip of the pincer loosened. Volos jerked free, twisted, and brought his arm down, blade extended, severing the claw limb at the elbow. Blind and howling, the monster stumbled and flailed, its blood spraying in a wide arc. Volos took the thing's head off.

Braxas had stopped his fall with a burst of his jump pack and landed back on the bridge. The whole team was present. Volos scanned for their next target. He happened to look up first, and so he saw the disaster happen.

Another nest cleared. They were better than halfway down the bowl now, and the purge had momentum. Toharan had seen three more identification runes turn red, three more Brothers killed. He had seen Brother Bumalin's body plummet past, head missing. But the tally was heavily in the Dragons favour. They were scouring the Swords of Epiphany from Flebis. A wave of burning purity was descending the bowl of the vault. This felt right. This was what he was made for: tracking down whatever was tainted and extinguishing it.

The Nychus team descended another ramp. The bridge skirted a pipe immediately ahead, and then soared out into the middle of the bowl, leaving a gap dozens of metres wide on both sides between it and the nearest pipes. Zero cover, zero interest. There was a staircase twisting back and forth next to the pipe and down to the next level. There the bridge spans were short and cut from pipe to pipe. But the auspex said there was an enemy on this level, just on the other side of the pipe. A stupid position. Toharan would be happy to explain the error to the Sword.

The Sword didn't wait. He left his position and sprinted down the bridge. Vritras, out in front, followed, Toharan a breath behind. The others were a second slower. 'There's something wrong,' Rothnove said.

As he spoke, his words became truth. The Sword stopped running in the middle of the bridge. Toharan's instincts screamed a warning, and he and Vritras slowed down. The Sword's armour collapsed as the creature inside poured itself out. If it had ever been even partly human, it was no longer. It was a pink, boneless pool of flowing muscle. Its many mouths giggled.

'A trap,' Vritras said. '*Back!*'

Toharan turned, but he had known from the daemon's

laughter that it was already too late.

Melta charges went off at either end of the bridge. Outside the vault, where subjects of the materium had hammered pointlessly at a construction based in the warp, they would have had no effect. But inside the vault, the melta bombs were of the same realm as the bridge's stone, and things were different. The terrible flash happened. In that split second, half-formed thoughts tumbled through Toharan's mind. He saw the fall of the bridge to Lexica. There was a bitter taste of symmetry and fate. Then there was nothing beneath his feet but air.

Squad Nychus fell.

Setheno didn't head back when Vritras yelled. Instead, she jumped. It wasn't quite a leap of faith. The last of those was well in her past. She was at the rear of the team, closest to the pipe. Down and to her left was another span. She leaped for it.

The explosion was a scorching hurricane blast. It buffeted her, shoving her through the air with a giant's incandescent hand. Her armour smoked, its purity seals ignited, and she careened, out of control, not to the bridge but to the pipe. She felt ribs shatter on impact. Her right shoulder popped out of its joint. Beneath her, as she fell, the bridge came up. She was going to miss it. She threw out her right arm and hooked it through the web of the bridge surface as she passed. The yank was agonising. Setheno dangled, a broken doll, as the worst happened below.

* * *

Volos saw them drop. The entire command team, plummeting past him into the crimson glow below. He shot after them, using the jump pack to accelerate his descent, ignoring the fire from the remaining Sword emplacements. He decelerated at the last moment. Toharan had smashed into scaffolding half-dozen metres up from the floor of the bowl. He was writhing, impaled on the wreckage. The rest of the team lay broken on the ground, at the mercy of the group of traitors who stood there. Volos descended on the renegades with a roar, but a ball of Chaos energy hit him in the chest and took him down.

Makaiel lowered his hand, the vibrations of the spell still travelling up and down his arm. The enormous Dragon fell to earth with a crash. The rest of his assault team was right behind, and engaged with Makaiel's brothers. They would be busy. He had the time to do what was necessary. He turned to the object that stood in the centre of the floor. He wished his father was here to see this. Nessun would have been delighted by the impossibility. All of the pipes narrowed at their base and joined together in a tube barely a centimetre wide. The tube ran into a plinth twice Makaiel's height. The plinth was the same crimson rock as the rest of the vault, but in the centre was a clear, crystalline block. He had been hammering at it with his force staff since arriving, and he had almost reached the prize within. He struck another two blows, channelling all of his psychic force to the end of the staff, where the serpentine symbol of Tzeentch glowed. The block shattered. The prize was his.

He was reaching for it when he felt something grab his leg. He looked down and saw that the Dragon captain had survived the fall. Both legs smashed, spine no doubt broken, he had dragged himself to Makaiel and had pulled a gladius from its sheath. Makaiel laughed.

VOLOS FOUGHT UNCONSCIOUSNESS. He rose to his knees. He was aware of combat all around him. His vision cleared, and he saw Vritras at the feet of the traitor, and the traitor was laughing. Anger gave him strength and focus, and he was on his feet. He had lost his bolter in the fall. He didn't need it. His body was the blade of the Emperor. He charged.

The Sword of Epiphany did not turn his staff on Vritras. Instead, he reached into a cavity in the plinth, and withdrew an object. It was about the length of his palm, and roughly tubular, though covered in short, twisted protrusions. It resembled a fossilised centipede. The Sword wore no helmet. His face was a nightmare of raw, oozing meat twisted into spirals, and beneath the surface of its flayed skin, other, worse faces moved and struggled. But his eyes were a terrible, beautiful blue, and they shone with ultimate joy and triumph as he raised one end of the object to his lips. He blew.

There are sounds too big to be heard. This was one. Volos heard nothing. Nothing at all. As if out of awe at the enormity of what had occurred, the entire universe observed a second of silence. And through that terrible, absolute silence, Volos could feel what had happened, what had been so loud as to murder all sound. The pipes of the vault had given voice to something awful.

The vault had sung. The games of echoes and threatened melody that he had heard and sensed at ground level had been but the hint of what the structure had been designed to do. Worse yet than the immense, silent song was its effect. Volos sensed a fundamental shift. Something in the materium altered. The Sword's simple act had consequences that touched the core of being. For the moment of the silence, Volos could do nothing. Nor could anyone else. All combat around him ceased.

The moment passed. Space Marines struggled to the death once more. Volos was again running toward his felled captain and the traitor.

Vritras struck with his gladius. Even in his critical state, the blow might have injured the Sword, but he was slowed by his wounds. The Chaos Space Marine stepped aside from the thrust, and raised his staff. His eyes were shining with such enormous joy that he barely seemed to be paying attention to his adversary. Still, when he brought the staff down, he did so with the power of centuries upon centuries of honed skill. The writhing sickle end flashed red as it stabbed deep into Vritras's head.

There was nothing but rage for Volos then. The world was a wash of black-streaked scarlet, with his prey illuminated in lightning silver. He was upon the sorcerer as he lifted his staff. It flashed again, and something hit Volos's chest hard enough to fracture ceramite, but it didn't stop him. He crashed into the Sword, who fell against the plinth. The sorcerer raised his hand and a vortex of strobing, cancerous light engulfed Volos. It reached through his eyes, into his skull. It spoke to his body and demanded that it change. It shouted the promise and freedom of formlessness, the emancipation from shape. It demanded he let go. Pain lacerated his frame as his bones sought dissolution. He blocked their escape. He held on to his self through sheer will, and rejected the light with the force of his rage. He pulled back his arm, and the movement took an age, but it was *his* movement and *his* arm. He expelled the light from his body, pushed it back and back until it was an envelope surrounding him. He was whole. His consciousness and will focused to the jagged adamantine bone that burst from his wrists, and he *was* the Emperor's blade.

He thrust his arm forward, and time was his again, and his action had the speed of war. He drove the blade through the sorcerer's mouth and out the back of his head. Teeth rattled against the plinth. The sorcerer slumped, suspended on the blade. Volos pulled the bone back inside, and the body collapsed.

Panting, Volos turned from the dead traitor and faced the aftermath. The other Swords were dead. The Dragon Claws were still standing, their body language as haggard as he felt. The gunfire from the other levels had ceased. The other teams were arriving, and with them came more despair. Brother Volturious of the Terminators carried the decapitated body of Standard-Bearer Kommodor, who had been leading the other half of Squad Nychus. Volos tore his eyes from that further loss to see Melus supporting Setheno. Qanel and Graal from Pythios worked to free Toharan. No one said anything.

They had won. The Black Dragons had exterminated the Swords of Epiphany on Flebis. Volos stared at the motionless Apothecary, Chaplain, and Librarian. He made himself look again at the corpse of the standard-bearer. Then at Vritras. There was bile in the back of his throat as he foresaw the dark times looming for his Chapter. And that was the darkness he knew about.

What he didn't know was what the sorcerer had done to the materium.

Victory had never tasted more like defeat.

CHAPTER 13
THE GEMINI MOON

PEREGRINE DELACQUO WAS working the orchards. Night farming wasn't his favourite thing. Never had been, never would be. It was hard to see what he was doing, and he was constantly tripping over roots and being raked across the face by branches. It was a stupid thing to do, or would be if it weren't so necessary. The growing season never stopped on Abolessus Gemini Primus. Nor on Secundus. He stopped harvesting the caldena fruit for a moment and stared across the night sky at the neighbour and rival. That was when it happened.

Gemini Secundus took up half the firmament. To look at it was to be looking at his own planet in a mirror, and it had always been the dominant of the sky, its reflected light strong enough to make the night farming possible, if not easy. It washed out the stars, and the distant reminders that there was an Imperium beyond the Abolessus system were visible only for the brief darkness between the setting of Secundus and sunrise. But tonight, as Delacquo looked up, another moon appeared. It did not rise. It was suddenly there, at the zenith. It was an eye that opened in the heavens. It was a sudden, incarnadine judgement.

Something stirred beneath Delacquo's feet. The movement was slight, but it was planet-wide. It felt like Gemini Primus was vibrating with anticipation. But that wasn't what made Delacquo scream. What made him howl, what made every living human, awake or asleep, on the Abolessus Twins cry out, what fused a billion souls into an abyssal choir, was the music. It was a single note. Its pitch and tone did not change. There was no melody. It was brief.

But it was enormous.

It was the sound of a moon whistling.

VOLOS TOOK THE object from the dead hand of the sorcerer. When he lifted it, he felt a tug toward the plinth. He looked closely, and saw that each hook-like protuberance along the shaft was connected to a flexible, tiny, almost-invisible tube running back to the stone. Volos brought his blade down and severed the connections.

When the Dragons finally emerged from the vault, they had lost a month.

HE HAD SENT the message. He had done that much. He had had an anonymous infantry career, and then led an even more anonymous life in the bureaucracy, but Bisset could say, if he had to sum up his existence, that he had warned the Imperium of a Chaos insurgency on Aighe Mortis. So that was something.

He stayed mobile. He had no firm goal in mind, but he had, if nothing else, a notion: get away from the rebel-controlled territory, if he could. Find a zone still under Imperial control. If he could. The curse of Aighe Mortis was how independent it was. The shallowness of the ties between Imperial administration and the local powers meant that he couldn't trust the loyalty of the government itself. But he had nothing else to try.

Bisset had travelled five hundred kilometres from the site of the Munitorum palace. He had skirted frontlines, ducked street fighting, and reached what seemed like calmer territory. He wasn't sure if that was because order was holding or if what passed for a regime on Aighe Mortis had already fallen. It was impossible to tell. Centuries of incessant gang warfare meant that signs of fresh damage on the rotting hive towers was meaningless. Still, he followed duty and idiot hope.

The streets were quiet, which worried him. He pushed on, until he hit one of the few clear spaces still present on Aighe Mortis. The Grand Square, kilometres wide, lay before the Palace of Saint Boethius. The building was one of the few on the planet that truly was palatial. Broad enough to seem squat in its dimensions, it still loomed higher than any of the towers within sight of its domed roof. It had been the seat of Aighe Mortis's ruling mercantile families. It was now, so Bisset hoped, still the planet's administrative centre, the headquarters for the planet's kleptocratic council.

He started across the square, acutely aware of exposure,

but there was no way to reach the main doors without being in the open. He watched the windows of the surrounding buildings, but saw no one. The emptiness unnerved him. There was never any calm on Aighe Mortis. The quiet was alien and wrong. Midway across, he noticed that the doors to the palace were ajar. He stopped. He knew, with complete certainty, that he was approaching an abandoned building, and now the only thing worse than discovering that it was empty would be to find that it was not.

The council had fallen.

Bisset turned away from the palace. He walked briskly, not wanting the building at his back for longer than necessary. He listened to the silence, searching for life. He found better. In the distance, to the north, he could just make out the *crump* of artillery. So there was still fighting. Combat was suddenly as good a sanctuary as any. He headed north.

IN THE PRINCIPLE chapel of the *Immolation Maw*, the ceremony of investiture of rank took place. On this occasion, there was no sense of elevation. All the notes sounded were wrong ones. The rite had the *appearance* of propriety. Volos and his brothers lined both sides of the chapel. Through the doorway shaped into a dragon's skull, Toharan entered. He walked the transept towards the altar, past tapestries of fiery glory. Behind the altar was an immense viewport in the form of the Black Dragons livery. The rearing dragon head snarled over the vista of the galaxy, the infinite expanse subject to the beast's strength.

That was the symbolism. Today, all Volos saw was indifferent space.

There was no Chaplain to conduct the ritual. Massorus was in a sus-an membrane coma. So was Rothnove. And Urlock. Chaplain, Librarian and Apothecary down. Captain and standard-bearer dead. Second Company had been decapitated. So now they were making do.

Brother Symael led the service. Volos didn't know why Toharan had asked that he do so. Volos didn't think of Symael as especially learned or theologically inclined, but he read the correct liturgy well enough. They all knew the call and response, and so the ritual was recognisable, and at the end, after bending knee and taking their oaths of loyalty and obedience, the Black Dragons had a captain again. Though they mourned the loss of Vritras, the continuity represented by the ascendancy of the first-sergeant should have been a comfort. Volos had been pleased to see Toharan become Vritras's right hand. He had been pleased to think he would one day call his friend captain.

But he wasn't pleased, and there was no comfort.

The presence of Werner Lettinger was part of the problem. The rite was sacred to the Dragons. It was not for spectators. But there the inquisitor was. It was possible, Volos supposed, that he had insisted, as part of his investigative purview, on attending the ceremony. But he had walked in behind Toharan before taking up a position to the left of the entrance. That arrival smacked of invitation, which puzzled Volos, given Toharan's earlier extreme hostility toward the man. It also worried him. He was now less inclined to dismiss the danger Lettinger represented. He particularly didn't like how the inquisitor had had the run of the ship for over a month while almost half the company had been in combat on Flebis.

Toharan left the chapel first, the new captain requesting his sergeants' presence in the strategium in half an hour. Volos and Nithigg were the last to go. Setheno and Tennesyn were waiting for them in the corridor outside.

'Canoness,' Volos said. 'You are recovering well from your wounds?'

'I am, thank you.'

'My condolences, lord, for your losses,' Tennesyn said.

Volos nodded his thanks.

Tennesyn went on, 'The canoness and I have found a few items of interest in the librarium.'

'Oh?' Volos asked. 'Do you know what it was that the Swords were trying to do?'

'No,' said Setheno. 'Not exactly. We came across some fragments that are suggestive, and they are not reassuring.'

'We have a few scrolls that are partial works by the ancient Terran remembrancer Ehmar Djaims,' Tennesyn explained. 'He appears to mention Flebis. Or rather, the name appears in a High Gothic phrase.'

'*Flabis, Flebis,*' Setheno quoted. '*You will blow, you will weep.* It appears in conjunction with another phrase, which translates as "What is this that is coming?"'

Volos took that in. Setheno was right. He wasn't reassured. 'And does Brother Ydraig know what that device is?' Volos had given the tube to the Techmarine upon returning to the *Maw*.

'A whistle of some kind, he thinks,' Nithigg said.

'A whistle.' The word was so trivial. It was obscene to have lost so much over something that could be given that label. 'Well, that's good,' he said, his frustration spilling into sarcasm. 'I was worried it was going to turn out to be a horn.' He sighed. 'A whistle for what? To do what? Where?' The other two didn't answer. He asked Nithigg, 'You've seen these fragments?'

Nithigg nodded. 'We were three in the librarium.'

'And you've told our captain?'

'Not yet.'

'Why not?'

'I thought you should know first.'

'Why? He needs to know anything at all that we can discover so–'

'So he can ignore it?' Setheno interrupted. 'I think you'll find that Captain Toharan's priorities lie elsewhere.'

'Such as?'

'Aighe Mortis.'

Volos shrugged, trying to come across as far more sanguine than he felt. 'That's perhaps as it should be. We can't ignore our responsibilities there.'

'At the expense of pursuing anything to do with Flebis?' Setheno asked.

'He wouldn't.' Volos turned to Nithigg for support. Nithigg looked him hard in the eye but said nothing.

'You were offered the position of first-sergeant, weren't you?' Setheno asked. When Volos nodded, she said, 'You were wrong to turn the honour down.'

He kept his temper, but he was tired of outsiders judging the actions of a Dragon. 'I was not suited to the job.'

'You are lying,' she said, and Volos was so startled by

the bluntness that he couldn't muster a suitable comeback. 'To yourself, if not to us.'

He counted to ten, then said, 'Do you have a reason for telling me this, canoness?'

She nodded. 'You have a destiny with your Chapter. And you have a responsibility not to deny it.'

Volos was having difficulty processing not just what he was being told, but who was telling him. The canoness had proven herself a valuable ally in combat, and the distance between her and Lettinger seemed more like a chasm all the time. Yet Volos still couldn't shake the impression that she represented a serious danger. 'You appear to be very concerned for our Chapter's wellbeing,' he said.

'I serve only the Emperor, and do what must be done in that service.' There was something terrible in her phrasing.

'And you can see the future?' Volos asked.

'That is not my gift. I can see clearly. That is all, but it is enough.'

'And what you can see is that we have the wrong captain.'

'That's right.' There was no hesitation before she answered. She was emphatic.

Volos realised that Nithigg had taken himself out of the conversation. The ancient veteran was saying nothing, but looking at Volos with a disconcerting intensity. 'If I understand you correctly,' Volos said to Setheno, 'you are counselling sedition. You would have me not only disobey my captain's orders, but try to supplant him.'

Setheno's golden stare was as direct and unmoved as it

always was. 'That might be necessary, yes,' she said.

'I don't want to hear this,' Volos said and walked away. He didn't want to think about it, either.

But he did think about it. He heard about it again, too.

Lettinger said, 'I'm troubled by some aspects of what happened on Flebis.'

They were in the strategium. They had another five minutes before Toharan was to meet with his officers. 'I'm troubled by everything that happened there,' Toharan snapped.

'Of course,' Lettinger said smoothly. 'I was thinking specifically of something you mentioned about Sergeant Volos.'

'Concerning what?'

'His arm-blades. You said that you had never seen them as deadly.'

Toharan nodded. 'They were cutting like a relic sword.'

'Which they did not do before.'

'No.'

Lettinger held the moment for a few seconds. He wanted Toharan to see the implications. He wanted him to feel even a hint of the chill that was crawling down his own spine. He said, 'So in an encounter with powers of the warp and Chaos, something changed.'

Toharan said nothing. His eyes, grim, stared into the middle distance over Lettinger's shoulder.

Lettinger said, 'Captain, both you and the sergeant have an avowed commitment to purity. Let me remind you that evil has its own perverted purity.'

* * *

Volos saw a lot of faces being kept carefully neutral during the briefing.

'Our mission now is clear,' Toharan was saying. 'The reports from Aighe Mortis are as spotty as they are dire. The planet is crying out for our intervention. All we have achieved here is to suffer grievous losses. I think we know now where the true trap was. We have been tricked by a diversion. No longer.'

Volos clamped his teeth together. He would not speak. Toharan was right about Aighe Mortis's need. But his dismissal of the events on Flebis was foolish. It was worse than a tactical error. It was some kind of political move, one that the Dragons could not afford. Toharan seemed set on repudiating Volos, and the Dragon Claw couldn't understand the logic of the move. He was no threat. He might not agree with the new captain, but he would never disobey his orders. Toharan was fighting a war where none existed, and turning his back on decades of comradeship. Toharan was baiting him, asking him to defend the Flebis action and step into some kind of ambush. Volos declined.

Setheno's words rattled around in Volos's head. He tried to push them away. Then the shake-ups were announced, and it was all Volos could do to keep his jaw from dropping.

'Nychus must be rebuilt,' Toharan said. 'Brothers Symael, Jemiah, Mattanius, and Kataros, I would have you at my side.' Volos's eyes widened. No Melus? He had known Toharan almost as long as Volos had, and had been his squad-mate for most of that time. 'In recognition of their actions on Flebis and Antagonis, I am pleased to raise a few of our brothers to the rank of sergeant,' Toharan went on, and Volos moved beyond surprise and into dread. Too sudden, too many changes, too much wholesale flouting of tradition. What did Toharan think he was doing? More disturbingly: *why* was he doing it?

Danael was one of the new sergeants, and assumed command of Squad Neidris. Omorfos was given Pythios, and the slight to Melus was complete. Volos barely registered the other names. But Toharan shocked him one more time.

'We remain without our Apothecary, Librarian and Chaplain,' Toharan said. 'The Emperor willing, they may yet recover. Until such time, I would ask Brothers Symael and Jemiah to act in their place.' There was some logic to that, Volos thought. Symael had done some apprentice medicae work with Urlock. He knew his way around field dressings, at least. And Jemiah was a Lexicanium, though so was Ennyn in Squad Exuros, and he, in Volos's opinion, had shown better battlefield ability. Then Toharan said, 'Chaplain Massorus has no clear successor. Initiate Bumalin was killed on Flebis. We thus find ourselves with no Chaplain until a truly suitable candidate can be found. No decision in matters of faith should be taken lightly or quickly. But neither should we be without spiritual guidance. Therefore, until Chaplain Massorus recovers, or his successor has been found, I have asked Inquisitor Lettinger to preach to us. Though he is not of our brotherhood, his ecclesiastical experience is considerable. I think, too, that, at the very least, we might find his perspective interesting and worth hearing.'

With a supreme effort of will, Volos kept his hands from balling into fists. He stood still, silent and, he hoped, expressionless. When the other sergeants, veteran and newly minted, said, 'As you command,' so did he. When Toharan looked him in the eyes, Volos met his gaze with a neutrality that took more out of him than his battle with the doubtworm. Toharan's violation of Black Dragon tradition in effectively naming Lettinger acting Chaplain was unspeakable. What he was doing was obscene. It was also perversely clever, in the short run, since it would be difficult for any Dragon to complain about the arrangement while Second Company was under Inquisitorial investigation. But the damage Toharan was doing to the Chapter in the long term might be incalculable.

Still, Volos did his duty, as he still saw it, for the time being. He held his peace.

He headed back to his quarters, hoping for some time to think quietly. But Nithigg was waiting for him by his door, and Melus strode down the corridor, scattering servitors, to catch up.

'You heard?' Melus asked Nithigg.

'Some. I can guess the rest.'

'What is he doing?' Melus demanded of Volos.

Still reeling, his thoughts thick and stumbling, Volos found himself giving a rote answer, defending the Space Marine he had long held a close friend. 'He is making his first decisions as captain. This is a huge responsibility that has been thrust on him, and he needs us...' He trailed off, the stares of the other two finally registering.

'Volos,' Nithigg said quietly.

The use of his name snapped him back to clarity. 'I don't know,' he said.

'Did you have a look at that group that is in command, now?' Melus fumed. 'I've never seen such a concentration of pretty faces.' Melus's skin was almost as dark as Volos's, and a single, hooked horn jutted from his brow, poking through lank grey hair. Melus was not pretty.

'Fire and bone,' Volos muttered.

'What was that?' Melus asked.

Volos shook his head. 'Nothing.' But he was thinking about the Black Dragons battle-cry, and about their liturgy, and about how warriors like Toharan might feel excluded. Had that been done? Were he and Melus and their other, mutated brothers reaping the whirlwind of an unintentional elitism? *Is that all this is about?* he wondered. *Maybe it will pass, then. Maybe this is a squall, not a storm.* He indulged in a brief moment of foolish hope.

Melus dragged him back to reality and dashed the hope. 'You know where this might lead,' he said. 'You should be our captain. We all know it. Even Toharan does, I'll wager. The day is going to come when he'll have to be stopped. And you'll find many who will stand beside you.'

'*The day is going to come?*' Volos snapped. 'He's barely been captain for an hour, and you would have me begin a mutiny?'

'No, brother-sergeant. Toharan started it. You'll finish it.'

CHAPTER 14
IMMACULATE ACTION

The guns fell silent in the hour before Bisset reached the site of the battle. He followed the smoke and the sporadic rumble of machinery. Now and then, there was the crack of a pistol. And yes, there were some screams. It was all better than the terrible silence of the Palace of Saint Boethius. As he drew closer, he started to encounter people at last. Before long, he was in the familiar suffocating crowd of street-level Mortisian life. Most of the people he saw were in worse rags than usual. Many were clearly refugees, clutching bundles of belongings and bearing scorch marks and tears on clothing and flesh. But the mood was, by Mortisian standards, surprisingly upbeat. Bisset picked up his pace, chasing optimism. Perhaps this engagement had gone the Guard's way.

He rounded a corner to find a contingent of Defence Militia troops relaxing around an indifferently maintained Leman Russ. Beyond them, a warehouse complex built into the lower stratum of the towers had been blasted open. Bodies lay in twisted, carbonised piles. Bisset approached a nearby trio of soldiers. He nodded to them. One of them gave him a cock-eyed salute. Bisset's uniform was long gone, but he couldn't disguise his posture and gait. Any military man would recognise him as one from blocks away.

The soldier offered him a tabac. Bisset accepted and gestured toward the bodies. 'What happened here?' he asked.

'Cultists,' the solider said. He spat.

'Did they put up much of a fight?'

'Some.' The solider grinned. 'Not enough.' He pointed to the street that ran alongside the warehouse. 'Gave us something to think about.' Charred vehicle wreckage blocked the passage. The solider lowered his voice. 'Don't mind telling you I thought it was last shift,' he said, his slang marking him as a product the southern manufactorum complexes. 'Lucky for us the Space Marines showed.'

Bisset's eyebrows shot up. 'They did?' He'd been praying for Adeptus Astartes intervention since he'd sent his message.

The solider nodded. 'Extermination time. Cultists didn't even have time to blink.' His grin broadened, and suddenly he shed his hard-boiled shell and a young man was standing in front of Bisset, his eyes shining with unexpected joy. 'I never thought we'd get their support, too. I guess they know a just cause when they see it.'

Bisset's words caught in his throat. The soldier's phrasing alarmed him. He glanced back at the warehouse. He could see the scorched remains of an eight-pointed star on one interior wall. It was almost reassuring. So the dead *were* Chaos cultists. But... 'I hadn't heard the Space Marines were here,' he said carefully. 'What Chapter are they?'

'Couldn't tell you,' the soldier said. 'Bright ones, though. Lots of gold. Look like angels.'

Bisset's mouth went dry. 'I suppose they are,' he lied. He wondered why the Chaos Space Marines would kill their own followers. He sensed a bigger, more sophisticated game than he had guessed.

The solider nodded enthusiastically. 'The revolution can't be stopped now,' he said, and gave Bisset a clap on the back. 'Justice for Aighe Mortis at last. Work on that for a shift.'

He didn't appear to notice Bisset's dread.

SOMETIMES, VOLOS FOUND strength in the reliquary. The huge, vaulted chamber was dark except for the minimal glow-globes casting a reverent shine on the machines and weapons of Chapter glories. There was the peace of certainty here, of the Black Dragons at their finest. He thought he might escape his doubts for a few minutes. Just a little bit of peace was all he wanted, a respite from thoughts of mutiny and heresy.

It didn't work. Instead, he was thinking of an absence. He stood before the empty Dreadnought armour. Its last occupant had died more than a century ago, and no worthy successor had yet been found. Warriors whose skill, bravery and age made them candidates for the grim immortality of the armoured coffin, and whose wounds on the battlefield did not kill them outright, were rare. Volos longed to speak with a venerable brother. He needed to hear wisdom tempered by the ages.

Footsteps behind him. He turned and saw Nithigg. Volos smiled. 'Why are you the only one who hasn't been telling me what to do?' he asked.

'Because if you don't act from your own conviction, we are all lost,' Nithigg answered.

Volos grunted. There was no comfort in his friend's words, but they gave him an anchor of strength. 'You're a wise man,' he said.

Nithigg was looking over his shoulder at the Dreadnought. 'No,' he said, 'not really.' His gaze was poignant with humility and reverence.

THE HALL OF Exaltation was a shaft that stretched from the top to bottom decks of the *Revealed Truth*. Both ends were covered in armourglass. The mad light of the warp flowed in, spiralling up and down the walls of the shaft, fingering runes, charging them, and setting them off on a writhing dance. Even when the *Truth* was in the materium, as it was now, waiting on the far side of the sun from Aighe Mortis, the Hall carried with it the energy and taint of the warp. It was as much a battery as it was a place of worship and meditation. Standing in the centre of the transparent floor, and looking up, Nessun couldn't see the stars through the distant ceiling. What he could see was the stored power, coiling and flexing over the expanse of the Hall. It invited his eyes and mind, and he surrendered to the whirl.

Dreamscape, warp space, it was all one, and in his

fugue state, Nessun's consciousness stretched over infinities. He was searching for a prize. The note on Flebis had been sounded, and the song would soon resound throughout the Imperium, but he had sacrificed much for this step. He wanted recompense. He was sure he would find it. He travelled the warp, swimming and tasting the currents of emotions and impulses, the knots of thoughts and the flesh of desires. The Black Dragons had been exposed to the strength of the vault. Not all of them could have emerged without being marked. The scars would be distinctive.

They were. He homed in on them, a predator summoned by the scent of blood. He found the lesions in the wounded soul, and slipped inside. He began to whisper. He began to teach.

He placed his hands on the threads of destiny, and, as his god showed by great example, plucked at them. Wove them. Tangled them.

THERE WERE STORMS in the warp. There had to be. Something was different about this crossing. Toharan couldn't pin down the precise nature of the difference, or how it was affecting him. He knew it was, though. He had started sleeping. Not just the microbursts of downtime that a Space Marine could get by on almost indefinitely, but real sleep, hours of it, as if he had that time to spare and didn't have the infinite demands of his new duties. And even with those hours lost to the luxury of full unconsciousness, he was exhausted. So he only wanted to sleep more. It was a drug. It was a hallucinogen. He had also started to dream, though he couldn't remember the details when he awoke.

Just as well. He didn't feel up to dealing with two sets of unrealised hopes.

He was in the prison chapel. He walked its length, running his fingers along the altar stone, breathing in the austere atmosphere of rigour, supplication and final extremities. After a few minutes, he knelt at the altar and prayed. He prayed for guidance, and for the strength to do what needed doing. Because it was clear that hope, reason, goodwill and daylight dreams were simply not enough.

He could be praying in the upper chapel. There was nothing compelling him to seek spiritual solace in a place designed to cow prisoners rather than elevate the thoughts of Adeptus Astartes. But here was where the Disciples of Purity had formed, and the collective dream that group represented had come to pass. Most of the key positions in Second Company were now filled by Disciples. The upper chapel, on the other hand, had become the site of dashed hopes and bitter disappointment. The promise he had felt during his rite of ascension had been an illusion. There had been a moment of unity that evaporated as soon as the demands of duty and purity had made themselves felt. The Disciples were in power, but they were resented. Training cage matches were turning into blood feuds. Hostile silences in the mess hall turned into brawls in the corridors. The conflicts were unseemly. They were, it seemed to him now, almost heretical.

The scenes in the upper chapel were demoralising. There were no fights there, no veiled insults or toxic debates. The services were solemn, dignified and, thanks to Lettinger's sermons, insightful. They were also sparsely attended. After the first one of his captaincy, when he guessed the ranks had been filled by the curious and the outraged, the numbers had plummeted. Almost every face he saw there, he knew from the meetings here. The upper chapel was becoming, for Toharan, a symbol of pointlessness. Here, in the depths of the *Immolation Maw*, he could feel the direction and impetus of mission.

He was still on his knees when Lettinger found him. 'I think I know why you're here,' the inquisitor said.

'And why are you here?' Toharan asked. 'Have you come to offer judgement or strength?'

'What do you mean?'

'Your mission on our ship seems to have undergone an evolution of sorts.'

Lettinger said nothing at first. He looked uncomfortable. 'Perhaps,' he said, thoughtful, not coy. 'I have been having dreams,' he continued, and Toharan held his breath. 'I feel a sense of...' he hesitated. He seemed embarrassed, which Toharan hadn't thought possible.

'Destiny?' Toharan supplied.

Lettinger smiled. 'You too?'

'I can't ignore all that has happened.'

'Neither can I. I thought I was here to render judgement.' He glanced in the direction of the cells holding the abominations. 'I certainly could. I have seen the monstrosities that are kept down here. But I now believe that I was sent to help you save your Chapter.'

Toharan believed the same thing. But he didn't feel the optimism he should have. 'Is that even possible?'

he asked. 'Have you seen what is happening? Have you seen how the simplest attempts to move us back towards Codex compliance have been received?' He sighed. 'This kind of conflict is unworthy of the Black Dragons.'

'Perhaps,' Lettinger said quietly, 'you have the problem reversed.'

'What do you mean?' Even as Toharan asked, something stirred in his brain. Memory or dream, vision or inspiration, he couldn't say. It was both new and familiar, enticing and maddening. It was the struggling scrabble of insect legs against his cortex.

'Maybe it is the Dragons themselves who are unworthy.'

'Then what would you have me do?' Toharan demanded.

'You should consider the possibility of something new arising from the ashes of the irredeemable. A new Chapter.'

Horror and promise stretched out before Toharan. The scrabbling in his head was almost unbearable. 'How?' he whispered.

'I don't know. But if this is destiny, if this is the Emperor's will, then the way and the means will appear.' Lettinger spread his hands. 'I could be wrong. Our task will be much simpler if I am. But I fear that I am right. I sense that the coming engagement on Aighe Mortis will give us the answers we need.'

Toharan heard, but said nothing. His sense of mission grew until it was an ecstasy. He looked around the prison chapel, at the dark stone and iron, and saw a reflection of the stark choices ahead. He placed his hand on the bloodied altar, and drew on its strength. He would make those choices. When they came, he would know what to do, and the way he would know was suddenly clear. The answer was so simple, so obvious, and such a basic fact of his existence that he had almost overlooked it.

Purity. The dictates of purity were the answer. He had but to follow the pristine road, and his actions would be immaculate in their power and perfection. And if it came to that choice, then yes, he would destroy his Chapter in order to save it.

Then the noise in his brain blotted out the world, calling him down to sleep and dreams.

CHAPTER 15
PARSING REVOLUTION

EVEN WHEN VIEWED from orbit, Aighe Mortis couldn't hide its essential ugliness. Some hive worlds glittered like spiked jewels from a distance, the cloud-piercing turrets of the elite creating a mirage of beauty. Others had mountain chains and oceans that defied the feature-eradicating virus of humankind. But Aighe Mortis was honest. It looked like an infected boil. The lance of Exterminatus might almost be a mercy. But the Black Dragons came to liberate, not to annihilate.

The atmosphere was a sluggish, brown-grey sludge. Where the clouds parted, which was rare enough, the urban blight of the surface was visible. From space, there was no architectural majesty to be seen. There was no detectable quality, only an endless, soul-numbing quantity. The impression Aighe Mortis presented was of a planet-wide scrapyard composed of clusters of rusted nails. The filth of the planet was so palpable that the strategium's hololith seemed to carry a stench.

As the Immolation *Maw* approached, and the planet filled the bridge's occulus, Toharan was struck by the irony of striving for purity in any form in such a place. It was, in fact, such a perfect irony that there could no longer be any doubt, he thought, that destiny was unfolding. He was staring at a test. He would be found worthy.

Volos looked at the planet and felt pity for its inhabitants. During the voyage here, he had spoken at more length with Tennesyn about what he had seen of the insurrection. Tennesyn's analysis of the planet's economy was depressing. No matter what happened here, its people were doomed to a squalid end. That this civilization's endgame brutality made it a fruitful recruiting planet for the Black Dragons filled him with shame.

It wasn't shame, though, that sent an unpleasant tingling down his fingers. Premonition was casting a long shadow before him. The awful conviction he had felt just before arriving at Antagonis was back. He could feel the blood of the innocents slicking his hands. There was an atrocity coming, and he would own it. His mouth was dry. He was Adeptus Astartes, and he knew no fear. But he did know horror.

The question in the strategium was where to make planetfall. There were no open spaces to speak of anywhere on Aighe Mortis. Vox traffic from the surface was a hopeless mess of fragments, conflicting voices, and garbling static. Some of the voices that came through were not human. Toharan ordered the reception terminated. There was no point in indulging the Chaos interference.

The *Immolation Maw* joined the Imperial Navy fleet at high anchor. The command ship was the *Irrevocable Fate*, an Overlord-class battlecruiser. Toharan hailed its commander. Admiral Keilor Hassarian radiated frustration over the vox. The Mortisian Guard had landed troops in the tens of thousands with the goal of taking and holding the government centres. The men had disappeared into the smog of war. Hassarian had no idea what progress, if any, had been made, though the state of communications did not bode well. Nor did the constant flashes that lit the clouds from below. The light did not come from storms. Battles were ongoing, widespread, and impossible to track. 'There is no front,' Hassarian sputtered. 'Or the front is everywhere. How do we know where to advance and what to defend?'

Only the front wasn't everywhere. A few hundred kilometres west of the northern hemisphere's administrative nerve cluster, there was a region where the clouds did not flash. The area covered a full hive quadrant, almost a thousand kilometres square. The zone appeared to be pacified, but Hassarian couldn't be sure. Its communications were no better than the rest of the planet's.

A staging area, Toharan thought. A starting point, a place where it might be possible to get a sense of the actual strategic situation. 'We land here.' Toharan pointed at the hololith, and designated the eastern border of the quiet zone.

* * *

The target sector had a functioning starport, and Second Company deployed there, transported in by Thunderhawks. Toharan wasn't going to use the deep strike muscle of the drop pods without knowing so much as the state of the conflict. So the Black Dragons landed, disembarked in force, and were greeted by filth and good cheer.

The filth was the hive of Aighe Mortis up close. As festering a vision as the planet presented from orbit, it was orders of magnitude worse at ground level. The pollution was so thick that ground fog was brown. The architecture was an unending forest of towers built of black iron and a rockcrete that time and smoke had turned just as black. Some buildings stood alone, barely shouldering aside their neighbours. Many others were connected by a tangled patchwork of walkways, or joined by afterthought annexes.

Volos was reminded of the scaffolding on the Flebis organ, and saw some of the same dense, embodied nightmare here, on an even larger scale. But where the vault had the awful inspiration of the warp behind it, and a kind of perverse grandeur, there was nothing awe-inspiring about the Aighe Mortis hive. It was hab towers and smokestacks that looked the same, hab towers and smokestacks that *were* the same, and industry indistinguishable from cancer. Hope was foreign to Aighe Mortis, and had been banished for millennia. The world-city was drudgery and despair made of stone and metal and choking air. Though Volos did not question the necessity or the rightness of the mission to bring the planet back under Imperial rule, he couldn't help but see the irony in the struggle. There was nothing to liberate here. There never had been. And what could Chaos possibly do to make life here worse?

This wasn't the first time he had entertained these thoughts. He had been to Aighe Mortis before. All of Second Company had during recruitment missions. Finding suitable candidates made it a necessity to walk among the inhabitants of the source planet, to get to know the culture, the challenges, the strengths and the weaknesses of the indigenous population. But for the Black Dragons, it was also a point of honour. They made use of the human resource of Aighe Mortis, but they did not plunder it. They took the asphyxiating civilization's hardiest, most promising sons and transformed them beyond all recognition into sacred monsters of war. Beyond the duty to destroy the foes of the Emperor, there was a debt the Dragons had incurred toward the people of Aighe Mortis. They would repay that debt with salvation.

Whether it was desired or not.

The ferrocrete expanse of the starport would have been one of the rare open spaces of Aighe Mortis, if it hadn't been for the fact that it was two hundred metres above ground level, built over a warren of miserable, light-deprived habs, which in turn rose over the squalid converted mine tunnels. As he joined his mustering brothers, Volos watched the approaching welcome party, and that was where he saw the good cheer. The crowd was a motley collection of civilians and militiamen, sprinkled with a few officers and the odd Guard uniform. Some wore field dressings, others were using makeshift crutches, but most were uninjured. Some of the work and military uniforms were in rags, others were intact, but all were grimy. And there was something in every one of the faces. Hope might have been exiled from Aighe Mortis, but it had returned, and it was coming to meet the Dragons.

Toharan walked towards the crowd. Lettinger was at his side. Volos followed close enough to be able to hear what was said. He heard footsteps behind him and glanced over his shoulder. Nithigg was right behind him, and ghosting along a step further back was Setheno, her eyes flicking with a cogitator's impassivity between the crowd and himself. Volos faced forward again, but he felt the canoness's gaze on him like a bad conscience.

A militiaman saluted Toharan. 'Sergeant Karl Feher, lord,' he said. The greeting and the salute were respectful, but carried off with a jauntiness that was completely un-Mortisian in character. It was, Volos could tell, a product of the hope animating the group, and it was clear that that hope had nothing at all to do with the arrival of the Black Dragons. Volos was used to humans reacting with awe and, quite often, terror in the presence of Space Marines. He saw neither here. It was as if the hope left no room for anything else. It was an emotion so long repressed that, when it returned, it was a narcotic.

Toharan nodded to Feher. 'You seem to have the situation well in hand here, sergeant,' he said. There was battle thunder in the distance, but nothing nearby. Feher and his fellows carried weapons, but slung over their shoulders. They looked relaxed.

Feher grinned, his teeth a bright flash in the dirt on

his face. 'Bit by bit, lord,' he said. 'It's slow, but we're getting there. I'm sure the work will go faster yet now that you're here.'

Volos noticed a man standing at the back of the group, and a bit to the side. He was the only one whose face wasn't lit by hope. He was watching Toharan and Feher intently.

'We are not a service of convenience,' Toharan told the sergeant. 'Are you telling me that your reassertion of control is inevitable? Have you won the war?'

'No, no,' Feher protested, wilting a little under Toharan's glare. 'We're working the shift hard. It's tough to the east, and if one side or the other comes out on top, then we'll be in for it.'

'One side or the other?'

Volos moved off, working his way around the crowd to the man at the rear. Volos took in his bionics and bearing. 'You're with the Guard?' he asked.

'A long time ago. Munitorum now, at least until…' He gestured vaguely. 'Jozef Bisset,' he said. He lowered his voice. 'There are traitor forces on this planet.'

'We know. A warning was sent.'

Bisset visibly sagged with relief. 'So someone received it.'

'You sent it?'

'Yes.'

Volos kept his voice low. 'Can you tell me what is going on? These people… there's something wrong. Are they–?'

'They aren't cultists,' Bisset said. 'They're not even heretical.'

'Aren't they?' Setheno put in. She had arrived without Volos noticing. Her question was a warning.

Bisset paled. 'At least, they don't think of themselves as such,' he amended. 'I think they still worship the God-Emperor after...' He caught himself.

'After their fashion?' Setheno finished. Volos heard a world's doom lurking in her words.

'After the fashion of anyone on a world like this,' Bisset answered.

'You mean rote, unthought, automatic,' Setheno said. 'Unfelt.'

'Perhaps. But they have had little reason to feel it.'

'You are defending them.' Another warning.

'I don't mean to... canoness,' he said, taking in her armour's engravings of rank. 'I'm trying to explain them.'

'Why are you with them?'

'I decided I would be more use to whoever finally came if I stayed alive and found out what I could than if I got myself killed before I could even reach a Guard contingent.'

Setheno's nod was slight, but Volos sensed the shadow of judgement pass over Bisset, leaving him unscathed.

'So if they aren't heretics...' Volos prompted.

'As far as I can tell, there are three forces in this civil war. The Mortisian Guard leads the loyalists, but apart from the Guard itself, that faction is very small. They have the military advantage, but little base of support in the general population. Less well-armed, but far more numerous, are the secessionist factions. There are the actual Chaos cultists, and then there are these rebels.'

'What's the make-up of the cultist force?'

'A mixture,' Bisset said. 'Very big mobs of former civilians, a significant chunk of the Defence Militia, and a fair number of the new Guard conscripts. They don't have the training of the loyal troops, but they did get their hands on weapons before they fell to Chaos. There are other cultists, too, who are very far gone. They came with the Traitor Space Marines, I think. I didn't get too close, but some didn't really look human anymore.'

Volos grunted, unsurprised. 'And these people,' he said, taking in the untainted rebels with a sweep of his arm. 'What are they hoping to achieve?'

'I think they just want to be left alone.'

Setheno said, 'This is not a universe where that is possible.'

Bisset gave a slight bow, acknowledging the point. 'Unfortunately, they believe otherwise.'

'And the Swords of Epiphany,' Volos said. 'The cultists are following them, I assume.'

Bisset frowned. 'That's the odd thing,' he said. 'I've only seen them the once, but I've seen the results of their passage. They've been acting on behalf of these people.' He pointed to the group. 'They've been killing cultists.'

Volos and Setheno exchanged a look. The strategic arithmetic assembled itself. The sum was dire. Guard versus cultists, turmoil and war everywhere except for the zones occupied by the faction that believed its rebellion was merely political. The archenemy was winning hearts and minds.

'One more thing,' Bisset said. 'You've seen these traitors?'

'We have,' Volos told him.

'At first glance, and from a distance, they look... Well... People are confused. I've spoken to more than a few who think *those* Space Marines have been sent by the Emperor.'

THE COMMAND CENTRE had been set up near the centre of the starport. Inside a large tent, Toharan called up a hololithic map of the area. It displayed the best intelligence the Dragons had of the combatants' dispositions. They had tried to raise the closest Guard commanders, without success. The vox interference made communication over more than a few blocks impossible. Toharan pointed to the nearest clash, about twenty kilometres east. 'It would seem that Admiral Hassarian is correct. There is no one front. Pushing back the enemy is not an option. This is a war of extermination. It falls to us, therefore, to smash the enemy's spine so that the Guard can then finish him off. We will begin here.'

Volos had no quibble with the strategy or the choice of initial strike. But there was the problem of their rear. 'What do we do about the local rebels?' he asked.

'They are not an immediate concern. I see no point in fighting two fronts at once.'

Volos nodded, and there was a murmur of agreement from the other squad leaders.

'Their heresy cannot be allowed to spread,' Setheno objected.

For the first time in days, Volos found himself at one with Toharan. 'Spreading heresy hardly seems to be their interest,' he said.

'All rebellion is heretical. There is no such thing as a

ANTAGONIS

ADEPTUS MINISTORUM
CEMETERY WORLD

CONTENTS

Extracts from the private journal of
Inquisitor Werner Lettinger..2
Antagonis Northern Continental Map...................4
The Battle of Concordat Hill Map..........................4

> *... circumstantial evidence overwhelmingly points to daemonic taint. The Black Dragons must be put to the question before they betray the Imperium.*
>
> -- Inquisitor Werner Lettinger to the
> Ordo Malleus High Council

File: 53L-653

The concept of randomly occurring, militarily useful mutations such as this is ludicrous. That these mutations are common makes such claims even more insulting. The Adeptus Mechanicus reports that gene samples, when they are provided at all, are so pure that mutations become inexplicable.

We are dealing with deception, pure and simple.

Anecdotal reports suggest that the retractable bone-blade is becoming more common. Its desirability, from a tactical point of view, is clear. Its increasing frequency points to deliberate, heretical genetic work on the part of Black Dragon Apothecaries.

I find any hesitation to take action incomprehensible.

The bony outgrowths on the forehead (opposite) are, if it were possible, an even greater indicator of corruption. They are frequently modified by the individual. They must therefore be taken as an expression of intent.

The daemonic inspiration is so obvious, it needs no further commentary.

Extracts from the private journal of
Inquisitor Werner Lettinger

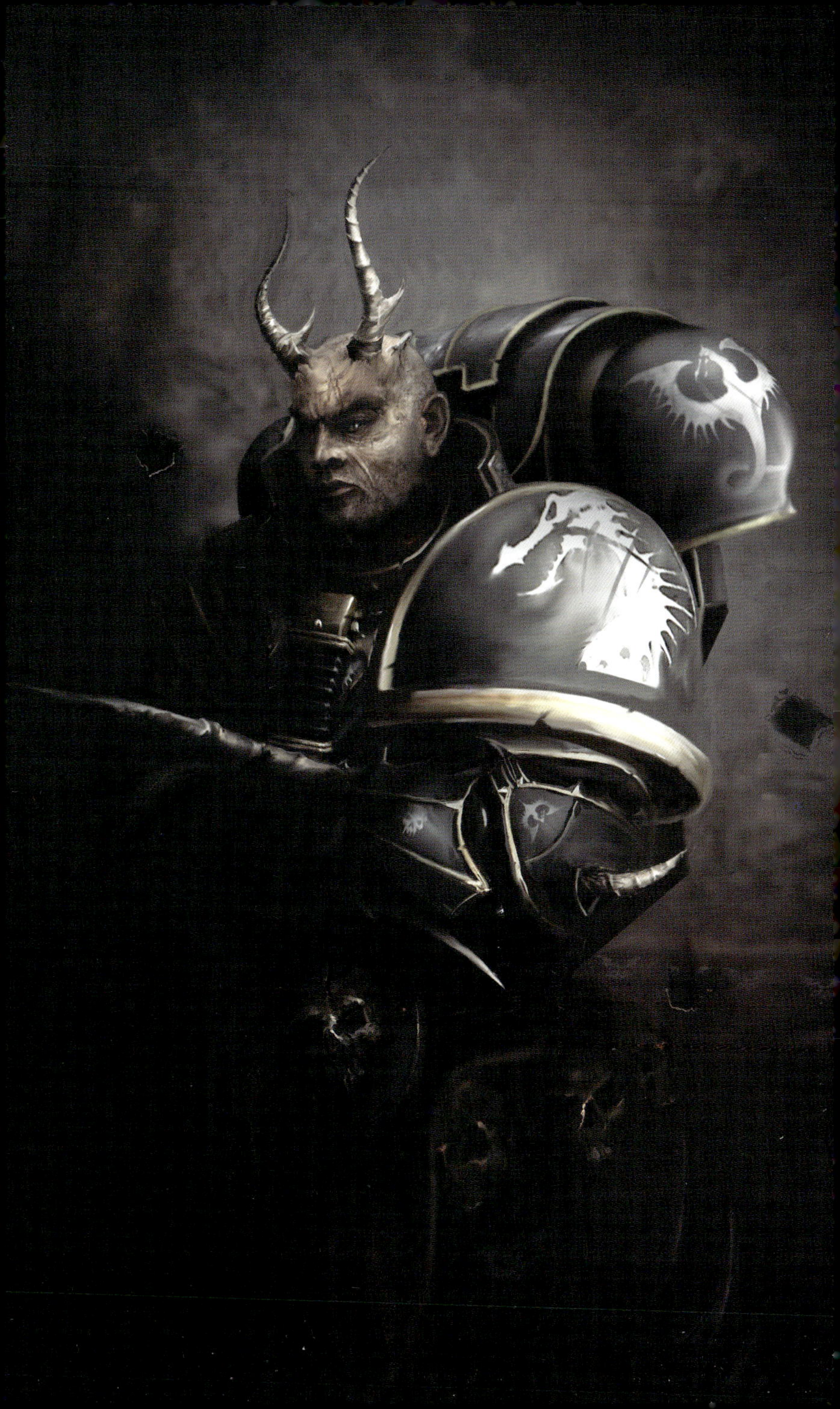

ANTAGONIS
NORTHERN CONTINENT
LECORB TO LEXICA KEEP

MAP KEY

LEXICA KEEP Ref 307	ECCLESIARCH ALEXIS XXII BRIDGE Ref 824		
FOREST Ref 903	CANYON ROAD TO LEXICA KEEP Ref 618		
FOOTHILLS Ref 451	LECORB Ref 386		
GRASSY PLAINS Ref 756	TEMPLE MOUNTAINS Ref 292		

REF: 02335/N00HE/98345

THE BATTLE OF CONCORDAT HILL

1. THE CONCORDAT
2. CONCORDAT RIVER
3. LAKE
4. MAIN ADVANCE OF BLACK DRAGONS AND MORTISIAN GUARD
5. CULTISTS' ADVANCE
6. INSERTION OF SQUAD ORMARR

purely political split with the Imperium.'

Lettinger was nodding as Setheno spoke, and for a moment, the universe seemed to have righted itself, with the Ecclesiarchy and the Inquisition allied and at odds with the Black Dragons.

Toharan stepped in. 'You are, of course, correct, canoness,' he said smoothly. 'But I think this is a heresy easily defeated. Once these people witness the truth, they will repent.'

'And how will they see this truth?' Setheno asked.

'Through the purity of our actions.'

There was a long, disbelieving silence. Setheno's expression didn't alter, but her eyes, if anything, became even colder. The heat death of the universe stared at Toharan, and found him wanting. 'I cannot dictate your war-making,' she said. 'But please believe that I know what I am talking about when I tell you that heresy cannot be ignored, coddled or reasoned away. It can only be punished.'

'And please believe that I know what I am doing. When I see the potential for redemption, I would give the wayward a chance to seek it before I destroy them.'

Volos heard, in Toharan's words, an agenda that had nothing to do with the rebels of Aighe Mortis, and he saw his beloved Chapter fall deeper into shadow.

His sergeants left to ready the troops. The mission would begin in an hour. Toharan's first battlefield command loomed. Lettinger offered to stay and talk, but Toharan asked him to go. He needed the solitude to think, meditate and pray. There was so much at stake.

He understood Setheno's argument. What she didn't understand was what he was attempting, and how desperate his gambit was. On it rested the future of the Black Dragons, and perhaps their very existence. His conversation with Lettinger in the prison chapel haunted him. He could feel the truth and necessity in what the inquisitor suggested, but still he couldn't bring himself to condemn many of his brothers without making one last attempt to show them the error of their ways. The rebels in this sector gave him the perfect opportunity. They offered little military threat, being content to let the other factions slug it out and then pick up the pieces. And though their actions were wrong, it was clear that they meant no harm. They opposed the cultists, and, at least in what Toharan could see, showed no inclination to indulge in depravity of any kind. They believed themselves righteous, and conducted themselves accordingly. They were simply misguided.

They could be saved.

They *would* be saved, once they saw the true nature of the conflict on Aighe Mortis, and how they were being duped. They would return to purity, and their redemption, in turn, would pull the Black Dragons to the light. It was a perfect circle of salvation. The hermetic simplicity of the scheme was so beautiful, it had to work. Toharan could see the strands of fate weaving together to culminate in this moment. To turn his back on the opportunity would do more than throw away the last best chance to salvage his Chapter. It would damn his soul.

And if everything came to pass as he knew it must, if

he fulfilled the quest that he had been given, perhaps peace would be his again. Perhaps the scrabbling in his head would cease. The impulse showed him what was necessary. It kept him walking the sure path to the pure and the triumphant, but his mind was agonised with buzzing, vibrating, anxious, irresistible movement. It was no longer just the crawling of insect legs in there. There was also the thrumming flutter of wings. It broke up his thoughts. His conversation stuttered. Behind his right eye, a sharp point stabbed and strobed. There was only relief when he took action, releasing the writhing impulses by following them. That part wasn't hard. He knew, down to the core of his soul, that he was doing the right thing. The problem was waiting. The impatience to save the Dragons blurred with the urgency in his head.

The wait was almost over. The attack was about to begin. Relief and salvation were at hand, and in the end, the purity of fire would restore the purity of bone.

THE REVEALED TRUTH and its small squadron hung in stationary orbit as near to Aighe Mortis's sun, Camargus, as void shields would allow. With the *Truth* were the Apostate-class heavy raider *Metastasis*, which had taken point in creating Aighe Mortis's civil war, and the Soulcage-class slaveship *Foretold Pilgrimage*. It still waited to play its part in the game. The squadron was as invisible to the Imperial ships as they were to it, but Nessun had no need of augur readings to tell him who was abroad in the Camargus system. Dancing with the empyrean in the Hall of Exaltation, he had access to minds. He caressed their surfaces, and tormented their depths with burning truths. He listened to their desires and obsessions, and they found in him a more sympathetic ear than they had ever encountered before. He soaked up the unwitting confidences, came to know his prey, and followed the paths of weakness deeper and deeper into the tender flesh of self.

He felt the truths he planted take root and flourish. They grew strong, spreading their branches ever wider. In full glory, they would strangle every other thought and hope, converting all drives to their own ends. Already, there had been so much progress. Nessun's empyrean-self laughed with unqualified delight, laughed with all the force of his being, while his material body let its mouth hang open and utter a low, moaning rasp.

Actions had been taken. Destinies loomed. There were still many branching paths ahead, but along every one, he saw nothing but the celebration of his Great Lord. Now, he had but to wait a short while before the moment would be ripe for his next move. During that wait, he could revel in the perverse, and watch the Black Dragons make their choice of dooms.

CHAPTER 16
THE COMMANDING HEIGHTS

If Hell had nightmares, Concordat Hill was one of them. Most of Aighe Mortis's features had been razed, consumed and buried. Thousands of years of industry's hammer had smashed them flat, leaving only the blackened towers of humanity's misery to reach for the toxic skies. But some traces of the planet's shape still showed through, a geological palimpsest. Concordat Hill was an echo of the mountain it had once been, a roughly conical rise distinct enough to lift the spires of its towers above those below. At its peak was a monstrous manufactorum cathedral, and this was the Concordat itself.

Even after the exodus of Aighe Mortis's ruling elite, the Concordat retained its force. It was a machine of unstoppable momentum. It was too big, too integrated, too self-contained, and too horrific to kill. The factory floor and the hall of worship were a single space combining machines and tapestries, assembly lines and stained glass windows, workbench and pew. Labour and liturgy were one and the same. Fanaticism changed work into an act of faith that could never be completed, and so the clangour and smoke-belching of the Concordat never ceased. Worker-supplicants slaved, prayed, and drank and evacuated grey meal substitutes until they collapsed at their post. When they revived, their penance for hours lost to sleep was to work twice as hard. Life expectancy was measured in months. But the doors were always open to new employees, while hundreds of vox-casters made the Hill resound with the hymns sung by a tireless choir tens of thousands strong. Whatever desperation walked the streets and warrens of the hive, there was employment to be had here, all applicants accepted. Within a day, new employees had become full initiates.

The Concordat ran its endless course, untouched by the tides and currents of the planet's political affairs. It paid no attention to the early infiltrations by the Swords of Epiphany, or to the first stirrings of resentment against the new founding. It ignored the insurrection. Not even the global civil war disturbed its relentless cycle of production. The Concordat had long since lost any sense of purpose or goal. While it did produce its share of small arms, it also spat out millions of components whose use had been forgotten for centuries, and an eternal flow of incomprehensible fusions of rods and boxes poured from the complex to fall straight into its sewage outflow. This was the Concordat River, and it ran down in discoloured cascades and brown-water rapids to become a moat at the base of the hill, and the closest thing Aighe Mortis had to a lake.

The Concordat was a mindless devotional machine that existed for its own sake, and even now, as war came to its doorstep, nothing changed. The maelstrom of arms that engulfed Concordat Hill seemed less to be closing in on the complex then to be just another product of the beast, its effluent transporting the blasted insanity of its interior to the outside world. And perhaps there was some truth to this. The convulsion that was devouring Aighe Mortis was the inevitable result of the Concordat's abomination.

But the immediate military truth of the battle of Concordat Hill was that the topography and the complex were invaluable. They were the means whose end would be the annihilation of a foe. The force that controlled the Hill would have the only true high ground for hundreds of kilometres in every direction. The elevation was such that the Hill really did look down on the streets and rooftops of the surrounding city. The Concordat's own roof had a broad landing pad beside its colossal crozius spire. Though fallen into disuse, the pad was big enough for cargo freighters. Big enough to install a battery of heavy artillery. The king of this hill would have the means to level any sector occupied by his enemy between here and the horizon. It was a prize so valuable that two armies were willing to destroy themselves in order to claim it. If, when the smoke cleared, there was no one left standing to make use of the position, the futility would be no more than a fitting tribute to the Concordat itself.

The Black Dragons came to bring an end to futility.

* * *

For all the vortex of street-to-street, building-to-building clashes, the struggle for Concordat Hill was, in its broad lines, quite simply defined, and Toharan's plan took advantage of this. The Mortisian Guard were advancing up the western slope, while the cultists had the east side. The race to the top had ended in a dead heat. The back and forth skirmishes at the summit had turned into a perpetual flesh grinder. There was no pause as opposing troops stormed into the maw of war, gunfire giving way to the butchery of melee weapons. A tide of blood had flowed into the Concordat River, giving it a slick shine visible even in the night. The wave of battle splashed up the sides of the complex, with more hand-to-hand massacres taking place on the Concordat's lower ziggurat levels. Anyone climbing above the first three terraces was taken down by opposing fire. The building's immense doors, metres thick, had closed automatically as the first combatants had arrived, and were still unbreached.

Toharan had the friendly rebel forces advance as far as the base of the hill. He didn't ask them to engage in combat directly. It would be enough, he thought, for them to witness what would happen, and they would clamour to fight in the Emperor's name. Tactically, all they had to do was hold and protect the rear. The Dragons, meanwhile, would move to support the Guard, pushing the advance forward and driving the cultists from the summit. The Dragon Claws were to strike behind the enemy lines, at the base of the eastern slopes, and disrupt the foe's march. The plan was a good one, Toharan thought. It was simple, it was adaptable, and it would make good use of the terrain and the Space

Marines' strengths. He felt the imminence of glory and redemption as he charged into battle.

THE BATTLE PYRE unleashed the Dragon Claws. It flew in from the south, coming around the curve of the hill to the eastern positions. Anti-aircraft fire from both sides denied all access to the airspace directly above the summit, but Keryon wasn't interested in that approach. All eyes were on that quadrant. He brought the Thunderhawk in from an ignored corner of the sky, weaving low between the filth-blackened towers. The gunship struck like a scythe: a slash from the side, deep into the enemy's flank. Hellstrike missiles cratered the target zone. The sponson heavy bolters chewed the enemy into so much meat. The enemy attempted to respond. Disorganised return fire clanged off the armour. The momentum of the march bled off. 'Give them a judgement of flame,' Keryon voxed.

'They'll be kindling for their own pyre,' Volos responded, and the Claws launched.

The squad split into two fire teams. Volos led the first. They hit the ground with the fury of an orbital strike, shredding cultists and heretic troopers. They struck the centre of the main advance. Four broad avenues, running along the cardinal points of the compass, went up in relatively straight lines to the Concordat. They were the means by which ground transport fed the beast raw supplies and received its still-usable output. The east road was now the main tributary of the Chaos flood. The Claws brought chaos of their own, a bloody turbulence in the middle of the flow, and the advance slowed even more.

Volos had opted for a flamer again. He didn't need range for this stage of the combat, just a maximum spread of death. He spun, torching cultists, and those who weren't instantly carbonised ran flaming into their fellows, creating an expanding ring of burning casualties. Five metres to his right, he saw an enemy-commandeered Hellhound. He burned a path to it, pounding over fragile bodies, shrugging at the rounds that glanced off his armour. The turret rotated his way. With a burst from his jump pack, he shot up out of the line of fire and landed on top of the vehicle. He extended a blade and, a part of him still unable to believe that he could actually do this, punched through the armour-plating of the Hellhound's promethium reservoir. He tossed an incendiary grenade inside and blasted back. He was still in the air when the tank exploded. A mushrooming fireball rolled over the cultists, gifting them with slashing shrapnel. Across the entire width of the avenue, Braxas and the other Claws of Volos's team were butchers with bolter and flame, creating barricades of corpses, interdicting the upward slope of the road.

They were a virus in the bloodstream of the Chaos ranks, and the army responded like antibodies to the invader. The advance contracted as troops from uphill and the side streets rushed to crush the Claws. Volos and his brothers welcomed them to damnation with open arms. They burned and shot and sliced and smashed: dark gods of black ceramite and white, murderous bone. They were giants, monsters of war breaking little human dolls into bloody, smoking shreds.

It almost wasn't sporting, Volos thought, snarling as

he tore into another clump of cultists. A traitor Guardsman got off a lasrifle shot at Volos's face, scorching his mouth grille. 'I just had this repaired,' he growled, his voice distorted into an electronic, inhuman rasp. He wrapped his fingers around the man's neck and squeezed. The Guardsman's head popped off. No, it almost wasn't sporting, but heresy deserved no better, and what the traitors lacked in force, they made up for in quantity. Given will and enough time, they could, like the doubtworm-infected on Antagonis, overwhelm a Space Marine. They were attempting to do that now as they choked the avenue with their numbers. It was exactly what Volos and his brothers wanted them to do.

Nithigg, heading up the other combat squad, voxed. 'At your leisure, brother-sergeant.'

Fangs bared, Volos grinned in anticipation of carnage. 'No, brother,' he said. 'At yours.'

'How very kind. On three, then.'

'On three.'

Two beats, two more savage moments during which dozens more cultists died, and then the Claws lifted off from the choked morass of the avenue. Above, the demolition charges set by Nithigg's fire team detonated.

Bisset had told Volos about the insurgents' opening salvo of the war and the fall of the Munitorum Palace. 'They should be repaid in kind,' Volos had replied.

Now they were. The charges took out the street-side façade and structural supports of an immense spire. The job, Nithigg had explained, was like felling a tree, and the art lay not only in making the tree fall, but in controlling where it did. With an outraged roar of murdered stone, the tower seemed to twist, its bulk fighting gravity for a perversely graceful second before it came down like the fall of the heavens themselves. It collapsed along the length of the avenue, destroying the network of upper level roads and walkways, triggering a chain reaction. For the cultists, it was as if an entire mountain chain descended on them. Volos and the Claws rose through a night filled with flying rockcrete and dust, and below them an entire swath of the insurgent army vanished, crushed out of existence.

The Dragon Claws landed uphill of the destruction, and began to burn and slash their way to the summit.

IS IT TIME *yet?* Rodrigo Nessun wondered. It was hard, sometimes, to keep track of minutes and hours in the materium. So much of his consciousness was at play in a realm where time was not just meaningless, it wasn't even a concept. But it was important that he remember he had things to do on the material plane. That was, after all, where the game was being played. That was where there were destinies. He reached out and touched the minds that were open to him, and read what was being experienced. The full picture of the Concordat Hill struggle coalesced before him. He saw that yes, it was indeed time. He sent another player onto the board.

THE MAIN FORCE of the Black Dragons surged through the Mortisian Guard and hit the front lines of the Concordat battle like a battering ram. Lettinger ran with them, doing his best to keep up, but it was a lost cause. Setheno, more than a head taller, was better able to match the pace, and he lost track of her power-armoured figure early in the charge. The Dragons used no vehicles. With this concentration of troops, even a bike would get bogged down. On foot, the Space Marines had a duck-weave-smash momentum that ate up distance and shredded opposition. Lettinger swallowed the humiliation of being the straggler. It wasn't easy. The secrecy of his actual ordo notwithstanding, he was unmistakeable as an inquisitor, and he was used to the awe and cringing he inspired when he emerged from the shadows. There was no such reaction from the Guardsmen he ran past. He was too pathetically human, too ordinary, in the wake of the storm of gods that had just passed.

It didn't matter, he reminded himself as he reached the upper quadrant of Concordat Hill. Today did not matter. The battle did not matter except as a test of the Black Dragons. A test not of their martial ability, but of whether there was anything worth salvaging, or whether he and Toharan should proceed with seeking an act of mercy for an irredeemably tainted Chapter. That decision was what mattered, and so, when all was said and done, he could put up with a little wounded pride. He held the fate of a Chapter of the Adeptus Astartes in his hands. That was true authority and power. He knew there would be no songs written about Werner Lettinger in the centuries to come, but his name might certainly be spoken in hushed whispers, and that would suit him very well.

Ahead, the Black Dragons must have already been having an impact, because the mass of Guard was moving faster. The vehicles were doing more than inching, and the men were actually marching. Lettinger ran a bit faster, his cloak flapping night. He was a wraith weaving in and out of the men, and at last he reached the battlefield. The summit of Concordat Hill was a volcanic eruption of blood and confusion, a hurricane of close-quarters fighting where unit cohesion and even a sense of direction fell apart. Within seconds, Lettinger didn't know if he was advancing or retreating. There were heretics on all sides, and he pounced from one to the next, a lethal shadow. He wasted no energy, putting one shot from his laspistol in the skull, point blank, of each target. He was a piece of the dark, and they couldn't see him coming, couldn't fight what they didn't know was there.

He heard a series of explosions, and then a rumble so huge it might have been an earthquake, and the ground did shake beneath his feet. The Dragon Claws mission had succeeded, then. He sensed a shift in the nature of the struggle. The current became more defined. He was moving consistently in one direction: the top, driving the enemy away from the Concordat.

Then there was another big sound. From the wrong direction.

THE IN EXCELSIS was a Goliath-class factory ship. It was almost five kilometres long. Amidships was a plasma refinery. The transport was Aighe Mortis-registered, and it now re-entered its home system for the first time in years. It broadcast its identity and destination, and slowly approached the position of the Imperial fleet as if the presence of the warships and the ominous flashes on the planet's surface were nothing out of the ordinary.

'*In Excelsis*, hold position,' the *Irrevocable Fate* demanded.

The factory ship did not. It came closer. After its first broadcast, it fell into vox silence, and no hails were answered. It moved with grace and majesty. And will.

Toharan was on the summit when the explosions happened. Without pausing his extermination of heretics, he glanced down the east slope and saw the billow of dust rise towards the invisible heavens, glowing from the flashes of fireballs. The enemy reinforcements were blocked. The troops on the hill were outnumbered now, with no way up or down. It was time to crush them, and place the Concordat in Imperial hands.

Then there were more blasts, like echoes, only they came from the rear lines. Toharan frowned and voxed on the entire command network. 'Does anyone know what that was?'

There was so much static and interference, the answer had to be relayed along line of sight from person to person until it reached Toharan. 'It's those Throne-abandoned rebels we left to guard our rear,' Symael reported. 'They've done the same thing as the Claws. They've dropped towers across the main avenues away from the hill.'

Both armies were boxed in now, Toharan realised. The traps weren't airtight. Egress was possible. But it would be slow. He felt a premonitory dread.

On the Immolation Maw, helmsman Maro listened to the unanswered message from the *Irrevocable Fate* to the

In Excelsis. As the type of ship he was looking at and its precise course sank in, he ordered firing resolutions for the factory ship. He sent an urgent vox to Admiral Hassarian: 'Cripple it! Cripple it now!'

Nessun sat in the mind of Captain Henrik Rogge of the *In Excelsis*. Nessun had brought the truth to Rogge years before, and had held him and his ship in reserve for just such a crossroads of fates as now. 'Send it out,' Nessun whispered to Rogge.

The *In Excelsis* opened its cargo bay. The missile inside was carried off the ship by two tugboats. They transported it a safe distance from the hull before its engine fired and it streaked toward Aighe Mortis.

The Immolation Maw's augurs scanned the missile, divined its nature, plotted its trajectory, and fed the data to Maro, who sat in the pilot throne, mechadendrites linking him to the being and spirit of the ship. The missile was ancient, of unknown make, and Chaos-distorted. It was also atomic, and its ground zero was Concordat Hill.

The laws of physics were unforgiving, and movement was glacial as Maro pulled the *Maw* at maximum acceleration out of orbit. He set a course perpendicular to the angle of approach of the *In Excelsis*. He divided the targeting servitors between the missile and the factory ship's engines. The ship had to be stopped, but not destroyed. And if the missile were hit too soon, it might take out the Goliath.

Hassarian had understood the danger too, and the

engines of the *Irrevocable Fate* were flaring hot, but the cruiser was even bigger than the *Immolation Maw*. It was too slow to start, and it would not reach a good angle until too late. Its escorts were no better positioned. Maro pushed the *Maw* to the limit, and the ship's machine-spirit seemed to recognise the threat. It responded with an urgency that matched Maro's own.

The missile was just reaching Aighe Mortis's outer atmosphere when the *Maw* breathed fire with its turrets.

The vox traffic was garbled, but Volos still caught the essential: Toharan was ordering an immediate retreat. Volos couldn't understand. They had the cultists at bay. The summit was about to be theirs. But he obeyed. The Dragon Claws pulled away from their slaughter. They shot up over the summit and back to allied lines. Volos was just landing when the clouds above flashed white with sudden sunrise.

The missile's death flash was a sear in the void above Aighe Mortis. The shockwave passed over the Imperial ships, punishing void shields and rattling hulls. Maro kept the *Immolation Maw* on course. The *In Excelsis* closed in. The window to stop it was slamming shut. Maro acquired his angle on the engines. Lances stabbed from the *Maw* into the stern of the factory ship. The strike was the slice of an Apothecary's blade. There was a bloom of fire, and wreckage trailed away from the ship. The *In Excelsis* lost its forward impulse, but inertia would carry it on in a straight line forever until something stopped it.

Like a planet.

Or another ship. The *Irrevocable Fate* finished its turn and approached the floating plasma refinery head-on.

'Captain,' Maro voxed.

'I am aware of the risk,' Hassarian sent back. 'It will be a controlled collision. We have to force it back.'

Through Rogge's eyes, Nessun saw what the *Fate* planned. In the Hall of Exaltation, his body's lips twitched, and would have smiled. The reckless bravery was charming, and so futile. He had never planned for the *In Excelsis* to come any closer to Aighe Mortis. He still had need of the planet and its population.

The Imperial ships, though. They were a nuisance.

'Now,' he told Rogge.

The plasma refinery exploded.

CHAPTER 17
THE NECESSARY MONSTER

A SUPERNOVA IN miniature lit up the Camargus system. The energy released by the death of the *In Excelsis* was, for a fraction of a second, greater than the sun's. The shock wave was a blinding sphere of superheated gas and dust. It expanded at a tenth the speed of light, hitting the *Irrevocable Fate* in less than a blink. The battle-cruiser vaporised, the sudden flash of its own death barely visible in the stellar apocalypse of the refinery. The wave hit the rest of the Mortisian fleet. Ships came apart and burned. Engines exploded, hulls were crushed, power systems surged and died. The craft that did not disintegrate became dead hulks, floating in listless orbits toward random collision or eventual destructive re-entry.

The *Immolation Maw*'s race to the proper firing angle had taken it further out from the Goliath than the fleet. It had, in Maro, a helmsman who had piloted the ship for centuries and knew it so well that he could, he had once boasted, make it dance a quadrille. He had foreseen what might happen, and had done his best not just to prevent the disaster, but get the *Maw* far enough away that it could survive if the worst happened. He was more successful than he could have hoped.

Less so than he could have wished.

The wave overwhelmed the void shields, popping them like gas bubbles. It took the strike cruiser in its jaws and worried it, trying to shake it apart. Explosions rocked the decks, engulfing servitors in flame. Power flickered, and then went down through much of the ship. Maro went blind as the ship's sensors were shut down or destroyed. The interior and exterior of the ship became a foreign territory to him. The *Maw*'s body was horrifically wounded, and the spirit, howling in pain, lost all connections to its component parts. The ship's agony flashed down the mechadendrites into Maro and he gaped in torment, his body arched beyond even Space Marine limits, blood pouring from mouth and nose and ears and eyes.

The *Immolation Maw* screamed and fell into a coma.

The shock wave reached Aighe Mortis. If the *In Excelsis* had been a few tens of thousands of kilometres closer, the explosion would have scoured the planet clean of air and life. Instead, the energy of thousands of atomic blasts was absorbed by the atmosphere. What had been torpid, weighed down by particulate matter into an oppressive, windless miasma of perpetual summer, now became a weather bomb. Vortices of hellish speed formed into hurricanes the size of continents. The furies had descended on Aighe Mortis, and none would stand before them.

On the ground, the furies first came as a light. It was a ripple, solar bright, that swept across the sky. In its wake, the clouds boiled. They became rage. Lightning exploded over the entire firmament, arcing from cloud to cloud to ground. It was electric judgement, come to condemn all. Thunder and wind were the same god-throat roar, so loud there was no room left in the world for the screams of the judged. The world's fist slammed into Volos. He staggered, but grounded himself, sinking his weight through his feet to the centre of the earth. He was rooted like a mountain, and he did not fall.

Around him, the retreat became a scything of wheat. He saw the other Dragons remain upright, but all the humans were flattened by the wind. Some who were exposed on the summit, Guard and cultist alike, were picked up and thrown through the air to smash like dolls against the towers. Glass erupted from windows, and for a long, terrible minute, the air sang with a million killing shards. They were caught in a murder vortex, tiny glints reflecting the lightning as they lanced through air and flesh. A sandstorm of glass ticked against Volos's armour.

As the atmosphere went to war, the battle on the ground paused. The humans were flattened, those who had tried to rise shredded by glass. This was a moment, then. The Black Dragons were the only ones standing. Toharan took it.

'Brothers,' Volos heard him announce on the

comm-feed, 'we have been betrayed, but the Emperor's hand has shielded us. Take the hill. Slay the heretics.'

Volos turned around. Toharan was right, though there was little glory in this victory. This was simple butcher's work, a massacre of the prone. All the Dragons had to do was walk into a high wind and kill whatever lay on the ground.

Then there was another voice, half-smothered in static, speaking to him. 'Sergeant, I would speak with you.' It was Setheno.

'I have been given orders,' he said.

'This is of vital importance.'

He hesitated, then took a chance and listened to his instinct. 'Where are you?'

'Meet me at the base of the hill. Where the avenue is blocked. Bring your squad.'

'Ormarr, on me,' he voxed, and the Dragon Claws made their way down the hill. Volos didn't have to specify that they be discreet about it. He left the main avenue, saw the others doing the same. But they were moving against the current, and it was less than a minute before Toharan was on the comm.

'Brother-Sergeant Volos,' he demanded. 'Where are you going?'

'A target of opportunity, brother-captain,' Volos answered. Toharan said nothing in response. Volos was surprised. No further questions, no demands, nothing. *He's giving me rope*, Volos realised. He had just acted contrary to a direct order. He was more than halfway to hanging himself.

Away from the crown of the hill, the wind dropped

slightly. It shrieked as it was funnelled between the towers, but the hive blunted some of its force, too. The glass storm passed. Debris still flew, and Volos saw some metal shards sing by like guillotine blades, but the Guardsmen were struggling to their feet and resuming the push forward. Volos's Lyman ear could just make out, over the wind, the sounds of war starting up again.

Setheno was waiting at the base of a mountain of rubble. Rather than stage a collapse along the main avenue, as the Dragon Claws death trap had done, the rebels had triggered a transversal fall. Volos was looking at a mountain chain of wrecked spire, stretching north and south for kilometres, blocking all roads back west to the starport. The retreat would have involved a slow, awkward climb over twisted metal and shifting rockcrete. Volos thought about how Squad Ormarr had lured the cultists into a concentrated area, and then dropped a chunk of city on them. The same stratagem had been used on the Imperial forces, only on a vaster scale. He had recognised the earlier flash as a high-atmosphere atomic blast. If it had hit as no doubt was intended, it would have eliminated the Dragons and a sizeable host of Mortisian Guard.

The rhythmic, pulsing lightning strikes cast conflicting shadows over Setheno. In her grey armour, she blended in with the dust and ruins, the shriek of her helm making her look like a gargoyle that had somehow survived its tower's fall. Volos saw symbolism, not camouflage, in her appearance, and it was symbolism that chilled with its abyssal bleakness.

'Sergeant,' she began. She was addressing him, but

using the squad channel. So she wanted them all to hear. 'This is a crucial moment, and you cannot waste it. Captain Toharan's action is necessary, but it is not sufficient to win the day.'

'How do you suggest we seize the moment, then?' Volos asked, wary.

'By recognising it for what it is, and by embracing what you are.'

'Go on,' Volos said, though he more than suspected that he would regret listening to her.

'Look at the skies. We stand on a cusp. The people of Aighe Mortis are gazing up and experiencing the greatest terror in the history of their civilization. They will be desperate to ascribe meaning to what they see.'

'That is not the function of the Adeptus Astartes. Our sole mission is to smash the Emperor's foes–'

'Using all necessary force,' Setheno broke in. 'One such application of force is the shaping of beliefs and fears, something that you are uniquely qualified to do *in this moment*. The opportunity will soon pass, and Aighe Mortis will be lost to the Imperium. I do not relish the thought of another Exterminatus so soon after the last.'

Volos shook his head. 'We are here to fight the Swords of Epiphany, not engage in a propaganda campaign, which is what you seem to be suggesting.'

'I am suggesting something far more lethal than that, sergeant. And tell me, where are the Swords of Epiphany? Why have you not been fighting them? This battle must still be a diversion. Nevertheless, the traitors have been very effective at creating a narrative for the population to believe in. We must take that weapon away from them if we are to save anything on this planet.'

'How?' Volos asked, curious in spite of himself, and feeling still that mounting dread. His hands began to tingle, and he was suddenly thinking of blood dripping from them.

'How can the rage of the skies appear as anything other than judgement? We must use that. You must be the incarnation of the Emperor's wrath.'

He began to see where she was going. A beat of denial began to pulse in his head. He did not want to hear her words, he did not want to follow her logic, and most of all, he did not want her to be correct. The Black Dragons were not uncaring of the civilians they encountered, whether in the course of prosecuting war, recruiting initiates, or engaged in the salvage and trade that kept Second Company functioning on its homeless crusade. There were Chapters who barely acknowledged the existence of unaugmented humans beyond the abstract awareness that this was, after all, the Imperium of *Man*. There were others who regarded civilians as a barely tolerable nuisance. But the Black Dragons did not. They knew for what and for whom they were fighting. They knew that destroying enemies wasn't enough: this was also a war to *preserve* something.

'You must embrace who you are,' Setheno said, and Volos now understood why he had always thought she was more dangerous than Lettinger. The inquisitor only wanted to destroy the Black Dragons. Setheno was here to mould them, to unleash their dark core. 'You must embrace *what* you are.'

What he was? He was defined by his actions. He always

had been, and had always lived by the catechism taught by the Chaplains. The mutations of his body, however much they enhanced his abilities as a killing machine, were also a warning. There had been so many Adeptus Astartes, from the terrible genesis moment of the Horus Heresy onward, who had fallen from grace, descending into monstrousness because they believed themselves to be gods. The Black Dragons had the daily, inescapable, physical reminders that they were not divine, and Volos had absolute faith in the lesson: the impurity of the body was a goad to find purity of soul through purity of action. Every act had consequences, for oneself and for others. That was not a platitude; it was a profound statement of reality that was forgotten by too many, too often.

'Take us over these ruins, sergeant,' Setheno said, her voice as calm as it ever was, and as implacable. 'Remove your helmet. Let the traitors and heretics and the fools beyond see what must be seen. Do what must be done, sergeant. Become what you must be. You are the Emperor's monster. And you are *necessary*.'

THE WIND WAS the gale of the planet's agony, but it had dropped enough that Bisset was able to emerge from the doorway in which he had taken shelter during the first moments of the horror in the sky. If he leaned into the wind and walked carefully, he could move without being blown off his feet. He looked down the road to where rubble filled the rockrete canyon, and cursed himself as a waste of oxygen. After speaking with the Black Dragon, he had asked to join in the assault on Concordat Hill. All he wanted was to be put in contact with the

Guard, to be given a gun and marching orders. But the Black Dragon sergeant had asked him to remain here, with the rebels, to be the eyes and ears of the Imperium. He had seen and heard much since the Black Dragons departure. He had heard the boom of explosives and the collapsing-mountain crash of the falling hive towers. He had seen the laughter and dancing of the gathering crowd as they imagined all their opponents boxed in and about to be removed forever from their lives. He had heard, as the celebrations began, that this outcome had been promised by the 'other' Space Marines, the ones who looked like angels and wore armour of gold, not menacing black.

Bisset had seen and heard all these things, and been helpless to do anything about them. He had been given a vox unit, but he'd been unable to raise anyone in the combat zone or back at the starport. Communication was reduced to barely more than line of sight. The only person within the reach of his voice who would be concerned with what he had to say was himself. He was stuck in limbo once again. He seemed fated to be the man with the important information that he could do nothing about.

Now he saw a new sight, as did everyone filling the cramped and serpentine streets. At the crest of the rubble barrier, some thirty metres up, figures appeared. They were silhouetted against the maelstrom clouds by lightning so constant and so pervasive, it was as if the sky burned with electric fire. They were massive, hulking, horned beings clad in armour the black of hell, except for one in the grey of the shroud. The black ones began a steady descent of the slope. The grey one remained at the summit and spread its arms.

Bisset knew, at the rational level, that he was looking at the Dragon Claws and Canoness Setheno. But the atavistic part of his brain reacted with bowel-loosening terror. These were not humans. They were nightmares from an afterlife of punishment. Then the voice spoke. The rational Jozef Bisset, late of the insufferably rational Departmento Munitorum, realised that Setheno's armour must have the capability to tap into any vox-caster within reach of her signal. The frightened primitive, who had regressed to little Jozef hiding under the blankets from thunder and monsters, reacted to a woman's voice that did not shout, but that made itself heard over the gale. The voice came from all sides, and it was a voice so shorn of pity, so closed to any form of human entreaty or emotion, that simply to hear it was to know one was damned.

'Oh faithless of Aighe Mortis,' proclaimed the cold saint. 'You have abandoned your God-Emperor, turned your face from his light, and made covenants with the archenemy. And behold.' She raised her arms, and her hands appeared to grasp the convulsing heavens. 'The Emperor sends his judgement with fury. You are vile, you are doomed, and you will know such agony that the world will crack with your screams.'

And it seemed that the world might, because the crowd began to scream. The sound was a duet with the wind, a howl of despair and too-late repentance, for as the sky above them exploded and the air itself attacked, how could the misguided, manipulated, desperate people of

Aighe Mortis not believe every word the terrible woman said? How could they believe anything else but that at long, long last, after millennia of being ignored and left to suffocate slowly in their industrial filth, they had the undivided attention of the God-Emperor, and did so to their woe?

The voice spoke again. It cut through the shrieks, and though the people wanted to run and hide from the face of their god, they were held, rooted as stone, by the creature who bore the flesh of a woman, but who had long ago ceased, by any sane measure, to be one. The Gorgon had not finished with them yet. 'Seek forgiveness. Seek it now or die unshriven. Prove yourselves worthy of a return to the light of the Emperor, if only after your final breath. Find the heretic. Slay the heretic. Stamp him into the mud and perhaps your deaths will be a release, and not the promise of torment unending. Kill the heretic now because the Emperor's vengeance will be at your heels.'

As she finished speaking, the descending figures in black shot into the air on comets of fire. They came down at the front of the crowd with the boom of a deity's hammer. They roared, the speakers on their armour turning their voices into the metallic rage of machines. Then they removed their helmets. Bisset was less than a block away, so he saw what they looked like clearly. They had all been wearing their helms when he had spoken to them earlier, and fearsome as the red eye lenses and snarling mouth grilles were, he had been around just enough Space Marines to know the general form of their armour. He had seen the horns, but had thought they were ornamentation on the helms. Now the faces were revealed and the horns slid through openings in the helmets because they were not ornaments at all. They were part of the monsters. The one in the middle, the biggest one, was one whose name Bisset knew but could not think of because right now his brain would say nothing but *Dragon, Dragon, Dragon, Dragon*. The monster with reptile skin and obsidian eyes bared his fangs, and raised his arms, and bone, sharp as wrath, shot out. He looked down at the man before him. Sergeant Karl Feher trembled and took a step back. The monster reached out a massive hand and closed it over Feher's head. Bisset could not hear the *crunch-crack* of skull, but he felt it in his chest and gut. As blood and brain matter ran down the monster's gauntlet, he gutted Feher with a bone-blade then threw the mangled corpse at the crowd. The Dragon roared, and with a voice that was deep and hissing and loud enough to be heard without speakers, he shouted, 'People of Aighe Mortis! We are the Adeptus Astartes! We are the Black Dragons! We have come to purge your heresy with fire and with bone!'

CHAPTER 18
TAINTED

THE NECESSARY MONSTER. *Necessary. Necessary.* Volos thought the words again and again as he slipped into a rage of herding, roaring, beating, and killing. Killing the weak and the fleeing. But killing traitors, he reminded himself, and he clung to more words Setheno had spoken: *All rebellion is heretical.* She was right. Curse her for what she was making him understand, and for what she was making him do to himself, but she was right. Toharan's lost sheep who needed only good role models to come around had tried to exterminate them all. All heresy must be punished, so all rebellion, whatever its initial justifications, must also be punished. In the final analysis, there were no justifications for turning against the Emperor. And so Volos and the Dragon Claws swam in the waters of damnation together and taught themselves another form of purity: the purity of terror.

The Dragons snarled, cursed, threatened, and fired

bolters overhead or into flesh. Most of all, they wielded the monstrousness of their own bodies. They brandished bone-blades and let loose the grotesquerie of their faces. They sacrificed their former sense of identity on the altar of necessity. They spread terror before them, and it tore through the crowd, a wildfire and plague. With it came anguish and fanatical repentance. Every lightning flash was now understood to be the anger of the God-Emperor, and having brought this on themselves, the people had but a single goal: to propitiate their deity. Volos and his brothers were here to show them there was only one route to salvation, and that was through the flesh of the enemy.

The terror and its gospel flashed through the hive faster than the crowd could run, and the population of Aighe Mortis, in hiding or not, guilty or innocent, poured into the streets, screaming their love for the Emperor and their fear of his monsters. The Dragons spread out, each becoming the master of a different quadrant, and they controlled the flow of the crowd. Setheno had caught up to Volos, and as she marched one step behind him, her voice travelled from vox-caster to vox-caster, driving in its message of damnation and bloody penitence.

They herded the crowds west at first, gathering the numbers until they were a colossal army. The terrified outliers were too far away to see the Dragons or hear the canoness, but the message and the horror reached them all the same. The gigantic mass of repentance turned south, then east, and then north, to where the rubble barrier ended and the way was clearest to Concordat Hill. Driven by thunder, wind and raging, armoured beasts, the masses were uncounted insects on a mindless charge. Volos found that he hated them.

Almost as much as he did himself.

THE CULTISTS WERE on their feet again. They were disoriented at first and unsure whether to attack or flee, and the Black Dragons cut swaths of them down, clearing the way for the recovering Guard. Toharan led the assault, his squads unbroken by the fire in the sky, unbowed by the rage of the wind. They took the summit of Concordat Hill. Toharan had the Devastator squads hold the position while his tactical teams moved down the eastern slope, tearing the enemy apart. He was surprised by how quickly the cultists found their footing again. They weren't organised now, simply attacking as a mob, their mouths open in raging howls whose sound was stolen by the wind. Rather than cowed, they seemed to be energised by the storm, as if it were a reflection of the Chaos in their souls. The delay that the Dragon Claws had bought with the dropped tower had run its course, and though reinforcements weren't as quick to arrive as they had been before, whether they came in a stream or a flood was academic. They were here, and they were numberless.

But the Concordat was taken, and the Guard consolidated the position. The transports arrived to place a Basilisk gun on the Concordat's landing pad. Soon, the endless roar of the wind was punctuated by the deep *crack-boom* of the gun, and the shelling of enemy concentrations had begun. On the ground, Toharan couldn't see the artillery targets, but from the sound of each shot he could tell that the bombardment was taking in all the points of the compass.

The gun couldn't defend the hill itself, so the cultists had to be driven back and back, until there was no longer any chance of the Imperial forces losing the heights. The Black Dragons plunged into their ranks like a knife in the belly. Though there were no organised lines to break, and the fighting reminded Toharan of treading water, the Space Marines drew the frothing cultists to them and away from the Mortisian Guard on the summit.

The momentum of both forces reached a standstill once again. The slaughter wreaked by the Adeptus Astartes was enough to hold the cultists at bay. But the heretics had such numbers that, midway down the hill, Toharan's advance slowed to a stop. Each shot of his bolter blew a head to paste, each sweep of his chainsword cut bodies in half, and every one of his brothers added to the tally of gigantic butchery. Lascannons annihilated dozens of cultists at once, blowing craters of flesh into their packed density. Flamers reduced advancing walls of bodies to ash. But there were always more. There were simply too many of the enemy to kill.

Later, Toharan would wonder what had made him realise a change was coming. Like a slight breeze that foreshadows a storm, a breath against the cheek just before the cloudburst, the premonitory moment came, he would decide, as a nuance in the way the cultists attacked. There was a slight decrease in intensity. When Toharan culled the immediate enemy with his chainsword, the breathing space he created for himself lasted one beat longer. It was as if the heretics were becoming distracted, their minds no longer focussed, to the exclusion of everything else, on killing the Space Marines.

Toharan had time to notice the shift, and a question was just forming in his conscious mind when the tide swept in with enraged shrieks and chanted, hysterical prayers. He looked south, and saw a crowd surging forward through the streets like a torrent churning through a narrow gorge. A few of its members carried firearms, and many of them wore Militia uniforms, though Toharan saw some Guard insignia too. The vast majority of the mob, though, was made up of civilians. They wielded makeshift weapons: short bits of metal for clubs, longer ones for spears. Many were unarmed, and simply had their arms outstretched to grab their foe. They were so frenzied that, at first, Toharan thought they were a massive wave of cultists, coming in on the flank. But then they fell on the heretics. Toharan's opponents were swept away by the foaming tide of exultant, vengeful, terrified faith. He almost lost his footing in the storm of penitence. Most of the cultists were armed, and they fought back, but the momentum of the surge was inexorable, and the heretics went down beneath a swarm of clawing, grasping hands and beating metal.

Now Toharan could make out, in the cacophony of screams and ravings, the God-Emperor being called on and praised, and begged for forgiveness. He looked to his right again and stared at the savage flow of the faithful until he saw the source of its impetus. Behind the crowd, raging with bone and bolter, came Volos. Toharan saw him gnash his fangs, saw him spear a man with an armblade and raise him high. He launched a fountain of blood over the running figures before him, driving them to still greater howling panic, before hurling the corpse through the air. Where it landed, the cries for mercy climbed new heights and the people clawed at those in front of them, urging them to go faster and faster yet, that they might show their devotion by ripping still more heretics to pieces. Setheno was just behind Volos, and as they came closer, nearby vox-casters picked up the canoness's excoriating liturgy.

Volos drew level with Toharan. He was a colossus risen from the most fevered depths of humanity's collective unconscious. His black ceramite dripping with gore and flesh, his face contorted into that of a saurian predator, he had become something that Toharan had never wished to contemplate, but now regarded with horrified understanding. He looked at his brother, and saw a daemon. 'Sergeant,' he said into the vox-link as Volos passed. The Dragon Claw stopped. The rout he had created ran on without him, the wind and demented lightning carrying on his work. Toharan looked past him at the mob. He saw no trace of reason in its rampage. This was not the redemption he had planned for the rebels. This was not the reasoned return to the light of the Emperor. This was a plunge down into the very pit from which he was trying to pull the Black Dragons. 'What have you done?' he whispered.

'What was *necessary*.' Volos spat the word like it was poison.

'I fear that I am seeing you clearly, brother, for the first time.'

Volos turned his head and looked down at him. His black eyes were as distant as the stars. 'With respect, brother-captain,' he said, and the only emotion in his voice was a resigned disgust, 'I doubt that very much.'

He moved off. Setheno followed. Her exhortations, as calm and closed to entreaty as ever, did not pause, but her helmet turned Toharan's way. Beneath the helm's fixed rage, he sensed cold-blooded appraisal. He returned the favour. He had thought her an enemy, and now he was certain. She was, in some way, responsible for this madness. And if he owed her a debt of thanks for bringing his brother's true nature to the surface, she was as tainted as he was. He watched them go, herding their monstrous sheep. Decisions that he had imagined would be hard to make were suddenly easy.

REFLECTIVE FLAK ARMOUR was no power armour, but it had saved Lettinger's life. He'd been caught on open ground, just below the top of Concordat Hill, when the first, most punishing blows of the wind had hit, and with them the razoring hail of glass. He had been knocked down with the other humans. When he had been able to look up, he had seen a scoured landscape. The black and brown of Aighe Mortis had changed into a flashing, roiling hell where the only things that stood were the black silhouettes of the rotting hive towers and the relentless shapes of the Black Dragons. From his prone perspective, abased in spite of himself, the Space Marines were more like gods than ever. They were monuments that moved, but would not *be* moved. His own status as a mere human was driven home yet again.

He rose as soon as he could, and mere human though he was, he was still up and taking the hill before any of the Guard. But once more, he was behind the Space Marine advance, and as he crossed the summit to the eastern slope, now with the Devastators at his back, his hunting was not what it had been earlier. Some cultists did get past Toharan's teams, but they were easily contained by the Devastators' heavy bolter fusillades. His own kills, it seemed to him, had a pathetic 'me too' quality, and until he worked his way a bit further down the hill, his martial skills were most heavily called on in avoiding the indignity of being cut down by friendly fire.

He killed what he could, and he was only a dozen metres away from Toharan when the surge happened. He watched the shrieking horde overwhelm the cultists, and saw very little to distinguish the behaviour of the heretic and the faithful. Then he saw Volos and Setheno. The Dragon Claw's tainted nature was now visible to all, and Lettinger felt some small satisfaction in being vindicated. But the power Volos wielded was disturbing. And the presence of Setheno made it clear to Lettinger how mistaken he had been to seek her as an ally. She was at least as corrupt as the Space Marine.

They passed, and Toharan stood still for a moment. Then, perhaps sensing Lettinger's gaze, he turned around. Lettinger nodded to him. The monsters of Chaos who had just passed below him were dangerous. But so was he, and so was his ally. They would not make the mistake of underestimating the threat before them. They would not turn from the measures that would have to be taken.

CHAPTER 19
THE SANCTUARY HORN

FOR THE THIRD time in quick succession, the Black Dragons tasted ash instead of victory. They had retreated from Antagonis, lost their captain on Flebis, and now the word spread of daemonic corruption. The dawning triumph on Aighe Mortis was a false one. It was being won through the archenemy's means, and so his military defeat became his spiritual victory. That was the word. That was the story. The damage, though, was not caused as much by what the story told, as by *how* it was told, and by who told it. Toharan spoke to the Disciples of Purity on a dedicated vox-channel he had set up. They, in turn, passed on the tale of Volos's taint to their squads. The whisper was a virus, and it travelled the landed contingent of Second Company with the speed and virulence of an epidemic. It was as if the Black Dragons had created their own strain of doubtworm and infected themselves. Some succumbed, others fought off the illness, but all were injured. The body of the company took sick.

There were those, like Toharan, who believed in the truth of the tale. These were the most fervent of the Disciples, those whose desire for purity of body, of dogma, and of Codex compliance had become the master drive of their identity. There were those whose resentments and ambitions made them want to believe, and choose to do so. There were those who looked to what they knew of the sergeant of the Dragon Claws, and considered the source of the tale, and felt their anger grow in the face of the lie. And so, even as the Dragons fought shoulder-to-shoulder, brothers together, to purge the heretics and consolidate the gains of Concordat Hill, the schism grew. Within minutes, alliances had been formed. They weren't spoken of, and in many cases their members did not know they had joined one side or the other. But they had, and oaths had been taken as surely as if they had been witnessed by the God-Emperor himself.

NESSUN RETURNED TO his body and left the Hall of Exaltation. After extended sessions of travelling the immaterium with his mind, his body felt like a suit of clothes cut a few sizes too big. His limbs were awkward, and didn't want to do as they were bid. His movements lacked grace. Sensation was too distant, seeming to come at one remove. He used the minutes it took him to travel from the Hall to the *Revealed Truth*'s strategium to master the physical. By the time he walked onto the bridge, he was serenity in motion once more.

Raphyle was awaiting his pleasure. 'What is your will, Father?' the Sword asked.

'It is time for the harvest,' Nessun said. The explosion of the *In Excelsis* had not had the effect planetside he had been counting on. Someone had read his move and countered it by using the devastation in precisely the fashion he had intended for his own forces. The tide of the war had turned, and the loss of Aighe Mortis was inevitable. He gave a mental shrug. Control of the planet itself was unimportant. Whether the world was his or not, he would be leaving soon, but would return to teach a new lesson, one that would make everything that had come before seem but the shallowest of prologues. He had seen, through eyes that belonged to him more and more with every beat of thwarted desire, the Black Dragons carve out another material victory. He had also seen them make, from the array of dooms that great Tzeentch had offered them, their final choice. On balance, he thought it a good one. The aesthetics of it pleased him. But for now it was time to complete the immediate task on Aighe Mortis, so that he might head off to meet his greater glory. 'Order the *Foretold Pilgrimage* to the surface,' he said.

'What about the *Immolation Maw*?'

'Does it still live?'

'As far as our remaining augurs in planetary orbit can tell. It hasn't moved since the explosion, but it is still intact.'

Nessun hesitated. The chance was there to swoop in personally on the crippled Space Marine cruiser and finish it off. The temptation was delicious, and he allowed himself a few seconds to indulge in it and savour its taste. Then he dismissed it. The mission was at too critical a stage to allow any risk. The *Maw* might be dead, and it must certainly be hurt, but it might still be capable of striking back. He could not permit harm to come to the *Revealed Truth*. Not now, when it was about to make the most important journey of its millennia of service to the gospel of Chaos. 'Avoid it,' he said. 'Take up position over the horizon from the *Maw*. Send the *Pilgrimage* in now. Sound the horns.'

The Swords of Epiphany squadron left its concealment behind the sun and closed on Aighe Mortis. As the endgame moves began, Nessun felt there was one indulgence he could allow. 'The warriors of the *Metastasis* performed their duties on Aighe Mortis well,' he told Raphyle. 'They have earned a reward. Tell Captain Meliphael that the *Immolation Maw* is his.'

The heavy raider split off from the rest of the squadron, hunting for its wounded prey.

VOLOS RETRACTED HIS blades and lowered his bolter. He didn't need to act the monster any longer. The penitent mob had its own momentum. It was gathering recruits far beyond the reach of his epicentre. It was a question now of directing the force of the mob, of sending its fury down the channels that would have the greatest strategic benefit. All that was required was for a Dragon Claw to make an appearance at the head of the kilometres-long rush and gesture. The flood would follow that path with renewed, shrieking fervour. The work, the *necessary* work, was accomplished.

He brooded over the look Toharan had given him. Their bonds were broken beyond salvage. He knew that now. There had been nothing but horror and disgust in Toharan's gaze. *How should he have responded?* he wondered. Should he have defended himself? Should he have explained that he had only killed men he knew to be traitors? And of this, Volos was sure. For all the raging and fury he had unleashed on the Mortisians, he had never been out of control. He had picked his targets with care. They had all been renegade militiamen or disaffected Guardsmen. They had all been part of the celebration at the foot of the rubble. They were traitors and heretics, even if they did not think so themselves, and by their actions had proven Setheno correct. There was only one verdict possible. So he had killed them, but no others. Anyone whose guilt he was not certain of, anyone who might simply be a civilian caught up in the religious frenzy he had created, he had not touched.

He could have said these things to Toharan. He hadn't. He doubted Toharan would believe him. He doubted, for that matter, that Toharan could afford to believe anything he said. But the deeper truth was that he had no desire to defend himself. He loathed what he had had to do. And though he had not hurt any innocent citizens directly, he knew their blood coated his hands. The forced march had taken many victims, some trampled, some beaten to death by their neighbours for imagined heresies, others ground into the muck in the attacks on the cultists. Volos was a realist. He knew that war and its unalterable demands made no allowance for the innocent. He had taken part in actions before that had had massive civilian costs. But this time, his role had not been one of direct action. He had not been fighting the enemy with the brutal honesty of bolter and blade. He had become the monster many feared him to be. Perhaps Toharan was right to look at him as he did.

The nightmare tingling in his fingers. Was this what his premonitions had foretold? No. This was only a start. There was worse to come.

Volos shook himself. Enough. He had done what was needed, and however distasteful it might have been, he also knew it to be right. He was wallowing in a self-pitying resentment that the Emperor had marked out a difficult path for him to tread. Where was his sense of honour? Or did he believe himself unfit for the duty that lay before him? That thought almost made him laugh. If Setheno was to be believed, he was singularly fit for that duty.

Breaking out of his reverie, he noticed that the canoness was watching him. She had removed her helmet, and stood a few paces away. She had given him space for his thoughts, but was unwavering in her scrutiny. 'Well?' he asked. 'Was I a proper monster?'

'You were. The people of Aighe Mortis fear you, and they fear the Emperor. That is as it should be.' She cocked her head slightly, an expression of curiosity that was the closest thing to an emotion Volos had yet seen from her. 'Tell me. Do you feel ashamed of the actions you took?'

'No,' he said after a moment's thought. When he had told himself a minute ago that his actions had been right, he now understood that that had not been a rationalisation. It had been a simple acknowledgement of an absolute truth.

'And did you enjoy what you did?'

'No.' Just as true.

'Good.' She nodded, and Volos sensed he had passed a test. He wasn't sure whether to feel resentful or not about that.

There was a metallic rattle off to his left. Volos turned his head. They were standing near the Concordat River, and a large chunk of discarded assemblage was tangled with some wreckage hanging into the effluent from the bank. Volos looked back up the rancid flow of water and filth to the industrial basilica at the top of the hill. The Concordat hadn't so much as paused in production during the battle at its feet. 'Is that what we fought to save?' he asked, half-rhetorically.

'Partly,' Setheno answered.

'Why?' Volos was verging on heresy, but at this moment he didn't care. He was staring at the wrecked bodies, allied and enemy, unknown and brother, that littered the hill and were stacked in mounds closer to the summit. 'What is worth saving in that? Is it *necessary* too?'

'In its function, yes it is. Or would you rather do without the bolter rounds that it produces? If a round from that manufactorum kills an ork warboss, would you still doubt the institution's necessity? As for its form,' she shrugged. 'Who is to say? But if it is in that form that the Concordat fulfils its function, then yes, the form is necessary too.' When she looked at Volos, he imagined that he saw a glint of regret somewhere in the void of her eyes. 'There is no joy in necessity, sergeant.

Not when all we know is war.'

His reply was arrested by something new arriving on the soundscape of Aighe Mortis's agony. Over the endless industrial chugging of the Concordat and the monotonous fanaticism of its vox-cast prayers, over the sluggish rush of the outflow river, over the periodic roar of the Basilisk gun, and over the more distant sounds of clashes and gunfire came the long blast of a horn. Volos parsed the sound with his enhanced hearing. The horn was many kilometres away, somewhere to the east, and its faintness was deceptive. Closer to the source, it would be deafening. It was a plaintive, mournful note that reached into the bone marrow. It was the sound of surrender. It announced not just the end of a fight, but the end of a dream. But it was also a siren call. It made a promise. *Come to me*, it said. *Run to me, and you will find succour. You will find sanctuary.*

'What is it?' Setheno asked.

'A summons,' Volos answered. One he would answer, to see who was calling and, he didn't doubt, to slit the caller's throat. He glanced back at Toharan. He was talking with a Mortisian Guard commander and gesturing at the hill. Giving orders for holding the territory, Volos assumed. Then he would be ready to move on with the Dragons and push the enemy even further back. If he had noticed the horn, he gave no sign.

The horn sounded again, and Volos's course was clear. The distant target required the rapid, deep strike of an assault squad. He voxed the other Dragon Claws, calling them to him. The penitents were legion, and would spread on their own. They could do without the supervision of monsters for now. Then he asked Brother Keryon for his services once more.

THE IMMOLATION MAW was slow in waking. The ship had been brutalised by the explosion, its machine-spirit battered by shock and damage. The Imperial Navy fleet was destroyed. Many of the ships were gone as if they had never existed, reduced to a stream of atoms. The rest were pitiable debris. The *Maw* was the only ship still to hold its shape. But it was dark as a tomb. A trail of wreckage drifted behind it. From shattered, pierced decks, puffs of vapour emerged as the last of the atmosphere from those levels leaked out. The ship was a long, silent ruin floating in the void.

Maro regained consciousness, and his immediate sensation was pain. It wasn't so much his own, though his body had been damaged when the shock wave hit. The painkillers flooding his system blocked the worst of his own injuries from his consciousness, but they couldn't block his sense of the ship's pain. Every hull breach, every tortured system, every blown bulkhead was as real to him as his own nerve clusters. As the ship revived, it screamed. Maro whispered to it. He repeated litanies of healing, doing everything he could to soothe the wounded spirit.

The ship calmed. One by one, support systems came back on line. Assessor servitors sent in damage reports, while their repair-tasked counterparts and serfs went to work. The data streamed in to Maro, and most of it was bad. The engines were down. They could be saved, and the efforts could be speeded up considerably if the resources of Aighe Mortis were available. Most of the habitat compartments had survived, though there were losses. Maro would mourn those brothers later. Shields were depleted, and would need time to power back up. The good news boiled down to two things: the *Immolation Maw* was not about to die, and most of the weapons systems were intact.

'Approaching contact,' a bridge servitor reported.

'Analyse,' Maro ordered.

The report came back: an Apostate-class heavy raider.

Maro ran scenarios through his head. There weren't many. The *Maw* was dead in the water, but she still had her teeth. 'Brother Ydraig,' he voxed.

'Yes, helmsman,' the Techmarine answered.

'We have a hostile contact.'

Ydraig cursed. 'The shields won't have a fraction of their force back in time. He'll cut us in two.'

'Then we will have to encourage him to take another course of action. We will be running dark. All available power to be routed to the weapons.'

'Understood, brother. The Emperor protects.'

'The Emperor protects,' Maro repeated, thinking, *Now would be a very good time for Him to do so.* He sent out a general order: 'Full dark. Vox silence.'

The *Immolation Maw* drew back into the shadow of the grave.

On the Metastasis, Captain Meliphael watched the *Immolation Maw* arrive within easy firing range. Impossible to miss at this distance, and the ship immobile, too.

The execution was so easy, his father's gift was almost an insult. He eyed the growing dark bulk of the cruiser. For a moment, as the *Metastasis* had first closed in, there had been a flicker of lights aboard, as if the ship were grasping at a fitful spark of life, but that ember had dimmed to nothing again. An idea occurred to Meliphael, a way of transforming the cardinal's gift into a boon. 'One shot,' he commanded. 'To the engines.'

THE MAW SHOOK, its agony spiking, as the lance strike punched another hole into the engine room. Metal groaned in sympathy with the machine-spirit. Maro whispered to it, soothing, promising relief and retribution, entreating the beast to be patient just a little bit longer.

NO RESPONSE FROM the Black Dragons. Meliphael's lip curled, and the daemon inside him squirmed in anticipation. 'Close in,' he ordered. 'Prepare boarding parties. We will be adding a new convert to our Father's cause.'

TENNESYN GROPED TO consciousness. He was ensnared by grav-webbing in the simple quarters he had been given since his arrival on the ship. He had retreated to the acceleration couch when the action against the *In Excelsis* had begun, and blacked out when the plasma refinery had gone nova. Now he fumbled through darkness, clawing at the webbing, frightened by the silence that surrounded him. The normal sounds of a ship were absent. There was no thrum of engines, no marching back and forth of men. Instead, there was a deep nothing.

He worked free of the webbing, and felt his way to the chamber's viewport. He looked out. The heavy raider he had first seen when he had fled Aighe Mortis was lining up broadside with the *Immolation Maw*. From this distance, even Tennesyn's unaided eye could see the torpedo tube hatches opening.

THE BATTLE PYRE skimmed over the rooftops of Aighe Mortis, keeping just beneath the volcanic clouds. Keryon was following the coordinates of the last horn blast. The call had stopped about an hour ago, but had gone on long enough for Keryon to triangulate the location. Far below the racing Thunderhawk, Volos could see columns of ants charging down the streets between the buildings and along the connecting walkways. Repentance was a grass fire, almost outpacing the *Battle Pyre*.

They were just reaching their target, and Volos could see nothing unusual about the location, when the Thunderhawk's sensors started picking up the horn again, still to the east, and many kilometres distant. 'It's a lure,' Keryon announced. 'We're being led to a trap.'

Volos thought for a moment. A lure, yes, but... 'I don't think it's meant for us,' he said. It was too clumsy, too basic, and the first horn had cut off long before any Black Dragons might have been able to make it on foot. The idea that the bait would be exclusively for vehicles struck him as too much effort for too specific a target.

'For whom, then?' Nithigg asked.

'Get us to the next one,' Volos told Keryon. 'If we can reach it before it shuts off, I think we'll have our answer.'

They didn't catch that horn, but they were almost in

time for the one after that, close enough to tell which building had been broadcasting the call. It was the Palace of Saint Boethius, and here they did find the answer. The Grand Square was filled to capacity, and every member of the crowd was pushing in the same direction. The rush was to the east, and the currents in the mob looked like wind over a field of wheat.

'I want a closer look,' Volos said.

'You want me to land in the square?' Keryon asked, incredulous. He would foul the Thunderhawk's landing gear with bodies.

'Get me low enough for a jump, then circle back. Look for me on the palace roof.'

Keryon clicked compliance over the vox-net and dropped the nose of the *Battle Pyre*. Volos slid back the door, and the storm blew in the interior of the ship. He hung on to the bulkhead, steadying his footing as the wind slammed against the Thunderhawk. Keryon plunged down one of the straighter canyons leading toward the square, and Volos took the jump, his pack pushing him away from the backwash of the *Battle Pyre* as it sped past him.

Volos landed on a walkway about ten metres up from the street level. He looked down into the Grand Square at the flood of humanity, and realised that, at least in part, this was his work that he was seeing.

Below him were not the penitent, but refugees. He saw cultists, distinguishable by their ritual scarification and the Chaos runes drawn onto their clothing. He saw traitor Defence Militia and Guard elements. But he also saw civilians, entire families with belongings tossed hastily into sacks. And when some of these saw him, they screamed and made the sign of the aquila, as if this would ward him off. The terrible truth sank in: here was Chaos so complete that large numbers of Mortisians didn't even know which forces were which. Perhaps, by the time the gospel of penitence had reached these ears, all that remained of the story was a tale of daemons pursuing the fearful. It was no longer about the wrath of the God-Emperor. These people, mixing and fleeing with the traitors, believed themselves to be faithful. And by his actions, Volos was sending them into the waiting arms of whatever was sounding the series of horns.

His fingers tingled with the phantom slick of blood.

Using large jumps, he made his way to the palace and up to its roof. He saw the *Battle Pyre* heading for him, and he concentrated on getting back on board. He tried not to think about the implications of what he had just seen.

He failed. Miserably.

THE METASTASIS'S BOARDING torpedoes were beginning their launch sequence when the *Immolation Maw* fired. The Space Marine cruiser was crippled, motionless before its predator. But Ydraig gave Maro all the power he needed, and the machine-spirit, raging with the fury of an injured animal, was eager to lash out. The entire starboard flank of the *Maw* lit the void with turret, lance and torpedo fire. The *Metastasis* was a much smaller ship, and it had just presented its length to the *Maw*. It didn't stand a chance. Its void shields collapsed beneath the overwhelming barrage, and its port side lit up even more brilliantly as explosions hammered its hull open. Secondary blasts rocked its interior, and it drifted off its orientation.

There was no return fire.

The top of the stern cathedral was spared the worst of the devastation. The space of the bridge was intact, but all power was gone. Malformed servitors continued their duties, even though the cogitators they operated were dead. Meliphael screamed orders, smashing to pulp any helot or servitor within reach. His demands were met with silence. His ship was dead. He was alone.

THE HORN WAS still blowing, and they were coming close to its source. They were catching up with the relay of calls. Each time the blast sounded, the fleeing millions below answered with their own cry of fear and hope. Volos heard the call-and-response when he made another jump and gauged the composition and mood of the crowd. That had been enough. He was just as glad, now, that the roar of the Thunderhawk's engines shielded his ears and conscience from the inarticulate prayer below.

They had travelled hundreds of kilometres from Concordat Hill, always moving east, the migration of refugees only growing larger. There was a detached part of Volos that was fascinated by how quickly the exodus had developed. The people they were passing over now would never have seen any actual conflict between the penitent and the heretics. But words and ideas spread faster than any physical virus. That was, he reminded himself, how doubtworm had infected all of Antagonis in a matter of days. Between the tale of terror and the call of sanctuary, a compulsion had been born throughout this sector of Aighe Mortis.

'We're coming up on another starport,' Keryon reported. 'That's where the sound is coming from.'

'Slow and careful,' Volos told him. 'Let's not announce ourselves before we know what's going on.'

Keryon took the *Battle Pyre* within a kilometre of the starport's perimeter, then cut the Dragon Claws loose. They jumped the rest of the way from rooftop to rooftop until they were overlooking the open expanse of the port. What they saw made Volos snarl.

There was only one ship present, and it was impossible to miss. It was two kilometres long, a bulky, clumsy, fat-bodied avatar of hate. It had once been an Imperial transport, but that was a memory so old it had been forgotten. The superstructure seemed to have both melted and grown, spreading spines and strangling vines of metal around the hull. Iron excrescences had formed immense runes over which the air turned brittle and fragmented into buzzing black swarms. Loading ramps gaped like open jaws, and into the ship's belly streamed the refugees in the tens of thousands. A large detachment of Swords of Epiphany guarded access points, backed up by Rhino armoured transports and Predator tanks.

'Soulcage,' Braxas muttered. '*Foretold Pilgrimage*,' he said, reading the molten Gothic letters on the hull. He spat the taste from his mouth.

'Brothers, we are witnessing a historical first,' Nithigg said with bitter humour. 'Have you ever before seen Traitor Adeptus Astartes acting as crowd control while people fought to get *on* a Soulcage?'

Volos hadn't. But he'd never seen people brandish the aquila against him, either. Even in the face of military defeat, Chaos still controlled the narrative of Aighe Mortis, and by the light of its inside-out non-logic, what was happening made a ghastly kind of sense. The slaveship was the same gold as the Swords' armour. It was the gold of grasping, greedy ruin, the gold of blasting knowledge. Light was damaged by it, and reality in its vicinity took on a greasy sheen. But it was still gold, and meant to be seductive, and to the panicked and the fearful, it might well seem more inviting than the unyielding black of the Dragons.

'Why is it,' Volos demanded, 'that we are winning every battle, but losing the war?'

The other Dragon Claws didn't answer. Abruptly, the ship's horn stopped sounding. The Swords and their vehicles began to withdraw inside the ship. The refugees continued to pour into the starport, rushing to be granted sanctuary from the anger in the heavens and the monsters at their backs. There was no room for the Swords to push through, so they went over, trampling people beneath their boots, crushing bodies to smeary pulp with the treads of their tanks. The screams of the dying travelled back to the Dragons, but still the crowd pushed forward. They had already walked over so many of their own, a few more smashed skulls and broken spines were not going to dissuade them from struggling to reach the ship.

'What do we do?' Vasuk asked. 'Do we attack?'

Volos felt the call of battle. He wanted to rend the

Chaos Space Marines into slabs of meat. But to engage now would be to throw his brothers' lives away. 'No,' he said. 'Our battle isn't here.' He watched the loading ramps begin to close. The rumble of the ship's engines powering up shook the building beneath his feet. The crowd screamed, hands beating at the hull, desperate for the salvation of the slaveship. 'How much human cargo can that ship carry?' he asked Braxas.

'Hundreds of thousands.'

'We should ask ourselves what the traitors need with all those people.'

'What do you mean?' Vasuk asked. 'They're always scooping up slaves. That's nothing new.'

'No, but everything they've done on this planet can't just be about gathering a few slaves. Do you think Flebis was all about blowing a whistle? No. These are moves in a game where we haven't been allowed to see the stakes.'

The Soulcage began to rise from the port. A cloud of flame lifted it from the ground and engulfed the crowd. The screams were different now.

'Our battle,' Volos said, pointing to the ship, 'is wherever that abomination is heading.'

CHAPTER 20
METASTASIS

Toharan didn't argue with Volos's conclusions. Given the frost between them, Volos was almost surprised, but it was clear Toharan hated being outmanoeuvred as much as he did. The captain of the Black Dragons issued new orders: re-embarkation on the *Immolation Maw* and pursuit of the Swords of Epiphany. Maro reported the *Revealed Truth* and *Foretold Pilgrimage* transiting into the empyrean together. There were only a couple of obstacles in the way of the Dragons furious crusade: their ship was crippled, and they didn't know where the Swords had gone.

On the ground, the battle for Aighe Mortis was all but won. Volos wasn't sure if he would call the planet *pacified*. The movement that the Dragon Claws and Setheno had triggered was too big a storm, and as it swept the globe, what little structure the civilization of Aighe Mortis still had collapsed further. But loyalty to the God-Emperor at its most fanatical had replaced the older apathy. Heresy would find the ground infertile now. In the region of the Concordat, something approaching a functioning order returned, and it was possible to have needed materiel sent up to the *Immolation Maw*. The healing of the shattered engines began. Once they were functional, and the Geller field generators were deemed warp-worthy, the pursuit could begin. Other repairs would have to be undertaken during the journey.

That left the question of the destination.

'The information will be on the *Metastasis*,' Toharan told Lettinger. They were walking the corridors of the *Immolation Maw*, inspecting damage, tallying the losses. Seventeen brothers had been vented to the void when the hull plating over their decks had peeled away. Deeper into the ship, in areas that hadn't been breached, the damage took the form of twisted, broken corridors, many of them blocked by wreckage. Toharan couldn't feel the ship's machine-spirit in the immediate, visceral way that Maro did, but he could still feel its pain and its hunger for retribution. 'The captain had to know where he was going.'

'Are you sending a boarding party?' Lettinger asked.

Toharan nodded. 'The enemy's bridge is still intact.'

'Who is going?'

They stopped at a dead end. The deck ahead of them had been ripped apart, and there was a gap now, a plunge of hundreds of metres through shattered stone and shredded metal, down to the depths of the hull. Toharan stared into the blackness, and felt an odd tug.

'I'm going myself,' he answered, a little absently.

'No,' Lettinger said.

'No?' Nothing but dark below, nothing but void. To fall into nothing, into the purity of non-being: there was an odd comfort to that idea. A seduction. A relief from the disappointments and betrayals. Perhaps even relief from all the movement in his brain.

'Send Volos.'

Toharan blinked and tore his eyes away from the drop. *What's wrong with me?* he wondered. 'Why?' he asked.

'The *Metastasis* is utterly corrupt.'

'And?'

'And so is Volos.'

'Yes, we both agree on that. I don't see the connection.'

'Old loyalties die hard,' Lettinger explained. 'We need all the evidence we can gather to convince your brothers of Volos's taint. If all know that he has been in direct contact with Chaos, the arguments will be easier to make.'

Toharan nodded. 'There's always the chance,' he said, 'that Volos won't come back.'

'The ship is dead,' Toharan had said. 'It lies open to the void. The two of you should be more than enough to find what we need.'

The argument was a logical one. Volos could find no reason to challenge it. Not formally. And it was true that every hand was needed to prepare the *Immolation Maw* for its return to battle. It was also true that all Dragons were joined in blood, and that Volos should be able to serve by the side of any brother, any brother at all.

All these truths. But as he transited from the *Battle Pyre* to the hatch into the spire of the *Metastasis*'s command cathedral, he had the ashen taste of lies in his mouth.

'Be on your guard, brother-sergeant,' Danael said. 'Let purity be our watchword as we travel this forsaken ship.'

'As you say, brother-sergeant,' Volos replied. He was reasonably certain he had kept the contempt from his tone. It was being assigned Danael as mission partner that, more than anything else, gave the whole exercise the stench of subterfuge. Why Danael? Never mind that it made little sense to pair off two squad sergeants for this task, and never mind that Danael should not have been made sergeant in the first place. Danael was a good fighter, but he was no leader. Worse, he was a malcontent and sycophant, a combination that made Volos's skin crawl. He had always found it an effort to remain civil with the Neidris squad member, and could remember many times in the past when Toharan had bemoaned his fate in having Danael under his command.

Things were different now. Danael had received the advancement he had always claimed was his due, despite all evidence to the contrary. He had attached himself to Toharan like a leech, and the new Toharan welcomed the slavering loyalty. And then there was Danael's incessant prating about purity. The concept was an important one to Volos, one that he had wrestled with in the complex catechisms of Chaplain Massorus. It was also one that he felt was being torn away from him by Setheno, or at the very least transformed into something he had yet to understand. Purity of action, of faith, of loyalty to the God-Emperor: therein, he hoped, lay truth and the counterbalance to the monstrosity of his physical being. It was not a monstrosity he rejected. It was one he embraced. He blessed the curse. But he knew, too, that a dark temptation could wait down that road. That was why Massorus's lesson was so important: the curse must be the spur to purity. The correct path was becoming increasingly tangled and hard to discern, making the struggle to find it all the more vital.

Danael's version of purity struck Volos as something shallow, a construction of words and gestures and nothing else. Danael had always seemed to resent his deformity. He hated his curse, and his embrace of purity seemed to begin and end with the physical concept embodied by Toharan. So his words rang false and weak in Volos's ears, especially in this place, where all purity except of the vilest kind had been put to death centuries upon centuries ago.

They were on a deck one level below the bridge. The interior walls, ceiling and decking had some of the same sickly gold hue as the hull, but were darker, and were so covered in runes that they seemed to pulse and jump in the corner of the eye. Knowledge, power and madness had lost all distinction, and they shouted for Volos's attention from every flat surface. The dim light came from the runes themselves. This was a place of illumination, freely offered, and hungry to devour. Footing was treacherous, not because the corridor was moving, but because it appeared to be. Then there were the whispers. Even though the ship was in its final agonies, the lesson that it embodied still ached to be taught, and a low, constant susurrus of half-voices enveloped Volos, murmuring litanies of paradox and change. Words clawed for purchase on his mind, looking for a way in. He pushed them away and moved forward.

He checked the glyphs on his retinal display. These decks still had a full atmosphere, though the power was off. 'No other breaches,' he voxed Danael. 'Be ready. Some of the crew might still be alive.'

'Not for long,' Danael muttered.

Bolters up, they moved silently through the pulsing, insinuating corridors, up stairs that were softer and more knowing than metal should be, and reached the door to the bridge. Volos gave it a tug. It was shut tight, either locked or frozen by the absence of power. Volos nodded to Danael, who backed halfway down the stairs. Volos mag-locked a small demolition charge to the door, set the timer to thirty seconds, and joined Danael.

The door blew open with *crump* and a shriek of murdered runes. The Black Dragons charged onto the bridge and stopped three paces in. Ahead and to their right, dozens of servitors sat before cogitators and ship controls, mindlessly repeating actions at stations that no longer responded. The once-human creatures all showed signs of surgical mutilation. Some had no legs but four hands; others had flesh replaced by tapestry. Each was different, but all had had their eyelids removed and their lips flayed to create faces that were expressions of perpetual tortured joy. The hololithic displays were dark. The only light, other than that of the runes, came from the reflected shine of Aighe Mortis visible beyond the main viewport. To the left was the upper level of the strategium. The command throne was empty. The bridge appeared to be abandoned.

'Auspex?' Volos asked.

'Negative,' Danael answered.

Volos moved in deeper. He took the steps to the strategium. On its table, he saw an array of maps and data-slates. He was reaching for the nearest when a blur of rancid gold shot out from behind the command throne and filled the air with bolter fire. Rounds glanced off Volos's pauldron and he dropped flat. He rolled next to the strategium table. Using its bulk as cover, he rose to a crouch. There was a pause in the gun burst and he was about to fire when a frag grenade came bouncing onto the strategium floor from the direction of the stairs.

Volos vaulted back, over the strategium balcony. He was in mid-air when the grenade went off, the blast sending him spinning, shrapnel embedding itself deep into the ceramite of his armour. He crashed onto the bridge deck, crushing servitors and smashing cogitator stations. More bolter rounds sought him out, but these ones came from the same deck. Danael was yelling incoherently as he fired, and all Volos could make out were the shrieked words 'tainted' and 'traitor' spewing out of the other Dragon's mouth like an idiot refrain.

Volos scrabbled backwards, desperate to get a wall at his back and not be pinned down in a crossfire. The Sword captain opened up again, and over the stuttering *chug-chug-chug* of the bolters, he could hear the traitor laughing.

It was almost funny. Volos conceded that much. The triangulations of who was a traitor to what at this moment were too complex and too ridiculous to sort out. Volos didn't laugh. He reached the back wall and began to crawl along the periphery of the bridge, staying out of sight behind banks of consoles. Bits of glass and plastek and iron filled the air, and servitors exploded blood and bone, but the shots were generalised, sweeping the space with destruction rather than zeroing in on his location. Between Danael's automatic fire and death raining down from the strategium, the bridge was a chaos of minor explosions and flying debris. Neither Danael nor the Sword was aiming at the other. The unspoken alliance had determined to kill Volos first. So be it. At this moment, neither knew where he was. He knew where they both were. He listened to the shots, identified the different guns, and placed the enemies at precise points on his internal compass.

He palmed a frag, pulled the pin, let the grenade cook, and then leaped out from his cover near the viewport. He took the impact of stray rounds, felt their punch and damage, but with momentum and rage, he completed his move. He felt the entire space of the bridge as an extension of his nervous system, knew precisely where each of his strikes would hit. He tossed the grenade at the strategium, twisted to his left and emptied the bolter clip at Danael. The grenade went off on the downward slope of its arc. Volos heard screams above him and to the side as he landed. The bolter fire stopped.

Volos ran in a crouch to the strategium balcony, jumped up and pulled himself over the railing. The Chaos Space Marine was prone, a massive hole in his breastplate revealing a suppurating mass beneath. Strange noises were coming from his helmet grille. They were buzzing, staccato groans, and Volos recognised them as the desperate, final gasps of ruined lungs. Volos fired twice into the wound, blasting the Sword's hearts.

He made his way back down to the entrance to the bridge. Danael was slumped in the doorway, bleeding from a dozen wounds to the upper torso and throat. Volos had concentrated his fire so the first shells would punch through the armour, opening the way to flesh for the others. Danael's right hand was twitching against the deck, fingers reaching for the fallen bolter just out of his reach. Volos stood over him, torn between pity, contempt and fury. He knew he would shortly feel something much worse, but there were a few seconds yet before that happened.

'Why?' Volos demanded.

Danael coughed. Volos reached down, released the locks and pulled Danael's helmet off. The wounded Dragon spat dark blood. 'Tainted,' Danael wheezed. 'Know what you did... Have to be stopped.'

Volos wondered if Danael really believed what he was saying. If a bandwagon jumper like he was could find a depth of belief, then Second Company was riven in a much worse way than Volos had suspected. And he didn't think that Danael was simply spouting rhetoric *in extremis*. Volos took a breath and asked the question whose answer he didn't want to hear. 'Did Toharan order you to kill me?'

Danael grunted. 'Going to finish me?' Volos wasn't sure if he'd heard the question. 'Going to slice me with your Chaos blades?'

Volos felt a chill in his soul. Danael had named the

concern that Volos had been trying to avoid facing. His arm-blades had changed, and their transformation had been caused by a Chaos spell. But he was no different. His essence had not changed. He had to believe this, and he had watched and prayed and guarded against any deviation on his part from the Emperor's light. There had been none. He was sure of it.

But the change...

He shook the thoughts away. 'Did Toharan order you to kill me?' he asked again.

Danael said nothing. He had stopped coughing and was very still. Volos knelt over him. He was dead.

Volos straightened, took a few steps back and grabbed at a console to steady himself. That other emotion, held at bay, now arrived, and it was worse than he had guessed it would be. He had killed a battle-brother. That he had acted in self-defence made no difference to the enormity of the act. He had tried to tell himself that the divisions that had begun spreading through the Black Dragons upon Toharan's ascendancy were political ones, and though injurious to morale and to the company, they would pass with time and sufficient good will. He'd been a fool. Now he had slain another Dragon, and the worst of it was that he knew Danael would not be the last. He looked down at his wrists. He extruded the blades. The pain of their emergence was, in this moment, more than physical. He stared at them, at the ultimate expression of his imperfect, corrupted body.

'I am not tainted,' he whispered. 'I am *not* tainted,' he repeated, praying now. 'The Emperor is my light, and my arm is eternally and solely at his service, until death releases me.' For a flashing moment, he found himself wishing Setheno were here. But her words came to him: *You are the Emperor's monsters. And you are necessary.* They were a dark comfort.

He retracted the blades and returned to the strategium. He sorted through the wreckage left by the two grenades, and found a few intact data-slates. There was a star chart, too, and it surprised Volos not only because it was still in one piece, but because of its age. It was printed on vellum so old it was cracking. He folded it carefully and collected the data-slates. Then he turned his attention back to the corpses. He realised the lie he would have to tell. Without knowing if Toharan had ordered his assassination, and lacking any proof to back up the accusation, admitting to killing Danael would only exacerbate matters on the *Immolation Maw*, and if he found himself imprisoned, Toharan and Lettinger would have a free hand. Better that the story be of Danael's heroic death in combat with a traitor. Volos's word would be doubted, but he would still have some latitude to act.

So he had to lie. And he had to cover his tracks. He grimaced. He wondered just how many black deeds the awful word *necessary* could swallow up. He hoped he would never know, because he feared the number might be infinite.

He hauled Danael's body onto the strategium. He gathered all the grenades both the Dragon and the Sword carried. The sacrilege he was about to commit made him pause. He was going to obliterate Danael's body and deprive his Chapter of the precious progenoid glands. An entire genetic legacy of Black Dragons would be no more. *Necessary*, Volos thought, accepting the guilt and self-loathing, and vowing he would make a greater good come of this, even if his own life were forfeit. Then he pulled the pins on the grenades. He strode away from the bridge as it erupted in flame.

CHAPTER 21
ACTS OF FAITH

THE DATA-SLATES WENT to Ydraig. The Techmarine wrinkled his nose at the tainted devices, but he pried some useful information out of them before he purged them in fire. The star chart became the study of Nithigg and Tennesyn. The ancient warrior and the scholar of the distant past found in the chart an object worthy of their shared obsessions. It was difficult to decipher not just because of its age, but because it was not, they soon realised, drawn by human hand. Between Ydraig's efforts and their own, a destination was identified. The Swords of Epiphany were on their way to the Abolessus system.

Three days later, limping but hungry for blood, the *Immolation Maw* plunged into the empyrean in pursuit.

VOLOS SAT IN the apothecarion, murmuring to Massorus's comatose figure. He had chosen here, rather than the chapel, to unburden his soul. Massorus could no more hear him than could the icon of the Emperor, but there was more privacy here, and there was an illusion of comfort in seeing the Chaplain. Volos could indulge, for a few moments, in the hope that Massorus might awaken in the middle of his confession and begin to untangle the theological knots for him. The Chaplain's breaths were slow and widely spaced, prompted more by the machines connected to his body than by his lungs themselves.

Nithigg entered the chamber and sat down quietly opposite Volos. 'Why did you want to meet here?' he asked.

'So we could talk.' They were alone, and more visitors were unlikely. Volos told Nithigg what had happened on the *Metastasis*.

Nithigg drew a sharp intake of breath. 'So we've reached that point.' He sounded sad, but not surprised.

'You were expecting this?'

'At the back of my mind. I kept telling myself I was wrong.'

Volos sighed. 'To tell you the truth, I think I was doing the same.'

'Was Danael acting on Toharan's orders?'

'I don't know.'

'But he might have been.'

'Being assigned to work with him was odd.'

'Then we have to assume the worst. The question is what we do now.'

'I'm open to suggestions,' Volos said, hoping Nithigg might have a plan, any plan that was different from the course of action that Volos saw looming ahead.

'You have to take over command,' Nithigg said. 'Arrest Toharan and his followers.'

And there it was: the action Volos dreaded, and had avoiding articulating to himself. *So much for alternatives*, he thought. 'On what evidence?' he asked. 'I have no concrete proof.'

'It won't matter.' Nithigg spoke as if he were trying to convince himself more than Volos. 'The loyalty of the company belongs to you.'

'Still?' Volos asked. 'Before Aighe Mortis, perhaps that was true. But after what we did… You must have heard the talk.'

With visible reluctance, Nithigg nodded. The divisions were deep, and they were broad. Volos didn't know any longer where the bulk of the Dragons stood.

'And it's still mutiny,' Volos said. 'Toharan is our duly anointed captain.'

'Mutiny against a criminal is a duty, not a crime,' Nithigg said. 'Are you saying that you wouldn't have mutinied against Horus?'

'Don't be ridiculous. Of course I would have.' But he conceded Nithigg's point. The time to worry about the ethics of resisting Toharan had passed. 'I would still need evidence,' he said.

They were silent for a moment.

Nithigg asked, 'Do you think he'll try again?'

'I'm not sure. It would be a bit more difficult to have me killed on the ship and not trigger open warfare. But he'll try something. Maybe when he does, I can counter it, turn the move against him.'

'And in the meantime?'

Volos hesitated for a moment. There was a line he was about to cross. Until now, he had advocated no action, and had been talking to no one other than Nithigg. When Melus and Setheno had raised the idea of moving against Toharan, he had shut them down. Now he was going to commit himself to the path of sedition. *Toharan has left me no choice*, he reminded himself. 'We speak to our allies,' he said. 'We tell them what happened. We warn them to be on their guard.'

'Do we know who our allies are?'

Volos thought he did. 'Ormarr,' he said. He trusted all the Dragon Claws with his life. 'And anyone else whom Toharan believes to be my ally, because whatever such a warrior might actually think of me, his life is in danger.'

'Agreed,' Nithigg said. 'So tell me, how does it feel to be engaged in conspiracy?'

Volos turned a regretful eye on the body of the Chaplain. 'Awful.'

TOHARAN PACED THE length of the prison chapel. 'Why do you make it so difficult?' he shouted at the icon of the Emperor. 'I am doing everything in my power to bring our Chapter into compliance with the Codex. I am trying to bring us closer to you. So why do you insist on thwarting my every effort?' How difficult, he wanted to know, would it have been to let events take their natural course aboard the *Metastasis*? There were so many reasons why Volos should never have returned from that vessel, but there he was, and though there were many whispers about what the daemon-tainted must have done to Danael, there were, Toharan knew, plenty of murmurers who saw things differently. The company was coming apart under his leadership, not unifying and moving towards a greater purity.

Then there was the humiliation on Aighe Mortis. Toharan's lip curled in disgust as he thought of the rebels. He had shown them mercy, and he had shown them an example. In return, they had proven themselves unworthy of either. They had betrayed him, and then become a mindless, howling mob in Volos's hands. He advanced to the altar and stared at the icon. 'Was there anything worth saving down there?' The black marble figure said nothing, but Toharan knew the answer. No, there hadn't been. The planet was unworthy of salvation. Exterminatus would have been too good for it.

The image hung in the air before him of the planet scoured of life, all that messy unpredictability and ingratitude and impurity wiped away. In the wake of the act, the purity of nothing at all. He thought again of that moment he had experienced looking down the gap in the ship's decking, of feeling the seductive grace of absence. If there was nothing, then the squirming in his brain would stop, because all those things that tormented him and set his mind to writhing would be gone. Then, and only then, would true purity be achieved.

The more he gazed at the icon, the more he resented it. The figure was nonsense. What was the Emperor doing, shackled to that rotting body? That material excrescence wasn't pure. It was just the opposite. If the Emperor were so perfect, why hadn't He transcended the body? Why hadn't He left it behind altogether to become pure and infinite will? Instead, His will was dependent on the survival of this hideous monstrosity, this shambles of deliquescent flesh and exposed bone, this helpless, perpetual reminder of death and weakness and the infuriating limits of the body. The Emperor's body *was* corruption. How had Toharan never seen this before? If the summit of human perfection was now this incarnation of the disgusting and rotten, then where was purity? What was there to strive for?

Toharan's hands tensed and he felt the urge to tear his hair from his scalp, and his flesh from his face. His body was an unbearable contradiction. It was so pure that the Black Dragons used it to disguise their fundamental impurity. And yet its lack of impurity, its missing excess of bone, ensured that he would always be an impure Black Dragon. He could never be at one with the full identity of the Chapter.

Unless he changed that identity. Unless he remade the Chapter in his image, body and soul. Perhaps, if he eliminated any reminder of the limits of the body, he could rest. If his body became the eternal and infinite model, perhaps he could find peace. But what an undertaking that would be, and in the name of purity, there would be so much, in the Chapter and beyond it, that would have to be destroyed. Well, what of it? That which was impure was already a form of destruction. He would simply complete the process.

He lifted his bolter and emptied its clip into the icon. He blasted it to stone fragments, and the fragments to dust. When he was done, there was a crater in the frieze above the altar. He was staring at an absence. In the moment of calm that descended, his task appeared before him in its full clarity. The first step would be one last attempt to convert Second Company. He would give his brothers a final chance at redemption, a chance that only existed because he did.

Volos was beyond redemption. That was clear. He was moving as rapidly toward total impurity as Toharan was racing to the opposite pole. He had to be destroyed before his contagion proved irreversible. But the problem was the same as it had been before the *Metastasis*: Volos had to be neutralised in such a way as to leave no doubt as to his corruption. He must not become a martyr. What he represented had to die with him. Maybe then there would be the possibility of salvation for the rest of the company.

It would be a welcome redemption if it came to pass. Toharan wanted unity for the confrontation with the Swords of Epiphany. He still had no idea what game they were playing, but he really did not care. However much he hated the morass into which the Black Dragons were sinking, he still felt the collective humiliations as acutely as ever. He would track the Swords down, and he would annihilate them. The mission was that simple, and that pure.

And yet... There was something about that scrabbling and scratching at his cortex. Amidst the throb in his head that sometimes pulsed in the corners of his vision, there was something like a black pearl of promise. The hook to follow the Swords was more than retribution. There was something they wanted, and they were going to enormous lengths to acquire it. Perhaps, the lure in his buzzing thoughts suggested, it should be his.

When he pushed this thought to the surface, acknowledged it and embraced his desire, then the scrabbling eased again, just a bit, and just for a short time. As it ebbed, it left excitement. To grasp this pearl, he felt, would be to clear the path to his goal. Every obstacle to his divine purity would be obliterated with a wave of his hand.

This would be so. Because he willed it.

Volos, then. Destroy Volos before they reached Abolessus.

He strode out of the chapel to find Lettinger. Behind him, the void over the altar gaped.

THE WARP WAS the raw stuff of thoughts and emotions. Every conscious and unconscious twitch of every sentient being formed its matter and shaped and fed its denizens. It was everything that Werner Lettinger held in abhorrence. It was what he had been created, through his nature and his training, to combat. In the makeshift meditation chamber he had established in his quarters on the *Immolation Maw*, he strengthened his will and his faith against the leeching temptations of the warp. It was especially important that he do so while the ship was travelling the sea of the immaterium. That was what he was doing now.

At least, that was what he told himself each time that he began the game.

As he meditated, he found himself travelling over the vectors and angles of his thoughts, tracing their intersections and leaps, following their twists to see where they might lead. What had begun as mere thought exercises – asking himself 'what if' and exploring the consequences to their logical conclusions – had become something deeper. He wasn't sure when the shift had happened. He thought it might have been during his period at Lexica Keep. But its origin didn't matter to him. What was important was the exploration he undertook, and how it made him feel. The game would begin as it always had, as a simple litany of questions and hypotheticals. But as he descended along the strings of logic, those strings gradually took on a pseudo-existence of their own. He could caress the lines of his own mind, and swim in its currents. It was intoxicating. It was empowering.

It was wrong. Part of him knew this, the part that still held to the credo of Monodominance, and it clamped down on him with iron ferocity, filling him with the most profound guilt. But the guilt was its own narcotic, leaving him tingling with the visceral reminder of his own fundamental morality. In forbidding his mental exploration, the guilt made the transgression even more enticing, and each time he crossed the line, the intensity of the cycle ramped up.

He was becoming stronger for the experience. He knew that he had reached a new level of understanding about his psyche when he had spoken with Toharan about destiny. That both of them felt the same premonition of greatness was, he felt sure, a confirmation of its truth. This certainty was his counter to the guilt, his invitation to plunge into the game again and again, and go deeper each time. Lately, the descent into the twisting depths of thought wasn't limited to his meditation sessions. His dreams carried the same charge. More than that, his dreams were inspiration. New possibilities suggested themselves each time he slept, and he woke with a nagging tug towards new realms. There was a consistency to the direction now, too. He was on the verge of something momentous. He could sense it just over the next mental horizon, and it came closer the more firmly he held the threads of the Black Dragons future in his fist.

Since the *Immolation Maw* had entered the warp, he had been twisting on the edge of gigantic revelation. The Abolessus system held the key. He was as convinced of this as anything in his life, and the fact that he had no concrete evidence on which to base this belief was itself confirmation that the knowledge came from somewhere other than the sad normalcy of the physical world.

It wasn't just destiny that waited around the corner. It was the supreme flowering of his potential.

That thought, the promise of his transcendence, was the one whose contours he was exploring when Toharan entered his quarters. The presence of another jerked Lettinger back to the here and now. It took him a moment to get his bearings. As he gathered himself, the guilt arrived, and he caught himself glancing furtively around the chamber for signs of his trespass. There was nothing unusual about the furnishings. Lettinger hadn't altered the layout of the quarters. There was a small bedchamber, barely larger than a closet, and a study, which was where he sat. This space held a chair and an iron desk.

Lettinger had pulled the chair out to the middle of the room, and he had been sitting facing the door, his back to the small viewport. He had drawn no circles of protection on the floor, had set up no wards. Why would he? He was just sitting here thinking, after all. But as he blinked his way back to full consciousness, he saw the flicker of an oily darkness withdrawing to the corners of the room.

If Toharan noticed, he didn't appear to care. 'Volos has to die now,' he said. 'And his corruption must be obvious even to the most blind.'

Lettinger couldn't argue the point. He agreed completely. What wasn't clear was how this necessity was going to come about. He opened his mouth to say so. The words caught themselves. He started, hit by inspiration so powerful it was a physical blow. 'Oh,' Lettinger gasped in wonder and shock. The idea was so perfect, such a round, hard, flawless jewel, and so foreign to him, that it could only have a divine origin. His smile, he knew, was beatific. It couldn't be otherwise, when destiny was so gloriously affirmed.

Toharan frowned at him. 'What is it?'

'We'll need a volunteer,' Lettinger said.

CHAPTER 22
THE DUELLISTS

Space tore open, the edges of the wound bleeding nightmares. Through this gap, the *Revealed Truth* and the *Foretold Pilgrimage* re-entered the materium. When Nessun saw the wonders of the Abolessus system, he could almost believe that he was still in the warp. The confusion delighted him. It was the first of many gifts Abolessus would give him. The multiplicity of his being exulted in the promise of what lay ahead.

There is no corner of the Imperium that can truly said to be forgotten. Somewhere, in some archive, no matter how remote from the pressing concerns of Terra, records exist of every system and every planet to fall under the Emperor's protection. But for some regions, the line between 'forgotten' and 'ignored' is a thin one. These are worlds whose value to the Imperium is minimal, and is outweighed by inconvenience of location, strategic worthlessness, doubtful character, or even embarrassing history. Abolessus had the unfortunate privilege of combining all these qualities.

It was located far beyond even the Flebis system, at the extreme southern edge of the Maeror subsector, itself a backwater of the Segmentum Tempestus bordering the Veiled Region. Like Camargus, Abolessus had only one colony, strictly speaking. But Abolessus Gemini was no Aighe Mortis, and the rest of the system had no equivalent anywhere in the Imperium.

There were wonders here. Orbiting the swollen, dull red massiveness of Abolessus were monuments. They were planet-sized monoliths of a geometry that was simple seen from a distance, as if they were not much more than impossibly massive oblongs, cubes and triangles fastened together in shapes of mourning. Closer up, they revealed ridges and lines as large as any mountain chain, and as intricate as any geologic formation, but carved with a regularity and precision no natural formation had ever possessed. They were runes in a language that had been forgotten before life on Terra had sparked in the primeval seas. They were unreadable, but they spoke.

Nessun did not hear what they had to say. His only interest in the monuments was the power that their existence implied. Growing in the viewport, in the orbit nearest the red sun, was the key to that power. If Nessun's eyes still had functioning tear ducts, he thought he might have wept in ecstasy as Abolessus Gemini presented itself to him.

The twin, perfectly spherical, 5,000-kilometre wide planetoids had been colonized for one reason alone. A system with such a massive xenos-taint would normally have been quarantined. But the Gemini bodies were composed of pure adamantium. Mining concerns had rushed to exploit this unheard-of bounty, ignoring the prefects in the Adeptus Administratum who feared what such a massive influx of the metal might do to the economies of the entire segmentum. In the end, the prefects needn't have worried. The adamantium was impossible to mine. The planetoids were fully finished, the metal forged to a density beyond human comprehension. They were indestructible.

By the time the last, most stubborn corporations had given up the cause, permanent colonies had been established, and an odd consolation prize had been won. Each of the Twins was striated with a dense network of mountain chains as uniform and straight as latitude lines given concrete being. The mountains were narrow and razor-peaked, and travel between the constricted valleys was possible only by air. But those valleys were covered by topsoil whose richness and fecundity was the envy of Ultramar's most luxuriant garden worlds. The colonists came as miners, and stayed to become farmers.

The departure of the corporations and the remoteness of the system meant that, within a few generations, trade with the rest of the Imperium ground to a halt. The citizens of the Abolessus Twins barely noticed. Their worlds were self-sufficient. After a few centuries, they ignored the Imperium as much as it ignored them. And yes, there were records of the system, and what it contained, so it could not be said, to the distress of an Administratum bureaucrat, that Abolessus had been forgotten. But those records had not been looked at for over four thousand years.

The Swords of Epiphany were here to correct that injustice. Rodrigo Nessun would give the Twins more attention than they had received in all of human history.

The identical worlds filled the main viewport, their new moon at the peak of an isosceles triangle formed by the orbits. Nessun gave the moon a look of promise. *Soon*, he told it. 'What we need is inside one of the planetoids,' he announced.

'Which one?' Gabrille asked. 'They're identical.'

'Scan them. There is a difference. Find it.'

THE DISCIPLES OF Purity met and prayed. Toharan didn't try to gloss over the damaged altarpiece. He stood aside while Lettinger began the service, but then took over once he felt the fervour in the room had reached the necessary pitch. He spoke with all the passion of his conviction, and he felt the necessary words coming to him as if he had been born to preach instead of fight. Before him was the largest number yet of adherents to his banner. They were still, to a man, the least mutated of the company, and perhaps that was as it should be. They represented the Black Dragons best chance to reach physical purity through the purging of the monstrous.

Toharan spoke to them of this purity, and they were with him. He spoke to them of power, and they were with him. He shattered the hold of the rotting corpse on the Golden Throne, and they were with him. When he unveiled the full extent of his illumination, he thought for a moment that he might have lost Lettinger. The inquisitor did start, and did look again with horrified fascination at the void above the altar. But then Toharan saw the play of guilt and exhilaration on Lettinger's face, and knew that he held the man more firmly than ever.

The call to prayer became the call to mission, and finally the call to war. There was never any question about who the enemy was. Volos had shown where the path of impurity led. He was a menace to the promise of what the Black Dragons could be. There was no question now of adopting Codex dogma. The Dragons could be so much more than the barely tolerated poor cousins in the family of the Adeptus Astartes. They were their own power, and the time was coming when that power would be known across the galaxy. The first step to unleashing that power was to eliminate that which threatened the Chapter's potential. Volos was not only a dark alternative; he had also killed one of the Disciples. There was no question that he had to die.

Toharan had no shortage of volunteers. He only needed one.

This time, Lettinger did use wards. He did place himself within a protective circle. He had no illusions about what he was doing. There were no rationalisations to be made here, not if he wanted to live through the next half-hour.

He was in his quarters. Toharan waited just outside the door. Lettinger drew steady breaths, slowing his pulse and regulating the beat of his heart. Then he began. There was a lot that Lettinger knew about summoning, but that knowledge, until now, had been academic in nature. He knew how to recognise the daemonic. He knew how to destroy it, and had done so times beyond counting. But to conjure something from the warp, to become that which he should exterminate...

That was the most forbidden. That was the greatest guilt. And in his new, enlightened, more powerful state of mind and spirit, that was also the greatest thrill.

He began the ritual as another thought exercise. It was his necessary rationalisation, a mental fig leaf. He pretended to pretend he wasn't doing what he was doing. Then he followed the thoughts until they became darker and more real. When he reached the point where he would previously have hung motionless in rapt contemplation, he kept going. He entered a new realm of flickering possibility and whispering obscenity. The guilt and excitement threatened to break apart his rational processes, but he hung on to them and pushed forward. And suddenly he was plunging his will into the stuff of the warp with the assurance of the born sorcerer. It was as if the mental chants and psychic defences were being given to him by a universe that had no choice but to recognise him and his deeds.

He sculpted an idea as if working in clay. It was an idea of doom and corruption, and he crafted every detail and nuance until it was a masterpiece of a curse. He scaled it down into an essence no less perfect, no less artistic, but as concentrated as it was toxic. Then it was time to haul it, newborn and wailing its soul-hunger, into the material world.

When Toharan entered the chamber, the curse hovered in the air before Lettinger's face. It didn't look like much more than an onyx marble. Lettinger couldn't take his eyes off it. Pride crushed guilt beneath its boot heel.

'Is that it?' Toharan asked. He was careful to stay outside the circle.

'It is.' Lettinger reached into a pocket, and produced a small wooden box. It had once held an icon: the molar of Ordo Malleus legend Saint Meruh. The icon had been a source of strength for Lettinger. He didn't need it any longer. But the box was useful. Wards covered its surface. Lettinger opened it, that it might receive its new pearl.

Volos had thought to spend some time in the training cage. For a short time, he could lose himself in the trance of physical exertion. Waiting for Toharan to make a move went against his grain, and his impatience felt more like a cursed impotence. He had no choice. He couldn't act first, unless he wanted to doom the company. So a few moments where his attention would be taken away from strategising a war no one should be fighting would be a boon.

But Toharan was in the cage. He appeared to have just arrived, and Volos couldn't shake the idea that Toharan had raced ahead of him to get there first. The notion was ridiculous. It also felt accurate. The Black Dragon captain stood stripped to the waist, longsword in hand, swinging the blade from side to side, just a bit too elaborately at ease. 'Brother-sergeant,' he said. His smile was thin.

'Brother-captain,' Volos returned, cautious.

'It's been a long time since we sparred together.'

'Really? I would have said we've been doing nothing but, lately.'

Toharan's smile didn't falter. He nodded once. 'Perhaps that's the problem. Shall we return things to the proper arena?' He bowed and presented the point of the sword in formal challenge.

Volos chose a blade from a weapons locker and climbed into the cage with Toharan. The duel began.

SETHENO HADN'T LIED to Volos. She didn't see the future. She had no visions of any kind. She had no psyker gifts. For all these lacks, she was grateful. The presence of any extra sight might hurt the accuracy of her true gift and curse: perfect clarity.

Volos had not spoken to her about what had happened on the *Metastasis*. He didn't have to. She saw his grim look when he returned, and that was all she needed. She knew how Danael had died. Now she stood in the shadows of an alcove partway down the corridor from Volos's cell. She was motionless, a thing of stone at one with the walls. She had been on post for several hours now, watching over the Space Marine who should be governing Second Company. She had been here while he rested and prayed, and she had been especially alert since he had left his quarters twenty minutes ago. She didn't know when the assassination attempt would come, only that it would be soon. Toharan's strategic position demanded that this be so. It was that simple

She heard the hollow echo of armoured boots against the metal decking. She pulled deeper into the shadows and waited. The approaching Space Marine might be one of Volos's number. Most of them had cells down this same corridor. But Volos's allies had no reason to be down here at this time. Work on the ship was ongoing, and preparations were ramping up in anticipation of war in the Abolessus system.

The Black Dragon appeared. He had his helmet on, but Setheno recognised the purity seals and insignia. It was Mattanius. She had seen him before, and noted him as part of Toharan's cohort. He was not as pure as the captain. No one was, and that, Setheno knew, was another reason why Toharan was so dangerous. But Mattanius's skull, though heavy of brow, had no actual deformities. Since the events of Flebis, Setheno had found herself eyeing the Dragons through a phrenological filter. Lack of physical deformity meant an equivalent lack of humility. A normal Ossmodula led to an overdeveloped sense of entitlement. She had made a mental list of Black Dragons she considered obstacles to the proper development of the Chapter. Now they were proving her correct.

Mattanius was carrying a small package. At Volos's door, he stopped and pulled out a key. He worked it a bit, and then the ancient lock gave way. The Space Marine disappeared into the meditation cell. Setheno followed him.

She stood in the doorway. Mattanius had his back to her. He seemed to be looking for something. He hovered before the bookshelves that lined the far wall. Setheno could see the titles on their spines. They were primarily works of military strategy and religious philosophy. Mattanius ran a finger along the books, testing the bindings. The book he selected was a collection of battlefield devotionals. It was very thick and very worn. It bore the marks of frequent, possibly daily, use. He let the book open in his palm. The pages flipped open to a favourite passage. There was a lectern in front of the shelves, and Mattanius place the book there, the small box beside it. He pulled out his combat knife and began to cut deep into the pages.

Setheno drew her bolt pistol.

Holding the hilt of the longsword, Volos was struck by just how long it had been since he had wielded a blade that was not part of his body. There was a distance between his will and the weapon. He was wrong-footed before the duel even began. Beneath the dome of iron bars that made up the practice cage, he circled Toharan, waiting for the other Space Marine to attack first. Any strike of his own would be countered.

For almost five minutes, neither warrior did anything but move around the perimeter of the cage, watching his opponent, studying how the other walked, how every twitch of muscle and nuance of breath might signal a move. To know the enemy as he knew himself could cut the actual swordfight down to an exercise of seconds. With each passing moment, Volos felt the stakes of the duel rising.

Toharan attacked. The move was lightning-fast. Volos had expected speed, but the strike came at an angle and at a moment that he hadn't anticipated. Toharan took a step forward and appeared to ground himself on the leading right leg. Then he pivoted on his left, coming in anticlockwise, his blade a streak of light. Volos brought his sword down and parried at the last second, but stumbled back, already on the defensive.

'Did you kill Danael?' Toharan demanded.

Mattanius reacted to the click of Setheno's gun. He spun, ducking low, and threw himself across the chamber. He slammed into her, knocking the pistol from her grasp. They crashed into the corridor wall. Their armoured bulk left a crater in the reptile-green stone. Setheno's ears rang. She slumped. Mattanius backed up a step to bring his knife to bear. He drew his arm back, the point of the blade aimed at the seam where her gorget met her cuirass. It was coming for her throat.

'Did you send him to kill me?' Volos countered. He blocked Toharan's flurry of strikes. They were hard blows, tiring to both of them, and he was still off-balance. He couldn't retaliate.

'Your evasion affirms your guilt,' Toharan snarled. He pressed the attack harder.

'So does yours,' said Volos.

Setheno jerked forward out of her possum feint and hammered Mattanius's ribs, her fists rapid-fire pistons. It was impossible for her blows to injure the Space Marine, but nor could he ignore the physics of hits strong enough to punch through walls. The impacts knocked him back, and his knife thrust went wrong, glancing off her right pauldron. She danced back out of his range. In a grapple, she would lose. She didn't have enhanced Space Marine physiology. Her power armour was almost the equal of his, but in a contest of strength, the result was preordained.

She drew her sword as he raised his bolter.

TOHARAN PRESSED VOLOS harder. His thrusts and slashes came with the precision and grace of a fugue. With the small part of his mind that was observing the duel with interest, Volos admired the art of Toharan's attack. It wasn't composed of individual moves. Each assault flowed into the next, the thrust turning into the parry of Volos's awkward counter, the parry becoming a slash, and so on, an unending flow that beat at his defence like steel hail.

'Why are you doing it, brother?' Toharan asked. His words came in a grunted staccato at odds with the fluidity of his swordcraft. 'Why are you standing in the way of what this Chapter can be?'

He doesn't want me to join him, Volos thought. *He just wants me to vanish.* He said, 'I'm more concerned with what we *should* be.'

The answer enraged Toharan, as if Volos had pricked a suppressed conscience. Toharan's rhythm broke into a moment of furious hacking, and Volos slipped his blade in for just a moment, nicking Toharan's cheek. Toharan spat and retaliated with renewed anger and rigour, his mistake corrected.

'You *will* be stopped,' Toharan promised. His glare was desperate, and Volos had a glimpse of the depth of Toharan's self-damnation, and the lengths to which he would go to justify the path he had chosen.

'What have you become?' Volos begged, as if the question might remind Toharan of what he had once been.

'Your conqueror,' Toharan answered. His blade cut long slices along Volos's ribs.

CLARITY COULD BE a curse. In battle, it was a gift. Setheno knew where she was weak against Mattanius. She knew her strengths, too. She wouldn't make a mistake. So all she had to do was stay alive until he made one.

Shooting her wasn't that mistake.

She threw herself forwards on her knees as he fired. The rounds burned the air just over her head. The far end of the corridor exploded stone fragments and dust as the mass-reactive shells blasted their way into the wall. Mattanius dropped his aim, bringing her into the line of annihilation. But she had her sword up now.

The blade had a name. It was Skarprattar, and it was a relic sword. It had once belonged to Saint Demetria, who had stood alone during the doom of Caedo III, taking countless bloodletters of Khorne down in her martyrdom. The sword had been the only artefact recovered when Imperial forces had staggered back to the ravaged world. It had done grim work since, and been Setheno's companion in wading the bloody tides of brutish necessity for nearly a century. Its spirit was her twin. It was foreign to hesitation, mercy, or the illusions of hope. Its existence was an endless severing of souls from being. Now it sliced Mattanius's rounds in half. Setheno's blow arced into his plackart, parting ceramite. Mattanius staggered into Volos's cell, blood rushing from his lower abdomen.

He was wounded. But he was Adeptus Astartes. He was Black Dragon. So he did not falter in his attack. He kept firing, and Setheno couldn't stop or dodge every round. Bolts stitched across her chest and ribs, punching through armour.

Her blood pooled with her enemy's.

TOHARAN WAS FIGHTING as if he meant to kill. The idea that the duel was a joust was fading into a lie. Volos abandoned any pretence of form and hurled his bulk into his captain. He took a deep gash in his left shoulder, but knocked Toharan off his feet. Volos rushed in to press his advantage, and he did so with his left fist extended.

The hand that did not hold his sword.

His rational mind caught up with his instincts and stopped him from impaling Toharan with a bone-blade. He stumbled right, and Toharan bashed him across the brow with the flat of his blade. Blood ran into Volos's eyes. He jumped away, blind. He swung his sword as a ward. He might as well have waved a parchment. Toharan did not reach his shoulder and was much lighter, but Volos didn't see the body blow come, and he wasn't ready for it. He hit the floor of the cage hard.

The edge of Toharan's sword bit into his throat.

SETHENO WAS NOT Adeptus Astartes. Her body did not start healing almost as soon as it was hurt. Her system was not flooded with pain-killing drugs. She *was* a Sister of Battle, and her discipline and will were no less than those of any Space Marine. Her need to kill her enemy outweighed her injury, and now she was the one who launched herself across the intervening space into Mattanius.

It was not a blind strike. There was strategy born of her hellish clarity. She rocked Mattanius against the lectern, jolting his right hand up. Bolter rounds smashed the ceiling. Setheno stabbed up with Skarprattar deep into Mattanius's armpit. Bone and tendons parted, and his arm fell limp to his side.

The Black Dragon roared in anger, not pain. His left arm flashed out and snatched the box on the lectern. He swung it toward Setheno.

'So you would kill me,' Toharan hissed.

'I did not.' It was hard to speak with the blade pressing so hard, just shy of sawing through his throat. Volos blinked until he could see again. Toharan's face was twisted with hate, yet Volos thought he also saw a desperate self-loathing beneath the surface.

'You are mutinous, degenerate muck,' Toharan said.

'Is that my death sentence?' Volos didn't hide his contempt.

Toharan straightened and withdrew the sword. 'This was your lesson,' he said. 'I won't stain my leadership or my hands with your death here, with no witnesses. You are going to answer for your corruption, *sergeant*, but not without exposing your true nature to the entire company.'

Volos got to his feet. He did not pick up his sword. He stared at Toharan. 'You are lost, brother,' he said. He felt a sadness that bordered on despair.

Toharan sneered.

His answer was cut off by a chilling thrum. It resonated not in the ears, but in the soul.

SETHENO SEIZED ON Mattanius's mistake. She grabbed his fist with hers and squeezed. The move surprised him and his grip tightened without thinking. There was a sharp *crack* as the box splintered. Mattanius froze. Setheno could not see his face behind his helmet, but she pictured his dismay. He spoke one syllable: 'Oh.'

She released his hand and jumped back. She sensed the arrival of something ruinous. The temperature in the chamber dropped below freezing. Skarprattar's aura burned a violent blue. Mattanius turned his head to stare at his outstretched hand. There was a low, almost subaural *whump* and his hand vanished. A point of absolute nothing hung in the space before his wrist, and then tendrils of dark, muscled thought whipped out of the singularity. They wrapped themselves around Mattanius, a kraken seizing a ship. Mattanius howled the agony of his soul, and then the strangling cables of dark contracted, pulling him into nothing. The sound as he vanished was a chord plucked from the strings of reality, a stab in the very essence of being.

Setheno retreated another step. The light in the cell was altering, the rays of the biolumes becoming individually discernible and bending towards the hole in the air. The point was now a circle, pulses growing it by tiny fractions. Tendrils coiled out of it, insubstantial as smoke but strong as madness, fishing for more prey. From a protective case on her belt, Setheno withdrew an aquila. Like her sword, it was a relic. It was porcelain, fired from clay made from the ground bones of a dozen saints. She held it up before the floating void, and began to speak a rite of banishment. The thing fought, but she was strong. She knew it for what it was. It wasn't an actual tear in the materium. That would have been beyond anyone's ability to seal without destroying the ship. The sphere was a thought construction, an abstract idea given substance and a rudimentary intelligence. If it developed past its current embryonic form, it might in time become a daemon. But for now it was too dependent on its creator's conception, and there was only one individual on board who could be responsible for it. Lettinger's pride and ambition coated the thing like a signature, and Setheno tailored the rite to be a counter specific to the inquisitor.

The tendrils reached towards her, wrapping around the aquila. They pulled. She resisted. Her chanting never altered from a calm, inexorable monotone. The tendrils found no emotions to feed on, and the prayers ate away at their strength. Setheno felt the warmth of her blood running between her bodyweb and armour. She held herself rigid and straight, and saw the rite through. The sphere stopped growing. Each pulse now saw it smaller. Setheno poured denial on the construct, and at last, instead of a pulse, there was a blink, and it was gone.

The light in Volos's chambers became normal again. A smell like old nightmares and new bones lingered for a few moments, then faded. There was blood on the floor, and a few slivers of wood. The room was otherwise untouched.

Setheno's wounds began to weigh her down, and she staggered as she left the quarters. More blood on the floor of the corridor, and battered stonework on the walls and ceiling. Now, too, the heavy boom of running, booted feet. The battle had lasted less than a minute.

Volos and Toharan, monster and god unarmoured above the waist, were the first to arrive. Concern and suspicion flashed over Volos's face as he took in her injury and the signs of battle. Toharan's expression was less conflicted. He simply looked at her with naked hatred before stalking away, a retinue of Space Marines at his heels.

CHAPTER 23
DEPLOYMENT IN FORCE

The trap was twofold. Setheno's words, echoing in Volos's mind as the *Immolation Maw* transited back to real space in the Abolessus system. *It was meant to kill you and disgrace you. You would have been eliminated, and corruption would leak from your cell until the inquisitor dispelled it. You would have been destroyed by your own daemonic magic.* That would have been the narrative, one to convert those who still doubted Toharan's leadership, and to silence those who would resist it. The naked pretext of the practice cage duel was laughably obvious now.

You must stop him. Do what is necessary.

The words of mutiny and sedition, spoken by a legend of the Holy Ecclesiarchy. But he had no argument with them now. They had become the expression of common sense, and of fidelity to the truth of the Black Dragons and to the Emperor. Yes, he would do what was necessary. But he still needed the means to do it, and what had happened in his quarters had left nothing but questions, few of which did him any good. A battle-brother was missing, somehow killed by a canoness whose reputation was as much for cold-bloodedness as it was for righteousness. The whiff of the daemonic fed into the darker stories about the penitence crusade on Aighe Mortis. It was becoming harder for Volos to act against Toharan.

The captain of purity was winning. Not as quickly and decisively as he desired. But he was winning.

In his cell, Volos said a prayer over the last of the rounds that he loaded into his bolter. Then, blades out, he crossed them over his chest, making an aquila of them, and he prayed some more. There was an anger to his prayers now. He prayed for the violent end of those who would hurt his Chapter. 'Make me your monster,' he begged the Emperor. 'Make me your dragon.'

TENNESYN STOOD ON the bridge. He kept himself out of the way, near the seat-bound servitors, far from the traffic of war near the strategium. His eyes were glued to the viewport, and the revelations of Abolessus. Before the recovery of the data from the *Metastasis*, he had never heard of the system. Afterwards, he had only known the name. Now, he saw the most impressive finds of his career reduced to the scale of pottery shards.

The monuments of Abolessus floated past the *Immolation Maw*. They crowded the space of the system. There were too many orbits, too many objects of planetary scale swarming around the aged red sun. Tennesyn's jaw hung open. He had never experienced such absolute awe. Every object was a massive demonstration of staggering pointlessness and power. The geometrical assemblages were not for habitation, and they were not bases. They were engraved art, and existed only for the sheer excess of being.

Or so Tennesyn thought at first. But as the ship moved deeper into the cyclopean gallery, the monuments began to speak to him. As he watched their slow ballet of endless, dead tumbling, what he heard was a silence. It wasn't the simple silence of airless void. It was the quiet of a mourning too deep and too vast to be expressed in words or cries. These objects were the creations of grief and despair. A species of unimaginable power had produced a valediction to itself. It had marked the fact of its existence on an entire solar system. It had transformed worlds so it would not be forgotten, and then, after all, it had been forgotten. The deeds and histories written in runes the size of mountains would never be read again. What really mattered – the content of the memory – was lost. Only the shape remained.

The lesson was humbling. Before Tennesyn's eyes, the past became a landscape of extinctions stretching back to infinity. The xeno-archaeologist quailed at the hopelessness of his vision. He tried to redirect his attention, but then wished he hadn't. When he looked away from viewport toward the strategium, he was reminded of the atmosphere on the ship. He knew that he was a trivial figure. Nithigg did him the honour of engaging in research with him, and Setheno had questioned him a few times on his theories, their evidence and his speculations. But most of the Black Dragons seemed to regard him, if they noticed him at all, as an underfoot nuisance. But even as far removed from the pulse of the *Immolation Maw* as he was, he could sense the tension aboard. They were going to battle. He knew that without being told. And they were going into battle deeply divided.

He didn't like thinking about that, either.

So he turned back to the view of the immense cenotaphs, and wondered how long he would be remembered when the inevitable happened.

Nessun felt the minds he owned arrive in-system. He had known, through them, of the demise of the *Metastasis* and its crew. Though his grip on the souls was growing strong, there was no pretending that the *Immolation Maw* had come for anything other than his destruction. So there were decisions to make. He needed a bit more time. He had to do whatever would gain him an edge, even if it were no more than seconds. In the end, he sent the bulk of his forces to Gemini Primus. It held what he was looking for. The rest, a bare minimum, accompanied him to the Gemini moon. Whatever happened on Primus, success or failure, that was the result that would determine the victory or loss on the moon.

Nessun wriggled into his captive minds. He planted suggestions, creating contingency plans for himself.

'Multiple contacts,' the servitor reported, its voice a dehumanised monotone. 'Deployment by troops of the *Revealed Truth*. Soulcage and primary ship moving from Gemini Primus to position of low anchor over moon.'

'What are they doing?' Symael wondered.

'It doesn't matter,' Toharan answered. 'What matters is that we stop them.' He spoke more from rote habit than belief. He wanted to know what was so important about Gemini to the Swords of Epiphany. For the greater glory of his Chapter (*his* Chapter), he would take their prize and wield it himself.

In the meantime, his gut told him that he was seeing the moment when he must begin the purge of the Dragons. His smile tight with hatred and anticipation, he gave his orders.

VOLOS WALKED ACROSS the launch bay toward the *Battle Pyre*. Around him was the cacophony of a war machine throwing itself into high gear. Munitions servitors ran their burdens to gunships. Space Marines performed last-minute weapon checks and spoke oaths of moment. New purity seals were affixed to armour. Second Company's largest mobilisation in years was under way.

Nithigg and Setheno walked with him. There was no hesitation in the canoness's stride. She had recovered from her wounds with great speed by the standards of mortals. Volos credited her ferocious will. He caught himself thinking this, and wondered why he was more aware of Setheno's will than of her faith.

'You won't be accompanying us this time, canoness?' Nithigg asked.

'No. I think I will be more useful on the ship.'

'Useful in doing what?' Volos probed, not really expecting an answer.

To his surprise, he received one. 'Whatever is necessary. You know the rest.' After a moment's pause, Setheno said, 'You do realise you are flying into a trap.'

'Every encounter with the Swords of Epiphany has been a trap of some kind,' Volos said. 'Why would this time be any different?'

'I am not referring to one of their ambushes. The trap is Toharan's.'

Nithigg grunted. 'Look at who is going and who is staying.'

Volos glanced around the launch bay, and saw what Nithigg meant. Toharan had shaken up the squad personnel yet again, but Volos hadn't noticed the pattern right away. Melus had finally been given Pythios to command, but Omorfos wasn't part of the squad at all now. Everywhere he looked, he saw that the Dragons heading to the surface of Gemini Primus were all the brothers he thought of as his allies, and any other warrior showing strong signs of mutation. Toharan had split up the company along physiological lines.

Nithigg pointed. 'The blessed, too.'

He used the word with both irony and reverence. Squad Solemnis was being led by Sergeant Lucertus to a drop pod. The abominations had been released from their holding cages. Chained and sedated, they would be unleashed on the planet's surface to revel in the full extent of their madness, becoming furies of ceramite, teeth, and slashing bone. Toharan was sending every reminder of Black Dragon identity off the ship.

Nithigg said, 'I don't think our captain expects us to return.'

'Then we'll disappoint him, won't we?'

AUGURS SHOWED THE traitor forces concentrated on the one geological anomaly of Gemini Primus. It was also the only feature that distinguished Primus from its twin. Running for a kilometre along the base of the equatorial mountain chain was a cave opening. It was no more natural than anything else about the planetoid, and in its length it suggested a seam more than a cave. Toharan's strategy was a triple assault, the Black Dragons coming in from east and west and the sky. 'Close the talon on them,' Toharan had commanded, 'and if they retreat into the cave, pursue them to the last man.'

And then what? Volos wondered. *Reward our victory with cyclonic torpedoes?*

But he had his orders, and more than that, he had a duty. Below was an Imperial world under attack by Chaos Space Marines. There was no alternative but to strike.

And so they struck. Drop pods rained down on Gemini Primus. The *Battle Pyre* was joined by its sister ships, the *Cleansing Judgement* and the *Nightfire*. With schism and betrayal snapping at their heels, the Black Dragons arrived to put the Swords of Epiphany to flame.

PEREGRINE DELACQUO HAD feared the nights since the appearance of the moon. Come the dark, he didn't harvest. He didn't set foot outside of his sod hut at all.

He didn't look out his window if he could avoid it. He took what comfort he could in the fact that he was not alone with his terrors. The orchards were deserted after dark. No one on Gemini Primus wanted to confront the moon's gaze.

But tonight, Delacquo was drawn outside despite himself by the shrieking roar of the heavens falling. To the west of the township of Fruition, in the dreadful light of the scarlet moon, there had first come ships like molten gold pouring from the sky. Now, iron tears were streaking to earth. Behind them came a trio of ships, black as night, with the force and blunt shape of metal fists.

'What is it?' His wife, Kaletha, had followed him.

'I don't know.' The only ships he had ever seen before were the venerable, barely voidworthy freighters used for what little trade went on between Primus and Secundus. He had never experienced war. The soil of the Twins was so fertile, the divides created by the mountains so difficult to cross, that regional conflicts were unnecessary and impractical. There had been no contact between Abolessus and the rest of the galaxy for uncounted generations. But the word *war* was now resounding through his mind and heart, and though he barely comprehended the term, it filled him with the same dread as the bloody moon.

He and Kaletha weren't the only ones out in the night. The good people of Fruition were spilling out of their homes. These were cabins built of logs and sod, the only building material available on an unbreakable world. The people were farmers, loggers, fishermen. Combat was as alien as the things that fell from the sky. But its serpent fascination drew them. Delacquo and Kaletha joined the procession heading west, that they might stare their fate in the face.

CHAPTER 24
THE DESCENT

THE VALLEY WAS so narrow and so straight; there was no way for a large force of the Black Dragons to surprise the Swords of Epiphany. The forests and agricultural lands ended long before the cave, giving way to bare adamantium. Lines of sight from the cave extended east and west to the horizon. The Swords would be able to see an advance coming from kilometres away. If the talon attack was going to work, it had to take advantage of the fact that the entrance to the cave was too wide to defend in its entirety, and it had to begin almost on top of the enemy.

So it did. The drop pods landed only a few dozen metres from the east and west ends of the cave mouth. The Thunderhawks swooped down over the top of the mountain chain, making a run for the centre of the opening, sending out a massive barrage of missiles and heavy bolter fire ahead of them. The Swords had the bulk of their forces inside the cave. The exterior was guarded by a mass of thousands of cultists. Their firepower was heavy, concentrated, and undisciplined. Rifle and las-fire stabbed out at the Dragons, so many lethal bristles exploding out. Some hit their mark. Most did not. Blind luck saw a drop pod blown up before it landed. But the Thunderhawks' inferno decimated the cultists. There was no cover, no dirt to absorb the blasts, nothing but the utterly unforgiving canvas of adamantium against which the bodies were splattered and painted by fire and concussive force.

'How close can you get us to the cave mouth?' Volos asked Keryon as the *Battle Pyre* raced to the floor of the valley.

'Watch and grovel before me,' Keryon's voice came back over the comm-bead.

Volos watched, and his eyes widened as the ground raced toward the Thunderhawk, eager for the kiss of impact. The doors opened just as Keryon levelled the ship at the last second, piloting the gunship as if it were a high-performance lighter.

'*Now*,' Keryon said, and as the Dragon Claws shot away from the hull, the *Battle Pyre* was already nose-up, its undercarriage breathing against the mountainside. Keryon had dropped them within metres of the roof of the cave mouth.

Streaking flame from their jump packs, the Claws stormed the cave. The floor, thirty metres below, was a perfect semicircle, reaching back a kilometre into the mountainside. In the middle of the floor was a circular depression, its diameter a third of the width of the chamber. The Swords had withdrawn to the depression, with half of them guarding its southern perimeter, facing the cave entrance. The others were busy slaughtering dozens of unarmed humans while holding hundreds of others at gunpoint. Strategically, the Swords were in an untenable position. There were about fifty of them, and though they had firepower and the buffer of their helots beyond the circle, they had no cover, and no retreat.

The Black Dragon tactical squads were already moving inside the cave, slicing through the cultists like they were cobwebs. Devastator lascannon shots scorched a path toward the defensive line. The Dragons advanced in a series of speartips, punching through the heretic mob. Moving up the centre of the cavern, ignoring such trivialities as enemy fire, was the whirling savagery of Squad Solemnis. Volos saw a gigantic cull ahead, and his fangs bared in hunger.

The Dragon Claws came down behind the Swords' line, between the defenders and the butchers. Bolter and blade bit into the enemy. The defensive formation came apart as the Swords responded to the threat at their backs. Volos stitched a traitor with explosive slugs from groin to head, and as the rounds detonated ceramite and body, he slammed his left arm out, decapitating another with his bone-blade. The jolt of the blade slicing through vertebrae ran up his arms, and he revelled in the tactile feel of the kill. To his right, Nithigg faced the other way, blasting the inner ring of Swords. One Chaos Space Marine made the mistake of coming at him from behind. Nithigg jabbed his arm back, the force of the hit enough to jam the forearm blade through the armour and disembowel the Sword.

Volos was surrounded by killing. Hungry for vengeance, raging at the harm that was befalling his company, he gave himself up to the rhythm of violence. He let his body be fire and bone. He became what he was designed to be. He was monster and he was death, and there was no stopping him. Every movement took a life. Finger pulled trigger and blew up a head. Arm thrust to impale, pulled out and swept to sever. Head ducked and horns gored face and throat.

Traitor Space Marines and heretic cultists rushing to their aid fell before him, and as the dance of war took him, there was no thought, and there was no grand purpose. There was only the perfect kill, the perpetual rending of body into pieces, the brutal pleasure of life ended again and again and again. Enemies landed blows on him. Blades stabbed through armour joints to tear muscle. Rounds chipped plate and took out chunks of flesh. But he was moving so fast, so fluidly, that his foes could never lock on to him with hands or with targeting sights long enough to bring him down. His Larraman cells rushed to fix the damage, clotting blood and knitting rips, but it was his frenzy more than anything else that took him beyond considerations of personal injury and bore him into the intoxicating nirvana of absolute war.

Then a Sword, as big as he was, wearing Terminator armour in the gold of sin, smashed him to the ground with a power fist. The traitor had lost his helmet, and as he raised his fist to reduce Volos's head to pulp, Volos took in the expression on his face. It was peaceful.

Volos's rage had already swallowed him whole, but now it spiked to a higher intensity yet. He had fought and killed all manner of Traitor Space Marines, but these were the only ones who were perpetually *delighted* in themselves and the wars around them. Volos felt something so close to envy it was sickening as he slammed both blades up into the Sword's groin. The warrior howled, his blow going wild as his entrails spilled over Volos and the floor. But as he fell, he gazed down at the ground, and the monster *smiled*, as if looking upon his work and seeing that it was good.

The incongruity of the expression slit through the haze of Volos's anger, and he was rational again as he rolled out of the way of the tumbling corpse. Volos examined the floor as he rose, bolter already up and firing into the enemy, and he noticed now the intricate runes that formed the texture of the adamantium floor. They were only present in the disc of the depression. He saw the blood flow over the shapes, and then be absorbed by a substance that could absorb nothing. He realised that a large portion of the Swords had continued to kill their prisoners, as if the deaths of these people who could pose no threat was more important than fighting off the Dragons.

And perhaps it was. Volos remembered the sacrifices that had activated the doors of the Flebis vault. His finger hesitated on the trigger as the thought came to him that with all the blood they were shedding, perhaps he and his brothers were doing the Swords' work for them. He looked to the advancing Dragons, saw how close they were, and realised that they were too far away to help.

The floor shuddered beneath his feet, and as the Swords roared their triumph, the circular platform (for that, Volos realised far too late, was what it was) dropped like a stone. Volos staggered while friend and foe around him lost their footing. He looked up. They were descending a shaft. A circle of light created by explosions and fire retreated to nothing in seconds. The plunge picked up speed. Volos felt himself growing lighter. He was almost in free fall. As the light from above vanished, the glow of the shaft became visible. Here too, the walls were covered in glyphs, and they shone, flashing by so quickly they were streaks of corpse-silver.

Faster yet, and when he tried to take a step, he floated. Though he knew he was falling, the three hundred metre-wide platform blocked the updraft he would normally have felt. The effect was of being in zero-gravity. In the second his body took to adjust to the new conditions, he processed the tactical situation. Hundreds of non-combatants, a few dozen cultists, the Swords of Epiphany down half their strength. But his squad had been hurt, too. The red runes of lost brothers flashed on his lens readout. Still with him, and already turning on the tumbling foe: Nithigg, Braxas, Vasuk, Liscar, Jesterka. That was all. It would be enough.

The Swords weren't slow in adapting, either. What had been the defensive line turned inward now, and the butchers left their prey alone, their job done. The battle resumed, but with an odd care and grace. There was an elegance to the strikes as the warriors contended with the laws of physics as much as with each other. A Sword hacked at Volos with a chainaxe. The movement was dream-slow, and Volos had all the time in the world to avoid it, except that his own actions were far behind his impulses. He used a brief kick from the jump pack to rise above the swing, then reversed thrust to smash into the traitor, impaling his skull. Blood fountained upward and was left behind.

And then the fight ended, because the platform fell even faster, burning past terminal velocity, and the moment it crossed that barrier, it grabbed its passengers. Artificial gravity kicked in, and Volos was slammed flat. The platform was keeping everyone alive as the speed became a blinding terror.

They had travelled for hours, passing through the planetoid's crust, when the platform dropped out of the shaft. Crimson light, the same shade as the moon, filled the world-sized cavern. Volos was near an edge of the platform. He dragged himself forward, looked down, and saw that the platform was actually a piston, retracting a length of thousands of kilometres. The core of Gemini Primus was hollow. The piston was off to one side of the empty sphere, and occupying the core was a bell the size of a small asteroid. The object was more terrible and awe-inspiring than any of the much larger monuments the *Immolation Maw* had passed on its journey through Abolessus. Those had been abstract shapes. This, like the organ on Flebis, was recognisable. It was something familiar, grown into a dark god.

The bell was the source of the light. It was suspended by a monumental yoke at the top of the cavern, and from the crown to the lip, it was textured with runes.

Volos could not read the dead language, nor did he wish to. But at a thousand kilometres' distance, these runes were not turned into smears by the speed of the fall. They mesmerised. They demanded contemplation. And they spoke. These runes were not those that the followers of the Ruinous Powers painted, carved and gouged onto every available surface. There was nothing here of the perverse, of cackling insanity and willed malevolence. Instead, the bell spoke of an unfathomable will indifferent to all but its own desires. The power that created this monster would think nothing of exterminating entire civilizations, not out of malice, but in the way a man crushes an ant hill that is in his way.

Volos saw a Sword crawling towards him. He waited, then managed to pull his legs free of the surface long enough to lash out. He kicked the Sword in the chest, and discovered that it was possible to overcome the piston's gravity. The Sword flew into the air, and then appeared to rocket up, vanishing into the stone sky. He was still falling, but at a normal speed. He would catch up and die when the piston stopped.

When the piston stopped…

Volos looked down again. He saw the base of the piston coming to meet them. The speed of the plunge hadn't slowed at all. They were rushing toward a series of linked, concentric rings. They looked like canals.

Pieces fell into place. The breathable atmosphere and the gravity that were keeping the civilians alive for the length of the journey. What would happen when the piston stopped? What would run down those canals?

Volos felt a moment of pity for the hundreds of

Mortisians on the piston. Some of them were rebels, but others, he knew, were just confused refugees. None of that mattered. There was nothing he could do.

'Ormarr,' he voxed. 'Jump packs for deceleration. Get off this thing. Now!'

He sat up, yanking himself away from the iron grip of the floor. Anvils weighed him down. He struggled to leap, and his jump pack blasted. There was a moment's hesitation when he was caught in a tug of war of forces, and then he shot up away from the piston. The rest of the squad was right behind him. He fired multiple bursts with the pack, slowing his descent. As the piston flashed down the last few metres, the Dragon Claws hovered briefly above the surface of the cavern. They were close enough to see the faces of those on the platform. Volos took in the terror of the civilians. A number of the Swords weren't wearing helmets, and Volos felt grim satisfaction in seeing their ecstasy shift, at the last second, to confusion. They hadn't been expecting this.

The piston stopped. There was no slowing down, no transition. One second it was a missile descending, and the next it was is if it hadn't moved at all. Volos couldn't imagine how its momentum was dissipated, but for a second the surface of the cavern blurred, as if the entire globe had vibrated. Everyone on the piston was crushed to paste. The transition from human being to liquid was instantaneous. There was, Volos thought as the Dragon Claws came down to land, an impressive efficiency to the sacrifice.

Blood and pulverised bone fragments flowed into the canals. The remains of a few hundred souls looked like a pitiful drop in the vastness of the cavern. The bell loomed overhead. He couldn't see how something so vast would be satisfied by an offering of this scale. Yet he knew it would be.

'Now what?' Vasuk asked.

Nithigg stared upward. 'I imagine we wait, unless someone has something like a teleporter stashed away in a belt.' After a moment he added, 'You realise that the gravity is still all wrong.' He pointed to the bell. 'I believe the actual centre of this world is in there. So we should be falling, not standing.'

Liscar grimaced. 'Like the Flebis vault,' he said. 'Space and time are twisted here.'

Nithigg nodded. 'This is more warp architecture.'

Volos watched the blood spread through the rings. Where the piston had been the bottom of a declivity on the surface of the planet, here it was the top of a rise. The entire ring structure was a few kilometres wide. It would have seemed big anywhere else. Here he resented how small it was, how quickly it would be filled, and how easily the coming event would be triggered.

Nithigg clapped him on the shoulder. 'I know,' he said.

'They're dead.' Volos snarled. 'They're crushed to nothing. How can it be that they're about to win again?'

Nithigg didn't answer. The Dragon Claws stood in silence and watched the blood fill the rings. It took less than an hour. Then a terrible day dawned as the red glow of the bell's runes became blinding. And with a ponderous, monstrous deliberation, the bell began to swing.

CHAPTER 25
THE MUSIC OF THE SPHERES

ON THE GEMINI moon, Rodrigo Nessun ran his hands over the embodiment of beauty. It was a musical instrument. Its shape made him think of an organ, in that there was a large primary body, ten metres high and twenty wide, and there were pipes of a kind. But these looked less like organ pipes than did the monsters of the Flebis vault. For one thing, once they emerged from the main mass of the instrument, they curved down and ran out of the temple before plunging beneath the smooth surface of the moon. For another, they were made of bone. So was the entire instrument. Where the keyboard should have been, Nessun was presented with a long chain of giant vertebrae. When he touched the backbone, he came into contact with something so smooth, so perfectly crafted to its purpose that it seemed to be stroking his hands rather than the other way around. The instrument was composed of individual bones. There were skulls, femurs, ribcages and hands of all sizes and variations, none of them human, none of them of any species he recognised. Thousands of bones, but the joins were so seamless, the machine also seemed to have been carved from a single, monolithic bloc of grey ivory.

The instrument held his hands and showed him where to place them. When the time came, he would be able to play it as if he were an extension of its being. His soul was legion, and so was this creation. Yet he and the instrument would also become a single expression of power and will. He bowed his head before the omnipotence of paradox.

Above the vertebrae was a large, smooth, convex surface of bone. It was in the shape of an eye ten metres across and blank as the gaze of a marble statue. He shivered with pleasure as he imagined the film drawn back. Soon. Soon.

The Gemini moon's temple was situated on its equator, its face precisely equidistant from Primus and Secundus. It rose from the surface like a cobra's hood, and was formed of the same rock as the moon itself: smoother than marble, harder than granite. It generated its own crimson light. The temple entrance was on the outer slope of the hood. The doorway was massive. Inside, a short corridor led to the main space of the temple. This was an enormous open area. Curving walls led up to a domed ceiling unsupported by columns. A stairway, its steps so huge they had to be climbed, wound around the wall, leading up to the transparent dome and, beneath it, a ringed observation platform. The dome appeared to be made of glass, though thicker than any Nessun had ever seen, and so clear that, at first glance, the temple appeared to be open to the air. Before the temple was a vast, fan-shaped, shallow depression. It stretched for kilometres. More than big enough to hold the tens of thousands of humans that stood there, disgorged from the *Foretold Pilgrimage*.

Other than the temple and its apron, the moon was featureless. There were no mountains or hills, not even any impact craters. There was no dust. The moon was as perfect and artificial as the Twins.

'Father,' Gabrille said.

'Yes?' Nessun listened with only half an ear. His hands travelled over the beautiful death of the instrument.

'We have lost all communication with the Gemini Primus contingent.'

The cardinal's hands paused. There was the possibility of enormous tragedy in this news. He might be about to find out that all his good work had been for nothing. He had, until now, resisted the temptation to attempt a mass conversion of the Black Dragons. The lure had been strong, but he had been virtuous in the pursuit of his goal, again and again trying to throw the Dragons off the scent. But they were as dogged as their captain was corruptible. He had begun to think that the conversion was not so much a temptation as fate, mapped out by the Changer of the Ways. He sensed that this was the moment of truth. 'What was the last report we had from them?' he asked.

'That the route to the resonator had been opened.'

Nessun smiled. The path before him became clear. The crucial step to completion had been taken, quite likely at the expense of a large portion of his forces. On board the *Revealed Truth*, there were only servitors now. He had twenty Swords of Epiphany with him on the moon. Not enough, depending on how many Dragons were still alive. But plenty to welcome new sheep to the fold.

He stepped away from the wonderful thing before him. He needed his full concentration. There were minds he had to touch. He did not need the amplifying power of the Hall of Exaltation here. The entire moon was impregnated with the magic of the warp. He asked, 'What is the disposition of the pilgrims?'

'They are ready.'

'Good,' he said, and went to work.

'WHAT CAN YOU tell me?' Toharan asked.

Maro consulted the data-slates before him. 'They're gathered at a point just over the horizon from us,' he said.

'Ship activity?'

'Minimal. The *Revealed Truth* is in low orbit, doing nothing at all, and the Soulcage has landed.'

'I see. Then prepare to assault the *Revealed Truth*.' The *Immolation Maw* was still limping from its wounds. But the ship was hungry, too, eager to get revenge on those who had hurt it. It was also a question of honour. He would destroy that ship and everyone aboard. There would be no running away for the Swords this time. Then he would go after what was left of them on the moon. And then–

His train of thought froze. As soon as the image of

being on the moon rose in his mind, he was hit by a staggering wave of desire. He didn't know what was on the moon. He didn't know what the Swords wanted. But he wanted it, too. He must have it. The scrabbling in his brain was frantic, but it would ease if he could win this prize.

He dragged himself back to the present. There was a pain behind his eyes, like the crawling of spiny worms. He shoved it to the back of his mind. 'Take us to the edge of the atmosphere,' he told Maro. 'We come over the horizon at the traitor ship with a full barrage.'

'We won't have any other moves after that one,' Maro said.

'I'm aware of that.' The *Maw* had its arsenal, but in its damaged state, its manoeuvrability would be far less than that of the *Revealed Truth*. 'So let our first strike be the fatal one.'

Maro said nothing, though Toharan could read his scepticism. The helmsman believed he was crossing the line between daring and reckless stupidity. His feelings were understandable. He was impure, his skull topped by a massive club of bone. Perfect for smashing doors open head-first, but clearly insensitive to intimations of destiny. Maro was another who would be left behind as the Disciples of Purity rose from the ashes of the Black Dragons. Toharan would deal with him when the time came.

Toharan watched the primary pict display in the strategium as the *Immolation Maw* made its attack run. Unlike on Flebis, the *Revealed Truth* was too low to approach from beneath. The assault was more frontal. The Chaos cruiser came into sight over the curve of the planetoid as the *Maw* opened up with its frontal turrets and a full torpedo salvo. Toharan felt the rush of destiny fulfilled when he saw that they had come upon the *Truth* on its starboard flank. Withering fire raked the superstructure, blasting apart the crown of the command spire. The torpedoes slammed into the hull, blowing open enormous holes. A series of hits to the rear detonated an engine compartment. The ship's stern bucked upward, while its bow dipped towards the surface of the moon.

'Well played, helmsman,' Toharan said.

Maro grunted. He sounded dissatisfied, not triumphant. He leaned back in the pilot throne and turned his head to look at Toharan. With the mechadendrites webbing him to the chair, he struck Toharan as even more disgusting than if he were standing free with only his natural deformities on view. 'There is no return fire,' Maro said.

'Then we have landed an even more telling blow than we could have hoped–' Toharan began.

'And where are their void shields?'

That gave him pause. 'What?'

'The Chaos ship had its shields down. I refuse to believe that was a mistake.'

Toharan had no answer. He looked from the pict to the viewport and watched the *Revealed Truth*, its hull shuddering with secondary explosions and gouting flame, begin its funereal plunge into the Gemini moon's atmosphere. A suspicion grew into a theory and, with a flutter of insect wings against his cortex, became a certainty.

'They wanted us to destroy it,' Symael muttered,

echoing Toharan's thoughts.

'Where is it going to hit?' Toharan asked.

Maro absorbed data fed to him by the ship's augurs. 'Very close to where the Soulcage landed.' After a pause, he continued, 'There is some sort of structure there, too.'

The sense of destiny ran through Toharan's frame again like an electric shock. 'That is our target. We land with full force of arms.'

NESSUN MOUNTED TO the observation dome of the temple. He looked at the assembled masses. Over a hundred thousand strong, the refugees were all looking up at the dome of the temple. He lifted his arms to them, and they lifted theirs back. Through the glass of the dome, he could hear the roar of worship and supplication. The people knew they had been taken to a holy place. But they didn't know why, or what was to become of them. He would answer both of their questions. He pointed to the heavens. The vision of gold and light that greeted him filled him with enormous joy, and his ecstasy was contagious. For the next few seconds, the crowd shared his emotion, and he heard them exclaim in wonder. It was a pity this perfect unity wasn't going to last, but he revelled in the irony while it did.

The moment stretched out until the crowd realised what the flashes and fire above them represented. Shapes defined themselves, and the play of light and flame became the burning, erupting hulk of the *Revealed Truth* plummeting down to spread its final gospel. The swell of wonder became the howl of terror. The cruiser filled the sky. It was comet and cathedral, and the storm of its destruction drowned out the cries on the ground. The observation platform was high enough for Nessun to see the delicious patterns that panic drew in the crowd. He thought he saw some familiar symbols in the shifting, hysterical vectors of blind flight. Refugees on the outer edges of the multitude fled the apron. Nessun wasn't worried. They couldn't get far in a matter of seconds. They would still be part of the burnt offering, and would give their souls to the imminent beauty.

The *Revealed Truth* hit. The explosion filled the world. Fire of stellar brilliance washed over the dome. Nessun put a hand against the glass. It was cool, but the atomic inferno beyond was so close that Nessun rejoiced he had lived to touch the face of a sun. The refugees were annihilated in the light of truth, incinerated by the breath of Chaos and crushed by the weight of fate. Nessun couldn't hear his own laugh, but he felt it threaten to tear his cheeks open. He exulted as the rage of the cruiser's death embraced the temple. This was the apotheosis of his existence.

And there was even greater beauty to come.

As the bell reached the height of its swing and started back down, Volos saw the mountain-sized clapper arc towards the mouth. The movement seemed leisurely, though he knew that, given the size of the objects and the distances they covered, he was looking at an event that was occurring at thousands of kilometres per hour.

There was time, though, time for Volos to anticipate the coming of the sound. But he couldn't prepare for its immensity.

The bell rang. It sounded a note that transcended the aural. The toll boomed out from the bell and expanded not at the speed of sound, but at the speed of light. There was no resisting it. The Dragon Claws fell as it hit, hammered by a fist the size of the universe. Volos felt Gemini Primus in its entirety reverberate. The resonance reached into his soul, and he had a momentary impression of the vibration stretching its grasp beyond the planetoid. He had the terrible sense of being *tuned*.

The bell swung once only, and then returned to its position, motionless. The moment it finished, the piston fired upward again. The Dragons lay where they had been flattened by the bell's ring. As the piston streaked toward its starting point, Volos was reminded of a gun mechanism. Gemini Primus was re-arming itself, ready for another sacrifice to be provided. Volos didn't think one would be necessary.

The whistle had been blown. The bell had tolled. One single note each time. That was all it took.

With an effort, he turned his head. Nithigg was facing him. He couldn't see his battle-brother's eyes behind the red of the helmet's lenses, but Nithigg managed a nod. Volos returned it. They had been reduced to ants by the scale of events. They had been outflanked and outmanoeuvred again and again. They had been betrayed.

But they were alive. They were Adeptus Astartes. They were Black Dragons.

They were the Emperor's monsters, and no matter what resources the archenemy had, no matter how many planets he threw at them, they would teach him fear.

* * *

Toharan knew some moments of indecision as he chose who would descend to the moon's surface with him, and who would remain on the *Immolation Maw*. He was torn between having sufficient force on the ground and ensuring he kept his grip on the *Maw*. In the end, he chose to hit the site of the temple with the entire contingent of the Disciples of Purity. He left the ship in Lettinger's care, making it clear to Maro on the bridge and Ydraig in the engine room that the inquisitor had the captain's absolute confidence and would be speaking with his voice. He did not like having Setheno out of his sight. He couldn't command that she accompany the landing party, though he could, he was sure, enforce her presence. That was a battle that didn't seem worth fighting. He would embrace his destiny on the Gemini moon, then return to deal with the canoness.

He landed by drop pod in the company of the thirty loyal Disciples. It was the first time he had gone into action solely with the pure and the converted. He looked at his men with pride. In their armour, they were indistinguishable from most of the other Black Dragons, whose deformities weren't sufficient to require helmet or vambrace modifications. But he knew what was under the ceramite. While only he was completely free of disfigurement, none of his troops had worse than a few bone gnarls on their heads. With time, and new recruits, he would reverse the damage done by the Dragon Apothecaries, and take his Chapter back to a physical ideal that rejected the corruption of being. Some drastic measures might yet be necessary to hasten the process. He was not afraid of taking those steps.

Transcendence awaited, and to hesitate or show mercy would be a surrender. He refused to be shackled to the filth of imperfection any longer.

As the Disciples closed in on the temple entrance, he was struck by a new revelation. Why was he so concerned with remaking the Black Dragons? He had already rejected everything the Chapter stood for. Lettinger was right: it was beyond saving. So was anything that knelt to that disgusting mass of being on the Golden Throne. The Black Dragons were dead. The armour he and his true brethren wore was a thing of the past and a celebration of imperfection. The name they had chosen as a mark of their will and their goal was, he now realised, the true expression of their identity. They *were* the Disciples of Purity. They were not a mere group of like-minded battle-brothers. They were his Legion, and he would be their primarch.

He was quivering at the touch of glory as they arrived at the temple doors. They stood open. There had been no defensive line set up around the temple. There was no one inside the corridor that stretched ahead. Toharan paused at the threshold. The space was rather wide for an ambush, but the absence of resistance meant something had to be waiting for them here. He turned to Symael. The sergeant was consulting his auspex.

'No one here,' Symael reported, sounding just as puzzled. 'I have multiple readings in the larger space beyond.'

Were the Swords waiting to kill them as they emerged from the corridor? But the hall was much too wide to be an effective bottleneck. The strategy was ludicrous.

If anything, the Swords were backing themselves into a corner.

Jemiah said, 'They can't be this stupid.'

'They haven't been so far,' Toharan agreed. He had the Disciples advance along three lines, one on either side of the corridor, and his reforged Squad Nychus up the middle. Halfway along, they could see what was waiting for them in the temple's great hall. Rodrigo Nessun stood before an immense device of bone. He was flanked on either side by the Swords of Epiphany. They stood at attention.

Their weapons were mag-locked.

Nessun was smiling.

Toharan knew that, from a tactical point of view, he should stop his advance immediately. He should retreat from the obvious trap. But destiny spoke louder, and kept him moving. The mind-writhing was agonising, and though the pain should have dulled his vision, instead it sharpened it. The world was crystalline. It was transparent all the way to the heart of existence, yet fragile, ready to shatter in his fist. This was the right thing to do. It was the only thing to do. He was walking toward the moment that the universe had prepared for him.

'Captain...' Symael began.

Toharan said, 'Walk at my side, brother-sergeant.' He aimed his bolter at the ground.

Nessun spread his arms. 'Welcome, my sons,' he said.

The Swords of Epiphany began to beat their hands together. The rhythm built as the Dragons entered the hall, the smack of ceramite gauntlets becoming a wave of thunderous applause. Toharan saw the tension in the body movement of the Disciples. Their instinct to open fire was a difficult one to overcome. The fact that they triumphed over it told him that they, too, felt the truth and inevitability of this moment. The scrabbling insects retreated as he felt his spirit soar. One look at Nessun's face, and at the exhilaration in his eyes, made it clear that he was in the company of a visionary. Toharan had been so wrong. They all had, to have seen the Swords as the enemy.

Nessun reached towards him. 'Will you take my hand?' he asked.

Toharan stepped forward and did.

At that moment, the very cosmos tolled. Everything shifted. The resonance thrummed through moon and temple, bone and mind. Toharan's vision shimmered as he staggered, then clicked back into place, and the moon was suddenly home as nothing had ever been in his life. He and Nessun caught each other, and he held the cardinal up. As they straightened, he looked around and saw that the other Disciples had lost their wariness as they recovered from the toll. They knew they belonged.

'What was that?' Toharan asked.

'It was the tuning,' Nessun answered. 'The moon and Abolessus Gemini are now properly synchronised.' He walked to the instrument and placed his hands on the massive vertebrae. 'And now, if our latest burnt offering was large enough... Ah,' he sighed, and the sound was almost humble.

The blank eye of bone above Nessun opened. It was a pict screen of some kind, and at first it seemed to be merely a viewport, looking out onto the temple's apron. There, the smouldering wreckage of the *Revealed Truth* lay in twisted fragments over a carpet of burned, crushed, melted and fused corpses. Nessun moved his hands. The corpses slowly flowed into one another, gristle and skeleton and blood becoming one, becoming nothing, thousands and thousands and thousands of souls absorbed by the capricious demands of the song of the warp. As the corpses disappeared into the glowing crimson surface of the moon, Toharan became aware of music. It did not play for his ear, but he sensed the melody all the same, gathering up his spirit, expanding his heart with the touch of the dark numinous as the song grew. The melody line was simple in the beginning, but as it repeated, it layered and doubled back on itself, intertwined with subtle variations, and gradually became a chorus that was majesty and power. As it reached its first enormous swell, Nessun cried, 'Look! Oh, look!'

The eye-shaped screen was not just a viewport. When Nessun shouted, the view shifted to Gemini Primus and Secundus. The screen blinked, and the planetoids appeared closer, filling the screen. Toharan noticed Nessun's head tilted back to look at the eye, and realised that it had become his sight, responding to his desire, following the focus of his attention and showing him what he wished to see. Toharan saw what had made Nessun exult. He saw where the music came from. It was the song of the Gemini configuration. The planetoids and the moon had become a choir.

And they danced with each other. The music swelled

again, and Primus and Secundus began to move. Their rotation was speeding up. Toharan could actually see their spin. He shook his head. At those speeds, the centripetal forces should have shaken the spheres apart. But they were adamantium, and what was one more impossibility in an entire system of miracles? One more was nothing. So why not another?

Why not?

As he watched and listened, the music sounded another triumph, and the planetoids began moving closer together.

CHAPTER 26
GRINDER

VOLOS EXPECTED THE piston to stop at its original position as suddenly as it had down below. He knew that his jump pack would not have enough power to counter his momentum, and that he and the other Dragon Claws would be splattered against the cavern ceiling. He knew this, but he would fight for his life anyway, as if sheer will could overcome the laws of physics. *It can*, he told himself. *The Emperor Himself is the living proof.*

But as the light of the surface cavern reappeared, a pinprick at the end of the shaft, the piston slowed. There was only purpose in its instant deceleration where it was part of the sacrificial altar. It eased into its slot in the cavern and became nothing more than the floor again, until the next time blood would spur it to action.

The Claws picked themselves up. They were greeted by Squad Pythios, knee-deep in dead cultists and a few dismembered Swords. Melus was standing by the edge of the piston. 'Nice of you to join us,' he said. 'Now if you don't mind, we should depart this Throne-accursed world immediately.'

'Dare I ask?' Volos said.

Melus led them out of the cavern. He pointed up.

DELACQUO HELD KALETHA to his chest. They were on the ground, lying where they had fallen when the toll of the bell had shattered their strength and their comprehension. Delacquo didn't want Kaletha to see the sky. He wanted to protect her from what he saw. But she was looking. They all were. The people of Fruition had come to see their fate, and now it was upon them.

Delacquo had watched the conflict between the iron gods. He had expected destruction to come in the form of bullets, swords or explosions, as he and his fellow villagers discovered the face of war. Then war had shown itself to be far vaster than he could have imagined.

The heavens had become a spinning insanity, but one that was not without a terrible purpose. Day became night and then day again. The sun rose and set in minutes, and it did so in fewer minutes each time. Gemini Secundus was spinning too. As it arced from horizon to horizon, again and again, Delacquo saw the lights of its colonies flash past. It seemed to be spinning at the same rate as Primus. Delacquo watched the same configuration of lights curve away each time the sister planet passed by overhead. And each time, the spin and the passage were faster. Delacquo felt he should be clutching the ground to keep from being thrown off into space.

He also felt flattened. He wished he could dig himself deep into the earth to hide, because each time Secundus appeared, he could see the cities a bit more clearly. Clusters of lights that had been a blob resolved themselves into distinct communities. Secundus was coming closer. The perfect lines of the mountain ranges took on an awful significance. It was so easy to picture what was coming, it seemed strange no one had conceived of the possibility before. The mountain chains of Primus and Secundus would interlock. The two adamantine spheres would roll together.

Grinding.

Delacquo began to weep. He hoped he was the only one who had realised the shape of doom. Kaletha touched his face. He looked down into her eyes. She knew, too. How could she not? Everyone knew. No one was going to die alone.

That was no comfort.

THE BLACK DRAGONS boarded the three Thunderhawks. There was enough room in the transports to haul all of the warriors back in one trip. The question was whether there would be somewhere to haul them back to.

'The *Immolation Maw* is not at anchor over Primus,' Keryon reported.

'I don't care if it's back on Terra,' Volos answered. 'Lift off now.'

As the assault ramp closed, Volos took a last look at the people of Gemini Primus. He had seen the crowd, lying prone and huddled, when he emerged from the cave. They were a few hundred metres east of the battlefield. They had been drawn to bear witness to their world at war. Now they were witnessing its end, and Volos could do nothing for them. He wondered if this was the shape of the new role of the Dragons, the role defined by Canoness Setheno: to be the monsters and bring the Emperor's terror and vengeance, but never to help the population of the planets where they raged.

If that was the Emperor's will, he would accept it. But he allowed himself the luxury of pity.

The *Battle Pyre*, the *Cleansing Judgement* and the *Nightfire* rose with the ponderous deliberation of Cretacia saurians. The atmosphere of Gemini Primus was becoming turbulent as the spin increased and Secundus closed in, gravitational fields and torque wreaking havoc with weather patterns. The wind picked up in a matter of seconds, shrieking down the narrow valley between the mountains, slamming into the Thunderhawks as if it were the gale of Aighe Mortis, come for unfinished business. Volos felt the *Battle Pyre* shake from the hammering gusts. In the time it took to climb to the height of the mountains, the spin became greater yet, and when Secundus flashed into view, it filled the heavens. As the gunships rose higher yet, Secundus and Primus appeared to be the same size. Volos realised the Thunderhawks were at a point almost equidistant between the two planets, and they were still within the atmosphere of Primus.

'WHAT IS IT?' Toharan asked, awed. The two bodies were almost touching now. He saw how they would interlock, and how the twin planetoids were really a single mechanism.

'An artist's tool,' Nessun answered. 'You saw the masterworks that make up this system. Where do you think the raw material came from? This is the means by which a planet is disassembled before its elements are recombined in a more aesthetically pleasing form.'

THE ATMOSPHERES OF Gemini Primus and Secundus touched. The friction superheated the air. *Battle Pyre* and its sister ships raced for the sanctuary of the void, their shields glowing as they were surrounded by hurricanes of fire. Strapped down by his restraint harness, Volos looked out a viewing block, and lost all sense of up and down. He could see little now but incandescence and tumbling immensity. Mountain peaks blurred past above and below the Thunderhawk. Two fists were about to connect, crushing everything between them.

TOHARAN SHOOK HIS head in bemused wonder. 'Was the species who built this mad? To expend so much power and effort in so nonsensical a fashion...'

Nessun's hands caressed vertebrae as delicately as if they were a hummingbird's wings. 'You do them wrong, my son,' he said. 'Do not mistake caprice for illogic. Perversity has a rigour of its own. You have fought in the False God's armies long enough to know that Chaos can have a very definite purpose. Every element of the art that you have witnessed has a reason to exist. Did you notice, for instance, how rich the soil of the Gemini bodies is?'

'In passing.' In the preparations for the invasion of Primus, he had taken in, as background data, the extensive farmlands and lack of industry.

'Now why would that be?' Nessun asked rhetorically, his voice lilting as his body responded to the shifts in the instrument's melody. 'Adamantium does not erode. The fertile topsoil would have to be placed there deliberately. What purpose would it serve? I'll tell you. It was a lure. Bait.'

'For what?'

'Sacrifice.'

DELACQUO GASPED. THE air felt like glowing embers in his lungs. Kaletha was screaming. So was he. They all were, but Delacquo couldn't hear their voices. They were drowned out by another scream: the shriek of the compressed and burning atmospheres. He saw the blinding rage begin in the clouds and descend towards him. It was the flaming grasp of a daemon god, come to obliterate everything. As the brilliance of the endfire filled his vision, he could still see the terrible spinning movement that was the engine of the destroying heat. In his last second before agony bright as wisdom reduced him to ash, he saw mountains falling towards him like descending fangs.

'AND WHY SACRIFICE? Because nothing comes from nothing. The machine of art needs fuel.'

GEMINI PRIMUS AND Secundus met, meshed, and rolled against each other. Mountain ranges filled valleys. The grinder absorbed the energy of two billion souls incinerated in a matter of seconds. The flaming ruins of cities and villages were smashed to dust. The only evidence that humans had ever set foot on the surface of either body was the operation of the machine itself. A civilization died, priming the mechanism that destroyed it for more.

'And why blood for fuel? It is, of course, one of the essential essences of warp sorcery. But the use of blood holds a lesson, too, as has every baroque step in the activation of this great machine. Its creators, it is clear, were beings possessed of infinite will and absolute amorality. How beautiful they must have been. Can you see the logic of the path they left for us? It was a test. To walk the path, we must prove ourselves worthy as artists. We must be able to hear the music, to see that there *is* music, and follow the logic from whistle, to bell, to organ. And we must prove our will. To use the machine is to be an annihilator. If we cannot provide blood, how will we have the strength to take it?'

The Battle Pyre was prey in the jaws of a wolf. Heat and gravity shook it, tore at it, squeezed it. Inside its hull, the only sense of movement was a lunatic, violent jerking, smashing its passengers in every direction. If they hadn't been fastened down, they would have been broken like eggs against the bulkheads. Volos felt its machine-spirit howl. From the comm-bead in his ear, he could just make out an imaginative stream of invective from Keryon as he fought to keep the

Thunderhawk on an escape course.

Then, something new was added to the shrieking roar outside the ship. It was the rumbling, cracking thunder of a planet-wide earthquake. It went on and on, a steady, endless apocalypse drum roll. The planetoids had met. Volos kept his gaze steady. If the end had come, he would stare it down.

There was a sudden piercing flash. He saw the death throes of the *Cleansing Judgement*. Flying on the *Battle Pyre*'s starboard, and half a length behind, it had been killed by the vortices of the colliding worlds. It broke apart as it burned, flinging wreckage and bodies to the insane winds. Thirty battle-brothers vanished. Volos's vision strobed red with rage.

It was as if his need for vengeance shielded the *Battle Pyre* and *Nightfire*. They found a trough in the storm and shot forward, slipping through the grip of Gemini. They touched the void. Their pilots threaded the needle, finding the one spot where the gravitation fields of the two bodies cancelled each other out, and the gunships streaked away from the grinder.

The shaking eased as the *Battle Pyre* put some distance between itself and the machine. Volos released his harness and made his way to the cockpit. Keryon gave him a quick nod as Volos slid into the seat beside him. 'Well flown, brother,' Volos said.

Keryon grunted. After a moment he said, 'A terrible loss.'

'A terrible crime,' Volos corrected. 'Our dead battle-brothers cry out for justice. Let us deliver it.'

* * *

'Sergeant Volos requires immediate docking for the *Battle Pyre* and *Nightfire*,' Maro said.

'Remain on station,' Lettinger told him.

Tennesyn turned from the hololithic display of the Gemini horror to watch the exchange.

'It was not a request.' Maro was staring at Lettinger as if he were a being several steps less impressive than a gretchen.

'Nor is this. Your captain left clear orders. No aid will be given to that traitor.'

Maro turned away from the inquisitor. He snorted in contempt. 'Coming about,' he said.

Lettinger drew his laspistol and placed the muzzle against the back of Maro's head. 'I know what you could do to me if you ever rose from that throne,' he said. 'So you should know that I will kill you if you so much as lean forward. Now. The ship remains on station. If Sergeant Volos's ships come into view, destroy them.'

The port-side bridge door slid open, admitting Canoness Setheno. She wasn't wearing her helmet, and Tennesyn found himself wishing that she were. The face of ice unnerved him more than the stand-off at the pilot's throne. She paused by the entrance, taking in what Lettinger was doing. She said nothing.

Lettinger cleared his throat. 'Canoness,' he began.

Setheno raised her bolt pistol.

Lettinger ducked around Maro, using him as a shield. Setheno hesitated, and Lettinger fired around the pilot. Setheno dived to the left as Lettinger's shot killed a targeting servitor and blew up his station. Lettinger stayed low and ran from the bridge, out the starboard door.

Setheno hurried to Maro's side. 'I am uninjured,' he told her.

She turned to Tennesyn. 'I trust I don't need to ask where your loyalties lie.'

'With the Emperor,' Tennesyn blurted. Setheno continued to stare at him. Tennesyn's mind wanted to shut down until her gaze went elsewhere. 'And Sergeant Volos,' he offered, and the paralyzing eyes moved on. She swept from the bridge after Lettinger.

'And now?' Toharan asked.

'Now,' Nessun said, 'we feed on Imperial planets. The deaths of the local Gemini populations have given us enough energy for some travel.'

'This thing can *move?*' Toharan.

Nessun nodded, his face rapt as he played. 'Oh yes,' he said. 'And the more it eats, the farther it can go. But let's begin with somewhere relatively near. Within the subsector. Captain, I give you the honour of choosing.'

The selection was obvious. Toharan smiled. He had tried to show mercy, and he had tried to teach through example. Both had failed. Now it was time to demonstrate that he simply was not to be trifled with. Better yet, the grinder would exterminate any trace of impurity. 'Aighe Mortis,' he said.

There. He had ordered an attack on the Imperium. The final line had been crossed. He drew his chainsword, pushed the activation stud, and marked the moment. He drew the whirring blade over his chestplate and pauldrons, destroying the Imperial markings. The Disciples followed his example. Dragons and aquilas disappeared, and Toharan rejoiced in the ecstasy of conversion.

CHAPTER 27
INTERNECINE

Lettinger raced through the corridors of the *Immolation Maw*. He could hear the canoness's footsteps. They sounded like a bell tolling for him. She was having no difficulty keeping up. He wasn't losing her. Good. He had guessed that, sooner or later, this moment would come. He was ready for it. He ran down the levels toward the prison chapel. There, he tore down the transept, activating wards behind him. He ducked down behind the altar, pistol out, and waited.

Setheno arrived at the chapel. She paused for a moment at the entrance. Lettinger sensed her evaluating the scene. He smirked. It was the least she could do to acknowledge the work he and Toharan had put into the space. He doubted she had ever been down here, but she would still know that changes had been wrought. Most of them had happened after the failed attack on Volos's cell, during the final hours in the warp, at the last meeting of the Disciples of Purity. The hole in the altarpiece where the icon of the Emperor had been was now a deeper void. The edges were rounded, and darkness dripped from them to the floor of the chapel. The stonework of the walls was blurry when looked at directly, and there was a subtle, twitching, oily movement just visible on the floor. There were no new symbols supplanting the ones that had been destroyed. Replacing one god with others was still, Lettinger believed, not what this struggle was about. It was about power, and who was worthy to wield it. This was what he told himself. It was a litany he repeated even now, as Setheno started forward again, striding right into the trap.

It triggered when Setheno was halfway down the transept. The attack came from two directions. Darkness bunched up behind and in front of her, and spat out two daemons. They were pink, giggling abominations, heavy bulks of flesh sprouting multiple arms and legs. Jagged-toothed mouths surfaced and sank, now in the centre of the mass, now at the top, now at the side, now at the rear. The horrors taunted and leered at Setheno as they rolled and bounded over pews, hurling gibberish insults at her that they seemed to expect she would understand. Lettinger had the unaccountable suspicion that perhaps she did.

The daemons cavorted about her, keeping their distance as they launched missiles from their palms. Setheno ducked and lunged forward as shifting, prismatic bolts passed over her head. She fired her bolt pistol behind, knocking one horror off-balance as it scrambled away from the rounds. She swept her power sword ahead of her. Aura crackling, the blade sliced through the lower limbs of the other daemon. The creature tumbled forward, snarling and laughing as it grew two new ones. But as it did so, it rolled towards Setheno. A joke caught in its mouth as she rose over it and brought her blade sizzling down through its chest. The daemon wailed. It bulged out on its sides, its flesh shading from obscene pink to a festering blue, and then, a hellish amoeba, it split.

Lettinger tried to get a clear shot at Setheno, but she and the daemons were moving too quickly. If he accidentally shot the horrors, he might redirect their attacks his way. So he waited for his opportunity, and smiled that Setheno now faced three daemons.

She seemed to have expected this. The two blue monsters, sobbing and screaming at each other, were just rearing back, hands upraised to unleash their warping assault, when Setheno struck again. The impaling move had been just the first step of her killing dance. She reversed the blade and thrust up, slicing the daemon on her left in half. With a babbling ululation, it vanished. The sword arced over and down into the other, and sent it back to the warp, too.

Setheno threw herself sideways, into a row between pews. Arms and multi-jointed fingers grasping air, the remaining horror landed where she had been a moment before. It fell in a heap, amused and ranting as it tangled its limbs. It sprouted others and righted itself. As it did, it fired a salvo of warp bolts Setheno's way. She deflected them with the sword. Lettinger gaped as Setheno straightened, the blade moving so quickly it became sheet lightning. Skarprattar wasn't harmed by the mutating powers of the daemon's missiles. Its aura grew blinding, and the chapel was filled with a piercing, purifying, flute-like song. Setheno lowered the sword and poured her pistol's entire clip into the daemon. The storm of explosive bolts blew the monster apart, spreading its flesh across the chapel too quickly for it to divide into coherent halves. The stench of ozone and slaughterhouse lingered after the remains evaporated.

Lettinger whipped around the altar, his pistol on full-auto, and bombarded Setheno with las-fire. She had barely released her trigger, and he hit her before she had time to react. He scored smoking holes in her armour. She dropped her empty gun and charged him. Lettinger leaped over two rows of pews and ran, firing all the time. She couldn't hurt him as long as he stayed out of reach of that sword.

They danced around the chapel, he keeping his distance and harassing her with las-fire, she closing relentlessly, the blade before her. She showed no interest in retrieving and reloading her gun. Not that she would have a chance. Lettinger knew where he stood in this battle. The reflective flak armour beneath his cloak wouldn't be worth a thing against the power sword. But it granted him mobility and speed he could use against Setheno. If she paused, if she looked away even long enough to grab her pistol, he would reduce her head to ash.

Setheno seemed to grow weary of the dance. Lettinger had circled back around to the chancel, and

Setheno stopped in the crossing. She watched him, saying nothing. He mirrored her confidence. He stood before the altar, in the open, taunting her for her lack of foresight in expending her ammunition. She didn't appear frustrated. There was still no emotion at all on that colder-than-alabaster face. Lettinger felt his blood pressure rise, infuriated by the canoness's sanctimonious calm. He had the urge to scream at her, to hurl imprecations and blasphemies until he finally provoked a reaction from that abyssal impassivity. With some difficulty, he mastered his temper. *Just kill her*, he told himself. He fired until his power pack came up dry. She deflected the head shots with her sword, but otherwise stood there, maddeningly stoic, absorbing the shots with her armour, and staggered only once. Fuming, Lettinger thumbed the release on his pistol. The power pack fell to the floor. He pulled out a spare from his belt. He glanced down as he slapped it home beneath the barrel. The Litany of Loading, so meaningless to him now, sprang unbidden to his lips. He looked back up.

He had underestimated Setheno's speed in the armour. She closed the distance between them while he was still realising what he was seeing. By the time he thought to react, she had brought the sword up between his legs, slicing until the hilt was just below his breastbone. He stared at it for a moment, frowning, wondering just how this turn of events could be compatible with everything he was supposed to accomplish. His eyes, growing sluggish, rose to meet Setheno's. The Gorgon towered over him, considering him with no more interest than she would a pinned butterfly. He waited for her valediction.

He knew the form. He had followed it himself, not that long ago (an eternity ago). He expected formal judgement.

He did not receive it, unless it was delivered in the sovereign contempt with which she yanked the blade back down, opening him wide. Lettinger emptied himself onto the chapel floor. The wet slap of organs against stone was the last thing he heard.

When there was no response from the *Immolation Maw*, Volos instructed Keryon to make for the Gemini moon. He voxed Lucertus in the *Nightfire* with the same order. 'Do we have enough fuel?' he asked the pilots.

'To get there, yes,' Lucertus answered. 'Afterwards, if the ship isn't near...'

'Then we'll have nowhere to go anyway. We end things there, or we end.'

'Maybe both,' Keryon mused.

'As long as that traitor's blood drips from my blades, I will accept that result with a grateful spirit.'

Toharan stared at the completed grinder. He drank in the sight of worlds transformed into an engine of perfect annihilation. There, before him, captured by the eye of bone, was the promise of something even more important than what Nessun was preaching. He could see the art. He could see the weapon this represented. The Imperium would fall before a beast that was fed by the very destruction it caused. But did even Nessun understand the gift of that destruction? Toharan could barely articulate it to himself, though he could feel it in his breast and in his soul. He had just been witness to the reduction of billions of lives to *nothing*. Aighe Mortis would be ground to dust. Exterminatus left the husk of the planet behind, but the grinder returned matter to the void. It would deal a death blow not only to the Imperium, but to existence itself. The terrible pressure of being would ease as he travelled on this chariot of oblivion. He would see the universe reduced to purity under its wheels.

Toharan smiled. Toharan laughed. He was giddy. He felt liberated. He experienced true joy for the first time in his living memory.

And then Volos had to spoil the perfect moment.

'Approaching ships, Father,' a Sword said.

Toharan saw them too: bright specks emerging from the grinder, streaking away from the very nexus of the destruction. Nessun noticed, and the eye-screen changed focus and perspective. It narrowed its attention to the specks, magnifying them, revealing their identity. 'Thunderhawks,' Toharan muttered, cursing.

'How long before they reach us?' Nessun asked.

Toharan ran some numbers in his head. 'About an hour.'

Nessun never took his hands from the vertebrae as he spoke. 'And you control the strike cruiser?'

'Yes.'

'Then there is nothing they can do to harm this temple.' There was a hint of strain in the cardinal's voice, and he spoke slowly, as if it were hard for him to keep track of his own words. The instrument was demanding his concentration, leaving little for the rest of reality. 'Deny them access, and they will shatter into foam against the rocks of our defence.'

The Thunderhawks were entering the moon's atmosphere when Maro broke the vox silence. The *Immolation Maw* was speaking to its children again. 'Apologies, captain,' Maro said. 'There has been some heretical activity aboard, but the ship bathes in the Emperor's light once more.'

'I am not your captain, brother,' said Volos.

'But you are. That pretty-faced traitor down there is no captain of mine.'

'You have my gratitude, brother-helmsman. Please stand ready.'

The gunships overflew the temple. Volos looked down at the ruins of the *Revealed Truth*. There were recognisable fragments: a twisted turret here, a blackened gothic arch there. He could tell what had happened, and though the impact of the cruiser had gouged the surface of the moon, there was no crater, and the temple looked untouched.

Volos thought through the options. He didn't like the prospect of assaulting the only entrance. He wanted a second avenue of attack. The transparent dome was inviting, yet it had somehow survived the annihilation of a Retaliator-class cruiser.

Nithigg had come forward to the cockpit and took in the scene. 'It would be nice to bomb the place flat,' he sighed.

'In through the roof, is what I want,' Volos told him. 'I don't care how sorcerous that dome is. It has to be a weak point. We smash it.'

'And how are we going to manage that?'

'If we can't shoot it out, we'll use the temple against itself. I doubt we can level it, but I think we might be able to wrench it out of true.' He turned to Keryon. 'We'll need some distance and altitude.'

Nithigg chuckled. 'This isn't going to be subtle, is it?'

Volos grinned, but he was also snarling in anticipation of crushing vengeance. 'I am Adeptus Astartes, not Inquisition. Of course it isn't going to be subtle.' Then he voxed Maro and told the helmsman what he wanted. If the move killed everyone in the temple, so much the better.

THEY SAW THE Thunderhawks pass overhead, and then head off beyond the curvature of the moon. Toharan wished for anti-aircraft weaponry. 'Make the jump,' he told Nessun. 'Take us into the warp now.'

Nessun gave a short jerk of his head. He had no concentration to spare. His fingers were a blur of music. 'Not ready,' he grunted.

The red glow of the moon's surface was leaking out into its atmosphere. It spread like a focused aurora across the gulf of the void towards the grinder.

The Sword, Gabrille, said to Toharan, 'We must prepare for an incursion.'

'Yes,' he agreed. 'Disciples, with me!' he called, and the Legion name sounded right when he spoke it.

'Orbital launch!' Symael yelled.

Toharan looked up, through the dome at the dark and stars. One star was rushing towards them. It became a streak, then a shape. In the eternal fraction of a second before it hit, Toharan had time to realise he was seeing a torpedo come for them. He had time to know that he had lost the *Immolation Maw*. He even had time to deduce, if only one torpedo had been launched, what sort of ordnance it must be.

He did not have time to brace himself.

His helmet shut down his senses to protect him from the worst of the flash and blast of the cyclonic torpedo. It couldn't protect him from the upheaval of the ground beneath his feet. The world shook and rolled. He was a storm-tossed ship. Blind and deaf, he felt himself flying. He slammed into a wall, fell to the floor, and then he was tossed into the air again as the earth bucked. The shutters over his lenses lifted, and the sounds were unfiltered once more. The destruction of the *Revealed Truth* was dwarfed by the searing madness of the new explosion. This was beyond fire, beyond heat, beyond comprehension. He was at the heart of the universe's birth and death. Reality's scream was so intense he could barely see the other figures around him as they were thrown about like dice in a cup. There was nothing to hear except the thunder of dying gods. Brilliance roiled. Waves of flame the height of forever smashed into and over the temple without pause. The ground writhed, caught in a tectonic seizure. The temple twisted with it, its walls torquing.

At the rear, the metal entrance doors blew off like leaves in the wind. On the top, the dome imploded. Jagged chunks of xenos glass hailed down into the great hall. Fire and heat rushed in with it. Toharan rose to his knees only to be knocked down by a chunk of glass the size of a boulder. He saw two Swords actually manage to stagger a couple of steps toward Nessun, their arms raised in an attempt to shield him. Then everything was glass, fire and the heaving of earth. He was slammed in every direction until he was completely disoriented. The blows of a world rained down on him, and even his Space Marine physiology was overwhelmed. He blacked out.

When he crawled back to full awareness, he found himself lying a third of the way up the staircase that circled the wall. He had no memory of landing here. He had gone limp in the jaws of the explosion, and rolled with the hits. A few ribs and teeth felt lose, but his limbs were all working. The fire was withdrawing, its fuel consumed, its work done. The temple still stood, but the walls were scored. Massive cracks ran their length. The staircase had numerous uneven passages and missing chunks. Toharan was astonished that the walls had not fallen. The rock had twisted like cloth, yet retained its integrity.

Not all the Swords of Epiphany had been as lucky. Toharan saw one who had died beneath a chunk of the dome three times the size of the one that had hit him. He saw another one who had been reduced to a smouldering wreck. He also saw one of his Disciples, Kataros, lying slumped against a damaged section of wall. The Space Marine lay at bizarre angles. He'd been shaken into pieces.

He looked for Nessun. The cardinal was hunched over the instrument. His white robes were scorched. Silk was torn where he'd been hit. So was his flesh. Toharan joined Gabrille at his side. 'How is he?' Toharan asked. He glanced up into the sky. The aurora was still there. Perhaps it didn't need Nessun after all.

The cardinal raised his head. His hair seemed to be hanging off his scalp, ready to slip off at the first sneeze. Blood poured from his forehead. Nessun licked his lips, tasting his own vitae. And still his hands moved over the giant backbone. He had nothing like Space Marine armour, but he had weathered the storm as well as, or better than, any of his acolytes. He had been protected by the machine, Toharan thought. The former Ecclesiarch was still being watched over by the gods. Nessun parted his lips in a bloody smile of triumph.

In the new silence, one barely broken by the metallic clunks of warriors putting themselves back together for the next battle, Toharan heard the snarling roar of the Thunderhawks on approach again. It sounded low to the ground.

Nessun heard the gunships too. His grin became wider. 'Too late,' he whispered. 'I am ready.'

The grinder jumped into the warp.

CHAPTER 28
THE WAR OF REDEMPTION

SETHENO RETURNED TO the bridge to find that the Gemini grinder had vanished.

'Is that worm dealt with?' Maro growled.

'He is. Helmsman, where…?'

'Into the warp.'

'Can your navigators track it?'

'Something that big? They would have more trouble trying not to see it. We are about to make the jump, canoness.'

'Good.'

THE THUNDERHAWKS WERE making a low attack run on the entrance to the temple when the sky disappeared. The stars and the healthy black of mere void vanished. A gaping wound opened up in reality. It engulfed the Gemini configuration. Volos saw the firmament swallowed by the sea of the warp. Things that pretended to be colours stabbed down in tornado formations toward the surface of the moon. What writhed overhead was not a storm, but something far more lethal.

'Oh, how nice,' Keryon grumbled.

'This changes nothing,' Volos told him.

'This ship doesn't have a Geller field.'

Nithigg said, 'If we were at immediate risk, we would already be destroyed. This machine is like the Flebis vault. It is already of the warp, and is able to maintain its integrity, and ours as well.'

Without looking up from his vector of approach, Keryon flicked a hand at the grasping warp-flow above. 'I'm sure you're right, and that that's as harmless as it looks.' He sounded grimly amused, as if the day had reached a certain perfection of vileness. 'Make ready,' he said.

Nithigg nodded and headed back to the crew compartment. Volos waited a moment longer. He wanted to see the next step in the retaliation.

Keryon brought the *Battle Pyre* within metres of the surface. He flew as if he were piloting a Land Speeder. The temple gates rushed toward them. Keryon fired a salvo of Hellstrikes and pulled up. The missiles flashed inside. The explosions were funnelled out of the entrance and washed over the Thunderhawk as it angled toward the temple's peak. 'Message delivered,' Keryon said. The *Nightfire* followed to make sure the message was understood.

Volos clapped Keryon on the shoulder guard and left the cockpit. He wasn't even on the field yet, and he could already taste the blood of traitors in his mouth.

* * *

The Death of Antagonis

THE MISSILE DETONATIONS were trivial after the cyclonic torpedo. But they did their work. Swords and Disciples were blown apart, armour and meat sent flying across the hall. Those not caught in the direct blast were knocked to the ground again, fire scorching their ceramite. Toharan cursed, shaking off the stunned ringing in his head. The Dragons were keeping them off-balance, blocking their attempts to regroup and prepare a defence.

He staggered up, saw Symael, and pointed at the entrance hall. Symael nodded, and was already throwing together a group to interdict that access point. The squad that formed was made up of both Disciples and Swords. The cooperation was good, but the organisation was improvised, driven by the demands of time and not strategy. They were losing the advantage of their numbers and of their defensive position.

Those were irrelevant concerns, Toharan told himself. His destiny was unalterable.

One of the missiles had flown straight into the instrument. Toharan looked at Nessun. Gabrille was beside the cardinal, arms out to support him. There was little recognisable in the creature that stood there, consumed by the music. Its shape was human, but flesh and robes had been burned away. Instead of showing the raw pink and black of blast injuries, Nessun had turned the cartilage-grey of the organ. He was becoming part of the machine. The entities of his collective being were transforming, building layers of ornamental bone over his actual skeleton. He turned his head Toharan's way, and for a brief moment, his eyes were able to see the room. The screen above Nessun's head was suddenly filled with Toharan's image. Nessun's skull was art now, an ecstatic expression of death and music. Bones whose new purpose was to replace the weakness of flesh had taken the place of his lips, and they arranged themselves into a terrible grin. 'Perfection,' Nessun croaked with the sound of twigs on slate. His eyes were scale reproductions of the screen. They were stones with the power of sight. They gazed at Toharan for one beat more, promising glory, and then their attention soared away. Toharan and the hall vanished from the screen, replaced by the hungry joy of the warp and the spinning grinder.

'He doesn't need us,' Toharan told Gabrille. 'Not anymore.' The instrument had been untouched by the rocket strike.

Gabrille nodded, grabbed his bolter, and ran with Toharan to the staircase. The *Battle Pyre* was passing over the shattered dome.

THE DRAGON CLAWS streaked into the temple on flaming promethium. They hit the observation deck, slamming down in a ring formation, slashing the space of the great hall with a web of interlocking fire. The *Battle Pyre* peeled off to join the *Nightfire* and drop the rest of the Black Dragons at the temple entrance, and for the next thirty seconds, the Claws were on their own. Volos felt no sense of being outnumbered. He felt the strength of holy war as he and his men brought justice down on the heads of the traitors.

Toharan was partway up the staircase, and Volos sent a concentrated burst of fire his way, forcing him and the Sword back down. Volos and the Claws ran along the platform and jumped across the space, shifting targets every few seconds, keeping their own movements unpredictable. There was no cover below. The hall was an immense killing field for them, and there were so many targets.

There was an instinctive resistance that Volos had to fight through, a moment of horror at shooting figures in the armour of the Black Dragons. But he knew what was necessary, and the rage at betrayal gave him strength. And when he saw that Toharan's troops had defaced their armour, renouncing their Chapter and their faith in the Emperor, then the killing was easy. 'Exterminate them all!' he roared. The righteousness of faith was with him, and he was invincible.

THE THUNDERHAWK'S ASSAULT ramp lowered the second the ships touched surface. Thirty-eight Black Dragons thundered down its length and rushed the temple entrance. Their blood was up. They were dark fury incarnate, a pounding juggernaut of war come for judgement and slaughter. Their numbers had been reduced to less than half of what they had been, and only two squads were fully intact. They had lost one captain, and been betrayed by a second. Their true Chaplain, Apothecary and Librarian lay in comas. They were on a xenos abomination travelling the warp, and they had no reason to believe they would live beyond this day.

They had never been more dangerous.

For Melus, there was an additional edge to the charge. This was a battle to restore the honour of Squad Pythios. The successive commands of Toharan and Omorfos had tainted him and his men by association. The time had come to purge their shame and burn the filth who had caused it. 'Fire and bone!' he shouted, and the cry was taken up by his brothers, their roar a weapon in itself, launched at the craven betrayers who waited for them inside.

The temple rose before them, its outer wall an ophidian slope of smooth, glowing rock. The entrance was wide, the enemy visible about ten metres in, where a mix of black and gold armour was gathered to meet the invasion. There was no cover inside or outside the temple. The strategy for both armies came down to a brute mathematics of force. The Dragons had to smash the defences with the speed and violence of their charge. The Swords and Disciples had to hold and break the wave of the advance.

As the unstoppable force raced towards the immovable object, the opening moves of the opponents mirrored each other. Grenades hurtled through the air, crossing paths in mid arc. Krak and frag munitions erupted in the corridor. The stonework of the temple was untouched. The bodies of the warriors were less fortunate. Melus saw a brother gutted by shrapnel, but the Dragons had the advantage of speed and movement. They dodged and rolled out of the way of the explosives, while the defenders had to break rank or suffer the consequences. 'First blood is ours, brothers,' he voxed. 'Press them hard.'

Devastators on his left and right marched forward with a measured, implacable gait, their heavy bolters chewing up opposing armour, punching the enemy further back and providing cover for Melus's tactical team to rush in faster. The return fire was steady and skilled, but none of it was heavy. No cannons were answering the Dragons charge, no missile launchers, no multi-meltas. Melus dodged a grenade, rolled, came up firing and took the head off a Sword. He wondered if perhaps the renegades didn't have any heavy weapons. Grinning at the thought of the enemy's tactical mistake, he closed the distance to the traitor front line.

THE FIRE FROM above was infuriating. It was so fast, so intertwined, that there was no opportunity to reclaim the initiative. Toharan was on the defensive, and Volos was forcing him and his allies out of the great hall and into the cover of the entrance corridor. Once there, they would be under siege on two fronts. 'We can't let them box us in,' he yelled to Gabrille as they ran across the temple floor in zig-zags, dodging rounds, firing over their shoulders.

'We won't. Are your men ready for the counter at the rear?'

'Yes.'

'Let's hit them now.'

'That doesn't help us here,' Toharan said as they reached the corridor.

'No, but *they* will,' Gabrille said as the Raptors pushed past them and shot up into the dome, bringing the fight to the Dragon Claws.

VOLOS HAD BEEN expecting them. It had been too much to hope that they had killed the Swords of Epiphany's only jump pack warriors on Flebis. The Raptors powered through the Claws' net of bolter fire, their own guns answering and disrupting the rain of death Volos and his brothers were sending down. For a few seconds, the two assault teams traded shots, every warrior moving too fast, jerking through the air too unpredictably, for his foe to target him successfully, and every warrior unable to score a telling hit. Then Dragons and birds of prey did as instincts and necessity commanded and flew at each other to grapple. The upper reaches of the great hall rang with the clash of armour and armour, cry of bird and roar of reptile. Giants smashed at each other as they rocketed beneath the shattered dome.

A Raptor slammed into Volos. The smaller traitor Space Marine was a swarm of clutching limbs as they tumbled end over end to the observation platform. They hit, but the Raptor didn't lose his grip. They rolled, clawing at each other's armour for purchase. They came to a halt with the Raptor on top. He pulled back an arm with a gladius. Volos reached up, shot out a bone-blade and impaled the Raptor beneath the chin. The other end of the blade came out the back of the traitor's helmet. Volos kicked the corpse away and sprang to meet the next Chaos Space Marine. The Raptors had to be dealt with quickly. He could feel the Claws' momentum bleeding away.

THE SWORDS AND Disciples held the counter-attack back until the bulk of the Dragons was almost upon them. The defenders had taken hard blows, but now they struck to annihilate. Their one heavy bolter stuttered to life, stitching fist-sized rounds along the front of the Dragon advance. But the main blow came from the psykers. What the traitors lacked in heavy weaponry, they made up for in numbers and in sorcery. The hail of bolter and las had begun to falter as the Dragons charged forward and blasted holes in the line. But the heavy bolter response forced a pause as the attackers evaded the fire or took hits. Melus felt the attack lose steam, and in the moment of hesitation came the energy bolts.

The sorcerous attack was a full salvo, multiple psykers unleashing their powers simultaneously. A flash that giggled side-swiped Melus, knocking him down. His left shoulder guard had vanished. The edges sizzled, and his upper arm was opened almost to the bone. Two other brothers weren't as lucky. Their helmets and heads were gone. Tendrils like coiling snakes danced over the stumps.

'Kill them!' Melus roared. There was no need to specify the targets. Already, his armour's auto-senses were feeding him the smell of ozone and hothouse flowers as the magic built up again. Too many brothers were on their knees, shaking off the assault, but slowed down for a moment. He knew that was all it would take for disaster if they lost the race to the next blow.

They lost. The sorcery came again, much too soon. The attacks had been staggered, and this one arrived with its targets slowed and primed for destruction. Melus howled his fury as he saw what came for them. It was an immense Space Marine made of fire, and it was the work of a psyker who had been a brother.

* * *

CHARGED UP AND running, the Gemini grinder was a thing of the warp. It travelled the immaterium with the ease and speed of a hawk through air. There were no obstacles in its path, and storms only sped it to its destination. The machine had known its target before its jump, and now it shot out of the warp, bringing doom to the Camargus system. Aighe Mortis lay ahead, and the power of two billion dead moved grinder and moon forward to an even greater feast.

ENNYN WAS OVERMATCHED. The Lexicanium was the Black Dragons sole remaining psyker. He could have taken on any one of the enemy's sorcerers in single combat, but now he was faced with a virtual phalanx of them. He didn't have the power.

But perhaps he had the rage.

The fire being that was falling upon him and his brothers was a blasphemy beyond anything he had ever seen or imagined. It was an avenger, and its reality was created by drawing upon the lore and tradition of the Chapter itself. It was a manifestation of the collective identity of the Black Dragons, and he would not permit it to be turned against the very warriors of which it was a part. He saw Jemiah a few metres back from the front lines of the traitors. Ennyn's anger, purified by his absolute faith in the truths of his Chapter, lashed out at the faithless Space Marine. Ennyn felt his entire being consumed in an expression of holy anger, and as he expended everything he had in this single strike, his mind erupted with new potential.

Jemiah clapped his hands to his head. His scream

was a brutish gargle, high pitched and cut short. It was shoved back down his throat. He fell to his knees, then on his face. His psychic hood flickered and smoked. His monstrous avatar did not dissipate. It had its arm raised to strike the Dragons, its four-metre sword about to cull them with fire. Then, as if the death of its treacherous creator restored its true identity, it turned around, and brought the sword down, setting traitors ablaze.

Snarling, the Black Dragons reclaimed the initiative.

THE RAPTORS FOUGHT with the assurance of the angels they thought they were. The Dragon Claws hit back with the savagery of what Volos knew they must become. They were dragons in every sense. They burned their foe and stripped the flesh from his bones. They met the Raptors, and what chance did mere birds have against the monsters of myth? None, the Claws proved. The Raptors fell. Volos landed on the back of one and brought him to the ground. The impact of Space Marines would have cratered a marble floor, but the temple stones gave nothing. Volos heard the Sword's bones shatter.

He stood from his fallen foe and saw Toharan's forces rush from the cover of the entrance hall. They came out firing, but there was a raggedness to their emergence, as if they were being forced to stage their counter-charge before they were ready. He decided to give them more cause for uncertainty. He used a blade to punch a hole in the Raptor's armour just below the neck. He slipped a frag grenade from his belt, shoved it into the opening, heaved the traitor over his head and threw him at the enemy. The Raptor exploded in mid-air, showering ignited promethium over the attackers. They stumbled just long enough for him to fell three of them with his bolter.

The other Dragon Claws landed at his side. They joined their fire to his, and they drove more of the traitors back. At the other end of the entrance hall, Volos saw smoke and uproar. For a moment, a wall of flame appeared to be a walking figure. Then it breathed fire forward. He grinned as the dragon flame pursued the faithless on two fronts.

Toharan launched himself through the fire. His defaced armour was scorched, and Volos thought he could see runes in the burns, Toharan's new masters branding him as their property. Symael and a Sword were at his side. They threw themselves forward and down, beneath the Claws' bolt stream and retaliating with their own as they slid across the smooth floor. Volos fired off a burst with his jump pack, taking a high leap to avoid having his legs shot out from under him. He came back down straight at Toharan.

THE BLACK DRAGONS push from the rear drove the traitor alliance into the great hall. Volos's brothers followed their foes inside. They were a juggernaut of vengeance, ramming forward with no thought to injury or death. The war lost all trace of coherence. There were no lines anymore. There was only the confusion of melee. Armour slammed into armour. Point-blank bolter fire was answered with dismembering chainsword. Giant predators tore at each other with weapon and fist, fire and bone.

* * *

NITHIGG JUMPED AWAY from Symael's power fist. The gauntlet passed close enough for its crackling aura to make Nithigg's eye lenses flare with static. Symael overbalanced and punched the ground. The invulnerable stone resisted the blow, and sent the force jarring up the warrior's frame. Nithigg stitched Symael's frame with bolts, blasting open his armour from ribs to helm. As Symael collapsed, blood and organs oozing from the hole in his side, he frowned at Nithigg. He looked more confused than in pain.

A streak of pity rushed through Nithigg's anger. The awful waste and tragedy of what had happened was a lead weight in his chest. His hearts ached at what had become of his company. In his centuries of service, he had never seen such division and betrayal. And he had always liked Symael, thought him a first-rate, if unimaginative, fighter. He had trained the younger man. The pain of killing him was as real as the need to do so. He knew Symael and the others had been tempted and manipulated, but they had still made the choices. Yet he couldn't help but hope for the possibility of at least a hint of redemption. There was so little hope to go around; he couldn't bring himself to throw away what little he could grasp.

He moved quickly. He knelt beside Symael. 'Do you repent your heresy?' he asked.

The resentment in Symael's eyes gave him his answer. He sighed and shot Symael once in the head. Feeling even older, he turned back to the needed job of killing his former brothers.

* * *

Toharan barely twisted out of the way of Volos's strike. Volos landed within a metre of him and lashed out with his arm-blades. His fury wouldn't be satisfied with a bolt between Toharan's eyes. He needed the betrayer's blood coating his armour. Toharan parried with his chainsword. Its motor whined as its teeth ground against Volos's adamantine bone. Volos brought his left arm around the hilt, aiming at Toharan's throat. Toharan jerked his head back and sidestepped, but the blow shattered the side of his helmet. Shaking his head to free it of the broken ceramite, he spun around and brought the chainsword down two-handed. There was the strength and speed in his strike to slice a cannon in half, but Volos moved inside his reach. He smashed his right fist and blade against Toharan's elbow. He heard armour and bone break. With his left hand, he grabbed Toharan's gorget and hurled him to the ground.

They were no longer in the practice cage. Volos wasn't holding back. No mercy, no quarter, no respite until he had killed the filth at his feet. He raised both fists, prepared to plunge the blades into Toharan's neck.

A flicker of movement caught his eye. He glanced up, and saw Aighe Mortis on the eye-screen. The planet was in magnification, but it was also moving closer. The simple truth hit him: Nessun had to be stopped, and there was no time for anything else.

Volos plunged his arms down to impale Toharan's throat and be done, his legs already tensing for the leap that would take him to the ossified cardinal. His shift in attention had lasted less than a second, but Toharan was already bringing up his chainsword to block. Something hit Volos from behind, knocking him over Toharan's head. He landed in a crouch and spun around. He stared into the barrel of a meltagun. Beyond it, the Sword of Epiphany stood in the tainted majesty of gold. Gabrille's finger squeezed the trigger.

The shot went wild as Nithigg threw himself against the Sword. He took Gabrille down and rabbit-punched his head until the helm split open. Nithigg's forearm blade punctured the traitor's forehead. Gabrille spasmed, limbs rattling against the ground. Something bitter and petty wailed as its host died, and with a writhing flicker, vanished back into the warp.

Toharan was on his feet and raising his sword again. Nithigg and Volos exchanged quick nods. Nithigg was closer to Toharan and turned to fight him. Volos rose and rode his jump pack on a horizontal flight into the cardinal. It was like colliding with a pillar. Volos grunted and fell against the enormous backbone that Nessun was caressing. Volos felt eldritch energies leach through his armour and into his core. The cardinal grunted mild annoyance, barely aware Volos was there, and batted him aside. Volos recovered his balance and looked at the eye-screen. The grinder was slightly off-centre in its approach to Aighe Mortis. The cardinal's grey skeleton fingers danced, and the course was corrected.

As Volos reached for Nessun again, the character of the war shifted as it acquired a focus. The traitors saw him attacking their leader and father, and he became their target. The Dragons blocked them. The butchering frenzy intensified. Volos turned his gun on Nessun and the instrument he played. The bolts ricocheted, almost taking his own head off. The cardinal paid no attention. The details of Aighe Mortis became clearer, and Volos prayed to the Emperor that the screen was still at a high level of magnification. He was about to grab a krak grenade when it finally registered that for all the flame, missiles and weapon fire that had filled the hall, he didn't couldn't see a pockmark or mar on the surface of the device. Nessun, or the thing that had once been him, transformed now beyond any memory of the human other than a silhouette, was made of the same impervious bone.

Volos spat at the cardinal's invulnerability. Seized by inspiration, he raised his bone-blades high. He struck with all his strength and rage. He was the dragon of the Emperor, and he blessed the curse. The blades, touched by Chaos but wielded by faith, hit Nessun's right forearm. Altered bone met altered bone. The touch of the warp moved over both, but the eye of the Emperor lay on only one.

Nessun's arm shattered like porcelain. He screamed, and so did the symbiosis between himself and the instrument. The music that had been thrumming at the base of Volos's spine since he'd entered the temple fell into a discordant shriek. Nessun turned. His left arm was still attached to the instrument, still clutching and stroking vertebrae, but now with a jerking, spastic, agonised motion. The images on the eye-screen fragmented. There was a last flash of Aighe Mortis veering off to the side, and then a kaleidoscope of impressions of the hall before there was nothing but pain given electric expression. The stump of Nessun's right arm lifted in supplication, and from it spewed a twisting sinew of energy. It was rope and tentacle and light. It was Chaos channelled through the cardinal. It hit the observation deck, and the walls of the dome. Stone writhed, then collapsed. Massive, agonised slabs fell to crush the combatants.

The fighting did not stop, but as the realisation of what had transpired rippled through the temple, there was a change in morale so pronounced its effect was almost the same as a hesitation. The Swords of Epiphany were losing their leader and creator. The Disciples weren't hit as grievously, but Volos was sure they were seeing the pointlessness of their struggle.

Toharan didn't. He stormed towards Volos, shaking off Nithigg and blasting through the other fighters like they were wheat. He had lost his helmet in the fight with the old veteran, and his face was contorted by a terrible desperation. Howling an inarticulate denial, he was the embodiment of fanaticism. There was nothing left of the noble Space Marine whom Volos had fought beside for decades. He saw only entitlement, pride and self-loathing transformed into a daemonic hate. Volos raised his bolter to gun down the rabid dog.

Behind him, Nessun's scream stopped for a moment, and there was the sound of a laugh. His final act one of revenge and merciless generosity, Nessun lowered his stump and hit Toharan full in the chest with the twitching strands of Chaos energy. Toharan stopped dead and sank to his knees. The energy poured into him.

Cursing his stupidity, Volos turned on Nessun and smashed his left arm. The instant there was no more connection between the cardinal and the instrument, the energy vanished. Nessun stood and rocked back and forth on his feet. The quality of the grey exoskeleton changed. It became more rigid, darker, brittle. His eyes dimmed as they receded into the bone prison, but they looked up at Volos with an air of bitter exasperation. Volos brought an elbow down on Nessun's head, and shattered the skull into hundreds of pieces. The scream returned, echoing out of the ether now, and the stump of Nessun's head spouted a fountain of shrieking warp spirits. They shot up like a geyser and did not come back down. The eye-screen went blank, becoming vacant bone once again.

Volos turned back to Toharan, half-expecting him to be dead. He was sure his former captain was incapacitated.

He wasn't.

TOHARAN'S DESTINY KNOCKED him down and filled him. He had thought the control and command of the Gemini grinder was that destiny, but he had been proven wrong, and now he was experiencing his full flowering. He wondered what it would be as the energy flooded his system. He was about to experience the fulfilment of every potential. He opened his mouth to laugh in triumph.

The change took him. It was not what he had imagined. His body expanded. Legs, torso and arms lengthened and thickened. He screamed as his nerve clusters were scraped raw by racing bone. Flesh and muscle metastasised. He grew too big for his armour. The plates pressed into his body. They crushed organs.

They snapped bones. But still he grew, and even Adeptus Astartes power armour couldn't contain what he was becoming. It split, and then fell off like a shed skin. He continued to grow. Now his screams weren't of pain but of disgust. The ugly, stupid, excess of being was consuming him. His dreams of purity were swallowed by rampaging flesh. His mind couldn't cope. Walls of bodily existence constricted it. He was a monster worse than everything he had despised in his brother Dragons. His last act of sentience was to give voice to his despair. Then he was nothing but anger. He lashed out at the source of his pain, and the source was all existence. The only relief would come if he could smash the universe out of existence and out of his misery with his bare hands. And so he began.

THE CREATURE THAT had been Toharan was twice Volos's height and he was still growing. He was a monster of corded flesh and sinew. His face and head were huge caricatures of Toharan's features. The noble profile was gone, replaced by grotesque growths of spreading bone that passed for a nose and chin. Toharan's roar wasn't mindless, but it was utterly mad. He lashed out with fists larger than power hammers. He made no distinction between friend and foe. He grabbed the nearest warrior, a Sword, and smashed him to the ground. Toharan pounded him until he was a swamp of blood and bone fragments. The Black Dragons trained their fire on the monster, but the Swords and Disciples did not. He was dangerous, but he was still of their number, and he was powerful. They continued to fight, forcing the Dragons to deal with them. The war raged in fractal clusters around the monster, while he shrieked and murdered at random.

Volos saw the bolter rounds thud, ignored, into Toharan's flesh. He didn't appear to know he'd been shot. The Dragons weren't going to bring him down through conventional projectile weaponry. But perhaps the monster could be cut down to size. Leaving the petrified corpse of Nessun, Volos leaped at Toharan and slashed him across the abdomen. His blade tore deep into meat, and the edge ground against a rib. Blood, thick and black, spat out at Volos, but the lips of the wound sealed as soon as he withdrew the blade. Toharan snarled and swatted at him. Volos dodged, but the tips of the growing fingers caught him and knocked him flying. He slammed into Nessun, reducing the body to dust.

Toharan reached for Volos, but Nithigg landed on his back. Nithigg reached around the monster's neck and sliced his throat with his forearm blade. More blood, and again the instant seal. The storm of flesh grew higher and higher. As Volos regained his feet, Toharan snatched Nithigg off his back. He held the Dragon Claw in a fist that was now as big as the Space Marine and squeezed. Volos heard the terrible crunching and saw Nithigg convulse. Volos hacked at Toharan's wrist, but it became thicker faster than he could cut. His jump pack propelled him into Toharan's face. He punctured an eye. His blade went deep. It should have killed Toharan's brain. Either the brain healed too, or there was no longer enough there to matter. Toharan didn't die, but he did feel pain. He shrieked and dropped Nithigg.

Volos saw his old friend fall boneless to the ground. He yanked his blade out and jumped to the observation platform, bathing Toharan in flaming promethium exhaust.

The monster howled at the injury and babbled incoherent rage. Toharan was regressing further and further as he grew. Language had abandoned him. He was little more than a pure loathing of flesh. Whether he knew who Volos was, or was simply focused on his tormentor, he followed, as Volos had hoped he would. Toharan pounded up the staircase, leaping over gaps with more power than grace.

'Keryon,' Volos voxed. 'Come over the dome. Full Hellstrike barrage at what you see there. Do not hesitate.'

'Acknowledged.'

Toharan reached the platform. He lunged for Volos. The Dragon shot over him, landed behind and slashed at his legs behind the knees. The tendons healed immediately, but the second during which they were severed was enough to drop Toharan. He squirmed around, his flesh bubbling like boiling tar, and his arm was suddenly longer than it had been a moment before. Toharan caught Volos before he could step out of reach and flung him against the temple wall like a rag doll. Through the ringing in his ears, Volos heard the roar of the approaching *Battle Pyre*. Toharan didn't let go. He smashed Volos against the wall again. Volos heard and felt his left arm break. Ribs were swimming in his chest. And he was flying again. He slashed with his right hand and parted enough of the wrist to make Toharan drop him.

Volos limped back a few steps. Now almost ten metres tall, Toharan advance on him. Volos stood his ground. He wanted Toharan to stay put for just a few seconds. He removed his helmet and showed the unwilling monster the face of one who embraced what he was. The mutation stared down at him. Toharan's eyes were endless reservoirs of stupid hate, but buried deep in the cancerous instinct, Volos saw a spark of the personal. Toharan knew who he was. Some part of him was savouring this moment. *Good*, Volos thought.

Toharan rose to his full height. His fists, big as pillars, came together. They began the descent that would smash his rival to nothing.

Volos whispered, 'Fire,' as the Hellstrikes flashed down through the dome. Keryon's aim was truer than he could have hoped. Toharan disappeared in the fireballs. Flames washed over Volos and the blast wave threw him to the wall again. His left shoulder popped out of its socket. But Toharan's bulk shielded him from the worst of the explosions. The light and fire faded, and Toharan was still standing. He was sluggish, though, stunned and shrieking. His flesh was a flaking, blackened crust. Pink muscle showed through deep crevices. Ignoring his own injuries, Volos launched himself forward on his jump pack, right arm out, blade as spear tip. He hit Toharan in the chest. Toharan toppled like a felled oak. Flesh disintegrated and bones shattered inward. He started healing, but not fast enough. Not this time.

With his good arm, Volos butchered his former friend, flaying open his chest. He stomped a boot through the ribcage and there, fire damaged but pumping madly, were the hearts. Toharan's hands closed in on either side to crush him like an insect. Volos sliced through aortae and venae cavae, severing the hearts from the body.

The hearts stopped beating. The hands fell back. Toharan breathed once, the air escaping in a sigh of fruitless denial, and he was dead.

Volos did not look back at the corpse as he returned to the floor of the temple. He was exhausted, but he did not slow as, one-handed, he joined in the final slaughter of the remaining traitors. The Swords and Disciples had nothing left to fight for. The Black Dragons had the Emperor, and justice, and vengeance. They had more than enough.

When it was done, Volos crouched over Nithigg. His armour had cracked like an eggshell, and there was very little left of his body. But he lived. One side of his face was a pulped ruin, but the intact eye fixed Volos with a desperate intensity. His lips moved. Volos leaned in, and heard Nithigg's whispered prayer: 'Let me serve.'

'You shall,' Volos promised, and didn't move from his side until, days later, the *Immolation Maw* finally transited out of the warp and found them.

EPILOGUE

THERE WAS NO end. Not yet.

The grinder had missed Aighe Mortis by a precious few million kilometres. It ran out of energy partway out of the Camargus system, and drifted into an eccentric orbit.

'It cannot remain here,' Setheno told Volos when she met him aboard the *Immolation Maw*.

THERE WOULD BE no end. Not yet.

Volos stood in the reliquary, surrounded by holy silence and sacred history. Several decks up, Nithigg lay in sus-an membrane coma, waiting. Before Volos, the blessed coffin of the Dreadnought stood empty, sleeping, also waiting. Second Company's losses were great. The Apothecary, Librarian and Chaplain were still in the death-sleep. There was no one with the skills and knowledge to do what must be done. 'There will be,' Volos promised. 'Have patience, brother. You *will* serve.'

* * *

'There must be an end to it,' Setheno said.

They were standing on a balcony of the Palace of Saint Boethius, overlooking the Grand Square. 'And this is the price,' Volos answered. He watched the tens of thousands of pilgrims pass through on their way to the starport. They chanted thanks and joy. Their robes were colourful sackcloth, fusing penitence and celebration.

'It is. Victory always has a price.'

Volos thought about his decimated company and said nothing.

Setheno must have read his expression. 'You have suffered casualties. Your numbers are reduced. This is temporary. You are stronger. That is permanent.'

'Stronger?'

'You are unified. You are purified. There has been a necessary purge.'

A terrible suspicion dawned in Volos's mind. 'You planned this?'

Setheno shook her head. 'No. But a purge was coming, thanks to Inquisitor Lettinger and his political allies. Better this be the form it takes.'

'So that we might be useful to you, instead of Lettinger.'

'So that you might be useful to the Emperor. You are discovering the true potential of your Chapter.'

'Necessity again,' Volos said softly, but he didn't disagree.

'Yes,' said Setheno. 'You have felt it. We must do *anything* that will preserve the Imperium. What we will be called on to do will only grow worse. The future is desperate. The Golden Throne was built by human hands, captain. It requires endless care and repair. Do you imagine that it will last forever?'

Volos's eyes widened. He was staggered by the blasphemy. 'You are without faith,' he said.

'You're wrong. There is no greater faith than the faith in a lost cause. I will fight to preserve the spark of humanity in the galaxy. The Emperor is our only hope, and I will give him my last drop of blood, and that of anyone else, should it come to that.' She gave Volos a hard look. 'So will you.'

He nodded.

There was the sound of footsteps on marble behind them. They turned to see Tennesyn approach. Standing with him was Jozef Bisset, now acting regent of Aighe Mortis. 'Canoness,' Tennesyn said. 'My lord.' He regarded them with a mixture of fear and resignation.

'You are ready?' Setheno asked.

When Tennesyn nodded, Volos said, 'Wait for us below.'

Tennesyn withdrew. Bisset walked with him, a supportive hand on his shoulder, and cast an uneasy glance back at the two giants.

'You are a monster of myth to them, too,' Volos said to Setheno.

'I hope so,' she answered. 'You and I need reminders of that sort. We must know the atrocities we commit for what they are. And the next one is mine.' She gave him a solemn nod. 'Captain.'

He returned the gesture. 'Canoness.'

She left. Volos watched the pilgrims a while longer, and accepted his responsibility for what was coming. Setheno was orchestrating it, but he condoned it. The millions of pilgrims thought they were travelling to the Gemini moon to pay due reverence to the site of the battle that had saved their planet. They were, but they would not be returning.

Necessity: the grinder had to be destroyed, or the threat of its use would forever haunt the Imperium. It had to be driven one more time, into the heart of the star Camargus. So it had to be powered up again. One more monstrous burnt offering. And someone had to study the device, and learn how to steer it. Tennesyn, the xeno-archaeologist, had the turn of mind that made him the logical candidate to be given that mission. Volos hoped the old man would survive, but was already wishing him a swift flight to his reward at the Emperor's side.

The pilgrims marched endlessly through the square. Not a few of them danced towards their doom. Volos's hands itched with the slick of innocent blood. The people sang. Their hymns were familiar ones, but sounded different to Volos's ears. He knew why. The songs of joy were really the lamentations of victory.

ABOUT THE AUTHOR

David Annandale is the author of the digital short story *Eclipse of Hope* and the novellas *Yarrick: Chains of Golgotha* and *Mephiston: Lord of Death* for Black Library. By day, he dons an academic disguise and lectures at a Canadian university on subjects ranging from English literature to horror films and video games. He lives with his wife and family and a daemon in the shape of a cat, and is working on several new projects set in the grim darkness of the far future.

WARHAMMER 40,000

BLOOD OF ASAHEIM

Chris Wraight

A SPACE WOLVES NOVEL

An extract from Space Wolves: Blood of Asaheim
by Chris Wraight

On sale March 2013

'So it's true?' asked Váltyr.

Gunnlaugur grunted.

'It is.'

Váltyr shook his head.

'When did they tell you?' he asked.

'Six hours ago.'

'*Skítja,*' Váltyr swore.

'He came in on a runner. They didn't send a warship. If they had, I'd have known sooner.'

Váltyr placed his slender hands together.

'Will he return, then?'

Gunnlaugur smiled wryly, a look that said, *Why would they tell me?*

The two were alone, hunched over a firepit and surrounded by lambent shadows. Gunnlaugur's chamber was high up on the eastern flanks of the Fang, close to the edge where the biting winds of Asaheim came over the Hunter's Gap. Ironhelmsshrine was within reach; on rare clear days, it could be seen from the narrow realview portal mounted on the external wall.

Out of battle armour, there was only marginal physical difference between the two warriors. Gunnlaugur, the one they called

Skullhewer, was a fraction heavier-set, a finger's width shorter. His shaven head still had residual traces of flame-red hair in the stubble, though his beard was slush-grey and stiff with age. His features were the same tight, brutal ones that had propelled him to clan chief of the Gaellings when he had been mortal, only now filled out and made heavier by aggressive muscular augmentation.

He sat on a stone slab in front of the fire, massive and stooped, his shoulders draped in furs. He ran a dagger through his hands, playing with the killing edge, flicking it between thick, dextrous fingers.

'We are wounded, brother,' Gunnlaugur said. 'Tally it up. We lost Ulf on Lossanal, Svafnir on Cthar, Tínd to the greenskins.'

As he spoke, his dark eyes reflected the warm light of the coals.

'We're under strength,' he said. 'He'll have to come back, just to make us viable. And where else can he go? Who else will take him?'

Váltyr listened intently. His narrow face was hot, and the glow exposed the many scars latticed across his cheeks.

His hands were still. Váltyr never played with blades. His longsword, *holdbítr*, was strapped across his back just as it ever was. The weapon was only drawn to be used in combat, or for veneration, or for ritual maintenance, and even then he never left its side, watching the Iron Priests intently as they invoked the sleeping spectres of murder that dwelt within.

Blademasters – *sverdhjera* – were a strange breed, guarding their weapons as if they were children.

'He chose to leave,' said Váltyr. 'He could have stayed, and we would have welcomed it then. He could have contested for the–'

'You'd have made the same choice he did,' said Gunnlaugur. 'I'd have done it too, if they'd asked.'

He hacked up a gobbet of phlegm and spat it into the fire. Trace particles of acid made it fizz angrily against the coals.

'I could protest,' Gunnlaugur said. 'Blackmane has a Blood Claw waiting in the wings as well, one he's eager to give us to knock into shape. That would make us six – enough to hunt again.'

Váltyr snorted.

'That's what we're reduced to now?'

Gunnlaugur nodded.

'Plenty of packs are running with losses,' he said. 'Every Great Year more come back diminished. Remember when Hjortur died? Remember how shocked we were? Tell me truly, would you be shocked now to hear of a *vaerangi* dying on the hunt?'

Váltyr grinned.

'If it was you, yes.'

Gunnlaugur didn't return the smile. He stared into the fire, and the blade spun and flashed absently in his fingers.

'I'll take the Blood Claw,' he said. 'We need new blood, and he'll learn quickly from Olgeir. But as for him…'

Váltyr looked steadily into Gunnlaugur's eyes.

'Blackmane will choose,' he said.

Gunnlaugur nodded slowly.

'That he will.'

He stilled the movement of the dagger.

'Our Young King,' he said, rolling his eyes. 'Barely fanged. What in Hel are we coming to, brother?'

For a moment it looked as though Váltyr had an answer. Then the blademaster shook his sleek head.

'I really am the wrong person to ask,' he said.

Order the novel or download the eBook
from *blacklibrary.com*
Also available from

and all good bookstores

READ IT FIRST

EXCLUSIVE PRODUCTS | EARLY RELEASES | FREE DELIVERY

blacklibrary.com

The hero of Armadeggon comes face to face with his greatest foe

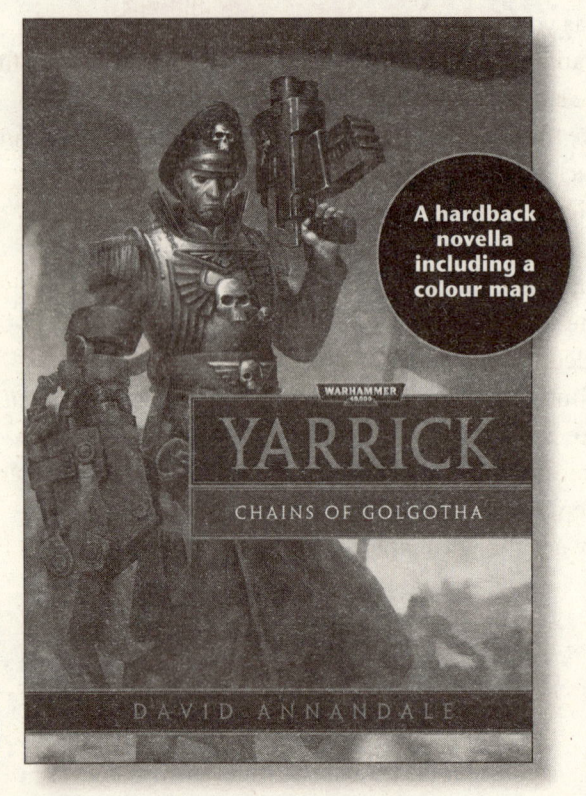

A hardback novella including a colour map

YARRICK
CHAINS OF GOLGOTHA

DAVID ANNANDALE

ISBN: 978-1-84970-412-0

Also available from

GAMES WORKSHOP

Hobby Centres